Anne Wyn Clark was born and raised in the Midlands, where she continues to live with her husband, a sweet-natured cat, plus a chinchilla with attitude. She has three now grown-up children and six grandchildren. Much of her formative existence was spent with her head in a book, and from an early age, she grew to relish the sheer escapism afforded by both reading and writing fiction.

She has a love of antiquity and a penchant for visiting old graveyards, often speculating on the demise of those entombed beneath.

The Cottage in the Ruins is her fifth novel.

You can follow her on X @EAClarkAuthor

Also by Anne Wyn Clark

Whisper Cottage
The Last House on the Cliff
The Secrets of Mill House
The Shadows of Hill Manor

ANNE WYN CLARK

THE COTTAGE IN THE RUINS

avon.

Published by AVON
A division of HarperCollins*Publishers* Ltd
1 London Bridge Street
London SE1 9GF

www.harpercollins.co.uk

HarperCollins*Publishers*
Macken House, 39/40 Mayor Street Upper
Dublin 1, D01 C9W8, Ireland

A Paperback Original 2025
1

First published in Great Britain by HarperCollins*Publishers* 2025

Emojis by Shutterstock.com

Anne Wyn Clark asserts the moral right to be identified as the author of this work.

A catalogue record for this book is available from the British Library.

ISBN: 978-0-00-876343-5

Set in Sabon LT Pro by HarperCollins*Publishers* India

Printed and bound in the UK using 100% Renewable
Electricity at CPI Group (UK) Ltd

MIX
Paper | Supporting
responsible forestry
FSC™ C007454

This book contains FSC™ certified paper and other controlled sources to ensure responsible forest management.

For more information visit: www.harpercollins.co.uk/green

For Mark, with love.
This one's for you!
xxx

There are no secrets that time does not reveal.

Jean Racine

Prologue

Gorton, Manchester

Monday, 6 November 1995

"In there?"

The young officer standing outside the door straightened. He nodded wordlessly, his eyes sunken from lack of sleep, haunted by the horror of what the previous night had brought. Detective Sergeant Cora Peters felt his pain. She peered through the little square of wired glass in the door of the interview room. Visible just a few feet in front of her was the back of a child's head: cropped brown hair; too-short trousers rising to reveal bare, twig legs with oversized, battered trainers at the end of them swinging beneath the table. Such a slight frame and small; so very small. It hardly seemed possible. Ten years old, but in appearance all of seven or eight. Something knotted in her stomach.

Taking a deep breath, she pushed open the door. The head turned sharply, and Peters found herself fixed briefly with a pair of huge, coal dark eyes, grimy streaks of recent tears dried on the pale cheeks. The interest DS Peters' sudden appearance had generated dissipated just as quickly and the child turned back to address the adult in the neighbouring seat, a woman in her late forties, from Social Services. The parents were conspicuous by their absence.

"When can I go home?"

The voice was timid, quavering. Cora felt oddly conflicted. She pulled up a chair on the opposite side of the table. The noise of the feet scraping across the floor set her teeth on edge. She nodded a tight smile to the social worker, who offered a grimace in return. Cora noticed how flustered the woman looked and wondered whether this was something entirely beyond her experience. It certainly wasn't every day that a child was brought in suspected of murder.

"Hello, JJ. My name is Detective Sergeant Peters. I'd like to ask you a few questions about what happened last night."

She pressed the tape recorder switch and glanced up at the clock. Only 8.50am. It had been a torturous night and she felt wrung out already. Cora stared across the table, waiting for some sort of acknowledgement. The child looked at the tape recorder, then down at the floor, fingers picking anxiously at the peeling edge of the table. The nails were chewed to the quick, Cora noticed. The kid's sweatshirt and trousers looked well worn, grubby and crumpled. A faint tang of stale urine hung in the air.

"D'you think you can explain to me what you were doing outside the Nowaks' family home with a box of matches in your pocket at the time the fire broke out?"

Still no response. The eyes remained firmly downcast, the fingers idly tracing patterns in the red Formica table top.

Cora exhaled. "JJ, you do realise that this is extremely serious, don't you? Both Mr and Mrs Nowak are dead and Olga is fighting

2

for her life. We're trying to put together a picture of what went on, why you would have done such a terrible thing."

A brief pause. Then, somewhat sheepishly: "She told lies about me."

The words were barely audible, but this was the first admission that the kid had actually been involved in some way – and of a possible motive. Cora cleared her throat. She and the woman sitting across the table locked eyes for a moment. It was an uncomfortable sensation.

Cora leaned forward in an attempt to make eye contact, but the child refused resolutely to look up. The leg swinging increased, causing the chair to rock slightly.

A tight band had begun to squeeze Cora's forehead. She massaged her temples with her fingertips. "Can you stop that, please?" She could hear the prickle of irritation in her own voice and realised she was losing her cool. She drew in a breath. The child, seemingly sensing this, stopped abruptly.

"Would you like to tell me what Olga said? It must have been really bad to make you do something like this."

The frail shoulders shrugged.

In spite of herself, Cora softened. "JJ, if we're to understand why you acted in such a way, you need to help us. Otherwise *we* can't help *you*."

"She said I was a thief. Her *and* her old man. In front of the whole street."

Cora and the woman exchanged glances once more. The air crackled with anticipation.

"What did she accuse you of stealing?"

The child hesitated for a few seconds, all focus on something apparently invisible beneath the table.

"Her nan's poxy brooch. She brought it in for show and tell and lost it, so she tried to blame me. 'Course, everyone believed her, din't they? I'm the Jackson kid. Why wouldn't they?"

"And that made you angry?"

"What d'you think?"

The retort was sharp. A spark of defiance leaching through the timorous front. The kid's face tilted upwards suddenly, eyes flashing.

"And did you? Take the brooch?"

"No, why would I want her crappy old brooch? She's a nasty little bitch, spreading bullshit to cover up 'cos she'd lost it herself."

"And that was a good enough reason to set fire to her home, was it?"

The eyes dropped once more. Cora couldn't decide if it was contrition or reluctance to cooperate.

The door opened and the officer who'd been standing guard entered, his face grave.

"Can I have a word, Sarge?"

Cora paused the tape and excused herself.

Re-entering moments later, she felt slightly sick. "We've just had word from the hospital. Olga has passed away."

The social worker gasped, paling visibly. JJ sat in silence, head bowed, fingers interlocked as though in prayer.

Three people dead, as the result of a petty playground argument. How needlessly tragic.

JJ's eyes lifted to meet Cora's suddenly, as if waiting for a reaction. An unpleasant chill crept along Cora's spine.

It was so fleeting that she couldn't swear to it. But she thought she detected the glimmer of a satisfied smirk twitching on the child's lips.

Wednesday, 9 November 2022

Police are appealing for witnesses following the shocking discovery of a woman's body in a quiet residential area, close to the centre of Warwick in the early hours of this morning. The woman, described as being in her late thirties to early forties, of average height and build with medium-length light brown hair, is as yet unidentified. The death is being treated as suspicious and anyone with any information should contact South Warwickshire Police on the number below. All calls will be treated in the strictest confidence.

Chapter 1

Georgia

Monday, 12 September 2022

In the orangery, Georgia sat wrapped in her taupe silk robe, the one Trevor had bought for her two Christmases ago, nursing a lukewarm cappuccino and staring out into the garden, her thoughts a thousand miles away. Beads of rainwater from the night's storm still clung to the lantern roof and window panes, jewel-like in the gentle sun that was beginning to peer through the clouds. The air was cool, although the forecast was predicting a mini heatwave over the next few days. A bit overdue, considering the apology for a summer they'd had. The glistening lawns, usually so manicured, were overgrown, spiked unevenly with rye grass. Dandelions blossomed through the patio's slate paving. She thought fleetingly of her daughter's pet rabbit, Thumper. He'd have loved those. How inconsolable eight-year-old Minnie had been when they'd found him stiff and cold in his hutch that terrible morning. He'd been young: a present for Minnie's fifth birthday. There was no obvious explanation, no outward sign of illness or injury. Trevor thought he had probably died of fright. Caught sight of a visiting fox, maybe, he'd said. They'd had to have a full, solemn ceremony, florist-bought flowers and a small stone rabbit to commemorate his brief existence. Minnie had cried at the little grave for days and refused to have another pet, saying it just wouldn't be the same. She'd been such a sensitive, caring child.

A notification pinged on her phone, bringing Georgia sharply back to the present. Glancing down to where it lay on the table, she saw that the camera on the hefty security gates had been activated. A darkly-dressed figure was retreating from the letterbox fixed to one of the lion-headed stone pillars, which stood either side of the gates. It didn't look like the regular postman. Georgia felt her stomach drop momentarily, but then reasoned that maybe it was just someone delivering flyers for something. There were frequent glossy leaflets deposited, advertising the services of people clearing gutters or cleaning driveways. Hopefuls offering shrub and tree-trimming at discounted rates. Probably another one of those.

She realised suddenly that it had been weeks since their own gardener had called; thought dispassionately that perhaps she should give him a ring. Everything had begun to slip since Trevor had gone. But she couldn't kid herself it was all about Trevor now. She had come through it – almost eighteen months had passed. She was hardly busy: she had no job to rush to, no obligations or responsibilities. She needed to give herself a shake, do something about it – and the state of the house. It was a huge pile: far too big for the two of them, let alone just her now that Minnie had flown the nest. Trevor had been all about size: the bigger, the better. It was like a security blanket for him. She understood, in a way. Like her, he'd had nothing while growing up and everything had come to him through sheer hard graft. And once his business had taken off and he was able to afford the finer things, he had gone the whole hog.

Georgia shuddered a little as she thought of the pearlescent mosaic-tiled pool in the basement, Trevor's tacky perky-breasted mermaid with flowing yellow hair shimmering the whole length of its base. She couldn't even bring herself to open the basement door in the hallway now, certainly not to venture down the steps leading to the bar area and the swimming pool beyond. She tried to block the image of Trevor, spread-eagled, face down in the turquoise water, the balding pate evident now without the expertly honed comb-over, a corona of dilute blood blooming around his head. He hadn't been a big man: five feet eight, medium build. But to Georgia it was as if he had stretched, cartoon-like, to fill the whole space. At least Minnie had been spared that sight. She'd have hated her to have that as her lasting memory of her father. The ambulance had arrived promptly but Georgia had known he was already gone. He'd been in there far too long.

Georgia couldn't allow herself to dwell on what had happened that day. It was futile. She snapped her thoughts back to the house once more, the jobs that needed tackling. She'd dispensed with the cleaner as soon as Trevor passed. Awful, nosy woman. Georgia had caught her watching them occasionally, beady-eyed; silently observing. Listening in. It had made her uncomfortable, but Trevor had laughed it off, saying she was paranoid.

"For God's sake, what's up with you? Let her gossip. We've nothing to hide. Probably brightens up her dull little life, poor cow. I don't mind being a topic of conversation."

But Georgia couldn't help but worry what the woman might have been saying. Who she might have been talking to in the village. Georgia was by nature an intensely private person and wanted to keep it that way. Although, she had to concede that the cleaner's housekeeping had been thorough. Everything was starting to look neglected since Georgia had let her go. She ran a finger over the thick, bevelled glass of the coffee table and pulled a face at the trails of dust the action had revealed. Either Georgia would have to employ someone else, or roll her sleeves up and get on with it herself. The prospect filled her with horror. There were en suites with gold taps, bidets and full-sized Jacuzzis leading off each of the six bedrooms. The parquet floor in the enormous living room needed buffing: she wouldn't know where to start. Two oversized cream leather sofas, each big enough to comfortably seat eight basketball players, were positioned around the heavy, intricate limestone fireplace which was now festooned with cobwebs, much like the multicoloured Murano glass chandelier suspended from the centre of the vaulted ceiling. It had cost an absolute packet but Trevor "just had to have it".

"Imagine swinging from that, Georgie!" he'd said with a wink as they toured the lighting showroom. She had rolled her eyes, knowing that the likelihood of Trevor doing anything quite so spontaneous would never arise. Safe and predictable were the two adjectives that sprang to mind whenever she'd thought of him. But that was how she liked things. Or at least, she had done initially. Maybe he'd been a bit more daring in his youth, but she hadn't known him then. When they first met, the sixteen-year age gap between them suited her perfectly. He'd had his wild times and was ready to settle down. Younger men were more erratic, more reckless. She'd learned from bitter experience. Her relationship with Minnie's real father could be summed up as a few drunken teenage after-hours bunk-ups in the pub car park. He'd been gorgeous, but even on her part, it was lust rather than love. She knew without asking if he'd stick around to support her and their unborn child. Trevor had come along at exactly the right time. She'd been five months pregnant, living in a hostel in Lichfield and despairing of how she would cope with a child to support and no real prospects. Trevor had been passing through: he'd recently signed a lucrative business deal and the house just outside Cheltenham was still under construction. A house with more than enough room for a family. It felt as if fate had been on her side for once in her life. It hadn't been about the money, although she couldn't argue that it wasn't a bonus. But money, she had come to realise, didn't necessarily equate with happiness.

She hated being in the living room now: it felt so cold and empty. Like a tomb. Gone were the days of lively gatherings, endless trays of canapés and free-flowing Moët, the laughter and inane chatter that such occasions brought. The stragglers emerging the next morning, having spent the night in one of the guest bedrooms only to congregate in the kitchen for a late breakfast, sometimes even staying for dinner. The house had always been full of people, full of energy. With Trevor's passing, any social life Georgia had had ceased abruptly. But those in attendance had always been *his* colleagues and acquaintances; his 'friends', as he'd preferred to think of them. She'd soon come to realise that not one of them had any interest in her as a person in her own right. Maybe it was her reluctance to share anything about herself, to engage in meaningful conversation. And she'd never been much good at making small talk. Hard work: that was how she'd overheard one woman describing her. But Georgia hadn't much cared: as far as she was concerned, Trevor always did enough talking for the pair of them. All she'd ever needed to do was look the part, smile sweetly (through gritted teeth when he'd made the odd thinly-veiled dig about her social ineptitude); make sure everyone's glasses were regularly replenished, that there was nothing anyone needed. She preferred being on the periphery, observing. People fascinated her.

After the initial gushing expressions of condolence and regret and "if you ever need anything, don't hesitate to call . . ." (not that she'd have dreamed of doing so), one by one, they had

10

drifted away. With her status as Trevor's spouse ripped from her, so was her link with any of the influential people he had built relationships with over the years. It had become just her and Minnie. And now, all too soon, it was only her.

It was so hard to motivate herself. All she could think about was her daughter. Minnie was spending her third weekend in Coventry, having moved into the new house she and a small group of her fellow students were sharing. Even though Georgia was financing things, Minnie had organised it all herself. A friend of a friend had told her about an enterprising associate of her father's, advertising a handful of wonderful high-end rental properties in the Coventry area, targeting students who preferred the idea of sharing a spacious house (and whose parents could afford it) rather than being shoved into halls with no choice as to who they might be stuck with as a room-mate. Though Georgia wasn't happy with Minnie moving away at all, having seen the photos and looked through the website's terms and conditions, she had to concede that it all sounded like the lesser of the two evils. And moreover, Georgia realised it would probably be easier to just 'drop in' on Minnie unannounced than having to negotiate her way into student halls. The idea was to put students in touch with those on the same course – the rental amount was for the property as a whole, so the total owed would be divided among the final number of occupants.

Including Minnie, there would be five sharing in all. Minnie had been put in touch with the others, who'd all been vetted by the owner and sounded decent, she said. Georgia was supposed to go along to view the house before the move, but had made a last-minute excuse not to accompany her. She really couldn't face it; the realisation that this was it, that Minnie was actually moving out. Minnie, however, had seemed fine about it, saying she'd prefer to go alone anyway. That she needed to start standing on her own two feet.

Georgia had tried, *really* tried, to appear enthusiastic about it all, though her heart felt like lead. When Minnie's form tutor had first broached the subject of further education during parents' evening two years earlier, it had all seemed so far into the future. Trevor had been enthused by the idea and began looking at the various options open to her.

"Dunno where she's got it from, but she's a bright kid," he'd told Georgia, proudly. "Oxbridge material, I'd say. The money's never going to be a problem for her, but it's brilliant that she's got the brains to go right to the top without a leg-up."

Georgia had nodded and smiled tightly, registering but not biting at the nod to her own academic inadequacies. Though it had rankled with her, she'd always tried to let Trevor's jibes wash over her. It wasn't worth getting into an argument. He could become quite unpleasant when he wanted to, delighting in reminding her who and what she'd been when they first met; that without him she'd have nothing. That she'd *be* nothing. He could be as nice as pie, but every now and then it was as if he felt the need to remind her of everything he'd done for her. That she *owed* him.

"See her, Georgie?" He'd leaned in to tell her once at a dinner party held by one of his associates, indicating an elegant-looking dark-haired woman at the far end of the table. "She's a multimillionaire. Could charm the birds from the trees, but she's shrewd. *Very* savvy. Everything she owns, she's worked her arse off for. That's the kind of woman I admire. One who can stand on her own two feet without having to rely on a bloke to support her."

She'd let it go most of the time. But there were occasions when Georgia felt the need to teach him a lesson, even if he was in ignorance of the fact. There were more subtle ways to get back at him. She smiled to herself, remembering the extra-strong laxatives she'd slipped into his coffee one morning before an

12

important meeting. The handful of rabbit droppings sprinkled into his muesli on another occasion. The best was when she'd squeezed hair removal cream into his expensive conditioner. His horror at finding the plughole clogged with handfuls of his own already thinning locks.

Oh yes. Trevor may have always believed he had the upper hand, but she knew better.

Naively, she'd never really considered the implications of Minnie gaining a place at university at the time. That it would leave her redundant and aimless. With a pang, Georgia realised now that, although Minnie had scraped passes, she would probably have done so much better in her A levels if it hadn't been for what happened to Trevor. It was inevitable that something so earth-shattering would have an effect on the girl's studies. Minnie had been given the option of resitting her exams, but was determined to go to university at the same time as everyone she'd been through school with. To 'move on with everything', as she'd put it. She didn't care about going to an ancient, prestigious institution like Oxford or Cambridge, nor even a red-brick university, and the history course at Coventry uni had ticked all the boxes.

Even at the start of the summer holidays, it hardly seemed possible: that Minnie would be moving away, spreading her wings and leaving home – leaving *her* – for good. The years seemed to have evaporated. It seemed like only yesterday that she'd felt the constant squeeze of Minnie's chubby arms around her leg wherever she stood, her small hand slipped automatically into her mother's the second they left the house for any reason. Minnie's soft curls resting against her arm as they watched her current favourite TV programmes. The endless nights when bad dreams had brought Minnie into Georgia and Trevor's bed to sleep between them. Neither had minded. Even though Minnie wasn't Trevor's biological daughter, he'd doted on her completely. Georgia could never fault him as a father, especially not compared with her own. And though she may not have been *in* love with him, she had been fond of him. At the beginning, at least. He had represented security, dependability. Everything Georgia had wanted in a father for her unborn child. Everything she herself had never had.

Georgia had tried – *really* tried, not to smother Minnie. But it was so difficult, given her own beginnings. She was determined never to replicate her own parents' failings and wanted only the best for her daughter, telling her constantly how loved she was, how precious. It was only after becoming a mother herself that the true extent of her own mum and dad's failings really hit home. She found it incomprehensible how anyone could have had such total disregard for their own flesh and blood, for a child they had created.

Georgia recalled bitterly an incident in her own childhood when, aged only five, she'd been in the school nativity play, cast, somewhat ironically, as an angel. The other kids' parents had made costumes, watched the performance from the packed assembly hall with glistening eyes; snapped endless images to keep for posterity. When it became apparent that Georgia had brought no outfit, one had been hastily cobbled together by her class teacher from an old sheet and a spare string of tinsel. Georgia's eyes had searched the audience hopefully for her mum and dad, but they hadn't bothered to turn up. Even at such a young age, she'd felt the need to hide the fact that no one had come to collect her at the end of the evening, slipping away before the teacher had noticed. Though the school was only a couple of hundred yards from home, she remembered being scared of the dark and running all the way, only to receive a vicious clip round the ear from her father as he opened the door. She couldn't even remember what she was supposed to have done to deserve it, only that her head throbbed for the rest of the night and she'd cried herself to sleep. Such was the pattern of her early existence.

No one had ever shown Georgia real attention or affection as a child and she wondered how differently her life might have played out if she'd had the backing of a caring family unit. As it was, she had pretty much dragged herself up with little input from her parents. Her mother was apathetic and weak, never backing Georgia when her father turned on her. The only person who'd ever shown the slightest concern for her welfare had been her grandmother, who lived at the other side of the city and died when Georgia was only seven. Georgia had never felt wanted. Her attendance at school had been sporadic, not least because she'd begun to dread what her next humiliation would be on a daily basis. She remembered with a shudder of shame being jeered at by a group of older girls when caught scavenging through her classmates' lunchboxes for leftovers; being mocked by the other kids for the sorry state of her clothes, her poor personal hygiene. The nits that seemed to be in permanent residence on her scalp. The horror when one had actually dropped from her head onto the desk where she'd been sitting, eliciting shrieks from the girl sitting beside her. Small wonder Georgia didn't have any mates. Consequently, she had become hostile, preferring to let everyone believe she was content with her own company rather than risk rejection and ridicule. Better never to set yourself up for an inevitable fall.

Maybe that was why, her whole life, she'd never felt able to form any genuine bond with another living soul.

Until the day Minnie was born, when the completely unexpected surge of fierce maternal love she felt for this tiny, helpless soul, the intense desire to protect and nurture, almost winded her. It was an epiphany. This, she realised, was what she had been created for. She had checked repeatedly, asked the nurses and doctors, unable to accept that Minnie would be okay; that there was nothing wrong with her. She couldn't believe that a child she had produced could be so perfect. A true gift. A second chance.

Georgia had woken in the early hours in sudden panic as she had so often over the last few months: those nights when Minnie had been out on the town or stayed over at a friend's. But now she had no idea what Minnie would be getting up to or who she would be with, nor any control over it, and every time she acknowledged the fact, the feeling of anxiety was overwhelming. It had been a gradual but inevitable part of growing up, this slackening of the apron strings, the subtle drift towards independence. There would be no more relief from the mid-morning key in the door as her daughter breezed in, all wild hair and smudged eyes, apologising for not texting but she'd been having *such* a blast; no more reassuring hugs and excitable chatter, and flakes of buttery croissant with dollops of raspberry jam to clean up from the marble island lost in the centre of the vast kitchen, Trevor's state-of-the-art Revo radio pulsing in the background.

Even though she'd known this time would come eventually, Georgia was finding it so painful. She couldn't even bring herself to switch on the radio today. The realisation that endless silent mornings like this were all she had to look forward to filled her with a deep melancholy – and dread. With Minnie so far away, how could she know her daughter was safe? She'd called her three times daily for the first week, checking that all was well. Minnie had begun to sound irritated whenever she answered the phone on the last few occasions, so in spite of the urge to check on her constantly, Georgia had forced herself to reduce the number of calls. But it seemed there was news almost weekly of young girls going missing or falling victim to a vicious attack on their way home. The thought of anything happening to her beloved child didn't bear thinking about. And Minnie was surely

16

more at risk than most, for obvious reasons. The thought made Georgia's coffee curdle in her stomach. She'd always been there to protect her before. Always.

*

Minnie was everything she hadn't been – bubbly, gregarious. Outlandish in her dress sense and choice of pillar-box red hair colour, tattoos snaking from her shoulders to her wrists. Confident in her looks: she'd refused point blank when Trevor had offered to pay for a nose job for her seventeenth birthday.

"It may not be perfect, but it's my nose, Dad. I don't want to finish up looking like someone I don't recognise when I look in the mirror." She hadn't been affronted, merely stating a fact. Unlike Georgia, who'd jumped at the chance and succumbed to everything going: nose refining, cheek implants, boob lift. Porcelain veneers. She bore little resemblance to the girl she'd been when she first met her husband, which suited her fine. She'd never liked the way she looked. But Minnie was perfectly comfortable in her own skin. Georgia flushed with pride as she thought of the strong, self-assured young woman they had raised. Minnie was the one thing she had got right. The possession she held most dear.

It was Minnie who had been her rock: supported her after Trevor's loss; got her through the fug of those wretched first few months, helped her deal with the practicalities. Ridiculous, *shameful* even, that her seventeen-year-old daughter had had to sort things out, prop *her* up when she must have been shocked and grief-stricken. Georgia was wracked with guilt, knowing how close Minnie and her father had been. The girl's strength of character was astounding.

Georgia carried her coffee cup through to the kitchen, tipping the dregs into the sink before shoving it into the dishwasher. On her way to collect the post, she glanced at herself in the huge, gilt-framed Venetian mirror in the hallway and looked away again just as quickly in disgust. She seemed to have aged ten years over the last few months. Her eyes were sunken, cheeks hollowed out and sallow. She hadn't had her roots done or her balayage refreshed in almost fourteen months.

Christ. What was happening to her?

Slipping her feet into the outdoor Crocs which she kept by the front door, she walked down the driveway and unlocked the letterbox from the near-side of the pillar. It had been Trevor's idea to install it, rather than having someone approaching the property directly to make deliveries.

"We don't want any Tom, Dick or Harry coming up the path, casing the joint," he'd said. Georgia wasn't going to argue. Though Minnie complained it was like living in a fortress, it had always felt reassuring for Georgia; even more so, now that Trevor was gone.

She pulled out the pile of post, locking the letterbox again, and leafed through as she made her way back to the house. The usual crap, most of it destined for the recycling bin. But one neatly handwritten A5 blue envelope bearing a first-class stamp looked as though it could be important.

F.A.O. Mrs T Parnell.

Something from the solicitor's, maybe? Though money wasn't an issue and she had more than enough to live on, the probate was taking an eternity. Perhaps they'd finally wrapped everything up.

She closed the front door behind her and took the bundle back into the kitchen. Pulling up a stool at the island, she reached for Trevor's paper knife to open the letter. As she withdrew the contents, something like a newspaper cutting fluttered to the floor. She glanced down to where it had landed and almost fell from her seat, her heart lurching. At once she recognised the photograph from the article – that day she and Trevor had met the mayor at the city hall, the oversized cheque from Trevor's fundraising effort for the local hospice held aloft in the foreground. With quivering fingers, she unfolded the sheaf of lined paper that had accompanied it, a single, portentous word blurring before her eyes as she read and reread it.

Gotcha.

Her heart hammering, she snatched up the envelope once more, peering at the stamp more closely. It hadn't been franked. She cast her mind back to one previous cryptic delivery which had played on her mind almost two years earlier: a single sheet of paper bearing a colour print-out of their home from Google Street View. It had arrived in a handwritten envelope via the usual post. No sender information, no accompanying note. Then there had been Trevor's drunken outburst the day he'd died.

This felt suddenly very real. Ominous. Frantically, she took her phone from her pocket and replayed the footage from the security camera. It showed the figure she'd noticed earlier approaching the house, their face largely covered by a loose hood, looking from left to right before dropping something into the letterbox, then briskly walking away. Her stomach tightened.

She'd always had a niggling doubt that there might be a penalty for marrying a man with money, for the luxurious lifestyle she'd embraced for the last eighteen years. She had waited after Trevor died; for what, she wasn't quite sure. But she'd known something would happen eventually. She wasn't so naive that she'd believed all of Trevor's business deals had been entirely above board. And now here was the proof that she'd been right.

It was payback time.

Chapter 2

Georgia

Tuesday, 20 September 2022

"Well, it's about as far removed from Warchester as you could've got, Mum."

Minnie cast a dubious eye over the uneven, darkly-stained floor, undulating to the extent it could almost induce motion sickness. It was just as well that neither she nor her mother were particularly tall, since the claustrophobically low ceilings clearly hadn't been designed to cater for anyone above six feet in height. The sharp incline of the rickety, narrow staircase they'd just climbed would be unsuited to (and possibly even treacherous for) anyone slightly unsteady on their legs. The soles of Minnie's trainers squeaked against the pitted floorboards as she crossed the tiny bedroom to peer from the small leaded window down to the cobbled courtyard below. It was a beautifully mellow early autumn day, the trees still clinging to their foliage but sprinkled now with saffron and amber. The tower from the old cathedral loomed before them, cloaking the lower end of the quadrangle and the small, walled graveyard in gloomy shadow, despite the afternoon sun.

Minnie looked back over her shoulder, eyebrows raised. "I'm really surprised you didn't go for something a bit less, well, *ancient*. There are some newish penthouse apartments not that far from town. Very plush. I'd've thought they'd be more your style."

Georgia smiled to herself. *More her style*. Minnie had known nothing but the grandeur and capacious rooms of Warchester Manor, and most of her friends came from similar, privileged backgrounds. The large, four-storey townhouse she was now sharing with her fellow students on the outskirts of the city had been modernised and equipped with every feasible facility. The owner had even hinted at converting the basement into a gym at some point in the future, although plans had yet to materialise. Having spent her own formative years in a cramped, damp two-bedroom maisonette, Georgia had never stopped appreciating the space and luxury of Warchester, nor did she take for granted the standard of living her marriage to Trevor had brought. Though Trevor had known she'd had a miserable childhood, he actually knew very little of her early years beyond the few carefully edited anecdotes she'd chosen to share. And she'd always been deliberately vague if Minnie ever questioned her about her upbringing.

"Oh, it was all a very long time ago, I don't remember much about it," was her usual flippant response if asked, followed hurriedly by a smile and a change of subject. As Minnie grew older, either she'd lost interest or had come to realise that Georgia didn't want to talk about her past and had stopped probing.

Georgia had been prepared to overlook the cracks in her relationship with Trevor for the sake of enjoying a life lived in comfort – but, above all, for Minnie. Publicly, Georgia and

Trevor had always presented a united front and she doubted Minnie had any idea of her true feelings. But then, since Georgia's teens, hadn't that been the shape of her whole life? A sham hiding the reality of who she was, of the cess-pit she had crawled from. It had got to the point where reality and fiction blurred in her own mind. Georgia didn't dare dwell on the past. For there lay the path to insanity.

That letter, the sudden reminder that someone out there was trying to drag up things she'd spent a lifetime trying to bury, felt like a very abrupt awakening from the stupor she'd been languishing in for months. She needed to protect herself. And she needed to protect Minnie from the truth.

It had been four weeks now since Minnie had moved out. Fearful of what might follow the unwelcome delivery, Georgia had been immediately galvanised into action. That very same afternoon, she had searched online, arranged transport for things she wanted to put into storage, then booked herself into an Airbnb apartment in the upper storey of an old half-timbered building in Coventry city centre, with the intention of visiting Minnie. It would be a nice surprise for her, she thought.

Hurriedly packing a bag, Georgia had locked up and taken a taxi to the station. Once on the train from Cheltenham, the overwhelming sense of panic began to wane. Her heart felt a little lighter, too. She could spend some quality time with her daughter and make sure she really was okay. And it would buy her time to make plans for herself.

*

Minnie had looked almost incredulous to find Georgia on her doorstep.

After dropping off her bag at the Airbnb, Georgia had immediately called another taxi to take her straight to Minnie's new house, brimming with excitement at the thought of seeing her daughter again after almost a month apart: the longest they'd ever been separated. There had been an awkward pause when Minnie answered the door, almost as though she wasn't sure whether to invite her in or not. Georgia felt hurt, her previously buoyant mood instantly squashed.

"What are you doing here, Mum?" Minnie had asked, glancing back sharply into the hallway. "You might've rung ahead first."

Georgia had forced a laugh, said jokingly she was doing a spot check; hoped Minnie wasn't up to anything she shouldn't have been. Minnie had rolled her eyes and made way for Georgia to enter.

"I mean, I might not even have been in." Minnie's voice had sounded almost accusing, with no trace of pleasure on her face.

"But you are, aren't you?" Georgia felt a barb of irritation now, her eyes scanning the lofty hallway as she stepped over the threshold, the row of unfamiliar jackets hanging near the front door. This wasn't the kind of reunion she'd anticipated. Still with the open door behind her, she held her arms wide.

"Where's my hug?"

Minnie leaned in to give her a stiff embrace. Georgia held her close for a moment, burying her face in Minnie's hair and breathing in the familiar scent of her herbal shampoo. Minnie always smelled so lovely. Georgia felt tears prick her eyes and blinked them back. She relaxed her grip on her daughter, squeezing a smile.

"I've missed you so much."

Minnie nodded, ever so slightly. But the smile was still missing.

Georgia looked her up and down, frowning a little. "Are you eating properly? I'm sure you've lost weight."

Minnie's eyes rolled skyward. "Mum, I'm eating plenty. You need to stop fretting all the time."

"That's my job, to worry about you."

"I'm okay, honestly." Minnie sighed. "It – it worries me that you always get so anxious. It's not good for you." She studied Georgia with narrowed eyes. "You didn't say why you were here."

"I wanted to see my baby girl. There's no law against that, is there?"

Minnie lifted an eyebrow. She made no response.

"Don't worry, I haven't come to stay. I fancied a change of scenery, so I've booked into an apartment in the city centre."

There was a pause. "In *Coventry*?"

"Yes, in Coventry." Georgia cleared her throat. "And while I'm here, I just wanted to check you're okay and have a look at where you're living. I mean, I am helping to pay for it all, in case you'd forgotten."

Minnie pulled a face somewhere between a glower and despair.

"Well no, of course I hadn't. And I'm very grateful." She made a half-hearted attempt at a smile.

Georgia bristled again. She didn't *look* grateful.

Minnie finally closed the door. "Come on, I'll make you a tea. Everyone else is out at the moment, so I'll give you the guided tour in a minute."

Finally seeing the house Minnie was living in had given her food for thought. The Airbnb had only been to buy her time while she considered her options. But why not move to Coventry, too – permanently? She could be near Minnie, and anyone with ill intentions who was looking for her at Warchester would be completely thrown off the scent.

Win-win.

After two nights in the Airbnb apartment, Georgia had begun house-hunting in earnest. She'd trawled through the websites of local estate agents, viewed a few places that didn't somehow feel quite right. Though the little house at the end of the row on Bayley Lane might have been small, Georgia had felt a rush of optimism the moment she'd walked through the black, studded door into the flag-stoned vestibule. Cuckoo Cottage wasn't twee exactly, but undeniably quirky, and she found it fascinating to think of the history of the place; the people who had made it their home over the last three centuries. The stories encased within the walls. A far cry from Warchester it may have been, but right now it was exactly what Georgia needed. She intended to treat this as an adventure, a new chapter in her life, rather than self-imposed exile. After the doldrums of the last few weeks, she was almost euphoric to be near Minnie once again. That, plus the feeling of being reassuringly anonymous and, for the time being at least, safe from whatever persecution might have been in store for her.

"No, this is perfect for me." Georgia surveyed her surroundings now, the corners of her mouth lifting. "I love where it is. And I'm surprised you don't like it, budding historian and all that. I thought it would've been right up your street."

Minnie spun round to face her, her blue eyes shining. She plonked herself in the threadbare Queen Anne chair positioned beneath the window and gazed up at the beamed ceiling. "Oh, it *so* is. So much character! I just didn't think something like this would appeal to you, that's all. I always thought you liked your home comforts."

"I do – of course I do. But I wanted a total change." Georgia's eyes flickered a little. "And this is exactly that. It's . . ." She sank down onto the edge of the narrow bed, running her fingertips absently over the old counterpane. The previous tenant, ostensibly a mature student, had left in a hurry, she'd been informed by the letting agent: payments still outstanding. The agency had been unable to trace them. She was welcome to the furniture, or the agency would arrange to have it taken away. For Georgia, it wasn't a deal-breaker either way.

She looked round the room again, noting the cracks in the

plaster, the original but very grubby cast iron fireplace, the addition of a clunky mid-twentieth century radiator on the wall beneath the window. Okay, so it wasn't going to provide the standard of living she'd grown accustomed to. But the cobwebs and grime could easily be banished. She would soon make her mark on the place. Only four days had passed since her first viewing, and she'd been itching to get in and make a start ever since. And now she finally had the key, it was becoming a reality. Georgia herself just needed transport to bring the few essentials from home that she'd already placed in storage locally. There was no need for her to return to Warchester at all. She intended to stay in the apartment she was booked into for another couple of nights until the cottage was more inhabitable, but the move was excitingly imminent.

Stephen, the lad from the letting agency, had seemed slightly surprised in the interest she'd shown when she told him at once she'd take it. The rent was really rather high, given the state of the property. He hadn't even appeared particularly concerned about conducting the relevant background checks on her. Maybe the killer Manolo Blahniks (ill-advised, she'd realised subsequently, given the precipitous staircase) and tailored Chanel suit were enough to persuade him that money was no object. Which, of course, in her case it wasn't – but she could easily have been faking it. Silly boy.

"We haven't had much interest, to be honest. It's been on the rental market for a couple of months now. A handful of viewings, but no one's bothered to take things any further. Same as the house next door – the old lady who lived there died over a year ago and the family are having no luck selling. I s'pose it's the fact these places are listed – limited what you can actually do to the buildings – and the décor, of course."

But Georgia was fine with it all. She wasn't buying anyway, and it was a base, tucked away but in the very centre of the city, and at a pinch, within walking distance of Minnie's digs. "When can I collect the keys?"

"I'll check with my manager. But as far as I'm concerned, you can have them by tomorrow. I think the owner will be pleased to have some income from the old place again."

"Who *is* the owner?"

Something like distaste crossed Stephen's face. "He's – Mr Jackson is, shall we say, connected. Owns several properties around the area. Fingers in a lot of pies." He shot her a knowing look.

"Oh?"

Though there was no one to overhear, the young man lowered his voice, leaning in towards her. "Jethro Jackson's a well-known figure in the town. Quite a colourful past, if you get me, but he's made good. Not short of a few quid now, which is probably why he wasn't that desperate to find a tenant initially. But something's happened lately and he's talking about moving abroad. He's been ringing the office a lot to see if we've found new tenants. So it'll be a box ticked for him and a relief for us, too."

And a relief for Georgia, to find just what she'd been looking for. She smiled to herself at Stephen's lack of discretion, wondering if the owner had been giving the agency a hard time. He sounded the type.

Jethro Jackson – she thought the name rang a bell. Trevor had known a lot of business people: maybe he'd mentioned him in passing. But then – Jackson was a common enough surname, wasn't it? Maybe she was thinking of someone else.

After the viewing, she'd bought a take-out panini from a little coffee shop round the corner, then wandered down across the cobbled quadrangle and into what remained of the bombed-out cathedral. She sat on a bench in the sunshine to eat her sandwich, looking up at the makeshift cross fashioned from the fallen beams of the old building that someone had propped on the original altar. Pigeons pecked for crumbs around her feet, tame and apparently oblivious to the handful of people who walked slowly by. Everyone seemed lost in their own thoughts and no one paid her any attention. Despite the fact that Georgia scoffed privately at religion, it felt so peaceful: a place for contemplation and reflection. A haven in the heart of the city. And only a stone's throw from where she was going to make her home. She dared to feel a tingle of optimism that here was somewhere she could shake off her past and build a new life for herself, whilst still being near to her beloved daughter.

*

She tipped her face in Minnie's direction now, a half-smile on her lips.

"I don't know; I just felt it somehow, that first time I walked in. I know it's a bit shabby, but that can soon be sorted. There's a nice atmosphere to the place. As though it's once been a happy home. Besides, I'd had enough of rattling around in Warchester. This is much more the sort of size I need. And it won't be forever, will it? I've signed a lease for twelve months and I'll review things after that."

"But – what will you do with Warchester? Are you going to sell?" Minnie's face clouded.

Something twisted in Georgia's gut. Warchester had been the only home Minnie had ever known. Even if she no longer lived there, it was going to be a wrench for her, never being able to go back. So many happy memories of her childhood. Of Trevor. Minnie had always been a home bird. And she'd adored her father. Though things between Georgia and Trevor had become increasingly strained over the years, begrudgingly she still had to credit him with always putting Minnie first.

28

Georgia took a breath and rose to stand behind her at the window, her eyes scanning the space below. The gentle autumn breeze ruffled the leaves of the trees surrounding the graveyard. A steady stream of pedestrians meandered by, some heading purposefully towards Holy Trinity Church and the shops beyond, many in the opposite direction: tourists eager to explore the cathedral ruins or to take on the challenge of climbing the winding steps inside the tower. None paused to cast their eyes upward in their direction and didn't appear even to notice the residential part of the square. Georgia looked across the quad and realised that, in the shadow of the tall surrounding buildings, all the upstairs windows opposite looked opaque, giving nothing away about what lay on the other side. It gave her a comforting sense of invisibility. She placed her hands on her daughter's shoulders and gave them a gentle squeeze.

"I think I'll have to sell eventually, sweetheart. I mean, it's far too big for me on my own – and with what happened . . ." She tailed off, feeling Minnie stiffen. "But not just yet, eh? There's no hurry. The money's not going to dry up overnight." Georgia peeped over Minnie's shoulder and tilted her face towards her, encouraging a small smile from her daughter.

"No, I guess not. And what you do with the house – well, it's entirely up to you. I mean – I don't know where this course will lead me. Who knows – I could even end up doing a master's abroad somewhere . . ."

Georgia's throat tightened. This was something she couldn't even contemplate. "Hold on – one thing at a time – you've only just enrolled! Focus on the here and now. And while you're busy studying, *I've* got to find something to do myself. I can't sit around here, twiddling my thumbs all day. I'm thinking of looking for a little job, keep me from going doolally."

Minnie drew back her chin in mock horror. "Mother! A job? *Really*?"

"Oi, cheeky. I have worked before, you know – I'm not completely useless." Georgia looked back out of the window. "Plenty of stores out there – no doubt some of them must be hiring."

"I'm joking. I think it's great that you want to get into the workplace." Minnie rose to give her a brief hug. "It may be the making of you. You need – I dunno, something to get up for in the mornings. To meet new people. *Nice* people." She gave an almost imperceptible nod of the head.

Georgia could see her daughter's brain ticking over and rolled her eyes. She realised this could be Minnie's new project: *find Mum the perfect career*.

"I just need something to fill a few hours every day. Nothing too taxing."

"I'll keep my eyes peeled." Minnie gave her an exaggerated wink.

Georgia smiled. This was more like the Minnie of old, the banter they would often exchange. But she realised she would have to find herself a job quickly before she was steered into something she didn't really want to do. Knowing Minnie, she would probably try to find her a vacancy at the university: clerical, or office-related in some way. Something mind-numbingly boring. This wasn't what Georgia had planned at all.

"I'll probably give it a while – check out the area and everything first," she said hastily. "I'd like to see the sights first."

Minnie considered for a moment. "I could show you around I suppose, when I've got some free time. One of the guys I'm sharing with is from Birmingham, but he's pretty familiar with the place – he took us all on a guided tour when we first landed here. There are plenty of bits worth visiting."

Georgia fixed her with a look of disapproval. "A guy? I thought it was all girls together in your house? You didn't mention anything about a boy living with you when I visited."

Minnie gave an exasperated sigh. "Just the one guy. His

name's Ajab, and he's gay – but not out with his parents. They're really old-fashioned and he's moved in with us to get them off his case. And before you ask, my other housemates *are* girls. So don't go getting any ideas about marrying me off just yet."

Georgia arced an eyebrow. Nothing could be further from the truth.

Georgia's inability, and later reluctance, to form friendships as a child had continued into adulthood. She, more than anyone, knew that no one could ever really know, much less trust, another person, and it made her wary and sometimes even hostile towards anyone Minnie had begun to grow close to. She'd suspected Minnie's last boyfriend, Scott, with whom Minnie had been involved for about eight months and was besotted, of being unfaithful. Georgia had taken an instant disliking to Scott. He'd seemed insincere, too gushing, overly eager to make a good impression.

"*Good evening, Mrs Parnell. I do like your blouse – it really suits you.*" That sort of crap.

He was overly sure of himself into the bargain – tall and blandly good-looking, the type that was obsessed with working out; always wearing a tight T-shirt to show off his physique. He used too much hair gel and couldn't pass a mirror without checking himself out. Georgia had spotted him one day as she walked through town one Saturday, when he'd told Minnie he was busy revising for an exam. Suspicious as to why he'd lied, Georgia had followed from a distance out of curiosity. She'd lost him briefly, then caught up to see him with one hand propping up a wall above the head of a pretty blonde-haired girl, the other low on the girl's hip as he leaned in towards her.

The next time Scott visited the house, Georgia told him in no uncertain terms that if he was messing her daughter around, she would see to it that he'd wake up one day with his testicles decorating his bedpost. The boy was some two years older than the then sixteen-year-old Minnie; from his red-faced reaction, he'd clearly been guilty of playing the field, when Minnie believed their relationship to be exclusive. Following Georgia's threat, delivered out of earshot from Minnie in a quiet, cold-blooded manner so that Scott was under no illusion about its veracity, he'd broken things off very quickly.

Minnie had been devastated, but Georgia felt quietly triumphant. Her intervention had shielded Minnie from heartbreak further down the line and she had every intention of continuing to keep an eye on her romantic attachments. No one was going to turn her daughter into a victim, not while she had breath in her body.

"Trust me, sweetheart, I've no desire to see you tied down. Plenty of time for that. You need to see a bit of life first. And focus on your degree, of course," she added, giving her a meaningful stare.

"I fully intend to." Minnie looked suddenly serious. "I mean, that's why I'm here, after all."

Georgia clapped her hands together suddenly. "Well, before you get too immersed in everything, let's have a night out this evening to celebrate. You know: you beginning your course, me making a fresh start."

A look of something like panic crossed Minnie's face. Georgia felt suddenly irked. She'd thought Minnie would want to spend time with her as they'd been apart so long.

"Oh, I'm sorry," she said curtly. "If you've already made plans, we'll have to do it another time, then . . ."

Minnie shook her head. "No, no. I've got nothing on." The corners of her mouth raised into an unconvincing smile. "Yeah, sounds good to me. Where d'you fancy going?"

"I had a wander round earlier – I noticed there's a couple of cocktail lounges in that shopping mall at Broadgate – you know,

Cathedral Lanes? It's nice and handy. We could start in there, grab a bite to eat."

"Cool. Right, I'd better get back to the house, grab a shower and that." Minnie edged towards the door. "See you back at your apartment, what, about seven?"

"Great – see you in a bit, then."

Georgia watched from the window as Minnie turned to wave from outside the front door, then moved at a brisk pace down past the cathedral and the medieval Guildhall, and towards the Herbert Art Gallery. She saw her pause and pull out her mobile to take a call, shaking her head as though all wasn't well, then disappearing round a corner. Georgia felt a twinge of disappointment – maybe Minnie had had plans after all and felt obliged to cancel. Or was she concerned that, by moving here, Georgia would be too close and cramp her style? But all Georgia wanted to do was to look out for her. And to keep their relationship as close as it had ever been.

The idea of Minnie growing away from her was unthinkable. Georgia had built her whole world around her daughter. Without her, what would she have?

She could never allow anything or anyone to come between them. Not ever.

Chapter 3

Minnie

Friday, 16 September 2022 – Four days earlier

The student union bar was a bit of a dive, but it was where everyone seemed to gravitate to on Friday nights, with the promise of cheap beer and good music. Minnie had had enough. It had been a long day and an even longer night.

She and her housemate Ajab had hit it off right from the start. The two of them had gone for a couple of rounds in an ancient pub called the Golden Orb, close to the cathedral and not far from the main uni building. But they'd arranged to meet the others in the SU, so after an hour or so, they finished their drinks and left, Ajab somewhat reluctantly. He'd seemed pretty taken with the guy serving, Yiannis, who'd started chatting to them as they stood at the bar. Minnie knew Ajab was sensitive and resisted teasing him. But she'd had a little grin to herself when he'd said what a great place it was, how they should go there more often.

So transparent.

By now Minnie had drunk herself sober and all she wanted to do was crash, but had stayed later than she intended because of the others. From the SU, it was a good twenty-minute walk across town back to their digs and she was sensible enough to know that it wasn't wise to venture through the city centre alone after dark. Sonia, one of her housemates, had become embarrassingly loud and Ajab, ever the voice of reason and respectability, wore a worried frown as he tried without success to get her to sit back down at their table. Sonia shook off his hand with a laugh as she teetered once more towards the bar, slender arms swaying above her head in time to the music booming from the sound system.

It was just two weeks into the first semester and a sort of hierarchy had quickly been established within the house. There should have been five of them sharing, but within days of moving in, they'd received notification that Joanna, whom none of them had met, had had a change of heart and was taking a gap year instead. The additional payment wasn't a problem for Minnie, but the others were keen to find someone to replace Joanna to bridge the gap in the rent. Following Minnie sharing her mum's bombshell that she was planning to rent somewhere in the city, Fatima had even mooted the idea of Georgia taking the room, which Minnie, aghast at the prospect, had been quick to squash. So they had put up a notice in the history department foyer, but as yet there had been no takers.

Minnie had quickly become fond of Ajab, who was quiet and studious and never took the piss with food supplies or cleaning up after himself. Which was more than could be said for Sonia and Fatima. Her lack of domestic skills apart, Sonia was okay and Minnie liked her. Fatima, however, was opinionated and could cause friction. Things generally felt more harmonious when she wasn't at home. But she wasn't all bad and could be a laugh at times, and Minnie felt that if you were in a tight spot, you'd be glad to have her in your corner. She'd resolved that, sometimes, you had to take the rough with the smooth. On the whole, the four of them were rubbing along quite nicely – most of the time.

Minnie looked on as Sonia sidled up to an equally inebriated lad near the bar and began to grind against him in time to the music. Within seconds the pair looked as if they were trying to eat one other's faces, with Sonia's hands clasped around the guy's buttocks. Minnie groaned, putting a hand across her eyes. She leaned in to Ajab. "*Jesus.* Shall I book us an Uber? Doesn't look like Sonia's going to want to leave any time soon. Dunno about you, but I'm wrecked." Without waiting for a response, she pulled out her phone and began to search.

Ajab looked doubtful. "D'you think we ought to wait for her?" He cast around fretfully. "And where did Fatima go?"

Minnie gritted her teeth. She scanned the room for Fatima's wild dark curls and homed in on the back of her head, jutting forwards aggressively from the edge of the leatherette bench against the far wall she was perched on. She was clearly drunk and involved in a heated debate with one of the boys Minnie recognised from a lecture she'd attended earlier in the week, jabbing a finger towards him and looking as if she'd like to throw a punch across the table. The lad had his palms raised in a conciliatory fashion, but from her body language, Fatima didn't appear to have been mollified.

Minnie sighed. "I think Fatima's in the middle of something. Anyway, she can handle herself." She rose, tipping her head towards Ajab. "You coming?"

He looked from Fatima back to Minnie and blew out his cheeks. "I'd better hang on, make sure the pair of them actually make it into a cab, the state they're in. I'll see you out to the Uber, though," he added.

Minnie tutted. "Thanks for the offer, but I'm a big girl. I'll be okay." She checked the app on her phone. "I'd better get out there. The car's six minutes away. See you in the morning."

Leaving Ajab looking anxiously after her, she weaved her way through the sea of bodies and headed out of the door. Standing on the kerb, she took in gulps of the cool night air, peering from left to right along the road for signs of the taxi. Her ears were still ringing from the ridiculous volume of the music and the din of drunken conversation and laughter. It was almost midnight. She felt wrung out and desperate for her bed. Crossing the road, she mounted the pavement at the bottom of the steps to the new cathedral, staring up at the huge bronze sculpture bearing down from its walls. In the darkness and against a sickly yellow backlight, it looked even more sinister: St Michael, wings spread wide and a spear in one hand, poised above the fallen, shackled Devil. A triumph of good over evil – though to Minnie, neither figure appeared sympathetic. It made her shudder.

The sky was a clear indigo, the moon almost full. The absence of other people made her uneasy and she checked the app again, hopeful that the car would be with her soon.

"You on your own?"

A male voice from behind caught Minnie unawares. She looked up sharply, suddenly on alert as a man descended the steps from the shadows and approached. Her pulse quickened.

"My Uber will be here in a sec." She clutched her phone more tightly, edging nearer the road.

The man smiled reassuringly. "I'll wait with you if you want. Not a great idea being out here all alone at night, you know." His accent had an Irish lilt. "You get all sorts hanging about up there." He gestured back towards the old cathedral ruins.

"I'm fine, thanks all the same." She glanced anxiously down the street, willing the car to appear. "The app says he's one minute away."

The man plunged his hands into his trouser pockets. He

took a step back, obviously sensing her unease. Minnie took a moment to appraise him. He was tall, maybe about thirty, with shaggy dark hair that skimmed the collar of his leather jacket. But his expression was open and friendly, not lascivious in any way.

"Look, I'm not a weirdo or anything, I promise. I noticed you standing there – I've just been for a few pints and I'm heading home." The way he pronounced 'pints' made her suppress a smile. It sounded more like 'points', but she bit back the urge to make some quip in case he took offence.

"Seriously," he went on, "you need to be careful, especially when you've had a drink." His brow had knitted into a frown. "Keep your wits about you. Lots of stories of people, especially girls, getting mugged and worse in city centres at night." His wide brown eyes studied her face with what appeared to be genuine concern. Minnie found herself staring at him. He was actually really attractive. She swallowed hard, looking away quickly.

"Yeah – I know. I thought my cab'd only be a couple of minutes." As if on cue, the rumble of an engine approaching caught her attention. A flash of headlights washed the road as a car pulled up alongside them. Minnie took in the number plate and flooded with relief. "Here it is now."

The driver wound down the window. "Uber for Minnie?"

The Irish man, still standing at her side, broke into a lopsided grin. "Like the car or the mouse?"

Minnie threw him a withering look. "Funny. Like the mouse."

"Well, you take care, Minnie Mouse. And don't get talking to any strange men." He gave her a brief wink and strolled casually across the street, then proceeded to descend in the direction of the main road.

The Uber driver made a U-turn and as they sailed past the man, he raised a hand to wave. Minnie surprised herself by returning the gesture. She sat back in her seat and, in spite of herself, felt a smile tug at her lips.

Minnie Mouse. A corny line she'd heard a thousand times before. Although – there had been something about him: a quiet, easy manner. And those eyes . . . Minnie tried to shake the thought. He was too old for her, of course he was. But all the way home she recalled the way he'd looked at her, and something skittered in her stomach. Part of her hoped she would bump into her Irish comedian again.

Chapter 4

Georgia

Sunday, 25 September 2022

The Golden Orb stood on the corner, between Bayley Lane and Cuckoo Lane – and within yards of Georgia's front door. So the A3 notice in the window declaring 'Part-time Bar Person Needed – Immediate Start' in bold, black felt-tip felt as if it was calling to her, even though she hadn't intended to start working quite so soon. After only a few days in Cuckoo Cottage, she was now beginning to get a feel for the city centre and where the various amenities were, which bits were pleasant, and the shadier places probably best avoided, particularly as a woman alone. It had been so useful to have Minnie to call upon for advice, too, since she and her housemates had already sussed the lie of the land. Georgia had been round to the student house a couple of times now, and though she had yet to meet the other girls, she'd taken a liking to Ajab, the boy who was sharing with them. She had taken him and Minnie for tea and cake in M&S a couple of days earlier and he seemed a polite, nice lad.

Georgia had scraped back her hair, now washed in a rich shade of chestnut with a semi-permanent home dye, into a high ponytail, and dressed down in faded jeans, Converse and a long-sleeved grey-marl T-shirt – designer labels were unlikely to impress anyone in here. It was almost 11.30am and the doors to the Golden Orb had only just opened, but she was determined to be first over the threshold since seeing the sign as she'd returned from Sainsbury's with her morning milk and Sunday newspaper.

The black and white half-timbered building was even older than her own house, all dark oak beams and wood panelling, with lots of nooks and crannies. The harlequin-like windows were leaded hexagons of coloured glass. The bar area was cool, empty except for a small lady wearing a headscarf, beetling around with a can of furniture polish and a duster. She glanced over at Georgia and gave a brief smile, before whisking through into the adjoining room. A huge fireplace stood adjacent to the bar, where a slimly-built man stood with his back to her, sleeves rolled past tattooed forearms, cleaning the coffee machine and singing along enthusiastically to the strains of Taylor Swift's *Shake It Off* blaring from the speakers at each corner of the room. Hearing Georgia approach, he turned, his mouth spreading into a slightly embarrassed grin. He looked about mid-thirties, buzz-cut hair, with piercings in his ears and lower lip.

"Morning. Caught me practising my karaoke. Not my usual playlist, I promise." He grimaced, indicating the Stone Roses tattoo on his arm. "Bear with me and I'll serve you in a sec – just finishing the steam nozzle."

"I'm actually here about the job," Georgia blurted out. "I – saw the advert in the window . . ." She hovered in the middle of the floor, indicating a little awkwardly over her shoulder with a thumb.

41

The man paused, frowned slightly, seeming to appraise her. "Got any experience, sweet?"

"It's been a few years, but I've done a fair bit of bar work in the past. I'm sure I can still pull a pint and give the right change. Smile at the punters. And I'm right on the doorstep, so I'll never be late."

The corners of the man's mouth twitched in amusement. "I'm not the one you'll need to convince – the gaffer's upstairs. He should be down soon, with a bit of luck. Still performing his ablutions at the moment." He flared his nostrils in apparent irritation. "Can I get you a coffee or anything while you wait? I'm Yiannis, by the way."

"Pleased to meet you, Yiannis. I'm Georgia. And thanks. A soy latte would be great. Just half a sugar, please."

"Georgia. Nice name. Have a seat if you like. Plenty of 'em." He gave a throaty chuckle.

"I'm fine – I'll just stand if that's okay." Georgia crossed the floor to lean an elbow on the bar, looking around as Yiannis busied himself with the coffee machine. She noticed the menus propped up on some of the tables and her heart sank. "Does the job involve food preparation, too?"

"Nah, we've got a chef for the grub, lunchtimes only. Lucas. Great cook but he can be a bit temperamental." He sucked air through his teeth. "Just the usual menial tasks for us lesser mortals – pulling pints, jingling coins; smiling a lot." He glanced back over his shoulder and threw her a wink.

"Sorry – I didn't mean . . . that must've sounded condescending."

"No worries, sweet. I mean, it's not rocket science, is it? This is just a stop-gap for me, anyway. Well, it was supposed to be. Aspiring barrister-turned-barista." He emphasised the last vowel.

"Oh? Are you between jobs, then?"

"Not exactly. Uni dropout." He grinned sheepishly. "To be honest, I decided law wasn't really for me after the first term. This is my fifth job in fourteen years. Been here the last six of those." He blew out his cheeks. "Still looking for my perfect niche, but it's not so bad. I live in, so at least I don't have to worry about bed and board. How about you? Shouldn't judge a book by its cover, I know, but I'd never've had you down as bar staff material."

Georgia thought back to the countless nights she'd spent in her late teens, collecting glasses and wiping down tables. Slopping out drip trays. Changing barrels in the cellar. Dodging the advances of lairy customers with a smile when she'd felt like slapping their bloated faces. Her life had changed beyond all recognition since then. As had she.

"I've been out of commission for too long. Stay-at-home mum; you know. I need to get back out into the real world, now my daughter's at uni. Give me something else to focus on." The sudden thought of Minnie invoked a flood of emotion and Georgia felt tears prick her eyes unexpectedly. She looked away, embarrassed.

"Aww empty nest, eh?" He tipped his head sympathetically. "Bet it takes some getting used to. I remember my mum when I moved out . . ." He paused, looking a little wistful. "So you've not worked in a while, then?" The sound of footsteps clattering down some unseen stairs beyond the bar prompted him to raise a finger. "Hark – sounds as if our lord and master's about to put in an appearance at last."

From the doorway to the left of the bar, a broad, silver-haired figure ducked beneath the frame and emerged theatrically, wrapped in a black velour robe and bringing with him an overpowering waft of aftershave.

"Yiannis, you been at my Tom Ford again? That bottle cost me a packet. I'll be taking it out of your wages."

Yiannis cast Georgia a sideways look, smirking a little. "But I thought you said you loved how it smells on me, babe? Anyway, I only had a quick squirt . . ."

Noticing Georgia, the man stopped and pasted on a smile. "Sorry, lovely. Didn't mean to involve you in a domestic. Drives me up the wall though, he does."

Georgia smiled back. "Don't mind me."

"Early bird, are we?"

"I was just explaining to Yiannis – I've come about the job."

The man's dark, almond-shaped eyes widened, then flicked from Georgia's head to her feet and back, in time to the building hiss from the coffee machine. "Well, you're quick off the mark – I only put the poster up last night. Our regular dropped a bombshell at the end of her shift – she's just decided to swan off on a hiking tour of the bloody Himalayas. At the end of this week. Imagine! And she can't work tonight either, as she's got a *'family gathering'*." He made air quotes with his fingers, his tone heavy with sarcasm. "Bloody kids. Can't rely on 'em." He rolled his eyes, following the gesture with his head.

"I can start as soon as you like – I haven't got any commitments." Georgia groaned inwardly as the words left her mouth, hoping she didn't sound too desperate.

"Have you worked in a pub before?" The man pursed his lips. "Only I need someone who already knows what's what. No time to train you up."

"Georgia tells me she's pulled plenty of pints in her time." Yiannis interrupted, handing her a steaming mug of coffee; winking again. "Go on Freddie, give the girl a go."

Georgia looked at Freddie hopefully. His round face softened.

"Okay. Come back this evening, 6pm on the dot. I'll give you a trial when we've got a full house. Sunday night's quiz night, so it'll be a baptism of fire. If you measure up, you can start properly on Friday. Five nights a week, two off for good behaviour, if that fits with what you had in mind."

Georgia's heart swelled. "Definitely. Thank you! I won't

let you down, I promise. And rest assured I'm not planning an expedition any time soon."

Freddie extended a deeply tanned, thick hand from the sleeve of his gown, revealing a huge diamond signet ring on his little finger, and shook Georgia's hand firmly across the bar. "Don't think I've ever filled a job as quickly," he said, smiling broadly. "And you never even asked about the pay. Shall we say . . . hmm – five pounds an hour?" His eyes crinkled a little as he studied her face.

Georgia hesitated, shooting a look at Yiannis, who promptly let out a bark of laughter, shoving Freddie's shoulder good-naturedly.

"He's such a wind-up. Nine-fifty's the going rate and that's what you'll be getting at the very least; don't you worry."

"I wasn't. Worried, I mean." Georgia would have worked for pennies, but she wasn't about to admit as much. A job would give her a foothold in the city, even more of a reason to stay close to Minnie. She couldn't stop smiling.

Freddie leaned across and gave Yiannis a playful slap across the buttocks. "No business sense, this one. Too soft by half."

Yiannis snorted. "You wouldn't have me any other way." The pair locked eyes briefly and Georgia dropped her gaze, feeling as though she was intruding on a private moment.

Freddie glanced up at the clock above the bar suddenly. "Ooh. Better get dressed. Can't look like this when the throngs start pouring in." With a toss of his head, he shuffled back towards the doorway, turning to wave a hand towards Georgia. "Six o'clock. Don't forget."

"Well, you obviously made a good impression. He's usually a lot more picky!" The thud of footfall ascending the stairs made Yiannis screw up his face. "Proper diva. Heart of gold, mind you."

Georgia placed the empty mug on the bar, nodding. "He seems really nice. Thanks very much for your help, though – I think it was you that persuaded him. And for the coffee – how much do I owe you?"

"On the house, sweet." Yiannis flashed her a dazzling smile. She wondered if he'd been helping himself to Freddie's expensive whitening toothpaste, too.

"Look forward to seeing you later, then! Enjoy your afternoon."

"You too. See you soon."

Georgia stepped out into the sunshine, shielding her eyes as she looked across to her front door. Her heart felt suddenly light, and she had to stop herself from doing a little skip. She couldn't quite believe her luck, landing a job just like that and only a stroll away from her new home. She was confident she wouldn't mess it up – past experience told her she was more than capable, full house or not. Her stomach fluttered in anticipation. Coming to Coventry looked like being the start of something positive and exciting.

It was going to be perfect.

*

As she had a few hours to kill before her trial run, Georgia decided to take a walk through the town. It was a pleasant morning and already quite busy for a Sunday. It would have been nice to meet Minnie for lunch somewhere. She tried to ring her, but there was no response.

She left a brief voicemail: *Hope you're okay today. Love you lots.*

She toyed with the idea of going to the student house, itching to tell Minnie about her trial run at the pub, but then thought maybe she should save the news until she had the job in the bag. Something to celebrate, another outing to plan together. She had a warm feeling about the position, certain that she would be successful. Yiannis seemed to like her: she was sure he'd persuade Freddie to take her on. As long as she didn't mess up.

Georgia decided to buy a sandwich from the little coffee shop she'd found near Cuckoo Cottage, then go and sit in the cathedral ruins again. She'd liked the panini she'd bought from there when she first arrived. The stocky middle-aged man who'd served her on the previous occasion recognised her as soon as she approached the counter. His face lit up, making Georgia uncomfortable. She'd obviously made some sort of impression and she'd rather she hadn't.

"Glad to see you back. Always nice to know customers enjoy our food." He'd smiled warmly, winked as he took payment for the avocado salad roll she'd selected. "Here – have one of these. Baked them myself this morning." He popped a cookie into a bag. "On the house."

Georgia smiled uncertainly, thanked him and left the shop, clutching the two paper bags. She didn't want to seem rude, but was uneasy about striking up conversations with people she didn't know. It was better to be civil but keep chat to a minimum. Chat invariably led to questions. Better to keep herself to herself. A brief moment of panic coursed through her mind as she considered the role in the pub suddenly – but then, speaking to punters was something else. Just banter – and most people forgot stuff anyway once they'd had a few. She could give away as much or as little as she liked. Or even make things up. It had always worked in the past.

She sat on the same bench in the old cathedral, her thoughts miles away as she gazed around her. In the enclave of the ruins, the sun was surprisingly warm on her head, the sky clear and cloudless. There were always people here in the daytime, taking photos, reading the plaques on the various sculptures. Staring through the huge glassless windows. People like herself, idly passing the time of day and minding their own business.

Georgia's attention was drawn suddenly to the tall, wrought iron gate in the south side of the cathedral wall facing her. Beyond it was the narrow passageway leading left to the Guildhall, or right, up Bayley Lane towards Cuckoo Cottage and the Golden Orb. The railings were overshadowed by the tall buildings to each side. She was just in time to see someone wearing a bucket hat and dark glasses, standing diagonally opposite the bench, staring through the railings, their face largely hidden behind the lens of a camera. But the person was positioned at an angle, their camera pointing straight at her.

Georgia gasped, her heart quickening. She jumped to her feet, dropping the remainder of her cookie in her haste. The flurry of pigeons landing to compete for the fragments of biscuit distracted her for the briefest moment, and when she looked back, the person had vanished. She rushed towards the gate, craned her neck desperately in either direction hoping to catch a glimpse of the photographer, but there was no sign of them.

The nape of Georgia's neck prickled, a coldness spreading through her limbs. She had no doubt that whoever it had been, male or female, the photographer's attention had been focused deliberately on her. It hadn't felt like someone taking an innocent, opportune snap, more as though they were pointedly letting her know she was being observed.

Screwing up the paper bags she'd been clutching, Georgia flung them into the bin next to the cathedral's gothic tower on her way out, and almost breaking into a run, hurried through the graveyard and back to Cuckoo Cottage. Only once behind the safety of her closed front door was she able to draw breath. Peering through the yellowing net curtains, her eyes darted round the quad outside, terrified that she might have been followed.

Someone had been observing her and she didn't dare contemplate why.

Chapter 5

Georgia

Sunday, 25 September 2022

Trying to shake off the thought that someone had been watching her earlier, Georgia locked up the house, glanced about her, then strode up Bayley Lane to the Golden Orb at precisely 5.55pm. She stopped to draw a calming breath before pushing open the door and entering. There were still a handful of regulars who had clearly been in the bar for much of the afternoon: two middle-aged men having a heated debate about the state of the city centre; a bleary-eyed fiftyish man and a scruffily-dressed woman a few years his junior, with numerous empty pint glasses on the table between them. They seemed to have nothing to say to one another and sat staring into space. As Georgia walked in, the unsmiling woman seemed to be giving her the once over, her expression hostile and almost suspicious. Normally Georgia would have glared back and asked what the hell she thought she was looking at, but she bit her tongue and forced a smile. She needed to create a good impression or she could wave goodbye to the job before she'd even started. An elderly, unkempt man with a bored-looking bearded collie at his feet seemed to have claimed the table nearest the fireplace as his own. He had nodded and smiled at Georgia, his eyes rimmed red and baggy, his face contoured with deep lines that implied a hard life. She later learned from Yiannis that the man was called Ned and he was virtually part of the furniture.

"Poor old sod lost his wife about five years ago. No kids. He doesn't usually drink a fat lot, to be honest, but he's here every day – just sits there striking up conversation with anyone who'll talk to him. Harmless. He could do with a good wash, mind you." He grimaced, waggling a finger in front of his nose.

Georgia looked around. It all seemed very manageable. "So when *do* the throngs start pouring in, then?"

Yiannis grinned at her use of Freddie's expression. "Oh, don't let *this* fool you. This is the calm before the storm. It'll soon be heaving, trust me. Quiz night's very popular – especially with the students." He glanced up at the clock. "It'll all kick off pretty soon. Make the most of the lull to familiarise yourself with the cask ales and stuff."

Yiannis had been right in his assertion that things would get more hectic in a short while. Georgia barely had time to hang up her jacket before people started to trickle in, the occasional solitary drinker, but mainly small groups of younger customers, laughing and chattering and filling the place with noise and heat. Within the hour, Georgia and Yiannis were rushed off their feet trying to keep up with orders and shouts from one end of the bar to the other asking about the draught ale of the week, what was cheapest and what flavour crisps were available. Gradually, as eight o'clock approached, everyone started to move through to the lounge, where the quiz was being hosted by Freddie, centre stage with a microphone and resplendent in a fluffy lilac sweater and fuchsia-pink chinos. The black, square-framed spectacles he was wearing were reminiscent of Michael Caine in his Harry Palmer era.

The bar area was mercifully quiet now, though Georgia's heart sank at the volume of empty bottles and glasses already covering the tables. She let out a long breath, running her sleeve across her damp forehead. It was good to be busy, but she really was out of practice.

Noticing her demeanour, Yiannis laughed. "Go on, sweet – take a breather for a bit. Have a gander at Freddie strutting his stuff." He waved a hand dismissively as she began to protest. "*Go*; I'll clear this lot up – won't take me long."

Georgia threw him a grateful smile, tossing her dishcloth onto the bar.

"I'll only be a minute."

With everyone now eagerly assembled around the room, Freddie, looking comically stern, rang a large, old-fashioned bell to signal the start of the quiz, and voices were reduced to whispers and smothered laughter.

"Right, settle down, you 'orrible lot. Good to see a few new faces, and welcome back to our usual suspects! Here we go with question *numero uno*." His eyes scanned the room, catching sight of Georgia as she stood against the wall and throwing her a surreptitious grin. Lifting a clipboard from the table next to him, he squinted at the contents.

He cleared his throat. "Okay. One for our slightly older clientele. Which Phil had a number one UK hit in 1981 with 'Don't You Want Me'? And in case you don't know the rules – *no shouting out*."

Georgia scanned the room. People sat in huddles, whispering

and nodding, then scribbling on the sheets of paper provided as Freddie continued to pose questions on all manner of topics. Everyone seemed to be taking it very seriously.

She became suddenly aware of a pair of eyes on her and jerked her head sideways to notice a dark-haired man, sitting alone at a table under the window, staring at her. As she met his intense gaze, he looked away quickly, putting a hand to the back of his head, his cheeks flushing slightly. She observed him for a moment, but he was clearly avoiding looking at her now, his focus unblinkingly on Freddie once more. Georgia felt a prickle of unease. She turned and headed back into the bar, where Yiannis had been efficient in restoring order, the tables clear and freshly wiped. He was just handing change to a latecomer and smiled as she approached.

"Had enough already?" His eyes travelled to the clock. "Enjoy the peace – it won't last long." He studied her for a moment, his brow furrowing.

"Everything okay, sweet?"

"Yeah – fine. Just – d'you know who that guy is, sitting by the window behind Freddie?"

Yiannis slung the tea towel he'd just picked up over his shoulder and walked out from behind the bar. He peered through the archway into the lounge, his eyebrows twitching.

"What – the really fit one with the cheekbones?" Yiannis turned back to Georgia, a smile playing on his lips. "Fancy him, do you?"

Georgia looked back at the man once more. He was undeniably handsome: short, dark hair greying a little at the temples, with striking bone structure and an aquiline nose. But the way he'd been observing her was making her uneasy.

"It's not that. He – well, he was staring at me, that's all. I wondered if he was a regular."

Yiannis shook his head. "Haven't seen him before. And

trust me – I'd have remembered." He gave her a playful nudge, lowering his voice. "Freddie'll be wrapping this up pretty soon. Why don't you go and clear the empties over there when he's finished – take a closer look."

The man looked up at her again suddenly. His mouth curved into a tentative smile. Georgia's chest tightened. She was wary of attention from strangers – particularly when they were quite obviously alone.

"I don't know. I mean, he might be a weirdo."

Yiannis huffed. "So every single guy out on his own is a potential sex case, is that what you think?"

"No; no, of course not. It just made me a bit, well, uncomfortable, him staring like that."

"You're a good-looking girl – he's a red-blooded male – why wouldn't he?" Yiannis tipped his head in the man's direction. "Go and say hello."

"I'm not interested in getting to know him," Georgia snapped, instantly regretting her tone. Yiannis seemed okay – she shouldn't take her anxiety out on him.

Yiannis looked taken aback. "All right, keep your hair on."

"Sorry. But I'm not looking to date anyone just yet. Too soon – you know . . ." She hoped this sounded convincing. Yiannis softened, his eyes scanning her face. "Fair enough. Look, if you'd rather make yourself scarce, one of the barrels needs changing, if you'd like to do the honours. Show Freddie you're not just a pretty face."

Georgia flexed her biceps, rearranging her features into a grin. "Just point me in the right direction. I'm stronger than I look. All those years ploughing up and down the pool paid off."

"Oh – you're a swimmer?"

She chewed her lip. Ever since they'd moved into Warchester, it had been part of her daily routine, her arms slicing the water, pushing herself to her limits. She'd loved the focus it had given her, the way it cleared her mind. The tone it had given her physique. But she hadn't been back in the pool since the day Trevor died. The very thought of it made her insides roil.

"Not really – just used to do the lengths, you know. Trying to stave off middle-age."

"Go on then – show us what you're made of."

She followed Yiannis behind the bar and watched as he raised the trapdoor into the cellar. Georgia peered cautiously down the wooden steps that led to the shadowy depths beneath. The escaping air was frigid and fusty.

Yiannis knocked the switch just inside the hatch and a fluorescent strip-light flickered into action, illuminating the aluminium barrels lined up below.

"You'll find the one you need just down there on the right – can't miss the label." He looked on for a moment as she ventured down, then retreated back to the bar.

She heard his slightly muffled voice call from above, "Just give us a shout if you need a hand."

Determined to complete the task unaided, Georgia wrestled with the cask and the connecting pipe, and within minutes had changed the old one for a fresh container. She heaved the empty one aside and climbed the steps back up to the bar.

"All done," she announced triumphantly, closing the trapdoor and brushing off her hands. The level of noise now coming from the lounge implied that the quiz was over and a queue of chattering customers was starting to build once again.

Yiannis was serving someone. He met her with an apologetic look. "Could you serve this gentleman, please, sweet?"

Standing at the other side of the bar was the man who had been watching her earlier. Her stomach turned a somersault.

The man smiled. "When you're ready. No rush."

Georgia felt suddenly flustered. She tried to smile back but it

54

was as though her teeth had stuck to her lips. "Erm – what can I get you?"

"Just make it a Coke, please. No ice."

"Draught or bottle?"

"Draught. It's cheaper." He looked sheepish.

Counting his pennies, then. With a slightly unsteady hand, Georgia poured a glass of cola from the tap and set it on the bar. The man was tall, slimly built; probably in his early forties, she guessed. He looked even more attractive close up: chiselled bone structure; wide grey eyes framed by thick, dark lashes. His hand brushed hers as he handed over a fistful of coins and she quelled the urge to snap it back. He might be a perfectly nice guy. She needed to stop being so suspicious of everyone – or at least, of appearing to be. Being hostile would get her nowhere. She wanted this job – the last thing customers wanted was to be served by a stroppy barmaid.

"Haven't seen you in here before, have I?" His deep voice bore the trace of a London accent behind the received pronunciation. He seemed to be studying her intently, a slight twitch of amusement on his lips at her evident discomfort.

"It's my first shift." The words came out more tersely than she'd intended and she almost winced. "I'm on a trial run."

Yiannis was closing the till. He whipped his head round, casting Georgia a wink. "You've passed with flying colours, sweet." His response was more for the benefit of the customer than her, she suspected. He turned to the man, running an eye up and down his lean torso. "I don't believe I've seen *you* in here, either."

"Oh, I've been here a few times now. Maybe it's always been on your night off." The man had been carrying a thick folder under his arm. He stooped to tuck it between his calves, then straightened, a tight smile directed at Yiannis. "I'm Cole."

Georgia glanced at Yiannis. His face was unreadable. He

proceeded to serve the old man, Ned, who'd been waiting at the end of the bar.

"I'm Georgia," she responded, still a little wary. She wasn't sure if she should introduce Yiannis or not. She needn't have worried.

"And I'm Yiannis," he said rather loudly, from the side of his mouth. "How did you get on with the quiz?"

"To be honest, I was observing rather than taking part. All pretty standard stuff, these things, aren't they?"

Yiannis drew back his chin, his lips setting into a thin line. "Hmm. Not highbrow enough for you, eh? What's your bag, then?" He peered over the bar, nodding his head at the bulging folder.

Cole smiled. "I'm an historian. Well, that's what I'm aiming to be. I'm actually writing a book about the history of the buildings in the old quarter of the city."

Yiannis handed the pint he'd been pouring to the old man, then moved to stand beside Georgia, suddenly more engaged. "Ah. Plenty to write about even in our little corner. Some pretty dark stuff – murders, executions and all that."

"Really?" Georgia turned to him with interest. Something to chat to Minnie about – she was so into her history. Yiannis opened his mouth to respond when Cole butted in.

"Oh yes, I know. That's partly why I like to come here, even though it's not on my doorstep. I can sit in a corner with my notes and work – gets me in the right frame of mind." He gestured over his shoulder. "The Slug and Lettuce, that bar just across the way on Cuckoo Lane, has a dungeon beneath it. The building used to be the county jail, back before Coventry's boundaries changed. And a woman called Mary Ball was hanged outside it in the mid-1800s, only a few yards from here. She's buried out there, somewhere under the cobbles."

The unwelcome image of a woman's body dangling from a

gibbet appeared in Georgia's mind, sending her hand flying to her mouth. "How vile." She shook her head, her eyes straying to the window. The thought that someone had been executed and then interred so close to her new home gave her an odd feeling in the pit of her stomach, however long ago it had taken place. That the fate of a murderer once meant forfeiting their own life if they were caught.

Yiannis gave her shoulder a quick squeeze, throwing Cole a warning look. "Probably best to change the subject. But before I forget – while we're on all things grim and grisly, look out for our resident ghost."

Georgia noticed Cole shift his weight a little, sniffing sceptically. "Is that one of those usual myths to help bring the punters in?"

"Oh no. I kid you not. I've seen him myself."

"Him? Who is he, then?" Georgia's eyes flicked nervously round the room, almost expecting to see an apparition summoned by the mere mention of it.

Old Ned, still standing at the end of the bar, had obviously been listening in. He moved along a few steps, setting his pint next to Cole's glass. "You on about our Jack?"

Yiannis nodded vigorously. "I saw someone, some*thing* once . . . well, not sure what it was. Out the back there." He indicated the door behind him. "Put the wind up me a bit, I can tell you." Yiannis lifted his shoulders in an exaggerated shudder.

The old man chipped in. "There was a fire in this building – about four hundred years ago. Legend has it a little lad called Jack was asleep up in the attic. His older sister was calling for him in distress, but couldn't get to him through the flames. Needless to say, poor little kid perished." He took a glug from his beer, licking the froth from his white moustache as his rheumy blue eyes searched their faces. "They say around the time of the anniversary of the fire, the girl can be heard screaming his name. And he appears on the top landing, screaming back."

Georgia's legs felt suddenly weak. "That's horrible. Him dying here – like that."

"Fires were commonplace in those times – you can imagine." Cole nodded, his eyes on Georgia the whole time. "All that timber and open fires; a recipe for disaster." He screwed up his nose. "Not so sure about the ghost bit, though."

"Scoff all you like, I know what I saw." Yiannis declared sharply. He glanced beyond them suddenly, indicating with a wriggle of his eyebrows. "And Freddie's heard him, too. He hardly slept a wink that night."

"Freddie's heard who?" Everyone looked round to see they had been joined by the landlord, who was standing behind Ned, sneaking a lustful look at Cole's backside.

Yiannis folded his arms abruptly. "The *ghost*."

Freddie smirked. "Ah. Well, I *thought* I heard someone shouting once. But we did have workmen in at the time – could've just as easily been one of them."

"Don't you dare backtrack now." Yiannis glared at him. "You turned as white as a sheet. And that's not easy, with all that St. Tropez you plaster on."

Freddie gave him a look that would have curdled milk. "I'm naturally dark. It just enhances my skin tone."

Yiannis gave a derisory huff and turned brusquely to attend to a woman who had been tapping her credit card on the bar to get his attention. He pasted on a smile. "Sorry, sweet. What can I get you?"

Freddie rolled his eyes. He swivelled to face Cole, smiling his whitest smile. "I don't think we've met. I'm Freddie, in case you hadn't realised. Your host with the most."

"Cole." He held out a hand, which Freddie shook lingeringly.

"Erm, Freddie – is it okay if I take a quick break, please?" ventured Georgia, tipping her head towards the exit from the bar. Freddie's attention shifted from Cole's slightly perplexed expression.

"Hmm? Oh, 'course; take five if you need it. You don't need to ask. I'm not a slave driver." He laughed heartily, winking flirtatiously at Cole, who threw Georgia a covert grimace. She might have found it amusing, but she thought him a bit full of himself.

Georgia went through to use the staff toilet at the back, glancing up the stairs with thoughts of the ghostly little boy still at the front of her mind. The air may have been cool, but it was the thoughts running through her head that made her shiver. She remembered her drunken mother, telling her with ghoulish delight tales of apparitions and weird goings-on when she'd only been quite small. That she was wicked, and some evil spirit would come to get her in the middle of the night because that's what she deserved. Though it wasn't something she wanted to believe in, she remained uneasy about the supernatural. The vengeful dead. Georgia had always been careful to shield Minnie from any such stories, worried that they might invoke nightmares as they had with her as a child. Some adults could be completely thoughtless. Cruel.

Georgia washed her hands, scrutinising her face critically in the oval mirror above the sink. Not wanting to appear 'overdone', she hadn't bothered with make-up beyond a sweep of mascara before coming to work, but now she looked blotchy and a bit the worse for wear. She felt old and washed out. She ran the cold tap for a few seconds, then splashed her cheeks. Removing her scrunchie, she raked her fingers through her hair in an attempt to tidy it, before pulling it up once more into a ponytail. Regarding her reflection again, she shrugged resignedly. It would have to do for now.

As she opened the bathroom door, Georgia's eyes were drawn to the landing above, where Ned claimed Jack's restless spirit could be seen. A whisper of breath seemed to brush her cheek. The hairs rose suddenly along her arms. Had she just heard her name spoken close to her ear? No. No, of course not; she was being ridiculous. It was her stupid imagination, running away with her. But still she felt the need to hurry back into the bar.

She was met with the sudden clang of the same bell Freddie had used for the quiz, followed by Yiannis's voice, calling time.

"See 'em off now please, folks. Some of us need our beauty sleep."

From where she stood just behind the doorway, Georgia could see Cole, surveying the room. He was looking for her, she knew it. She wasn't sure whether she should feel worried. It had been so long since she'd had male attention, she didn't know how to take it. Or was there more to it than that? Despite him saying he'd been in several times, neither Yiannis nor Freddie remembered him.

She thought again about the photographer outside the cathedral ruins and a chill ran through her. Was it more than coincidence that Cole had appeared in the Orb just as she had?

Could it have been him?

Chapter 6

Minnie

Saturday came, and with it the daunting prospect of catching up on coursework, laundry and shopping, and all with a hangover after their regular outing to the SU the night before. Minnie and Ajab had, as usual, agreed to do the supermarket run, with a list of requests, mainly from Fatima.

"I need oat milk for my cereal. Bagels – you know, the wholegrain ones. Some of that nice red pepper hummus. Get me a couple of those organic smoothies, too. Oh – orange juice with the bits – and make sure it's not that *from concentrate* crap," she'd almost demanded from where she was sprawled out on the sofa, still wrapped in her leopard-print dressing gown and scrolling through her phone. "No, wait. I'll text you a list, so you don't forget anything."

She didn't even look up to notice Minnie glowering at her.

Ajab began genuflecting behind where Fatima's head was leaning against the arm of the settee, edging backwards with palms pressed together. Minnie gave a snort of laughter.

"What?" Fatima raised her eyes briefly, darting a look round the room. Ajab straightened quickly.

Minnie shrugged. "Nothing. Just remembering a joke I heard last night."

Fatima gave her a withering stare before resuming the scrolling.

Sonia had been too hungover to care about much other than putting in a request for Alka Seltzer and paracetamol. Since arriving home, she'd spent the morning making urgent dashes to heave into the toilet, between hiding her shame and batting off texts from the boy from the SU she'd spent the night with, only to regret it bitterly in the cold light of day. In the end she'd switched off her phone.

"I'm never drinking again," she'd groaned, flopping back down into a bed that looked as if it could be the scene of a crime and pulling a pillow over her head. "What was I *thinking*? Somebody shoot me."

"Don't tempt me," Minnie had muttered. She and Ajab armed themselves with shopping bags and headed for the town centre. It was already turned midday. It would take around twenty minutes to walk from their apartment on the Kenilworth Road to the nearest Sainsbury's, in Trinity Street. They could have easily taken the bus, but Minnie hoped the fresh air would help to clear the fog from her head. It was breezy, the pavements slippery with fallen leaves, but the skies were clear. They could catch a bus later – she'd seen the amount of stuff that Fatima had asked for and knew she wouldn't have the energy to haul all the groceries back. She thought guiltily that she should perhaps call in on her mum, but it would eat into her day and she still had an essay to finish. Besides, it was important that Georgia didn't get too reliant on her. She appeared to be enjoying staying in the city and Minnie felt pleased that she seemed to be focused on carving out a life for herself that didn't always have to involve her.

It wasn't that Minnie resented Georgia living close by. Not exactly. She'd understood how hard it must have been for her mother to be left all alone, especially since she had no close friends or any real interests to occupy her mind. But Minnie *had* resented the idea that she was under scrutiny. It wasn't as if she was going to start doing drugs or sleeping with someone different every night. That just wasn't who she was at all. She had come to uni primarily to study, but equally to gain some independence – and to feel liberated for once in her life. Though Minnie was sure she had the best of intentions, sometimes Georgia's attention could be stifling. And even if she wasn't living right on her doorstep, the knowledge that they could bump into one another if Minnie was out with friends, or that Georgia might just "pop round" unannounced as she had done a few times already, had made Minnie less than comfortable. More than once, Georgia had reminded her that she was paying her rent and subsidising her lifestyle, and on reflection Minnie wondered if maybe she wouldn't have been better taking out a student loan and moving into halls as so many of her peers had. It wasn't nice, having to feel beholden to her mother.

Talking to Ajab, however, had made her realise that perhaps her mum wasn't so bad after all. At least she wasn't trying to force her into marrying someone she didn't know – and someone she was never even going to be able to fall in love with, at that.

"They'd cut me off if they knew about my sexuality," he'd told her miserably. "Maybe not my mum, but my dad, definitely. He's very old school. Wants me to get the best grades; have the best wife. Make the family proud."

"But he should be proud of you, regardless," Minnie had protested. "You're a sweet, decent guy – and parents are supposed to love their kids unconditionally. It's really unfair."

Ajab had been introduced to Georgia for the first time when they'd met up for tea and cake in M&S the previous week. He couldn't believe how laid-back she seemed about everything compared with his own mum and dad. How young she looked, too.

"If you hadn't told me, I'd've thought she was your older sister," he'd whispered to Minnie when Georgia went to place the order at the counter, making her roll her eyes but bringing a flush of pleasure to Georgia's face as she overheard.

"I do like your new friend, Mins," she'd said, winking at Ajab. "You can bring him again."

Ajab and Georgia had really hit it off. His face had lit up when he'd learned that the house she was renting was only a few yards from the Golden Orb, raving about the history of the building and its atmosphere. But Minnie suspected the lure of the place had more to do with seeing Yiannis than the pub's historical significance. She'd noticed the pair giving one another admiring glances when they'd popped in again the previous night en route to the SU. Ajab's coyness about it all made her smile.

He must have been reading her thoughts. "Erm – is your mum home this afternoon?" he asked lightly. "We could call round and see if she wants to nip in the pub – just for a soft drink," he added, as Minnie mimed being sick at the prospect of more alcohol. "I like your mum. She's cool."

"Nah, I'm not up for it today, to be honest. And I've got too much to do anyway – that essay won't write itself and I'd like to chill tomorrow once it's done. We could maybe take her on Tuesday evening if you like, though." She screwed up her nose resignedly. "I should make a bit of an effort, I suppose."

"Great. I've got stuff to get on with as well – Tuesday would probably be better," he conceded, nodding more to himself than to Minnie. "Yeah – something to look forward to."

Minnie smiled. She wondered if he'd realised she was on to him.

They jostled their way up and down the aisles in Sainsbury's. It seemed half of the students in the city were stocking up after a Friday night bender and it was a relief to step back out into the crisp air, even though laden down with the spoils of their trip. They made their way up the street and paused to sit on the wall outside Holy Trinity Church, where buses were pulling up continuously, passengers spilling out onto the pavement whilst others queued to board.

"Shall we jump on a bus, then?" asked Ajab wearily.

Minnie looked down at the bulky carriers at her feet and puffed out her cheeks. "Our stop's a bit of a trek. I'm knackered, to be honest – let's just jump in a cab. My shout," she added, seeing his worried face. "The taxi rank's only in the next street."

They crossed the road and headed down towards the Burges, then joined the line of people waiting as taxis began to roll up. The sound of a familiar voice stopped Minnie in her tracks.

"Well, if it isn't Miss Minnie Mouse. We'll have to stop meeting like this."

Minnie jerked her head round to see the Irish man she'd met the other Friday, walking slowly up the street behind them. She felt Ajab's questioning eyes burning into her and colour crept up her cheeks.

"Oh, it's the joker." She tried to sound casual, but her heart quickened at the sight of him. In daylight he looked younger and even more attractive than she'd remembered, those earnest dark eyes beneath heavy brows, a square jawline. There was an appealing dusting of freckles across his nose. He held her in a steady gaze, making her squirm self-consciously.

A grin spread across the man's face. "Been to do your messages, have you?"

Minnie frowned. "Sorry?"

He waved a hand at the carrier bags. "Your shopping." His

eyes travelled from Minnie to Ajab, his smile wavering slightly. "You helping this young 'un out, pal?"

Ajab eyed the man uncertainly. He shot Minnie a look, prompting her to interject.

"This is Ajab. We're housemates." Minnie didn't know why she felt the need to explain. "Sorry – I don't think I caught your name."

The man held out a hand to Ajab, the grin restored. "I'm Jake. I met this young lady briefly a couple of weeks back."

He turned to Minnie once more. "That's a pile of stuff for the pair of yous."

"There are four of us in the house," Ajab offered. "And a lot of it's for the others."

"Ah." Jake nodded. He hovered awkwardly for a moment. "Well, better get on. Nice to bump into you again, Minnie. See you around."

Minnie nodded. "Yeah. See you."

She and Ajab looked on as Jake strode up the road, turning to wave as he reached the top.

Ajab nudged her gently in the ribs. "Good-looking bloke. And he fancies the pants off you. Go and give him your number before he disappears forever."

"What? Don't be daft." Minnie felt her cheeks warming once again. "He never asked for it. And he's too old for me, anyway."

"Oh, *please*. Age is just a number. And what's wrong with *you* making the first move?" He arched an eyebrow. "Go on – we can get the next taxi."

Minnie hesitated for a moment. She watched as Jake disappeared round the corner towards the shopping mall.

Then: "Fuck it."

She broke into a trot as she headed after him, with Ajab looking on in amusement.

"Jake," she called breathlessly. "Wait."

He glanced over his shoulder and came to a halt, turning to meet her. "Did you forget something?" His brown eyes glinted with mischief.

"Do you want – can I give you my number? We could go for a few drinks some time if you like." It sounded so lame. She shrivelled internally, fearful she may have misread the signals.

He grinned, his gaze drifting from her eyes to her mouth and back. "Yeah, why not. You seem okay – I think I can probably trust you not to try and take advantage of me."

Minnie's stomach flipped a little. "Here; give me your phone then."

He delved into his jacket pocket, entered the pin and handed his mobile over, watching as she added her name to his contact list. She passed the phone back and watched as he searched the screen, tapping at the keys for a moment. Her own mobile buzzed in her pocket.

"Don't read it now," he said playfully, the tip of his tongue at the corner of his mouth. "I'll be seeing you soon for those drinks then, Miss Minnie Mouse."

With a half-smile and a wink, he continued on his way, raising a hand to wave behind him without looking.

"*Cocky git*," thought Minnie, rolling her eyes. But she felt a warm tingle pass through her. He wasn't that much older really and God, he looked good. There was something indefinable that drew her to him. She pulled out the phone to read his message and laughed out loud.

No text: just a GIF, a drunken Minnie Mouse with heavy-lidded, unfocused eyes, a burning cigarette dangling from one hand, a bottle of vodka from the other.

Idiot. But she had a feeling this could be fun.

Chapter 7

Georgia

Sunday evening, 25 September 2022

Inhaling deeply, Georgia re-entered the bar. Cole's eyes landed on her suddenly, a smile lighting his face. She returned a polite nod, then headed briskly through to the lounge to clear the tables.

One by one, people began to drain their glasses and drift away, and things gradually grew quieter. Without all the extra bodies and with the continual swing of the exterior door, the space had developed an unwelcome chill. Georgia carried a stack of empties back into the bar and found Cole still in the same spot. He had remained standing close to the bar for most of the evening, chatting with Ned, who had resumed his position at his usual table, the dog asleep at his feet. Cole was listening now with a slight frown as the old man regaled him eagerly with stories about the city's history. From time to time, Cole glanced back at Georgia as she put the glasses through the rinser, and once he actually winked, sending heat rushing to her cheeks and a feeling of unease in her gut. *Could* it have been him watching her earlier? The thought niggled at her constantly now.

"Proud Coventrian, I am," Ned was telling him, the old man's enunciation growing increasingly slurred. "Born and bred. As was my Jeanie, God bless her. You want to know anything, you come to *me*." He thumped his chest with a knobbly fist, his eyelids half-closed.

Cole darted another look at Georgia, his eyes dancing with amusement now. "I certainly will, thank you."

"You seen what they've done with the old undercroft? Tha's a proper find, I'll tell you."

"Yes – very impressive. I interviewed one of the archaeologists that were in charge of the dig." Cole nodded enthusiastically, sipping the third Coke that Georgia had served him. She really wished he would leave now, but there was no sign of him wanting to. "Makes you wonder what else hasn't been discovered yet."

"Now there's another likely place if you want to see ghosts." Wobbling a little, Ned sat up suddenly, a slow smile spreading across his face. "Monks. All that digging's brought one of 'em out of the woodwork."

Georgia shuddered. Minnie had taken her to the priory undercroft to show her what had been uncovered, and though fascinating, she had found it quite eerie. It wasn't beyond the realms of possibility that the extensive excavation work could have stirred a disgruntled spirit or two. She had begun to feel even more on edge, with all this talk of paranormal activity.

"Pfft. Some people have overactive imaginations," said Cole scathingly. "More than likely just one of those dummies they've dressed up to set the scene down in the old refectory."

Ned shook his head. He sounded earnest now. "I'm telling you. Well, you can imagine, can't you? All that misery, that – what

69

d'you call it – self-denial, when they walked the earth. You can see why they'd be restless spirits. Charlie tries to steer me away if I ever walk 'im round there. Bares 'is teeth and everything. They sense these things, animals." He stooped shakily to pat the sleeping dog, whose eyes remained closed. One ear lifted slightly, making Georgia think Charlie was more awake than he was letting on.

"Of course, he's *never* been keen to go anywhere near the Guildhall. There's supposed to be one who wanders past there at the dead of night. Friar Benedict, that's who they say he is. Story goes he usually appears to people before something nasty happens. If you're unlucky enough to spot 'im three times, it's curtains, they reckon. So my dad told me. A sort of harbinger of doom, or whatever they call it."

"Have *you* ever seen the monk?" The hairs on Georgia's arms prickled at the thought of a hooded figure roaming the cobbled area by the Guildhall, only a stone's throw from her house on Bayley Lane.

"Well, I couldn't be sure, but when I left here one night, I did think . . ."

"You still here, Ned?" Freddie, who had retreated upstairs after the quiz, suddenly reappeared in the doorway leading from behind the bar to the living quarters. "Haven't you got a home to go to?" He looked pointedly at the number of empty glasses crowded onto Ned's table.

The old man narrowed his eyes and swilled the dregs from his remaining pint. "I'm not one to outstay my welcome." He staggered unsteadily to his feet, tugging at the dog's lead. "C'mon, Charlie. Time to go." As if a switch had been flicked, the dog sprang to life, his tail beating against the table leg.

"'Night, all. See you tomorrow." Ned tapped his fingers to his temple in a sort of salute and swung out of the door, pausing to steady himself on the frame as he stepped over the threshold.

"Will he be okay?" Georgia asked anxiously. She crossed from the bar to watch as the old man snaked his way across the quadrangle. Yiannis, who had just come back from making a final sweep of the lounge, gave a throaty laugh.

"Don't worry, sweet. He doesn't often get drunk like that, but he can hold his beer. Constitution of an ox. Sober as a judge by morning and ready to start all over again."

Her brow folded into a worried frown. "I'm just concerned he's a bit vulnerable."

"Doubt anyone'd try to mug the old bugger. Awful to say it, but apart from the dog, he's got nothing worth taking."

Georgia felt a stab of empathy as she thought of Ned returning alone to his empty house. Was this the shape of things to come for her, too? And now once more, the fear of being alone was not just about loneliness. It was about someone exploiting her solitude. Hunting her down.

She began to clear the table where the old man had been sitting, awkwardly steering herself around Cole as she felt the weight of his stare. By now he was the only remaining customer and his presence had actually begun to feel oppressive.

He placed his empty glass on the bar. "Well, s'pose I'd better make tracks myself." He stretched his arms above his head, smiling at Georgia. "You got far to go?"

Georgia felt a flutter of panic. She hesitated, casting a look at Yiannis, who was observing their exchange with obvious interest. "No, not that far."

"I could walk with you, if you like – or is someone collecting you?" He studied her hopefully, running a hand across the back of his head.

She picked her response carefully, not wishing to give anything away about her circumstances. *Polite but firm.* "I'm all good, thanks. You carry on."

Cole's face clouded. "Ah. No worries. See you, then." He

71

smiled briefly, nodding at Yiannis and Freddie. "Goodnight, gentlemen."

Freddie raised a hand. "Goodnight, sir. Hopefully we'll have the pleasure of your company again soon." He inched back into the doorway behind the bar, turning to Yiannis and Georgia with a pained expression. "Can I leave you two to deal with this lot? I can feel one of my heads coming on."

The muscles in Yiannis's cheeks flexed. "Oh you can, can you? Go on up, then. I'll catch you up in a bit." He looked on for a moment as Freddie waved a hand and retreated through the door.

"Drama queen," Yiannis muttered. He went to bolt the door behind Cole, watching for a moment as the man disappeared up a side street. Turning to Georgia, his eyes widened in surprise. "You were well in there. Didn't you fancy him, then?"

"Look, he might be perfectly all right. I don't know him, though – and I'm on my own. Not the best idea to let a strange man see where I live. I mean – I don't want to take chances and bring trouble to my own door, do I?"

Yiannis pursed his lips, considering this. "Fair enough. Dunno when he's been in, but I'm sure I haven't seen him before. Maybe he was wearing a balaclava or something." He sniggered, then cocked his head, scanning Georgia's face. "You look all in, sweet. You've done a great job this evening – why don't you get yourself off home, then pop back in tomorrow morning and we'll talk shifts"

"So I've definitely got the job?"

"Yep. You're no slacker. Freddie gave you the thumbs up hours ago. I reckon we're going to get along just fine."

Chapter 8

Georgia

Sunday, 25 September 2022

The quad felt totally different after dark. The cemetery was one thing, but apart from the unnerving incident with the photographer earlier in the day, what Georgia had learned about the macabre history of the area: the hangings, the bodies buried in unconsecrated ground beneath the old prison yard, had put a completely different complexion on her new dwelling. And the thought of being confronted by ghostly apparitions, particularly one foretelling death . . . Had she imagined that voice in the pub? Though it was only a minute's walk from the Orb to her house, a feeling of cold dread had begun to mount inside her as she hurried across the cobbles, passing the low wall of the cathedral graveyard, her eyes darting constantly from left to right to ensure no one was lurking in the shadows. Georgia's thoughts turned again to Cole. His presence had left her uneasy.

The way he'd watched her all evening, that unflinching gaze. She half wondered whether he might have been waiting for her somewhere, out of sight and ready to approach from behind. This notion disturbed her even further. Blood rushing in her ears, she fumbled with the key, and once through the door, bolted it hurriedly. She leaned back against it for a moment, letting out a breath of relief. It had still been daylight when she'd left the house earlier, but now everything was shrouded in thick darkness that made eerie, unidentifiable shadows of every object in her path.

An odd, solid-looking lump resting against the wall near her feet made her stop in her tracks. Heart pounding, she felt along the wall for the old-fashioned light-switch and almost laughed when the shape turned out to be the old iron doorstop she'd stubbed her toe on earlier. The front entrance opened onto a small vestibule at the foot of the staircase, the door to the right leading into the small sitting room, where the old-fashioned, filthy net curtains had been hung from the leaded rectangle of window, affording the room a little privacy from the street. Georgia went through to tug the thick brocade curtains across these, and then switched on the light. It smelled musty and there was a definite chill in the air, making her shiver. After her first impression of the place being warm when she'd viewed it originally, she'd begun to realise this had been a reflection of the weather outside. She should have remembered that old buildings lacked insulation and were prone to damp. Though she'd thought initially that the house had a pleasant atmosphere, things seemed very different now. Threatening, almost. As though the place resented her occupancy.

Georgia felt suddenly very much alone. The realisation unnerved her. She found her eyes scouring every corner, her ears alert to any unusual sound. She needed warmth, daylight; the banality of a TV sitcom. Anything to distract her from the

74

thoughts running through her head. But it was late, far too late in the day to start faffing with the log burner that sat in the old brick fireplace. It had taken her an age to light it the last time. And the television still hadn't been unpacked from the box room. She wondered now why she hadn't prioritised it.

Georgia filled her lungs, then exhaled in an attempt to calm the rapid fluttering of her heart. A mug of Ovaltine, then bed: she persuaded herself that was what she needed. Things would feel better after a solid night's sleep. But her mind was still racing.

She went through the door at the far end of the sitting room that led into the galley kitchen. Her own reflection in the window above the sink made her clap a hand to her chest in fright. The enclosed courtyard at the back would make the ideal hiding place for anyone who wanted to observe her from the gloom, and the idea filled her with panic. She yanked down the roller blind as the strip light stuttered into action, then paused to collect her thoughts. This was ridiculous: she was being irrational. All that ghoulish talk earlier had sent her imagination into overdrive. And Cole was probably perfectly harmless. The person taking the photo – it could easily have been a tourist. She was being paranoid.

Georgia filled the kettle and flicked the switch. The room was freezing. As she waited for the water to boil, she leaned against the old gas stove rubbing her arms, and looked round. It was pitiful. There was limited storage, with what felt like a token gesture of 1970s yellow Formica cupboards and drawers. As with everywhere else downstairs, the floor was the original flagstones, worn and slippery with age. The rectangular enamel sink had a crack running through it, the mixer tap dull, its chrome scratched. One of the doors beneath needed its hinge repairing – the thing had fallen off completely when she'd first opened it to put away her cleaning products, and was now just propped against the kick board. There was no room even for a small table and chair. Even the bin in the corner seemed to clutter the floor. Though she'd just thought everything a little tired before, now it seemed almost as if the place was decaying.

What the hell had she done? The contrast between this tiny, barely functional space and the vast expanse of her expensive bespoke kitchen in Warchester was stark. She missed the comfort of her old home so much. She thought of the fun she'd had choosing the décor and furnishings. The luxurious little extras that had put her stamp on everything. Trevor had pretty much given her free rein – he'd signed the cheques and she'd gone all out. She'd felt proud that he trusted her judgement. Given her own beginnings, she had "impeccable taste and an eye for detail", he'd said in one of his more generous moments earlier in their marriage. It had come naturally to her, she had found. She fancied that in another life she could have gone into interior design. Carved a successful career for herself. One up on all those snotty wives of Trevor's business associates who hung on the coat-tails of their husbands' success. She'd never considered herself in that category. But though he admired working women, Trevor hadn't wanted *her* to work; had been adamant that her place was in the home. She'd been content to do so, to take care of Minnie. *A proper nest builder*. That was how she liked to think of herself. No nanny was going to be raising *her* daughter. She could never understand these women who popped out babies, then handed them over to someone else to take care of them. It made no sense to her. And how could you ever truly trust anyone you didn't really know with the welfare of your child?

Her thoughts were interrupted suddenly by a dull thud. Georgia held her breath. She wasn't sure where the noise had emanated from, but it seemed to be the direction of the sitting room. Steeling herself, she tiptoed through the doorway to listen. There it was again. Not in her own house, but coming through the wall from next-door. She was sure Stephen had told her the place was standing empty. Maybe someone had broken in. The photographer? Cole? Or were they one and the same?

The thought increased her anxiety tenfold. Heart thumping, Georgia waited, statue-still, listening for a repeat of the sound. But next came a series of slow, hesitant creaks, as though someone was trying to climb the stairs quietly. She pressed an ear to the wall above the fireplace, holding her breath as she listened. Would she be able to hear from there if anyone was moving around upstairs next door?

All seemed quiet for a few moments. And then the same cautious creak of footfall, this time descending the stairs. Georgia was sure she could hear voices, whispering. The walls were fairly thick, so maybe the sound was being carried through a gap somewhere, an airbrick she hadn't noticed. She strained to listen, but the words were indecipherable. Although . . .

A sudden realisation sent a flash of cold fear through her. There was only one person speaking. From the tentative movements, whoever was in the house obviously felt the need to conceal their presence. Why would an intruder be talking to themselves?

There was a sudden, unmistakeable laugh, smothered and low, but from Georgia's perspective, with more than a hint of malice. The muted click of a door. And then everything was quiet once more. Georgia looked about her in trepidation. With legs like jelly, she went back into the kitchen, half expecting a shadow across the window blind, a hand rattling the door handle. But there was nothing.

Georgia watched and waited, hardly daring to move from where she stood. It felt as though her legs were weighted with concrete. She was shivering now, from fear and the cold. It must have been ten minutes before she was satisfied that whoever had been in the house had gone. She boiled the kettle once more to make the Ovaltine, then, trying not to spill any with her still-trembling hands, went back through the sitting room and padded carefully up the stairs. She switched on the light, set the mug on the bedside cabinet and was about to close the curtains, then hesitated. She turned off the light again for a moment. If whoever had been in the house was still out there, she didn't want to be seen. For a moment she stood, looking out across the quad, her eyes flicking from one side to the other. All was still, the headstones in the graveyard crouching shadows in the gloom. The street lamps to the top end along Cuckoo Lane cast just enough light to wash the cobbles with a faint, warm-white glow. Her heart quickened suddenly when, as if from nowhere, a small group of rowdy students staggered out of an alleyway a few yards to her left, close to the Orb. She gasped, then exhaled deeply, watching as they turned left and disappeared towards the town centre. It made her wonder about Minnie; what she had been doing with her evening. Students always seemed to hang about in clutches and it reassured Georgia to think that Minnie seemed to have settled in with her housemates: any talk of outings always seemed to involve them. Ajab seemed a decent lad. The landlord had vetted every one of them prior to accepting their applications, so she was confident they were all a respectable bunch. And besides, Minnie was a sensible girl; Georgia knew that. Even so, she couldn't help but feel anxious about her. She would call her first thing, make sure everything was okay. Maybe they could meet up for coffee – lunch, even.

Georgia was about to pull the curtains across when something drew her attention to the terrace of houses on the opposite side of the square. Her eyes were growing accustomed to the low-level light and things had gradually become clearer. There, in one of the upstairs windows and against almost total darkness, a silhouette appeared to be standing, looking slightly to one side. At first she thought she might be imagining things, that it could just be a dressmaker's dummy or something similar. But as she watched, the head turned sharply, until its focus appeared to be directly on her. She blinked rapidly and looked again, wondering if her eyes were playing tricks on her. She couldn't tell if it was male or female, but there was definitely someone there. An unpleasantly icy feeling crept through her veins.

Georgia withdrew sharply from the window, her heart hammering. She waited for a moment, then peered round the edge of the curtain. The person, if indeed it had been a person, had vanished. Her eyes flew round the space below, fearful that somebody had left the building and was now outside in the square, possibly approaching. But there was no movement; no sign of anyone. All was quiet once more. Almost *too* quiet, an ethereal stillness settling over the quad.

She let out a breath, trying to steady her nerves, to think logically. Okay, so what if there *had* been someone there? It didn't necessarily mean anything, did it? But the thought that it could easily have been the same individual she'd heard laughing through the wall sent Georgia hurrying shakily back down the stairs to check the front door. She *had* locked it: of course she had. She was never that sloppy. She remembered the heavy iron doorstop in the hallway and, summoning all her strength, hefted it across the flagstones to wedge against the door as an extra measure. *That* would take some getting past if anyone tried to gain entry. It made her feel a little better.

The church bells tolled the quarter-hour suddenly, approaching midnight, a hollow, unearthly sound which echoed round the quad and sent needle-like shards through her nerve-endings. As she stood stiffly in the sitting room doorway, to her right and lit by the street lamp, she saw the shadowy upper half of a tall, grey figure drift slowly and silently across the window outside, almost making her heart stop. Slow, deliberate footsteps rang out as someone walked past the house in the direction of

79

the side entrance. Where had they come from? There hadn't been a soul in evidence when she'd looked out only a moment ago.

Georgia's stomach turned a somersault. The front entrance was safely blocked now – but what about access via the kitchen? There was a high-walled passageway round the side of the building – the thought that someone agile enough could easily have climbed the iron gate to creep through it and round the back sent something like an electric shock shooting up her spine. Stumbling her way through the murk of the sitting room, she inched along the wall and to the rear of the house where an old, stable-type door opened onto the tiny courtyard beyond. There was a bolt across the top; she'd thought earlier that it didn't look especially robust, but now it seemed imperative to make it secure. Her breathing shallow and rapid, Georgia stood for a moment, ear against the door, listening for evidence of anyone outside. She could hear a rustling noise, as though something was moving in the shrubs around the periphery of the yard. Was this the same intruder or was she being targeted by someone else? That photographer from earlier – could it be the same person? Frantically, she looked round for something to create a barricade. The loose cupboard door beneath the sink wasn't heavy enough. There didn't appear to be anything. Suddenly she remembered the sturdy fireplace tools sitting on the hearth in the front room – maybe she could thread the poker through both latches to prevent them from being opened.

This proved to be an excellent idea: the poker was just the right size, the handle preventing it from dropping all the way through. She stood stock-still for a few minutes, waiting with bated breath for more noises from beyond the door. All seemed quiet now. Could she have imagined it? No. She was certain: there had definitely been something out there. *Someone*, even.

Once reasonably sure that any immediate danger had passed, her legs unsteady, Georgia climbed the stairs back to the bedroom. She was tempted to peep round the curtain again to view the terrace opposite and the space below, but resisted. She felt as though she'd been put through a mangle. It was doubtful anyone could get in now though, even with a key. But she would keep the light on, for her own peace of mind. How she wished Minnie was here. For a brief moment she was tempted to call her, but then decided it would be unfair, in case she was asleep.

Taking a few deep breaths, she sat on the bed to sip the Ovaltine, recoiling at the tepid temperature and the skin which had formed over the surface. The adrenaline gradually subsiding, she felt drained and couldn't face going back down to make another. Replacing the mug on the bedside cabinet, Georgia undressed and pulled her nightshirt over her head, draping her clothes over the chair near the window, then crawled under the duvet. She lay almost paralysed with dread for what felt like hours, her ears straining to hear more footsteps or voices.

The church clock began to strike four. Georgia was exhausted. Just as it finished chiming, in spite of everything, she finally succumbed to a torturous sleep, her dreams filled, as they had been so often in the past, with a faceless, menacing figure, its gnarled hands reaching like claws to drag her into the unknown.

If she had looked across the quad at that moment, she might have seen the curtain twitch a little in a darkened upstairs window. The outline of fingers, pulling the voile across as they withdrew from sight.

Maybe Georgia had been right. Maybe her fears weren't unfounded at all.

Maybe someone was watching her.

Chapter 9

Minnie

Saturday afternoon, 24 September 2022 – One day earlier

"Some woman called Angela's emailed about the spare room." Fatima had finally dragged herself off the sofa to make tea. She stood in the middle of the kitchen, hands wrapped around a mug with a wisp of steam rising in front of her face, hindering Minnie's attempts to put the shopping away and making no attempt to move aside. "She's been looking for a houseshare – says she's been given a place on the same history course as us through clearing after someone else dropped out and a woman from Reception pointed her in our direction. She sounded keen so I said she could come round to have a look later this afternoon – I didn't think it'd be a problem."

Minnie's heart sank a little. She'd been quite happy with the dynamics but knew the others were anxious to have the rent burden lightened. "Oh, right. Did she say where she's from?"

"Yorkshire or somewhere, by the sounds of it. She's a mature student, apparently – not sure how mature." Fatima grimaced. "But I guess her money's as good as anyone's and I'm not going to argue if she helps pay the rent. Let's face it, we've had no other offers. And my dad's seriously pissed off it's costing him more than he originally thought. I need to keep him sweet." Her eyes flickered a little.

Minnie suppressed a smile. Sonia was constantly bemoaning the fact that Fatima's dad seemed to be paying for everything. No student loan for her. But it appeared that even *he* had his limits.

Ajab appeared in the doorway. "What's that – someone's coming round this afternoon?" He chewed the inside of his cheek, casting Minnie a dubious look. "Is Sonia still hanging? The booze fumes coming from her room earlier were enough to knock you sideways. We don't want to put the woman off."

"I've told her to get dressed, give herself a shake. I went round with the Febreze."

Minnie nodded approvingly. "Good idea. We can light a couple of smelly candles, too. It'll all help."

"Oh – did you remember the painkillers, by the way? She's been whingeing like mad." Fatima cast an eye around the kitchen. Dirty cereal bowls and mugs were piled around the sink, the surfaces littered with cornflakes and spilled sugar. "We'd better do a quick blitz of the place. Don't want Angela to think we're a bunch of slobs, even if we are."

"Speak for yourself," said Ajab indignantly. "I always try to tidy up after myself."

Fatima glared at him. "All right, Mr Domesticity. This is no time to be holier than thou. I'll clean up in here – you can sort the living room. Mins – you take the bathroom."

Minnie shot a look at Ajab, eyebrows raised. "Er – excuse me. Don't forget while you've been doing your lady of leisure bit, *we've* just been to get the shopping in – we could both do with a coffee and a sit-down before we start anything."

Fatima chose to ignore this. She glanced up at the clock. "We'd better get a shift on. She'll be here in the next hour or so." She waved a hand in the general direction of Sonia's room. "And I think the most we can expect of our dirty stop-out is to get herself looking half-presentable. No, better still, she can just stay out of sight. We'll just have to make sure her bedroom door stays shut."

Minnie felt a bit sorry for the woman when she arrived, flustered and red-faced, apologetic for being an hour later than she'd originally stated, having first miscalculated how long it would take her to walk from the B & B where she was staying in Earlsdon and then somehow missing the property completely. She'd been walking up and down the Kenilworth Road, "like a lost sheep" she'd told them breathlessly, until she'd eventually asked a passer-by for directions.

"I'm Angela – Angela T-Tandy," she'd announced, setting down a tatty tote bag and smiling uncertainly at the three faces greeting her in the hallway. The woman's clothes were dated, her straight, shoulder-length hair a dull brown. She was in her late thirties at least, slightly scrawny and not much over five feet tall. Minnie stole a glance at Fatima, whose nose had wrinkled as though a bad smell had just wafted in.

Everyone introduced themselves. Things felt stilted, as though no one really knew quite where to start. Fatima wore a stony expression. She seemed to be appraising every inch of their visitor. From behind tortoiseshell-framed glasses, Angela's green eyes widened as they travelled from the chrome spiral chandelier suspended from the high ceiling to the polished parquet flooring and heavy oak doors leading from the vestibule.

"Wow, this is *plush*," she remarked. "I hadn't expected anything quite so g-g-rand." She looked anxiously from one face to the other. "I'm definitely k-keen to take the room – if you're all happy to have me, of c-course."

"But you haven't even seen it yet." Fatima's tone was brittle. She cast Minnie an odd look. "And we're waiting for a call back from another prospective tenant, so nothing's set in stone till you've battled it out." She gave a hollow laugh.

Ajab's eyes met Minnie's, his expression quizzical. "What's she on about?" he whispered, as Fatima almost frogmarched Angela through the corridor to show her the rest of the house.

"I don't think Angela's quite what she was expecting," said Minnie in a low voice. "But if Fatima's daddy's piling on the pressure to plug the rent gap, she's going to have to grin and bear it."

Ajab smirked. "Whatever happened to 'her money's as good as anyone's'?"

"I know. Priceless."

Within minutes, Fatima and Angela were coming back towards them, Fatima now wearing a tight smile. "Angela says she can pay nine months' rent up front to secure the room so she can move in right away, so I think we're all agreed she can have it."

"But w-w-what about the other p-person?" Angela's brow creased. "Are they travelling any distance to come and view? I mean – I don't want to push anyone's n-nose out of joint."

"Oh, like I said – nothing concrete had been arranged." Fatima flapped a hand dismissively. "I'll call them to say the room's taken." Her eyes settled pointedly on Minnie, who arched an eyebrow in her direction.

"Well, welcome then, Angela! Good to have you on board." Ajab grinned broadly. "I'll make us all a coffee – you do drink coffee, don't you?"

Angela's face lit up. "Thank you. White, one s-sugar."

*

They took their drinks through to the living room, where, perched on the edge of the huge settee, Angela continued to survey her surroundings, a slightly vacant expression on her face.

"So, you've just been accepted onto our course – is that right?" Minnie put down her empty mug onto one of the coasters arranged on the glass-topped table, marvelling at the neatly piled magazines, lack of dust and usual cup rings. The absence of toast and crisp crumbs on the rug. The Jo Malone rose and oud candle Georgia had bought Minnie the previous Christmas had been lit, infusing the air with a delicious perfume. Ajab had done a sterling job. But it was clear not much would have been needed to persuade Angela to bite their hands off for the room. Still, at least everything was clean and tidy for once.

"Hmm?" A bemused expression clouded Angela's face. "I didn't quite c-catch . . ." She leaned forwards a little, turning her head to one side.

Minnie enunciated her words more clearly. "Fatima says you've just landed a place on the same history course as the rest of us."

"Sorry – I'm d-deaf in my left ear. I should've explained." Angela pulled a face. "Oh, yes. I – well, as you've probably g-gathered, I'm a bit late to all this. My mum . . . she died suddenly, a c-couple of years ago." Her voice quavered a little, but she composed herself, clearing her throat. "I needed something to take my mind off everything and Mum left me a little money. So I went back to c-college to take my A levels. I've always been k-keen on history. I'm pinching myself, to be honest. Never in a m-million years thought I'd be going to uni." She smiled shakily.

"Good for you." Minnie's heart went out to her. Angela seemed vulnerable, unsure of herself. Minnie turned to the others. "Great that Angela's following her dream, isn't it?"

"Awesome." Ajab nodded. "You'll have to come with us to your first lecture, Angela. We can introduce you to some of the others on the course. Most of them seem pretty decent."

Fatima shot Ajab a filthy look, then mumbled something about needing to call her dad, and excused herself.

"Is she all right?" Angela's eyes followed Fatima's figure as she flounced out through the door. "She seems a bit – well, p-prickly."

"Oh, she's okay. She can be a bit of a diva sometimes. Probably still a tad hungover, too. Friday night's party night." Ajab grinned. "I was the only one who behaved myself. Reprobates, this lot."

Minnie pretended to punch his arm. "Oi, you."

Sonia appeared in the doorway suddenly, yawning widely. Her copper, urchin-cut hair was wild, her eyes puffy. She tipped her head in Fatima's direction.

"What's with the face on her ladyship? Looks like she's been slapped with a wet fish." Her gaze shifted to Angela and she faltered. "Oh. Sorry. Are you the lady that's come to look at the house?"

Angela nodded, smiling up at her. "Yes, I'm Angela. You must be Sonia. Fatima said you were sleeping. I hope we d-d-didn't disturb you?"

"No, I've been awake ages. Feeling a bit . . . rough today." She locked eyes with Minnie for a moment, then turned back to their visitor with a weak smile. "Will you be moving in, then?"

"Yes." Angela nodded enthusiastically. "It's a f-fabulous house. And you all seem so n-nice. I c-can't w-wait."

"Cool." Sonia hovered for a moment. "I'll just jump in the shower. Try and liven myself up a bit. Good to meet you, Angela."

She flashed Minnie another look, then disappeared back down the corridor. The sound of lowered voices having some sort of conflab carried through from the kitchen.

87

Minnie wondered what was going on. She turned to Ajab, who shrugged his shoulders briefly, giving an almost indiscernible shake of the head. The atmosphere felt suddenly thick with uncertainty and Angela had clearly sensed this, her face betraying disappointment.

Ajab cleared his throat. "'Scuse me a minute – I just need the loo." He left the room, closing the door behind him. Minnie sat opposite Angela in awkward silence, as Angela fiddled with the hem of her corduroy skirt, her eyes skimming the floor.

She lifted her head suddenly, fixing Minnie with an unreadable look. "I s'pose it's a bit w-weird at first, moving into a house with t-total strangers. It must take t-time to get to know everyone p-properly. And then it's t-tough luck if you f-find out you don't really l-like each other." She gave an odd little laugh, which made Minnie shudder slightly. It wasn't what she'd said so much as the way she'd said it. As though there was some meaning behind the words.

Minnie was thinking of a suitable response when Ajab reappeared, grinning. "Sonia thought Fatima had been at her cranberry juice again, so there's been a bit of a debate going on in there. I don't know, those two." He clicked his tongue.

"Oh d-dear. I'll make s-sure I don't use anything without asking, th-then." Angela smiled up at him. She smoothed out her skirt and rose from her seat, depositing her empty mug on the table.

"Thank you for the coffee. I'd better g-get back to my B & B – the landlady's c-cooking this evening. She seems a bit of a d-dragon, so I don't w-want to be l-late." She laughed nervously. "Erm – I don't w-want to seem p-pushy, but when d'you think I can move my stuff in, p-please? I'm p-paid up at the g-guest house for three nights. It's not full," she added, "so I don't think it'd be a p-problem if I extended for a c-couple more."

Ajab turned to Minnie, eyebrows raised. "We'll speak to

Fatima and Sonia in case they've got something planned, but I can't see any reason why you can't move in soon as," he said.

Minnie nodded hesitantly. "Fatima's got your number, hasn't she – we'll call you later to confirm."

"Great. Right, I'll leave you in p-peace, then. N-nice to meet you all." Angela extended her own hand to shake first Ajab's, then Minnie's. As she did so, she held Minnie's gaze for a moment. For some reason it felt slightly unsettling. Minnie withdrew her hand, forcing a smile.

"Yeah, you too. See you soon."

Minnie watched from the doorway as Angela ambled from the driveway and back onto the street. It hadn't been immediately obvious, but the woman had a barely noticeable limp, as though one shoe was slightly higher than the other. As Angela reached the end of the wall outside the house, she turned to look at Minnie, nodding and smiling as she did so, before disappearing from view. Something niggled in Minnie's stomach. She couldn't put a finger on it, but still the feeling persisted that there was something slightly off about Angela. But that was silly. The woman hadn't done or even really said anything untoward. She was much older and clearly a bit socially awkward. Minnie thought of her mother, how irrationally suspicious she always was of people, sometimes even those she knew. Maybe it was rubbing off on her. Minnie shrugged off the notion as ridiculous and went back into the house.

Fatima appeared from the kitchen as soon as the front door closed, peering through the spyhole to check Angela had gone.

"Jesus." She pulled a face. "She's going to be a barrel of laughs. I know we need the rent money, but seriously . . ."

"I dunno. She seems okay." Ajab had begun to make his way towards the stairs.

"But she's so *dowdy*. And *old* – I mean, you get some people in their thirties who seem really, well, youthful. She's thirty-nine or whatever going on, like sixty. Even Mins's mum would've been better."

Minnie glowered. "It was never an option to have my mum moving in here, I told you. How would you feel about having your dad looking over your shoulder the whole time?"

Fatima huffed, but her silence spoke volumes.

"Well *I* don't have a problem with the woman." Ajab paused at the foot of the stairs. "And you seemed happy enough earlier when she said she could pay in advance. If she can hand over that much moolah in one go, that's us out of the woods for the first year, at least. Can't have your cake and eat it." He cast Minnie a smirk. "Anyway, I need to crack on. I've got work to do."

"Me too." Minnie began to follow. She felt her phone vibrate in her pocket and pulled it out. Jake's name flashed up on the screen.

You free for a drink Tuesday evening, Minnie Mouse? x

She smiled to herself, quickly tapping in a reply.

Maybe. Will be in touch x

She definitely wasn't going to pass up on the invitation, but didn't want to sound too eager. *Treat 'em mean, keep 'em keen.* That's what her dad had always said. The memory of Jake's appealing grin gave her a warm, tingly feeling. Her heart light and all thoughts of Angela pushed to one side, Minnie took the stairs two at a time.

She needed to finish that essay. She had a date to look forward to.

Chapter 10

Georgia

Monday morning, 26 September 2022

The hammering at the front door woke Georgia abruptly. Her heart pounding, she sat up, disorientated. She had forgotten for a moment where she was and her eyes travelled the room in confusion until everything came back into focus. Sunlight streamed through the thin curtains, though the air was frigid. She could hear activity outside, people moving about and bird call: the beginnings of a new day. Peering at the bedside clock, she saw with alarm that she had slept in. It had just turned nine thirty, far later than she would usually stay in bed. After the night she'd had, it was a miracle she had slept at all.

The loud knocking from below persisted. She could hear a man's voice, grumbling vociferously. Dragging herself to her feet, Georgia pulled on her dressing gown and slippers and made her way downstairs. Seeing the iron doorstop across the threshold, the memory of how anxious she had felt the previous night seemed slightly ludicrous in broad daylight, though the suspicion that someone had been observing her still niggled.

Georgia dragged the doorstop back to where it usually rested and unlocked the door, opening it only a small amount. She was greeted by the sight of a stocky, fiftyish man with short, greying hair and bloodshot eyes. There was a purplish bloom to the skin of his rather bulbous nose, making her think he must enjoy his whisky. He wore an open-necked white shirt under a pricey-looking grey suit, though the jacket looked as though it had been made for someone two sizes smaller, his chest pushed forward, biceps bulging.

"Ah. There you are. I was gonna let meself in to save you the bother, but the door was jammed."

Georgia glanced back at the doorstop. It had obviously done its job. She looked the man up and down, disturbed by the idea that he had a key to the house. Though expensively dressed, he looked like a thug.

"I'm sorry? And you are . . . ?"

"Getting ahead of meself there! I'm Jethro. Your landlord?" he clarified, as her brow folded into a perplexed frown.

"Oh – Mr Jackson?"

"One and the same. And you must be Mrs Parnell."

Jackson held out a leathery but manicured hand which Georgia shook warily through the gap, most of her still concealed behind the door. Whether he owned the building or not, the man had no right to try to gain access without prearrangement. "Are you in the habit of letting yourself into your tenants' homes, Mr Jackson? I mean, as it happens I'm not in the middle of anything, but it might not have been convenient."

"I'm sorry. I've been knocking for ages and when there was no answer, I thought I ought to open up. All the curtains were shut, so I assumed you must be home. I mean, you could've collapsed in there or anything and no one would've been any the wiser. As it is, I can see you're perfectly okay."

"Yes, I am, thank you." Her tone was sharp. She kept one hand on the door.

His eyes darted quickly from her head to her feet and back. He ran a finger under the collar of his shirt and smiled broadly. "Nice to meet you, anyway."

Georgia narrowed her eyes. "What can I do for you, Mr Jackson?"

"Jethro, please. It's a courtesy call really; just wanted to introduce meself seeing as I'm in town at the moment, find out if you're happy with everything in the house. Only I've a handy lad who does repair jobs for me and if there's anything needs sorting out, I can send him round to deal with it."

"Isn't it usual for the tenant to approach the letting agency if there are any maintenance issues?" Georgia regarded him dubiously. She remembered Stephen, the young man who had originally shown her around, implying her landlord was a bit dodgy. She wasn't sure how she felt about Jackson sending one of his lackeys round, nor about him being able to let himself in whenever he felt like it. She would need to have a word with the agency.

Jackson's mouth spread into a wry grin, revealing tobacco-stained teeth. "Ah – but they'll bill me for any jobs done and I'm not always happy with the way their workmen do stuff, to be honest. My lad always does a great job and he comes cheap."

Georgia sighed. "One of the doors has come off its hinges in the kitchen. And the radiators need bleeding – it was freezing in here last night. Not helped by the gaps in the window frames."

"Not a problem. I can get me laddo out to do all that for you – say first thing Wednesday – or even tomorrow morning?"

Georgia considered this. She was meeting with Yiannis later to discuss her shifts at the Orb, but mornings weren't going to be an issue. Although if today was anything to go by, it seemed she might have to set an alarm.

"Tomorrow will be fine."

"Erm – d'you want me to have a quick look to see if there's anything else while I'm here?" He looked hopeful.

Georgia suspected he just wanted to have a snoop round to see what she had brought with her. She stood firm in the doorway. "No, that's fine. If I find anything else, I'll jot it down and tell your – man."

Jackson seemed deflated. "Right you are. Well, nice to meet you, anyway. I'll tell me fella to call about eight thirty on Tuesday then, if that's okay." He turned to leave. "Oh – while I'm here – has there been any mail for the former occupant at all? Only she bailed out in a hurry and left me out of pocket. Haven't been able to trace her."

So it was a woman who'd lived there before her, then. Something flashed in the man's eyes and his face hardened for a moment. For all his outwardly amiable demeanour, Georgia could easily imagine he could be quite the opposite if someone got on the wrong side of him.

She shook her head. "Sorry. If anything turns up, I'll be sure to pass it on."

He nodded slowly, though she wasn't convinced he believed her. His manner seemed suddenly less friendly. "I'd appreciate it. Have a good day, then – see you again sometime, I expect."

Georgia closed the front door and went into the sitting room to open the curtains. She watched through the nets as Jackson crossed the quad, with the swagger of someone who thinks he has the whole world in the palm of his hand. She tutted aloud.

But her scorn turned to sudden apprehension as she watched him unlock one of the doors in the terrace opposite and disappear inside. Her eyes travelled upwards as she remembered the figure in the window the previous night. Something cold seemed to be creeping up her spine.

Wasn't it the same house?

*

Mid-morning, Monday, 26 September 2022

"So Jethro Jackson's your landlord, eh?" Yiannis arced a perfectly-shapely eyebrow. "Lucky you."

It was only 10.30am and the bar was deserted. The floor was still damp from the swab of the cleaner's mop, the air cool, a hint of cleaning fluid lingering. Yiannis was sitting at the table usually occupied by Ned, the rota sheet spread out in front of him and two steaming mugs of coffee at the ready.

"D'you know him then, Jackson?" Georgia tried to sound casual as she hung up her jacket and bag behind the bar before joining him.

"Not personally. His reputation precedes him, shall we say."

"What's he done? I mean, the lad from the letting agency sort of hinted he was a bit iffy, but he didn't elaborate."

"I only know bits of gossip. Nothing concrete." Yiannis glanced at the door, lowering his voice. "But it's rumoured there's dirty money behind his property portfolio. *And* his building company. One guy who used to work for him reckoned he tipped a bloke who owed him money out of his car on the dual carriageway – when he was doing sixty."

"Jesus. All round nice guy, then." Georgia felt something twist in her gut. How glad she was now that she'd left the doorstop at the threshold. "It sounds as if the woman who lived in the house before me still owes him rent. I hope for her sake he doesn't catch up with her."

"Better make sure we get you paid on time so he doesn't start hassling you, too." Yiannis grimaced.

Georgia grinned. She had more than enough set aside to pay for a couple of years up front if she wanted, but Yiannis didn't need to know that. It was quite touching that he seemed so concerned. "I'm sure I'll be fine. But thanks." She lowered herself onto the stool opposite him and he pushed one of the mugs across the table.

"Soy latte, half a sugar. Did I remember rightly?"

"Yes, thank you." Georgia's eyes landed on the rota. "So when have you pencilled me in, then?" She sipped the coffee, rotating the page to see which days she was expected to work.

Yiannis tapped his index finger on the paper. "I know Freddie said five nights, but if you want more shifts – you know, for the extra dosh, I'm sure we could wangle something."

"Five's great for me; for now, at least. I'm doing okay – my husband left me a little money, so I'm not desperate. I just really want to get out into the workplace, you know."

Yiannis nodded. He sat back in his seat. "That's fine, then. I've put you in for this Friday, then you can start properly next week, Tuesday to Saturday evenings, six till eleven thirty – that sound okay? We can tweak it each week to suit you. I mean, I'm always on site, so it's never much of an issue for me. But I'd welcome an extra pair of hands on Sunday quiz nights now and again."

"Sounds perfect. Gives me a few days to sort the house out. And I'm more than happy to help out on Sundays if I'm needed. So Mondays will be my night off, then?"

"Yep; for now, anyway. Suck it and see, eh? 'Course, you're welcome to join us just to socialise – it's pretty quiet at the start of the week as a rule, but I wouldn't mind betting that Cole fella'll be putting in an appearance if he thinks you'll be in."

Georgia wrinkled up her nose. She recalled how Cole had

made her feel the previous night and shuddered. "I'm not sure I want him to."

Yiannis drew back his chin. "He seems okay. Very easy on the eye, anyway."

Georgia widened her eyes, making him laugh.

"As long as he's not making a nuisance of himself or anything . . ." Yiannis slanted his eyebrows in a question.

Georgia hesitated. Cole hadn't actually done anything. Maybe she was being unduly cautious. "No. I'm just a bit, well – I'd prefer to keep him at arm's length until I know him better, put it like that."

Yiannis smiled. "I'll look out for you, sweet; you don't have to worry." He knocked back the rest of his coffee, and got to his feet, replacing his stool beneath the table. "Well, if you're happy with the rota, I can tell Freddie we're good to go. I'd better open up in a minute. Any plans for today?"

"Nothing specific." But Georgia did have one plan. She'd got a locksmith coming round at two o'clock – she wasn't going to risk Jethro Jackson letting himself in, whether she was at home or not. Plus, she wanted a more secure bolt on the stable door. And sod the ramifications – she hadn't read the small print to see if there was a clause in the contract about not altering anything. She'd worry about that later. If it had been him watching the house the previous night, the thought was even more alarming. Maybe he even had access to the neighbouring property – he might well have bought it to add to his portfolio. Guarding against him entering uninvited would give her peace of mind.

"Hope to see you this evening," Yiannis called, as she collected her belongings and made her way towards the door.

"We'll see. Have a good day, anyway. Ciao for now."

Chapter 11

Georgia

Monday, 26 September 2022

Georgia decided against visiting the Orb later. She'd be starting work soon enough and spending half her week in there. More productive to use the day to clean and sort through the boxes of stuff from home. In the cold light of day, she felt a little better, but after the previous night, top of her list was to bring the small TV she'd brought with her downstairs. She hoped that some background noise would help her to relax a bit as darkness fell. Apart from that, as the house was so small, she had packed only the essentials and a few nostalgic items she treasured. Things that she definitely didn't want to leave behind. And a few other items she couldn't risk anyone, especially Minnie, finding. The very thought made her heart tap out an uncomfortable rhythm.

She carried the old banker's box she'd commandeered from

Trevor into the bedroom and knelt on the floor. Though there was no earthly reason anything should have been removed, she felt an irrational compulsion to check, to make sure nothing had somehow gone astray. Or, perish the thought, been discovered by her husband and filed away elsewhere at some point as some sort of insurance.

She lifted the lid and began to remove the contents carefully, checking from the top where she kept precious mementos of Minnie's childhood, handmade Mother's Day cards; her glowing end-of-year school reports. There was an A4 wallet of class photos, one for each year she'd been at the local primary. A film of tears covered Georgia's eyes as she scanned each picture for Minnie's beaming face, her then fair, wavy hair. *Her lovely little girl.*

She remembered every teacher, every year group. As though it were only yesterday. She had gone to that school twice daily; every day of the school term, other than when Minnie had had chickenpox or an upset tummy, for seven years. Smiling inwardly, she recalled the time when Minnie was in year five, and Victoria, a particularly spiteful, sharp-featured girl in her class, had begun picking on her for no apparent reason. One day, she'd pulled Minnie's hair and made her cry. After dropping Minnie off the following morning, Georgia had waited in the school playground and beckoned Victoria, always a latecomer, over before she'd had chance to go into class.

"Hello, Victoria. Do you know who I am?"

The girl had darted a hesitant look across the empty tarmac. "Um – you're Minnie's mum."

"That's right." Georgia pasted on a smile, inclining her head to one side. "Do you love your mum, Victoria?" she had asked in a sweet voice.

"Of course," the girl had replied, a little defensively.

"I'm pleased to hear it. Because I love my daughter. And if

99

you're mean to her again, I'll do something *really* mean to your mum. Do I make myself clear?"

Victoria had looked horrified, but nodded mutely, her eyes filling with tears.

"Good. I'm glad we understand one another. Now off you go, you're already late."

Georgia had looked on in satisfaction as Victoria tore across the playground. She'd been right to feel confident that her little chat with the child would prevent any recurrence of the bullying. Minnie had come home later the same day grinning from ear to ear.

"Victoria actually said sorry to me today, Mummy," she'd announced. "She even offered to help me tidy up the book corner when Miss Jessop asked me to do it."

There were never any further incidents and Georgia felt pleased that her words had had the desired effect. Any time she'd seen Victoria's mother afterwards, the woman had never been anything other than civil towards her, so Georgia knew the girl had kept their conversation to herself. But would she have been mean to Victoria's mum if it had been necessary? *In a heartbeat.*

As she neared the bottom of the box, the familiar sick feeling rolled in Georgia's stomach as her eyes landed on the folder she'd been looking for. So, it was still there. The one containing every detail of her past life: her birth certificate, National Health card, medical letters; one particularly damning school report. Grim photographs. Letters. Details that she lived in constant fear of Minnie ever uncovering. She riffled through the paperwork within, trying to remain detached. Maybe she could have burned it all. But paradoxically there were things in there that she felt she *needed* to keep, reminders of how she had been failed by her parents and how far she had come. How long ago it all was. She wasn't that person now. She was a good mother, had done her best to be a good wife most of the time. She had to remind herself of the fact every day.

Having tidied everything away, Georgia secured the lid on the banker's box with a length of cord, removed the folded pile of knitwear from the top shelf of her wardrobe and shoved the box to the back, replacing the sweaters in front of it. She went back into the box room, then carried the small TV she'd brought with her downstairs and set it atop a shelf in one of the alcoves next to the fireplace, then connected it to the aerial point and power supply.

Georgia sat back in the armchair and blew out a breath. She'd had enough already. She decided to call Minnie. It was too late to arrange a lunch date and the locksmith was due to arrive in the next hour, but it would be nice to meet for afternoon tea, unless she had a lecture or something. Georgia dialled Minnie's mobile, but it rang out several times and then diverted to voicemail. She waited a few minutes and tried again, but this time the voicemail service was activated immediately. Georgia felt vexed. She knew Minnie always had her phone to hand – she must have been able to see she was ringing her and had rejected the call. The least the girl could do was to drop her a text to say she couldn't talk for whatever reason.

Georgia tapped out a message asking Minnie to get back to her, then looked around aimlessly. She ought to do a bit more while she was waiting for the locksmith. She'd call it a day after that.

Though she didn't want to clutter the place, she still had a small box of hardbacks to stack on the shelves built into the other alcove. Georgia had discovered a love for books when Minnie started secondary school and liked the familiarity of reading matter that she had consumed over and over, mostly classics, such as Daphne du Maurier's *Rebecca* and H.E. Bates's *Love for Lydia*. Despite Trevor's scathing insinuations – *Wouldn't you be better sticking to your celebrity magazines?* – she often used to return to them when she had a spare moment. They helped her to escape for a while, inhabit another person's existence. But since Trevor's passing, she'd had no inclination to read anything. Hopefully that would soon change.

She gave each shelf a wipe with a damp cloth, then began to arrange the books neatly. As she slotted them in one by one, she noticed one of the worn bricks covering the side wall of the alcove wobble a little. It was loose. Georgia inserted her fingers into the gap where the pointing had crumbled away and the brick lifted out easily. She groaned, thinking more might follow and the whole wall would need repairing. Another job for Jethro Jackson's handyman. But as she removed it, she realised that this was the only one which was unattached, as though someone had deliberately chipped away the mortar which held it in place. Behind it, the wall had been hollowed out and something tucked into the recess. Carefully, Georgia pulled out a small, faded-blue tin, rectangular and rusty, maybe two inches deep by four across at its widest point. The raised capital letters on the top declared *FARRAH'S ORIGINAL HARROGATE TOFFEE – EST'D 1840.* Though it was tight, she managed eventually to prise off the lid. She hadn't really expected to find toffees – but what Georgia *did* find made her stomach drop.

There, wrapped in a rubber band inside a plain brown envelope, was a small bundle of photographs. Not, as one might have expected, old and dog-eared, but glossy, colour images, looking as if they'd been printed fairly recently. Georgia unwound the elastic and began to leaf through the pictures. The other people featured were unknown to her, but on closer inspection she recognised Jethro Jackson in each of the photos. She wasn't sure of their relevance initially, but quickly it dawned on her that there seemed to be some sort of transactions taking place. A shaking of hands; the blur of something being slipped into an inside pocket with a cagey backward glance from the recipient. Judging from the awkward upwards angle, it looked as though each had been snapped covertly. She turned the pictures over to find places, dates and times on the back of each, written in clear black ink. But it was the final photograph that made her chest tighten. The swollen, bruised face of a dark-haired woman, age indeterminate, the eyes sunken, racoon-like, into their sockets. On the reverse of the image was the date *15/03/21* and one word: *COPY*.

Georgia's mind was whirring. Who was the woman? And why had the photos been concealed in the wall? What had gone on in this house? She felt slightly sick.

Stuffing everything back into the tin, she replaced it in the aperture and pushed the brick in front of it. The pictures were obviously of some significance. But what should she do with them? Maybe the person who had hidden them would come back for them at a later date. Another good reason to change the locks.

Before she'd had much time to muse over her discovery, there was a loud rap on the window, almost making her leap into the air. She turned to see someone attempting to peer through the grimy nets, hands cupped around their eyes. It must be the locksmith.

Casting a hurried glance at the shelves to ensure everything looked in order, Georgia went into the vestibule, pausing to be certain before opening the door.

"Hello? Can I help you?" she called.

"Mrs Parnell? Come about your locks," came the muffled response.

Georgia unbolted the door. A short, fiftyish-year-old man with receding grey hair was standing on the step, clutching a black canvas tool bag bearing the logo *Smithy's Locks* embossed in gold letters around the picture of a keyhole. She managed a polite smile and stepped aside to let him in.

The man squinted around.

"Where'd you want me to start? Front and back, wasn't it?" He chuckled bawdily. "That sounded a bit off, didn't it?"

Georgia's smile vanished. She pretended to ignore his quip, gesturing towards the rear of the house. "You can do the one in the kitchen first, if you like," she replied brusquely.

The man closed the door behind him, his eyes widening as he entered the hallway.

"I been here before, I think. Couple o' year ago; no, maybe a bit less. There'd been a bit o' bother. You wasn't here then, was you?"

Georgia shook her head. "No. I've not long moved in." She wondered about the 'bit of bother', but after the man's inappropriate joke decided not to engage.

He nodded slowly. "Ah. I remember now. Different lady." He inclined his head again, as though recalling something. "*Right*. Okay if I go through?"

Georgia drew back a little as the man took his bag into the sitting room, disappearing into the kitchen. She paused before following, then resumed placing the books on the shelves, her eyes constantly drawn to the loose brick. She thought again about the trouble the locksmith had mentioned. Maybe she *should* ask him about it.

Tuneless whistling warbled from the kitchen, drowned intermittently by the noise of a power drill. After a few minutes, both ceased abruptly.

"'Ere, looks like someone's left you a present," the man called suddenly. His voice sounded strange. Georgia looked round to see him approaching, his brow knitted, a gloved hand holding out something at arm's length.

"What – what is it?" As Georgia registered the item, she drew in a breath, the colour draining from her face. It was a small, very basic human-shaped figurine fashioned from unglazed clay. Like something a child might have made. And uncomfortably familiar.

"Just noticed it lying right there on the ground, outside your back door. Placed like it was sort of, well, *watching*." The man's mouth gurned in distaste. "I don't like owt like that. I remember my old mum saying witches used to curse people who'd crossed them and send 'em those things. Reckoned they were meant to bring bad luck – death, even." Registering Georgia's horrified expression, he forced a smile, though his brow was still knitted. "'Ere, don't take no notice of me. Probably kids mucking about. Getting near Halloween and all that. Shops are full o' the stuff already. Yeah, kids playing silly buggers."

For a moment, Georgia was horribly transfixed by the little model. It was almost identical to one she'd made herself in a pottery class, many years ago. But she neither wanted nor needed anything to dredge up memories of her childhood. She found herself scrutinising the man suddenly, wondering whether *he* could have planted the thing there. Whether he could have been sent to torment her.

But how was that possible? She had contacted him herself, hadn't she? She was overtired: she wasn't thinking clearly. Someone else must have left it. Was she being deliberately targeted – or could it be a stupid prank, as the locksmith suggested? Her stomach churning, she reached out and snatched the figure from his hand.

"All that crap about curses and stuff belongs in the fucking Dark Ages," she declared, failing to disguise the tremor in her voice. "It's bound to just be someone pratting about."

Taking the figure straight to the pedal bin in the corner, she threw it inside with force, staring in as the thing bounced against the side. The head fell off and cracked in two as it landed with a loud clunk at the bottom. Georgia was standing with both hands balled into fists, her jaw tight. She turned back to the man, who appeared startled.

"How long's this going to take you? Only I have to go out soon."

The man scratched his head. "Um – shouldn't be more than three quarters of an hour." He tipped his head towards the back door. "That one's nearly done."

His eyes travelled awkwardly from the bin back to Georgia. It occurred to her suddenly that she must look slightly deranged. She gave a small cough.

"Don't let me keep you, then." She looked pointedly at the man's drill, lying at his feet. He nodded mutely, picked it up and returned to his work. There was no more whistling.

Georgia marched back into the living room. Her hands felt uncoordinated now as she arranged the last few books on the shelves. A mystery photographer. Noises through the walls; someone rooting around in the yard after dark. Pictures concealed in the wall. And now *this*.

She felt tears threaten and was suddenly desperate to see Minnie. She picked up her mobile once more to see whether she'd had any new messages, but there was nothing. Angrily, Georgia tossed the phone onto the armchair. Why was she ignoring her?

Stuff it. She'd wait for the locksmith to leave, then go round to Minnie's house – if she wasn't in, she would just wait. There couldn't be anything *that* important that Minnie couldn't afford to spend an hour or two with her at some point. Surely it wasn't too much to ask.

There was no one home at the student house. Georgia had been waiting anxiously under the portico for almost an hour when she saw the glow of Minnie's red hair appear at the end of the road. She waved frantically, almost tripping in her haste to meet her halfway. Minnie had been oblivious, eyes down, scrolling through her mobile as she walked. Hearing Georgia approaching, she jerked her head up, visibly startled.

"Christ, Mum, you scared the life out of me. Is something wrong?"

Georgia threw up her hands. "I've been trying to reach you all day. Why the hell didn't you get back to me?"

Minnie's lips tightened. "I was in a lecture?" The inflection at the end of the sentence felt like a rebuke.

"Well, you can't have been for at least the last twenty minutes and I've only just tried to ring you again. I've been waiting here bloody ages. I'd hoped we could've met up this afternoon. I . . ." Georgia paused, seeing Minnie's face darken. "I've been at a bit of a loose end today."

Minnie sighed. "I'm sorry. I was going to ring back – it's just – I came out of uni and sort of got distracted." She studied Georgia, her eyes narrowing suspiciously. "But you're okay, though? Nothing serious?"

"Well no. Not really." Georgia felt suddenly sheepish. She thought about the things that had unsettled her in Cuckoo Cottage, but there was nothing tangible to report – not anything that she wanted to share with Minnie. Nothing that wouldn't have made her sound paranoid and pathetic.

"I haven't slept well. I feel a bit . . . restless today. I just wanted some company, that's all." She peered at the phone, still in Minnie's hand. "So who's messaging you then, that you had to reply to before me?"

Minnie stuffed the mobile into her pocket, mustering a smile. "Oh, no one. Just checking TikTok. Come on, I'm gasping for a brew."

They walked together towards the house in silence. Georgia hovered as Minnie unlocked the door, and followed her through the hallway and into the kitchen. She perched on a seat at the breakfast bar, watching as Minnie set about making their drinks, asking half-heartedly whether Georgia would prefer builder's tea or some herbal concoction. About what she'd been doing earlier.

It was weird, being in this strange house as her daughter's guest. The unfamiliar smells, belongings she didn't recognise. Just another visitor. It only seemed to highlight the fact that they no longer shared a home, that a chasm was opening between them. Instead of making her feel better, being there made Georgia suddenly sad and she remembered why she hadn't wanted to come to the house when Minnie first moved. She felt tired and emotional. Tears pricked at her eyes and she brushed them away, dropping her gaze so that Minnie wouldn't notice. She had wanted so badly to see Minnie, but now felt unwelcome. She couldn't tell Minnie about her fears, nor about the reasons for her deep insecurities.

What was the point in being here? Maybe she should leave.

"Actually, don't worry about the tea. I've just remembered I need to call into the letting agents' for something before they close." Georgia slid off the stool, summoning a quick smile. "But we'll catch up properly soon, won't we?"

Minnie looked surprised. "Oh. Okay, then." Her shoulders relaxed visibly. "We'll grab a coffee or something, maybe later in the week, yeah?"

"Yes, that would be lovely. Sorry I've got to dash – stupid of me to forget." Georgia rolled her eyes, faked a smile. She gave Minnie a brief hug. "Don't worry about seeing me out. I'll call soon."

Georgia turned up the collar of her jacket and kept her head down. She walked all the way back to Cuckoo Cottage, hoping no one who passed her would notice the hiccupping sobs that shook her torso. The empty feeling of redundancy, of no longer being needed, was more than she could bear. Without Minnie, she had nothing, no one to turn to. And now, on top of being alone, she had the awful sense that she was being preyed upon by someone.

But worst of all would be if that someone knew about Minnie.

Chapter 12

Georgia

Monday, 26 September 2022

As night drew in and with the door to the cottage closed behind her once more, all of Georgia's uncertainties resurfaced, overshadowing her feelings of misery. The first few nights in Cuckoo Cottage had felt strange, disorientating. More than once, she had awoken wondering where she was. But although she was now completely alone, with the door securely fastened behind her, Georgia had felt, albeit tentatively, safer than she had in months. And not being in the same room she'd shared with Trevor for all those years was somehow helping her to reclaim herself. For the first time since he'd died, she had been able to sleep without a light on.

That had all changed after last night. The feelings of paranoia and anxiety were back with a vengeance. Even with the new locks installed and makeshift barricades across both entrances, lying here now in the darkness, the street lighting bathing the thin curtains in an almost ethereal yellow ombre, every scrape or clunk as the house groaned and eased into the night had her catching her breath, straining her ears for evidence of someone next door or attempted entry.

It was almost 3am and Georgia hadn't slept a wink. Her eyes felt gritty, her limbs aching with tiredness. She tormented herself with the thought of the noises through the walls, the person watching her from across the quad. Could it have been Jackson? It seemed too much of a coincidence that she'd seen him enter the very same building. Unless, of course, it was another of his rental properties. Another uninvited house call on his part.

She blew out a long breath. Sitting up, she eased herself from the bed, and crossed to the window. Through the gap between the drapes, she could see the deserted street below, her eyes travelling to the house where she had seen the person the previous night. It was in shadow once more. No sign of life. Everything was deathly quiet, though the carpet of fallen leaves was being displaced and scattered by a breeze which seemed to have come from nowhere. To her left, the moon was high and full, its aura bronze. The wind sent islands of grey-white clouds scudding across the dark liquid sky between them. There was an odd sense of anticipation in the air, as though something might happen at any moment.

Georgia startled at the sight of a scrawny lone fox padding across the cobbles, then disappearing down the alleyway at the end of the terrace opposite. Her eyes scanned the façade of the building opposite a moment longer, until, satisfied there was no one about, she withdrew.

She tried to reason with herself. The locks had been changed: unless someone managed to jemmy a window at the back – perish the thought – there was no other way to access the building. She pulled on her dressing gown, tightening it around her against

111

the chill, and tugged the duvet from the bed, then headed for the small square of landing. The unwelcome thought that a malevolent hand at the small of her back would be enough to send her tumbling forward had her reaching for the incongruous twentieth-century banister. She gripped the thing for dear life, then placing her feet carefully, made her way downstairs, still clutching the duvet. It seemed pointless trying to sleep. She had no plans for the following day – she'd have to try to rest later in the afternoon, if need be. It felt safer to stay awake; to catch up on her rest in daylight.

Switching on the table lamp in the living room, she wrapped herself in the duvet and curled into the armchair in front of the window, her heart quickening as the wind whistled eerily down the chimney. The curtains rippled with the breeze, making Georgia pull the quilt more tightly around her. She could hear the roller blind rattling in the kitchen. The warm glow of the lamp should have been comforting; instead it only accentuated the shadowy recesses of the room. Georgia's anxiety began to build further, her eyes darting. Though the tip of her nose felt frozen in the cold air, she couldn't bring herself to kneel to light the stove. She felt less exposed somehow, being enveloped by the chair.

From its arm, she picked up the remote control and switched on the TV, but as she flicked through different channels, was dismayed to find the picture pixelating constantly, the soundtrack breaking up into incoherent stuttering. There must be something wrong with the signal – maybe it was the weather. Georgia switched it off, looking round in frustration for something to distract her. Her eyes landed on the book that Minnie had lent her about the city's history, lying on the small side table next to the chair. She reached across to pick it up and began leafing through the pages. The photographs were sepia, images of an era long past; the streets populated with people in Edwardian dress and the odd old-fashioned car and bus. Remembering what Cole had said about the old jail and the unfortunate Mary Ball, Georgia flicked through the index to find the section about crime and punishment, and was pulled up sharply by a photograph of the young woman's death mask. The detail showed every line on her face. The fine brows. Her delicately pointed chin. Georgia studied the image in morbid fascination. The woman looked so young and oddly serene, given the horrific circumstances in which her life had ended. She had been just thirty-one, convicted of poisoning her violent, adulterous husband with arsenic. Only one of the six children she had given birth to had survived. The execution had attracted crowds of around twenty thousand people, which seemed a disproportionate number, given the smaller population of the era. No sympathy for the wretched life the girl had led. No mercy.

There was a photograph of the plaque on the wall of the old courthouse next to the Orb, which stated the date of the last hanging to take place outside, but no mention of its victim, Mary, was made. Georgia felt suddenly aggrieved on her behalf.

Through the increasing howling of the wind, Georgia heard a muted clopping sound. It seemed to be coming from somewhere beyond the window immediately behind her, the one that opened directly onto the street. Georgia froze, pricking up her ears to listen. Slowly, she put down the book and sat up, her senses sharpened.

There it was again. The sound was growing louder now, as though whatever it was, was nearing the house. The clopping paused for a moment, then resumed.

Hardly daring to breathe, she turned off the lamp and rose reluctantly from the chair. There was someone outside, she was sure of it. Georgia was torn between flinging back the curtain to look and hiding beneath the duvet, praying who or whatever it was would go away. Maybe – maybe it was just the fox she

113

had seen earlier, or another of its kind, scavenging for scraps. The students regularly discarded bits of kebab, or the unwanted remains of Nando's takeouts, as they weaved their drunken way home – she'd seen a disgruntled-looking man from the council clearing the road of their debris in the early mornings.

But that sound – it was more like something being scraped across stone. A fox dragging its spoils back to its den, she thought hopefully. Chicken bones, or something similar. Or even the regular council road sweeper, doing an early shift.

Peering round the side of the curtain and praying to catch sight of either a bushy orange tail or a high-vis jacket, she pulled back at once, rigid with fear. She felt suddenly light-headed. Though terrified, she felt compelled to take another look.

Shrouded in a strange mist, a tall figure, dressed from top to toe in dark, shapeless clothing, head bowed, the face completely hidden beneath a huge, loose hood, was emerging from the narrow street between the cathedral wall and the old Guildhall, only a few feet from her door. As it passed beneath the street lamp, Georgia was able to see its form more clearly. The arms were held across the chest, hands concealed beneath the baggy sleeves of a cassock, the feet covered by the same billowing, floor-length garment. The wind whipped the leaves around its feet, encircling the bottom of the robe. But one leg seemed to drag behind the other, as though it was trying to pull a great weight. Something pinged against the window; a pebble maybe. But Georgia dared not look again. Still wrapped in the duvet, she squatted, trembling, next to the wall beside the window, blood pumping so loudly in her eardrums she feared they might burst. She could hear what sounded like some sort of mumbled incantation, reaching a crescendo as the figure seemed to pause right outside her front door. Georgia held her breath. The figure was only feet now from where she was crouching. Eventually, the apparition began to retreat, the chanting petering out. And then an ominous, deathly quiet descended.

It took several minutes before Georgia felt able to move. Once certain that whatever it was had definitely gone, she gradually straightened her stiff legs and peeled back the edge of the curtain. The quad was deserted once more, the wind calming suddenly. It was unsettling.

Her eyes travelled to the clock she'd hung on the wall at the opposite end of the room. Through the gloom she could just make out that it was almost 3.45am. What the hell *was* that? Could she have seen the ghost of Friar Benedict? She desperately wanted to share her uncanny experience, to speak to someone – most of all, to her daughter, but what would she say? And at this hour? It really wasn't an option.

Georgia needed something to calm her shredded nerves. She reached for the light switch, then made her way shakily through to the kitchen. There was a boxed, unopened bottle of a rare single malt whisky in the cupboard that had been bought as a gift for Trevor by a client. It was something she never drank herself, and had intended to pass it on to Minnie, since Trevor said it could be worth a packet in a few years.

Georgia took out the bottle, her fingers fumbling with the seal. She poured a large measure into a tumbler, knocking it back almost in one. The liquor burned as it trickled through her gullet, making her splutter. She shuddered, then poured another. This time she sipped. The taste was revolting to her, but within minutes she began to feel slightly more relaxed, and a little light-headed.

She added more to the glass, then replaced the cork in the bottle and took the drink back into the sitting room. Her stomach still churned. All the time she kept thinking about what old Ned had said about the ghostly friar from the Guildhall. Was that what she had just witnessed? But wasn't it supposed to appear to someone before some terrible event? Though lulled slightly by the whisky, Georgia's fear still failed to dissipate. Could it have been a prankster – or someone in fancy dress? But the likelihood of this in the middle of the night seemed improbable. She kept picturing the mist around the figure, the noise of the chanting echoing in her ears. Despite Georgia's earlier concern that she was being watched, this felt totally different. Other-worldly.

Gradually, she began to feel drowsy. Ensconced in the armchair, she nestled into the duvet once more and finally succumbed to fitful sleep, her restless dreams filled as so often before with images of a faceless, malevolent creature but now dressed in a cowl bearing down on her.

This wasn't quite the sanctuary she'd been hoping for.

Chapter 13

Georgia

Tuesday morning, 27 September 2022

"A *monk*? You sure you didn't overdo it last night?" Though still heavy with sleep, the scepticism in Minnie's voice was ill-disguised. Ever the realist, thought Georgia, though she felt slightly hurt that Minnie didn't seem to even consider the possibility she could actually have seen something. Despite her earlier resolve not to contact Minnie for a while, Georgia hadn't been able to resist calling her. There was no one else she could turn to.

"No. I hadn't been drinking at all. Not at that point, anyway. Maybe I wouldn't have seen anything if I had." Her tone was sharper than she'd intended. She stared down from the bedroom window, remembering the vision which had met her during the night and felt the hairs on her arms prickle.

There was a pause from the other end of the line. She heard Minnie exhale. "Well even if it *was* – not saying I believe in stuff like that – from everything you've said, it didn't *do* anything, did it? Didn't try to get into the house or make threatening gestures or anything? And it's not impossible it was someone in fancy dress – I mean, we *are* in a city full of students."

Georgia sighed. Whatever she said, she knew Minnie wasn't going to be convinced.

"Let's change the subject, shall we? We'll obviously have to agree to disagree." She still didn't want to mention the person watching her from across the quad the other night, nor did she want to talk about Jethro Jackson or the hidden photographs. Whilst Minnie might be dismissive about the likelihood of her having seen a ghost, Georgia knew she'd worry if she thought her mother had a criminal, and an apparently violent one at that, for a landlord.

She tried to brighten her tone, remembering she hadn't yet told Minnie about the new job. "Oh, by the way, I'm starting work at the Golden Orb on Friday; five nights a week."

"God, that was quick! The Orb, you say? But I thought you were going to wait a bit and see what else was out there . . ."

Georgia could picture Minnie's mouth curling in disapproval. She gritted her teeth. "I hadn't intended to grab the first thing that came along – but it's so handy for me, and the people seem nice. Anyway, it doesn't have to be a permanent thing, but at least it'll get me out of the house for a bit. I need something to occupy me now that you're so busy with your course."

She hadn't meant it to sound accusatory, but that was clearly how Minnie took it. She sounded defensive.

"Look, I know I haven't been round much. And I'm sorry I didn't return your calls yesterday. But I'm still finding my feet – once I've settled in and got to know what's what at uni, I should have a bit more free time."

Georgia sighed. "I know, love. I'm sorry. I don't expect you to keep coming over. It's just nice to know you're not far away."

There was a telling hesitation before Minnie responded. "Yeah, I get that."

Georgia's heart sank. That first night, when they had gone out for cocktails, sensing Minnie's apprehension about her proximity, she had promised not to turn up at the student house uninvited, not to keep phoning every five minutes; to give her daughter as much space as if she was at the other end of the country. But once Georgia had settled in, the temptation to call on her was too great. She'd hoped that Minnie might warm to the idea of her being close by, that she might actually want to spend more time with her. But Georgia had realised now that this wasn't going to happen. Not initially, anyway. She could only hope that, with time, Minnie would relax a bit and they could see more of each other. They were mother and daughter: surely now that Minnie was older, they could be friends, too?

"Anyway, enough about me. We didn't really get the chance to chat properly yesterday." Georgia paused. "Anything exciting to report from your end?"

"Nah. Getting used to the house and the others. Fatima's grating on me a bit. Ajab's good at keeping the peace, though. We put up a poster at uni to advertise the spare room and someone came to have a look on Saturday. Think she's moving in tomorrow." Minnie sounded flat, disinterested. She yawned audibly. "Sorry, still a bit dazed. Listen, Mum, I'd better go. I've got a lecture in an hour – need to get my act together. But we'll catch up over that coffee soon, okay?"

Georgia wished her a good day and ended the call, feeling slightly bereft. She looked down again at the quad, now filling with students and people walking past in every direction on their way to work. It was almost 8.30am; the sun was breaking through, lending everything a more cheerful aspect. Even with the view of the graveyard and the old jail, it seemed a world apart from the eerie, shadowy place she had looked out on the night before. She resolved to take a sleeping tablet later, early enough in the evening that it wouldn't impact too much on her the following day. Maybe her imagination *had* been running away with her. All that talk in the pub of ghosts and executions, and her being all alone. The thought of someone watching her, too. A good night's sleep could work wonders for anyone's perspective on things.

A sudden rap on the front door gave her a jolt. Georgia peered down to see a tall man, his hair covered by a black beanie hat, standing at the door, looking round. He was dressed in air force blue overalls and carrying what looked like a tool bag.

Shit. It must be Jethro Jackson's handyman. She'd almost forgotten he'd arranged for someone to call on her.

"Just a minute," she called out, peeling off her pyjamas and hurriedly pulling on jeans and a hoodie. She dragged her fingers through her hair, then made her way down the stairs, heaving the doorstop aside before opening the catch. Even with the new locks installed, she wasn't taking any chances.

"Mrs Parnell?" The man cocked his head, his blue eyes scanning her face uncertainly. Dark hair curled slightly from beneath the edges of his hat. There was something odd about the way he was looking at her; almost as if he thought he recognised her from somewhere. Georgia drew back a little, suddenly self-conscious.

"Sorry – are you . . . ?"

"Jethro – Mr Jackson sent me to fix a couple of things in the house." He looked uncomfortable. "I thought he'd sorted it with you – I can always come back later if . . ."

Georgia studied the man for a moment. He looked about thirty and was good-looking in a quirky way, with a strong jaw and full mouth. He had the slightly crooked nose of a boxer, or someone who'd enjoyed a scrap or two. His voice was deep, the accent thick Scouse.

"No, no – please, come in. I'm sorry – bit of a rough night. I overslept." Georgia stepped aside to let him pass.

The man seemed to relax, his face breaking into a half-smile as he crossed the threshold, wiping his boots on the mat. He smelled strongly of cigarettes, making Georgia feel slightly queasy. She hoped it didn't show on her face.

"You'll have to excuse the mess – I haven't managed to sort everything out yet."

The man grinned. "All looks fine to me. You wanna see where I live." He glanced round. "Shall I start in the kitchen? You can go back to bed if you want."

"Oh, it's fine. I'm fully awake now." She motioned towards the sitting room door. "It's just through there."

He nodded. "'S'okay – I've been before, to fit a new washer in the tap. When the last lady was here, like."

Georgia's interest was immediately piqued. "Really? I hear she left suddenly – do you know anything about her?" She was desperate to ask about the photographs, but then, the guy was Jethro Jackson's employee and she couldn't be sure what their relationship was like. Maybe it wouldn't be wise to alert him to their existence.

His jaw seemed to tighten. "Nope. Just that she didn't pay up. The gaffer's none too happy. And he ain't a man to get on the wrong side of, if you catch my drift."

"So I understand." Georgia closed the front door behind him, a queasy feeling turning in her stomach as she remembered the woman's battered face. "I'll come and stick the kettle on – d'you want a cup of tea?"

"Ta very much. Never say no to a brew. White, two sugars, please."

She followed him into the kitchen, quickly realising that there was only enough floor space for one of them, so hurriedly filled the kettle and squeezed past the tobacco-reek of the man's bulk, retreating into the doorway as he knelt to open his tool bag.

He indicated the cupboard door propped against the wall. "Job number one?"

"Please. And can you tighten the others, as well? – they all feel a bit wobbly."

It took him only minutes to reinstate the door and to nip up the fixings on the remaining ones with a few whizzes of a cordless screwdriver. He hauled himself to his feet, wiping his hands down his trouser legs and smiled briefly.

"Job done. Right, I'll go and have a look at your rads if you like, while you come in here – Jethro says they all need bleeding."

"Yes, it's been really cold. And there's been a howling gale coming through the windows – I don't think any of the frames fit properly."

"Well, we can fit some draught-excluders around the edges – and we've got these plastic sheet things he's bought as a job-lot, too – I've got some in the van." He indicated with a sideways tip of the head towards the quad. "They fit round the frames with these suction-cups. Not too pretty I'm afraid, but they'll do as a temporary fix." He sucked air through his teeth. "They might look nice, these old places, but it's a pain in the arse not being able to do this and that 'cause of them being listed."

"But surely the windows could at least be replaced with ones that fit properly?"

He grimaced apologetically. "Ah. But that'd be a costly little exercise. Specialist job. And I don't think the gaffer's planning any major improvements to any of his houses – not this financial year, anyway."

Georgia folded her arms across her chest. "Hmm. Maybe that's why the last tenant left without paying – perhaps she felt short-changed." Here was an opportunity for him to share what, if anything, he knew. She studied his face hopefully.

The man's eyes flickered. He swallowed, as if about to impart something, then seemed to think better of it. "Who knows?"

"Well, the rent's not cheap considering the size of the house – the least he could do is make sure the basic requirements are sorted." The noise of the kettle boiling distracted her and she went back through into the kitchen. Minutes later she returned carrying two steaming mugs, placing one on the little coffee table next to the man, who was now on his knees wiping black gunge from the side of the antiquated radiator beneath the window with an old rag. He turned to look up at her, his mouth widening into a smile.

"Cheers. That's me first cup of the day."

"Sorry – I didn't catch your name."

"Everyone calls us Heggs."

Georgia frowned slightly, making him laugh throatily.

"The surname's Heggarty. Nothin' to do with chickens."

"Oh, right." Georgia stood hugging her own mug, watching for a moment as, still kneeling, he paused to take a mouthful of tea, letting out an appreciative sigh.

"So have you worked for Mr Jackson long?" She watched as he drew himself to his feet, reaching into his overalls' pocket for his cigarettes and lighter, which he placed on the windowsill.

"About four years now." As though it was an automated reaction, he proceeded to take a cigarette from the packet, tucking it behind his ear. "Got a job with him up in Liverpool and then he asked me and a couple of the other lads I was working with to come here for a big contract. I sort of ended up staying. He's all right to work for – as long as you don't take the piss, like. And I'm a grafter, so he seems to like me." Heggs grinned.

Georgia nodded. "Erm – the woman who lived here – what was she like?"

His face grew taut once more. "She seemed a bit . . . weird, to be honest. Stuck-up. Jethro reckoned she was an art student or summat, but she was quite old. Quite posh, too. Sounded like she was born with a whole canteen of silver spoons to choose from. I know you can't always tell, but I'd have said she wasn't short of a bob or two. I'd've thought she could've afforded somewhere a bit better. No offence, like," he added hastily.

Georgia considered this. She wondered what conclusion Heggs must have drawn about her own circumstances and felt the corners of her mouth twitch.

"When you say old, how old?"

"Old for a student. Late thirties, I'd have said. Forty, maybe."

Georgia pictured the photo. Difficult to tell from the swelling, but the woman could easily have fallen into that age bracket.

Heggs paused. "Anyway, she was only here a few weeks; did a moonlight flit. Disappeared into the woodwork. Jethro was spitting feathers when he found out."

Georgia sipped her tea. "So how much money did she actually owe him?"

He shifted from one foot to the other, his hand drifting to the cigarette behind his ear.

"Couldn't have been that much in the grand scheme of things. I mean, he's loaded. But Jethro doesn't like anyone putting one over on him. It's more to do with his pride than the dosh, I think." His eyes travelled to the window, almost as if he thought someone could be observing him. "Fair enough, I s'pose," he added quickly, clearly not wanting to sound disloyal.

Georgia could well believe this of Jackson. She thought of her own encounter with the man, and of what Yiannis had said about him tipping someone out of a moving car. She felt the hairs on her arms prickle.

Heggs quickly drained the last of his tea and handed her back the mug, smiling briefly. He seemed uncomfortable, as though he thought he'd said more than he should.

"Thanks very much for that. Right, I'd better crack on – I'll go and do the rads upstairs, then I'll nip out for a quick fag and fetch some of those sheets to stick round the window frames. It's not been too cold yet, but I've heard it's gonna get proper chilly over the next few weeks. I've seen frost on the insides of these windows, y'know."

Georgia remembered scraping the layer of ice from her bedroom window when she was a child. That, and the mould embedded into the frames and creeping from the corners of the ceiling, that no amount of bleach could deter. Though she'd had her faults, her grandmother was the only one who'd bothered to try to remove it.

"That kid'll finish up with bronchitis," she'd warned Georgia's half-soaked mother on countless occasions. But it had been too much trouble, like everything else. Thank God Minnie had never had to live like that.

Georgia finished her tea, then took both mugs through to the kitchen to wash them, listening to the creak of Heggs's footsteps as he climbed the stairs. He hummed an indeterminate tune as he worked in the bedroom above, the sound carrying through the house. She stared through the window into the small courtyard, wondering again about the woman who had occupied the space before her. Well-spoken, clearly, from Heggs's impression of her. And if she *had* been wealthy, as Heggs had surmised, she may have thought nothing of leaving owing payment. Those for whom cash flow wasn't an issue often didn't seem to appreciate the significance of non-payment of bills. It was a sort of arrogant self-entitlement, as though the rules didn't apply to them. It might have seemed trivial to her and merely slipped her mind. On the other hand, maybe Jackson had done more than make a nuisance of himself and she'd had enough. She might even have left in haste because she feared for her life. Georgia suspected Heggs knew more than he was letting on. He had definitely appeared a little edgy when she'd started asking questions. This seemed quite feasible. The more she learned, the more convinced Georgia became that it was more than likely the woman who had hidden those photos. That maybe they were some sort of insurance policy. That it could well have been her, with the swollen face and black eyes.

But where on earth had she gone?

Chapter 14

Georgia

Tuesday, 27 September 2022

Once Heggs had left, Georgia felt on edge. Trying to banish the negative thoughts constantly whirring through her head, she filled the remainder of her morning with frenzied cleaning and taking stock of what she wanted to do with the house to make it more presentable. A fresh lick of emulsion would help to lighten the walls, but without a car to collect the paint, Georgia decided she'd need to have some delivered. She set about placing an online order for a large can and a couple of rollers to arrive by the next day, to give her a chance to at least give the bedroom a coat before starting work on Friday. The sitting room could wait for another day. Georgia knew she needed to keep busy. Sitting around and worrying that she was being watched was going to send her spiralling towards some sort of breakdown. She had to at least *try* to be philosophical. What was it her grandmother used to say? *Never meet your troubles halfway.*

After lunch, Georgia thought a walk to the shops might do her good. She couldn't hide indoors for ever. Maybe she could buy some new bedding to brighten up the bedroom and maybe find something for dinner from M&S. She took a quick shower in the dingy bathroom, followed by a generous mist of perfume to banish the smell of bleach from her nostrils, then pulled on a clean pair of black skinny jeans and a cream roll-neck sweater. Though the sun was still bright and the sky clear, the air was cool, so she slung a jacket around her shoulders before heading out. Closing the door behind her, she cast a cautious look around the quad before heading in the direction of Broadgate. As she walked, her eyes travelled to the house opposite once more, though the sun was reflecting off the windows, making it impossible to see if anyone was looking down at her or not.

Soon she was sifting through the homeware section of M&S, and had filled her basket with a floral Egyptian cotton duvet set, a grapefruit and ginger reed diffuser and an artificial succulent in a pretty ceramic pot. *Minnie will love these*, she'd thought. Having paid, she moved into the food hall and began to scour the fridges for a treat for tea. She felt suddenly lighter, all thoughts of the weird monk from the previous night and the mysterious watcher from the terrace opposite almost eradicated.

Almost.

A deep voice from behind caught her unawares and she nearly dropped her shopping.

"Hello again."

Her heart quickening, Georgia clapped a hand to her chest as she spun round, only to come face to face with Cole, also carrying a shopping basket. She glanced down to see that he had been filling his own with various marked down items:

an unappetising-looking cottage pie for one, a dented tin of vegetable soup, a small white loaf and some scones.

"You made me jump." She managed to stop herself from adding '*you idiot*'.

"Oh, sorry. I noticed you from the other end of the aisle – thought I'd come and say 'hi' before you disappeared."

Cole peered into her basket at the Coquilles St Jacques, butternut squash ravioli with sage, and fresh fruit tartelettes she'd just picked up. "They look nice." He smiled, almost ruefully, she thought.

"The tarts are delicious. I recommend them." Georgia paused, groaning inwardly. It must sound as though she was rubbing it in. She'd been about to pick up a half-bottle of chilled champagne, but thought better of it. From the looks of things, he didn't have a lot of spare cash and Georgia found herself suddenly curious about his circumstances.

"Have you just finished work?" she ventured, placing her shopping basket at her feet.

"Ah. No. I've had a bit of a flat day, to be honest. I abandoned the writing this morning as things weren't really flowing. Best to leave it and come back to it later with a clear head when I get like that. I've just been in the library to have a browse and return a couple of books."

"So do you have a publisher for your own book when it's completed?"

"I hope so. I've been talking to an editor from an indie company who sounds interested. But of course, I need a complete manuscript to submit before I'll receive a concrete offer." Cole paused. "I've still got some way to go. Feels like an insurmountable task some days." He attempted a cheerful smile, but Georgia detected an air of hopelessness in his tone. To her surprise, she felt suddenly sorry for him.

"Um, I thought I might go into the Orb this evening for a

couple, just to get me out of the house for a bit. Hoping for a bit of inspiration, too. That old Ned's a mine of local information." Cole scanned her face her hopefully. "Will you be in there at all? I'd like to buy you a drink."

Georgia studied him hesitantly. His eyes looked earnest, slightly sad. It would have felt like kicking a puppy if she'd said no outright. She felt pretty sure now she'd misjudged him when they first met. It had probably been her anxiety kicking in, the omnipresent paranoia that anyone looking at her must be up to something. Old habits die hard. But she didn't want to send out the wrong signals.

"Dunno. I might pop in for an hour or so after dinner, I'll see. I'm starting work properly on Friday, so I suppose it'd be nice to get to know the customers from the other side of the bar. I'm planning on decorating tomorrow when my paint order arrives so I'll probably be fit for nothing by the evening."

His face brightened. "Great. Maybe see you later, then." He lifted his basket. "Better go and pay for these." With a broad smile and a nod, he headed in the direction of the tills, leaving Georgia wondering whether she should have just given him a polite brush-off. He was good-looking, but embarking on a new relationship wasn't on her agenda. It all felt too soon – and might complicate things. Yet despite her earlier misgivings, her gut feeling now was that he was harmless. Surely a casual drink wouldn't hurt.

*

Before entering the Orb, Georgia peered through the window, cautiously scanning the faces of the few people inside. She was constantly on the lookout now, though for whom, she wasn't sure. Confident that she recognised none of them, she pushed open the door and stepped inside. Yiannis broke into a grin as he saw Georgia coming into the bar.

"Couldn't stay away, eh?" He was pulling a pint, but gave a covert tip of his head towards the seating area near the window. Georgia glanced over to see Cole, already having found himself a table, a large glass of Coke sitting in front of him. Seeing Georgia, his face lit up.

"Hi." He rose, gesturing towards the empty seat at his table. "Can I get you a drink?"

Yiannis arched an eyebrow at her but made no comment, the bulge of his tongue in his cheek saying everything. He handed the pint he'd been pouring to the waiting customer, then turned back to Georgia, who gave a small warning shake of her head. She felt like a hypocrite. It was contradicting everything she'd originally intended, everything she'd said to Yiannis, but it would seem churlish not to accept.

"Okay." She locked eyes with Yiannis. "I'll have a gin and tonic then, please."

"Ice and lemon?" Yiannis was still smirking.

"Yes. Thanks."

Cole crossed to the bar to collect the drink, fumbling in his trouser pocket, but Yiannis raised a palm. "It's all right, mate; the lady can have the first one on the house."

"Oh, cheers."

Georgia accepted the glass from Cole with a brief smile, then, doing her best to ignore Yiannis's obvious mirth, settled herself on the stool opposite Cole. She looked across the room to see old Ned sitting at his usual table by the fireplace, Charlie at his feet. He beamed at her, raising a hand to wave. Georgia waved back. There was a steady flow of customers coming and going, some familiar faces, some new. The hum of conversation and the 1980s soundtrack from Freddie's jukebox made for a pleasant, relaxed atmosphere. There were definitely worse places to work, Georgia thought.

"So, you all geared up to do your decorating tomorrow,

131

then?" Cole studied her across his drink, taking a small sip before replacing it on the table.

"Just waiting for the paint to turn up – it's supposed to be arriving in the morning, so hopefully that'll give me a full day. There's quite a bit to do."

"If you want a hand, I can always take a day off." He sounded overly eager.

Georgia felt caught off-guard. Accepting help would mean inviting him into her home. That was a step too far.

"No, it's fine. Thanks for the offer, but I'd like to do it myself – I actually enjoy it." This wasn't strictly true – she hadn't done any painting for years and it was a pretty boring task, but the fewer people who knew where she lived, the better. A casual mention to the wrong person could spell disaster for her.

"Oh. Well, if you change your mind . . ." He lowered his eyes and there was an awkward pause. "So – how long have you lived in your house? Is it an old property?"

"Uh-huh. It's pretty ancient, but I love it. I've only been there a couple of weeks, but it already feels like home." Did it? Feel like home? Maybe with sunlight streaming in and the hustle and bustle of people passing by. Not so much under cover of darkness. Remembering the noises in the night, the figure in the window and the ghostly monk, the fact that she was all alone, sent an uncomfortable prickle travelling up her neck once again.

Cole was smiling and nodding. "I overheard Yiannis telling Ned that you're a widow. I was sorry to hear that."

Georgia fired a look at Yiannis, who grimaced, mouthing *sorry* across the bar. She wondered what else he'd let slip.

"Yes. I lost my husband just over eighteen months ago. This is a sort of fresh start for me."

"I'm assuming you're not from the area? You don't have the accent." He inclined his head towards Ned. "Not like our friend over there."

Georgia took a breath. She had learned her spiel by rote. "I'm from the north west originally. Lost my parents and married young, then moved down south, which feels like a lifetime ago. So I suppose any accent I might've had has disappeared over the years."

North west was vague enough. Her father was long gone. And where her mother was, whether alive or not, she neither knew nor cared. If she'd been found lying dead in a ditch somewhere, Georgia wouldn't have batted an eye.

Fortunately, Cole didn't seem inclined to probe. "I'm sorry – about your parents, I mean. That must've been tough."

"Yes," she lied. "It was a real blow. But I was resilient – well, you have to be, don't you? And getting married was the making of me." She smiled tightly. He hadn't asked about Minnie – hopefully Yiannis had managed not to mention her. Time to steer the conversation before he started asking anything awkward.

"Anyway, what about you? You're not local either, are you?"

"No." He took another sip of Coke. "I was brought up, if you could call it that, in Essex. Left home as soon as I could. My own parents – well, they weren't the best I'm afraid." Cole pulled a face. "The old man liked his beer and was a bit too handy with his fists. Mum left when I was nine, buggered off with some bloke she'd taken up with from work. I obviously wasn't very high on her priority list. Let's just say my childhood ended pretty abruptly."

He gave a wan smile, but dropped his eyes. Georgia saw a lump move up and down in his throat.

"Oh dear. I can see why you got out, then."

Cole lifted his head, the hurt and anger in his grey eyes evident as he met her gaze. Georgia felt a sudden rush of empathy towards him. Here was someone else who clearly knew what it meant to have their formative years blighted by their own

133

family. Though she knew she couldn't open up to him, it might have been cathartic to compare notes.

"Yep. I wasn't going to stick around to be someone's punchbag." Cole paused as though remembering something particularly unpleasant, his jaw tightening.

"I suppose coming here was a kind of clean sheet for me, too," he went on. "I got divorced last year. Messily." He took a swig of his Coke. "We were living in North London, a little place I'd bought before the prices sky-rocketed. She took the house – took *me* to the cleaners, and I couldn't afford to stay in the area. Renting's much more affordable here, but I'm hoping to save enough to buy myself somewhere eventually. Pinning all my hopes on this bloody book." He gave a hollow laugh.

Georgia felt a bit sorry for him. It sounded as if he wasn't having a great time.

"Well, let's drink to your book being a resounding success, then." She clinked her glass against his and Cole smiled.

"And let's hope the future's a whole lot brighter for both of us."

The evening seemed to fly by. Cole proved to be entertaining company and, despite her earlier misgivings, Georgia found herself engaged and amused by his various anecdotes. He used his hands a lot as he talked, looked into her eyes. Listened with genuine interest whenever she spoke. She had warmed to him considerably, especially after discovering about his abusive childhood. And his ex-wife, from everything he'd said, sounded like a financial nightmare.

"She's got no concept of the meaning of money. She couldn't hold down a job, so all the bills were my responsibility. If she wanted something, she'd just buy it. Couldn't resist the designer labels. The beauty treatments. Lunches with friends whose husbands earned a small fortune, trying to keep up with them and splashing cash that wasn't hers. Like an idiot, I tried to ignore it, until one day a nasty letter arrived from some debt collection agency, threatening legal action unless I paid up immediately. Apparently she'd taken out a store card in my name when she failed the credit check."

"Oh, God. How awful." Georgia sat forward, aghast. "What did you do?"

Cole blew out a long breath. "I'd just been for a couple of drinks after work. I completely flipped, grabbed hold of her by the shoulders and shook her. She actually laughed. She said if I was half a man, I'd have been able to provide for her properly, and it was her way of escaping the miserable life she led as my wife."

He shrugged sadly. "I'd played right into her hands. She manipulated the whole thing to her advantage, made me sound like a tyrant. She found herself a shit-hot divorce solicitor, through one of her rich friends. Claimed I'd always been abusive and controlling, that I'd refused to give her money for housekeeping. I was forced out of my home and made to pay damages. It absolutely broke me – financially and mentally. I just thank God there weren't any kids involved and I've been able to sever ties with her completely. I pity the next poor sod she gets her claws into."

Georgia studied Cole's face. There was real anguish behind his eyes. With some people she might have questioned such a story, but somehow she had no doubt that everything he'd told her was true. No wonder he was watching his spending. She felt the urge to reach for his hand, but resisted.

"Well, it's all in the past now. If there's anything I've learned, it's never to look back." She gave him an encouraging smile and stood up. "My round. D'you want something a bit more exciting than Coke?"

Cole grimaced. "That's very kind, but I'll stick with the soft drinks, thanks. I hit the bottle in a big way for the first few months after the split and I don't want to risk going down that slippery slope again. Coke's fine."

So he was on the wagon, then. No bad thing, Georgia thought – at least he was aware alcohol was becoming an issue for him, rather than throwing caution to the wind. Ironic, though, that he chose to hang out in a pub, whether for research purposes or not. She headed to the bar. Yiannis, who had just been round collecting glasses, was over like a shot. He lifted the hatch and ducked behind, ready to serve her.

"Christ, you two haven't stopped rabbiting all night," he remarked, his voice low. "Looks like some deep and meaningful conversation going on over there."

She prodded his arm playfully. "We're getting on okay, thank you for asking. And I forgive you for your indiscretion." She dropped her head, regarding him pointedly from beneath her eyebrows.

Yiannis gave her a nervous grin. "Sorry, sweet. I was just telling Ned, you know. Seeing as he's lost his wife. He was very sympathetic."

Georgia smiled tightly. "No harm done. Just be careful what you repeat in public, though."

He nodded, his cheeks flushing slightly. "I will. Definitely." He paused. "So you'll be seeing Cole again, then?"

"Who knows? We're only having a drink."

Yiannis clasped both hands to his heart melodramatically. "From little acorns . . ."

Georgia huffed. "Whatever."

"I'm telling you – you make a pretty pair – and he seems a nice enough bloke. I can usually tell if someone's a bit iffy."

Georgia smirked. "I'll always make sure I consult you in future, then."

She ordered another round of drinks and returned to the table. Cole had pulled out his mobile and was frowning at it.

"Everything okay?"

"Hmm? Oh, yeah – just had a call from a number I don't recognise." A sudden ping implied a text message had been left. Cole scanned the screen, screwing up his eyes for a moment, then smiled up at her hesitantly, slipping the phone back into his inside pocket. "I'm sure it can wait. Probably someone trying to flog me health insurance or something." He flicked a look around the room, shifting a little in his seat.

"Yeah, I get plenty of those." She nodded in agreement.

"Where were we? Oh, that's right, I'd just finished dumping all my woes onto you. Maybe we need to talk about something a bit less – depressing."

Georgia laughed. "Like I said, always better to live in the moment. No good dwelling on what's been and gone. So where d'you live now, then? Not far I take it, if this has become your local."

Cole pulled a face. "I thought we weren't going to talk about anything else depressing. I'd rather not think about the poky hovel I'm staying in. Hoping it's a very temporary arrangement."

"Oh dear. Is it that bad?"

"A bedsit over a pharmacy. With a shark for a landlord. At least I won't have far to go to collect my prescription when the damp spores get onto my chest." He laughed bitterly. "I'd invite you back for coffee, but it wouldn't be fair to ask you to risk life and limb."

Georgia thought for a moment. "You can come back to mine if you like." Her stomach gave an odd little flip. She'd said it now. It was too late to retract the offer. But he seemed nice. Genuine. And the more time they'd spent together, the more she was finding herself drawn to him.

To her surprise, Cole looked suddenly uncomfortable. He glanced at his watch.

"Erm – that's very kind, but I think I'll pass this evening if it's okay with you. I ought to be getting back soon. Early start tomorrow."

"Oh. Another time then, maybe." She felt suddenly foolish and slightly hurt by this rebuff. Hadn't he offered to help her with the decorating earlier? What had changed? Maybe he wasn't as keen as he'd first seemed. Everything seemed to have shifted after that text. Maybe it was from another woman – his wife, even. *Had* he been telling the truth about her?

The remaining half-hour in his company consisted of stilted small talk. Cole seemed suddenly preoccupied with the time, though it was only just after 10pm.

"Well, thank you for a lovely evening. But I really must be off. Hopefully see you later in the week – are you working at the weekend?"

Georgia dipped her chin. "Yes. See you soon then, I expect."

He leaned forward and planted an awkward kiss on her cheek. "Take care, then." Lifting a hand as he headed towards the door, Cole waved in the general direction of Yiannis and then Ned, before disappearing into the night.

Georgia and Yiannis stared after him.

"Has he gone?" Yiannis hurried across to the table, a baffled expression on his face.

"Yep. I must've misread the signs. Like a tool, I even invited him back to mine, and he turned me down." Georgia shook her head. "Ah well, never mind. Probably a bit soon to start seeing someone, anyway."

"Weird. I thought he seemed really smitten. Maybe he's not feeling well or something."

"Who knows?" Georgia knocked back the rest of her G&T with a shrug. "It's his loss." She forced a smile. But the thought of the dark, empty house waiting for her sent a prickle of fear along her spine. She had begun to dread nighttime, anticipating what she might face next. Meeting it halfway. Exactly what she

138

shouldn't be doing. The thought of having company had been appealing; comforting, even. "I'll get back now, anyway. Lots of painting planned for tomorrow."

Yiannis tipped his head, smiling at her sympathetically. "Sorry, sweet. Hope you're not too gutted."

Georgia waved her hand dismissively. "I'm glad in a way. At least he didn't get to find out where I live, if he's turned out to be a non-starter."

But what was worse: mild-mannered Cole knowing where she lived, or whoever it was who'd left that clay figure? The more she'd thought about it, the more deliberate it had seemed. Not just kids messing about, as the locksmith had suggested. She hated that she was so alone, that she had no one to talk to. That Minnie didn't seem to want to see her. It was eating her up inside.

Yiannis's voice cut through her thoughts. "Every cloud, eh? By the way, though – I did remember him afterwards. He used to have a beard – must've shaved it off recently. No wonder I didn't recognise him."

Georgia nodded but said nothing. It didn't seem to matter now.

"Ah well. 'Night then, lovely. See you Friday evening, if not before."

"Yeah. See you." Georgia began to head for the door, her shoulders sagging. She had really enjoyed Cole's company. It was disappointing that he didn't appear to feel the same about hers. And now she was having to head home alone, to face another night in Cuckoo Cottage and whatever new torment that might bring with it. After how comfortable she'd felt in the house at first, everything seemed to have taken a sinister turn and anxiety started to bubble in her stomach once more.

"Oh, hang on a sec!"

Georgia turned back to see Yiannis stooping to retrieve something from beneath the stool where Cole had been sitting.

139

"He's dropped something." Yiannis straightened, holding a small white card aloft. Georgia watched his face fold into a frown as he looked more closely. "Jesus." He looked back up at her, grimacing.

"What is it?"

"Looks like our Cole could be mixing with the wrong crowd. Maybe you've had a lucky escape."

Georgia crossed the bar to see what had provoked Yiannis's reaction as he handed the item over. Stunned, she held his gaze, open-mouthed. A cold feeling crept up her neck. It was a business card. And the name emblazoned across it was one she was all too familiar with.

Jethro Jackson.

Chapter 15

Minnie

Minnie's pulse quickened when she spotted Jake already waiting under the clock at Broadgate as she turned the corner. They'd agreed on seven o'clock, and the chimes began to toll the very moment she approached, Peeping Tom's huge, leering face appearing from the window to ogle the juddering clockwork figure of Lady Godiva atop her horse as it passed beneath. Minnie had laughed when Ajab had shown her the clock, which repeated the action every hour, the first day they had explored the town centre.

"Seems a bit inappropriate really, immortalising a perv like that," she'd remarked.

"It's part of the city's history," Ajab had said, with a shrug. "And he's not exactly being glorified, is he. I mean, look at that mug." He lowered his voice. "I wonder if our own Doc Smith could be a descendant."

They had broken into fits of laughter. One of their less popular lecturers bore an uncanny resemblance to the wooden caricature. It wasn't intended as a compliment.

Minnie had felt a bit bad about cancelling on Ajab. But there was no way she wanted to take Jake to the Golden Orb to be scrutinised by her mum, certainly not on a first date, so as soon as she'd got Jake's text, she'd tapped on Ajab's door to tell him apologetically about the change of plan, with the assurance they would go to the pub later in the week.

"Of course, there's nothing to stop you going without me," she'd said. "If Sonia or Fatima don't want to go, I'm sure you could find someone to talk to. That old boy with the dog's always in there."

Ajab had drawn back his chin, an eyebrow cocked. "Seriously?"

"Okay, maybe not," she'd conceded. "But anyway, I doubt Tuesdays are usually that busy, so Mum would probably be able to stop for a chat."

Ajab seemed to consider this briefly, but concluded it would be best to go along with Minnie at some other point.

"I don't want to turn up there like some Billy No Mates. Besides, I should probably polish my essay a bit more – I've made a start but it's been a bit of a rush job. And I'd quite like Sunday off. I really ought to go to the library, too – there's some stuff I need to research." He managed a small smile. "Anyway, far be it for me to stand in the path of true love."

Minnie threw him a mock glare. "Don't be bloody daft – it's just a date. I'm not looking to get into anything heavy right now."

"You never know. These things happen." His face became suddenly serious. "Just watch what you're getting up to – and where you're going. After all, you don't really know anything about the guy, do you?"

Minnie laughed. "You sound just like my mum. Don't worry, I'm not going to let him lead me up any dark alleyways. And I'll be home by eleven – I've got a lecture first thing tomorrow morning."

Ajab nodded. "Just keep your phone handy. If you need to bail out, you can just drop me a text and I'll come and get you."

Minnie felt a small rush of affection towards Ajab. He really was a good mate. But she had a gut feeling that Jake was decent. After all, he'd seemed genuinely concerned about her being on her own that night outside the SU. And she wasn't stupid, either. She knew how to read the signs if there was an alternative agenda.

*

"Your man up there's a bit of an old lech, eh?" Jake's eyes slanted upwards towards the clock, his mouth spreading into that already familiar grin. "Weird thing to have in the middle of the town, if you ask me." He turned back to Minnie, who felt suddenly and uncharacteristically tongue-tied. All she could do was nod and smile back inanely. *Oh God* – she *really* needed a drink.

"Glad you could make it. You're looking very nice, by the way." He nodded appreciatively at her more-conventional-than-usual choice of outfit. Her mum would have liked it – she passed no comment on Minnie's outlandish dress sense generally, but on the rare occasions Minnie relented and tried to conform a bit, Georgia always expressed her approval.

"You should wear things like that more often, sweetheart," she'd told her when they met for cocktails the other week and Minnie had worn a silky floral bodycon dress. "It really flatters your figure. You might not notice yourself, but you turn a lot of heads." Minnie had thrown back her head and laughed when her mum's eyes had travelled to her feet, pulling a face as she noticed the chunky biker boots. Some things were never going to change.

Jake was wearing the same old leather jacket, but had put on a freshly pressed navy-blue shirt. He smelled lovely, too. "Did you eat before, or d'you want to go for a bite somewhere?"

"Erm – I'm not that hungry, to be honest. Could we – shall we just go for a drink for now? Maybe get something later on?"

"No problem. Any suggestions?"

Minnie had already decided the Old Windmill on Spon Street might be a good place to start as there was a local band playing that night, plus it was far enough away from the cathedral to eliminate the risk of bumping into her mum. And there was a decent Indian restaurant just across the street if they wanted food later.

"Yeah. How well do you know the town?" She studied his face.

"I've only been here a few weeks to be honest, so not that great. I've usually tagged along with the lads I'm working with, but they don't seem to care where they go as long as the beer's cheap." He looked slightly unsure, the cocky front vanishing for a moment. Minnie found it endearing.

"Follow me, then." Without really thinking, she slipped her hand into his. It felt warm, the palm slightly hardened as though he must be a manual worker. It occurred to her that she hadn't even asked what he did for a living. Suddenly there was so much she wanted to know about this man. The realisation startled her a little.

He turned to smile at her, his brown eyes meeting hers for a moment. "Okay, Minnie Mouse, you're the boss."

They walked down through the precinct. The shops were closed, but several people were milling about: like them, probably en route to somewhere to spend the evening. Minnie noticed a man huddled into a doorway, a filthy duvet spread beneath him on the ground. A small brown dog lay at his side. Jake stopped suddenly, releasing Minnie's grip.

"'Scuse me a minute." He went over to the man, crouching for a moment to speak to him and stroking the dog's ears. As she studied the man on the ground, she realised he was much younger than she'd first thought, maybe only in his late teens. He wore a knitted green hat and an old combat jacket. His face was drawn; unshaven and pale.

They exchanged a few words and Jake straightened suddenly, nodding and smiling at the young man. Minnie saw Jake delve into his trouser pocket and pull out a twenty-pound note, then lean forward to hand it over. The lad's eyes widened in surprise.

"You take care now, you hear," she heard Jake say, before he rejoined her and took her hand once more. Minnie could have hugged him.

"That was a kind thing you did there," she said, as they continued on their way.

"That young fella needs it more than me." Jake's tone was suddenly abrupt, his eyes focused on the pavement as they walked. "Been there myself. It's a bag of shite, believe me."

Minnie was taken aback. She wondered what on earth had happened in Jake's life that he could have ended up on the streets. She wanted to ask but he was quick to change the subject.

"So where's this pub, then? I'm getting a thirst on."

"Not far now." She was looking forward to a drink herself. Things suddenly felt a little tense. Maybe he would loosen up once the alcohol kicked in.

They made small talk for much of the way, Jake passing comment on the stark contrast between the city's older buildings and the multi-coloured high-rise flats now dominating the skyline to accommodate the growing student population.

"It's like two places in one," remarked Jake. "Personally I prefer the older parts, even if they're a bit run-down. More character."

Minnie was pleased to hear this. It seemed they shared an appreciation for old architecture, at least. That was a start.

They arrived eventually at the Old Windmill, known locally as Ma Brown's. The pub was almost as old as the Orb, with lots of nooks and crannies, low, beamed ceilings decorated with bunches of dried hops, and a huge stone fireplace. The band were setting up towards the back of the building and it was already filling up, though many people were choosing to stand. Jake directed Minnie into a snug just inside the door while he went to the bar.

Minnie's phone pinged in her bag. She unzipped it and stared at the screen. Ajab.

Everything okay? x
I think so. Will keep you posted x
Think???

She was about to respond when Jake reappeared, carrying a pint of Guinness and half a cider. He placed the drinks on the table and slid into the seat opposite, then took off his jacket. "Phew. Warm in here."

His lips curved upwards as Minnie nodded a little awkwardly, then took a huge gulp of his stout, which went down alarmingly quickly.

He let out a long breath. "Needed that," he said, licking the froth from his upper lip. "So where do we start, then, Minnie Mouse? Tell me all about yourself."

Minnie drank a mouthful of the cider, rather hoping it would go straight to her head. "What – what d'you want to know?"

"The usual. Where you're from, what star sign are you, what you like for breakfast." He grinned and she relaxed a little.

"I'm nineteen in a few weeks, so that makes me a Scorpio. I was brought up in Gloucestershire. Just me, no brothers or sisters. I'm studying for a degree in history. I like indie bands; I'm a bit addicted to tattoos, I'm an aspiring vegan and I adore animals. Oh – and I love a croissant in the morning."

Jake laughed. "*Aspiring* vegan? How's that, then?"

Minnie grimaced. "Struggling to give up cheese."

"They do vegan cheese, don't they?"

"Yeah, but I haven't found one I really like yet. I'll keep trying, though."

"I'll ask around. One of the fellas I share with is a vegan. He buys all sorts of weird and wonderful things."

He pronounced 'with' as 'wit'. It made her smile. "So you live with some other lads, too?"

"Uh-huh. Two of 'em." He rolled his eyes. "Just for the now. I mean, they're okay, like, but it'll be good to have my own space when I can afford it. Trying to save up, y' know."

"What do you do? For a job, I mean?"

"I'm a brickie. Working on the construction site near that old priory – that bit that's all fenced off. D'you know it?"

Minnie nodded. She wondered whether to mention that her mum lived quite close to the priory, but decided that might be something to divulge once she knew him a bit better.

"Yes, where they've uncovered the undercroft's really interesting. I'm a bit of a geek when it comes to history and ancient stuff."

"You don't look like a geek to me." His eyes locked with hers suddenly and that warm tingle flooded through her again. She felt heat rush to her cheeks.

"Ha. You haven't seen me with my specs on."

"I think you'd just look – what's the word, studious." He grinned. "You must be brainy. Not like me. I flunked everything. Didn't even finish school."

"You seem pretty switched on. I mean, you could always go back to college – some people are just late developers . . ."

He laughed throatily. "Nah. I'm happy enough doing what I'm doing. Always felt like I was in prison in the classroom. Anyway, there's money in the building trade when you can get the work."

"I s'pose so." She paused. "Do you have family back in Ireland?"

Jake's face hardened suddenly. "Not any that I want to see."

"Oh dear. Why's that – if you don't mind me asking?"

He picked up a beer mat and started peeling the edges, pursing his lips "Let's just say we had – a difference of opinion." He chewed his cheek. "Look. I was born in England. My mam and dad died in an accident when I was a baby and I was shipped off to live with my auntie in Ireland. My mam's younger sister. But nobody actually bothered to tell me she and her husband weren't my real parents. I'd always called them Mam and Dad. But her man let it slip one day when he was smacking me about; it all came pouring out. How he couldn't stand the sight of me, how he'd never wanted me there in the first place. How I'd brought them nothing but grief." The muscles in his cheeks twitched. "Everything started to make sense. The way he always treated me compared with their other two kids. The way he looked at me like I was something he'd picked up on his shoe."

Minnie was shocked. "God, that's awful. What about your auntie?"

"Oh, she wasn't so bad really. But she was under that fecker's thumb. Nothing was gonna change, y' know? So the minute I found out, I thought '*fook this*' and I packed a bag and left. Never went back." He looked up at her, his dark eyes filled with sadness. "I'd just turned fifteen."

Minnie instinctively reached across the table to squeeze his hand. "I'm so sorry. Is that – was that the reason you were homeless?"

"Yep. I had a couple of quid saved up, from this paper round I'd been doing, like. Hopped on the first ferry I could get and hitched my way to Liverpool – thought, like the eejit I was, that I'd find a job and get the money rolling in. 'Course, no one was gonna take on a skinny little bollocks like me with no experience or papers, were they? So I finished up sleeping rough for just over a year. It was a scary time. Freezing your tits off in winter, dying of thirst in the hot weather. Never know where your next meal's coming from. Frightened to go to sleep in case someone attacks or robs you when you're off guard. That's why you see so many homeless people sleeping in the day. It's safer – plus you're less likely to wake up with someone pissing on you."

Minnie considered the horrors of living on the streets – particularly for someone so young. Her heart went out to him. "But – someone gave you a break? I mean, you've obviously got things back on track. And you've got a useful skill now."

He nodded slowly. "I landed lucky. Met this guy, quite by chance. He was sitting on a bench in Liverpool city centre, not looking too clever. Not drunk, like, just really peely-wally, like he was going to collapse or something. I helped him back to his hotel and stayed with him till a doctor came to check him over. Turned out he had a heart complaint and had forgotten to take his pills. Anyway, cut a long story short, he's a business man. Feckin' *loaded*." Jake's eyebrows shot up briefly.

He took a swig from his pint and smacked his lips. "Asked me if I was fixed for a job and would I like to work for him. He's from Coventry but owns a couple of properties up in Liverpool and other places round the country, as well. He moved me into a big old house near Birkenhead with a few other lads. The place needed a fair bit of work but it was like heaven having a roof over my head and a bed again. Couldn't quite believe it. I started

149

off working up there, just your general dogsbody to begin with, got pretty handy with this and that. Then the guy got one of the others to show me how to lay bricks. Piece of piss after a bit. We've had other contracts all over since. And then this one came up a couple of months back, so here I am." He spread his hands wide, grinning. "Pretty much my whole life story in a nutshell."

Minnie thought of her own background, her doting parents. Never having to worry about money or food, or any of those things that Jake had had to contend with from such a young age. Taking everything very much for granted. She felt suddenly incredibly guilty.

"Wow. That's some story."

He leaned back in his seat. "I'm fine now. Had to do my share of ducking and diving to get by, but we won't go into that." He gave a raucous chuckle. "But everything's worked out okay in the end. And I guess it did me good, in a way. You always live for the moment when you don't know what's round the next corner, don't you?" He tipped his head to one side, his eyes scanning her face. "Anyway, enough about me. Tell me more about yourself. What's your family like?"

Minnie thought for a moment. "There's just me and my mum. My dad, he – he died – just over eighteen months ago." She cleared her throat. Even now the words tasted bitter in her mouth. To think of her dad as someone who only existed in her past still cut her to the quick. Though she loved her mum, at times she felt stifled by her. It was hard, being an only child and permanently the focus of so much attention. Being checked up on wherever she went, quizzed about who she spent time with at school and, as she grew older, when she went out with friends. Since Trevor's death, things had got worse. Minnie felt so desperately needed that sometimes it made her want to scream. There had been occasions in her earlier teens when Georgia had wanted to accompany Minnie if she went out with friends. Minnie had found it cripplingly embarrassing, to the extent that she'd turned down a few invitations rather than risk having Georgia tagging along or turning up uninvited. But she and her dad had shared a special bond. She'd once heard her parents arguing, Trevor telling her mum that she was being over the top and needed to give Minnie space.

When Minnie was about fifteen, Trevor had told her that Georgia hadn't had a great start in life; that Georgia had been sparing with details, but her own mum and dad had been pretty inadequate. Maybe even abusive. Apparently she'd just left the care system when he met her. Minnie tried to make allowances for her, reasoning that maybe Georgia was intent on never making the mistakes her parents had. She just wished she'd lighten up a bit.

Georgia and Trevor had explained gently to Minnie when she was very small that Trevor wasn't her biological father. They'd thought she had a right to know. But Minnie had never given her real father a second thought. Trevor had been her dad in every possible sense, the best dad she could ever have asked for. They'd had the same sense of humour, the same taste in films. How she longed every day to pick up a phone and call him to tell him about things that were happening. To ask his advice when she encountered a problem. She had to look forward, didn't dare dwell on her earlier life. It was too painful.

"Ah, I'm sorry to hear that. Was it expected, like?"

Minnie really didn't want to go into the details but Jake had been so candid. "No. It was an accident. He – he drowned. A horrible, horrible shock." She shook her head and looked away, hot tears pricking her eyes. She felt one roll down her face, landing on the table.

Jake leaned across and brushed her cheek with his thumb. "That must've been tough," he said, his voice gentle. "I don't remember my real family, so I couldn't really miss them. Just

151

later on, once I found out what had happened, I started thinking about them. But it was more the idea of who they were and how things might've been different for me, y'know? You can't really grieve for something you never had."

Minnie lifted her head to look at him. She'd known this man all of five minutes and she already seemed to know just about all there was to know about him. It all felt very intense, but not in a bad way.

"How old are you, Jake?" It suddenly occurred to her that this was the one thing she hadn't thought to ask.

"How old d'you think I am?" He narrowed his eyes mischievously.

"I really don't know."

"I'm twenty-eight. An old fart compared with you." His brow puckered slightly. "But that won't stop us being friends at all, will it?"

There was a hint of anxiety in his voice. Minnie reflected on her parents' relationship. Her dad had been sixteen years older than her mum and that hadn't been an obstacle to their happiness. A nine-year age gap didn't seem so bad. And she rather hoped that they could be more than just friends.

She pulled a tissue from her pocket and blotted her eyes, managing a smile, "No. It makes no difference to me at all."

Jake's lips curved upwards tentatively. He paused briefly, then blew out his cheeks. "Jesus, let's lighten things up a bit." He slapped his thighs, then rose from his seat, glancing round the opening of the snug towards the bar. He nodded towards her glass. "Come on, get that one down your neck and I'll get us another. I heard the band tuning up. Shall we go through there in a minute?"

By now the pub had filled with students and older customers alike, and the room was buzzing with chatter, people squeezing past one another balancing glasses on their way to and from the bar. Suddenly the strum of an acoustic guitar sent a hush over the room as people jostled to get nearer to the band, four lads in their twenties, two playing guitars, one a violin. The singer held a tambourine. They proceeded to deliver a selection of their own folk tunes, the vocalist having a unique, melodic voice.

Minnie stole a glance at Jake, Guinness in hand and standing next to her near the front, mesmerised as the band broke into a haunting ballad. Noticing her stare, he turned his face towards her, holding her in his gaze for a moment. She detected a sadness beneath the light-hearted façade, a vulnerability, and it made her want to wrap her arms around him. His free hand sought hers once more and their fingers interlocked.

She couldn't explain it: she'd known Jake all of five minutes, but already she felt as if she never wanted to let him go. Getting into a relationship with anyone right now was not what she had planned at all. But she was fairly sure that was exactly where this was heading. And she was more than happy to be swept along with the tide.

Chapter 16

Georgia

Wednesday morning, 28 September 2022

To ensure a half-decent night's sleep, Georgia had taken a sleeping pill. It wasn't burying her head in the sand, she'd told herself: just looking after her mental well-being. She *had* to sleep: if she didn't, she was going to go round the twist eventually. Both main doors were bolted, the extra barricades in place. Not completely failsafe, but as good as it was going to get.

She'd set the alarm to make the most of her day, knowing she'd need to allow an hour or so to shake off the grogginess the tablets always brought on. The paint was due to arrive at some point in the morning, and she wanted to move the furniture aside in the bedroom to sugar-soap the walls and woodwork in preparation before starting to decorate. She dressed in her scruffiest long-sleeve T-shirt and jogging bottoms, had a mug of strong coffee and a bowl of granola on a tray in the sitting room, then logged into her laptop to check her inbox for the delivery slot. It was still only 8.15am; the paint wasn't due to arrive until ten o'clock, so she had plenty of time.

Georgia began to leaf through her personal emails, realising she needed to unsubscribe to a huge number of the expensive designer shops which were clogging her inbox. She moved onto to the spam, groaning at how many had accumulated since she'd last looked. She always made a point of checking through them, in case something important had been mistakenly identified as junk, but she had let things slip because of her move. After deleting a good four hundred in one go, she was about to close the laptop lid when a notification flashed up at the bottom right of the screen. Georgia frowned.

Borealis.A1082@gmail.com

She didn't recognise the sender's address, but it hadn't gone to the junk folder so she assumed it must be something genuine.

Georgia hesitated briefly before clicking on the email. It opened in the centre of the page, the subject line making her freeze.

Re: Class of 1996

But it was the message that sent her heart rushing into her throat.

Ah, Found you again at last!
Look forward to catching up very soon 😊

Slamming the lid shut, Georgia leapt from her seat, just managing to grab the laptop before it fell to the floor. With trembling hands, she replaced it on the armchair, her mind whirring.

Someone had discovered her personal email address. She was always so careful not to give it out unless absolutely necessary.

"Don't ever give anyone access to you who you don't know well or want to correspond with, Georgie," Trevor had warned. "There are people out there savvy enough to hack your account and get your bank details and all sorts. Always pays to be cautious."

And she'd heeded his words, fearful of what it could open her up to. She had used Trevor's old email account for the odd business transaction, which she had given to the letting agency and her bank. But somebody had got hold of her own personal account from somewhere. Georgia was almost a technophobe. Beyond internet shopping and checking emails, mainly for orders she'd placed or for special offers, she'd never bothered with her computer much. Trevor had laughed at her lack of interest, calling her a Luddite. The very idea of social media filled her with dread: she'd never have dreamed of setting up an online profile for fear of what can of worms it might open. She had no idea whether opening the email could have been risky, or if responding might open her up to something potentially even more harmful.

She rushed into the kitchen and rooted through the drawer for a pen and notepad. Hurriedly, she copied the email address, then promptly deleted the message. Obtaining her email details was bad enough, but the sentiment behind the contents had sent a chill through her. All she could hope and pray was that whoever had sent it was bluffing and hadn't physically traced her but had just somehow obtained her email address.

Peering anxiously through the net curtains, she could see the usual stream of people walking past on their way to work. Her eyes travelled to the house opposite where she had seen the person watching her, but it was impossible to see beyond the window clearly in daylight. *Could* it have been Jethro

156

Jackson? But then – what reason would he have for spying on her? It made no sense. Unless – unless it wasn't *her* he was watching, but the house itself. Maybe he was waiting for the woman who'd left in such a hurry to come back, thinking she might turn up in the middle of the night. But now, with the new locks, neither of them would be able to gain access. Remembering the woman's battered face in that photo, the thought of how Jackson might react when he realised this made her gut roll.

Almost involuntarily, Georgia let out an angry scream, tugging at her hair with both hands. She needed to get a grip. It was just an email, for God's sake, but it had sent her into a flat spin. Someone was playing games, trying to put the wind up her. Why was she letting them freak her out like this? She was completely paranoid: she might even have just imagined the person watching her the other night in her overwrought state. The photographer outside the cathedral. The noises through the walls. The monk.

But the clay figure, the photographs in the fireplace. They couldn't be denied, could they? The thought of finding anything else made her stomach clench once more. Georgia drew in a long breath, then let it out slowly. She went to the kitchen and poured herself a small whisky. However unpleasant the flavour, it had definitely helped to calm her the last time. Even if it was only just after breakfast, she had to have *something*. Suddenly remembering the diazepam she'd been prescribed after Trevor's death, she hurried upstairs to the box room, rooting through the handbags she'd brought with her until she located the packet. A feeling of momentary relief washed over her as she popped one into her mouth. She knew she probably shouldn't have taken it with the whisky, but one shot wasn't going to be enough to quell her nerves, and the taste was awful. There weren't many tablets left, though – maybe enough to last another week or so – and she was going to need more sleeping pills soon, too. She'd need to register with a local GP before she ran out altogether.

Georgia decided she'd ask Yiannis about emails tomorrow, find out whether it was possible to locate the sender's IP address or whatever it was. She'd heard Trevor talking about those. Yiannis was pretty switched on. In the meantime, focusing on something mundane would be the best thing she could do to take her mind off it all, before she finished up sitting in a corner rocking: an incoherent, gibbering wreck.

Gradually feeling the effects of the alcohol and the pill, the thought of the email suddenly didn't seem so momentous. That was better; she was feeling a bit more rational, if slightly woozy. Taking a deep breath, Georgia rolled up the sleeves of her old T-shirt and went to fill a bucket of water from the tap. The paint would be arriving soon and this was no time to sit fretting. She had a room to prepare.

*

Georgia spent most of the morning scrubbing the walls and woodwork and plugging any holes with Polyfilla, then the afternoon painting her bedroom in the subtle shade of Farrow and Ball matt light grey she had chosen. Though she felt shattered, she was pleased with the end result. She couldn't wait for Minnie to see it, to see what an improvement she'd made. Georgia hoped Minnie would be pleased, realising she was keeping herself busy, being productive. But having finished for the day, the temporarily suppressed worries began to circulate through her mind again. The thought that if she opened her laptop, there would be another taunting message, made the loosened knot tighten once more in her gut.

This was no good, no good at all. After a light supper, Georgia washed down another sleeping pill with more whisky, took a shower, made up her bed in the new linen, then collapsed into it. Despite her earlier anxiety, she was asleep within minutes, as much from pure physical exhaustion as the Zopiclone and the alcohol. This was temporary, she'd told herself before swallowing the tablet. A sticking plaster.

She wasn't going to make a habit of it.

Chapter 17

Minnie

Wednesday, 28 September 2022

Their new housemate moved in on the Wednesday afternoon which followed her first visit to the house. The room which had originally been allocated to Joanna had remained untouched, so there was nothing to do other than help carry what few belongings Angela had brought up the two flights of stairs to the top floor, and leave her to her own devices. She had one rather battered suitcase, secured with a belt as the clasp had broken, an old Adidas holdall and a bulging laptop bag, which she seemed reluctant to relinquish even though Ajab offered to take it.

"I'll bring the holdall, then." He raised his eyebrows at Minnie, eliciting a covert grin from her.

After their initial meeting, Minnie had been thinking about Angela and decided that her awkward manner and stilted conversation could probably be attributed to leading a sheltered existence. And maybe her hearing loss affected her, too. It couldn't be easy for her. Minnie hated to be judgemental about anyone. The woman had clearly been through a tough time, losing her mother. She needed friendship, not suspicion.

"We must try to make her feel at home," she'd told everyone the night before, her focus very much on Fatima. "And if you can't be nice, just don't say anything at all. I'm not being funny Fatima, but you can be a bit, well, you know . . ."

"What d'you mean?" Fatima had immediately been on the defensive. "I'm nice to people if they deserve it. Anyway, I can't see us socialising much with her, can you? I doubt we'll have much in common beyond the course."

"We can at least offer to take her along now and again when we go into town – she's probably lonely."

"I doubt she'd want to come, anyway," muttered Fatima.

"Well if she doesn't, that's fine. But let's give her the option, eh?"

Fatima rolled her eyes. Ajab and Sonia seemed happy enough to include Angela in things, although Sonia was dubious as to whether the woman was going to fit in generally.

"She *is* a bit old, isn't she?" she'd said. "Can't really see her strutting her stuff down at the SU, can you?"

Minnie sighed. "Look. Can we all behave like adults for once? All we have to do is be civil and make a bit of an effort so she doesn't feel excluded. We've all got to live here and I for one don't want an atmosphere. Okay?"

Everyone agreed that they would try to get along. Fatima had welcomed Angela upon arrival with the offer of tea and a slice of carrot cake, with a nod of approval from Minnie. So far, so good. They sat around the living room, making painful small talk for almost half an hour, until Angela, who had taken forever to nibble through her cake, finally got up.

"Th-thank you all for m-making me feel so w-welcome," she

161

said with a smile, picking up her plate and empty mug. "I n-need to g-go and un-p-pack my stuff now, though."

Fatima shot Minnie a look of relief. She stood up too, stretching her arms above her head. "I've got work to do myself."

The pair left the room, leaving Ajab, Minnie and Sonia looking at one another. Sonia let out a sort of whistle.

"Well, this is going to be interesting," she said in a low voice, her eyes following the back of Angela's head as she approached the stairs.

Minnie sighed. She threw back her head, her eyes cast to the ceiling. "Aww come on, give her a chance. I don't suppose she's got a lot to talk about if she never goes out or mixes with anyone. Maybe living with us'll bring her out of her shell a bit."

Sonia looked dubious. "Hmm. We'll see."

The three of them headed for their respective rooms.

Minnie turned to Ajab as they reached the first-floor landing. "D'you think I ought to pop up and see if Angela's got everything she needs?"

He shrugged indifferently. "Up to you. I'd just let her get on with it for a bit, personally."

"Oh. Okay. I don't want to seem pushy."

"No, it's not that. If it were me, I'd just want be left to settle in myself first. I'm sure she'll let us know if she wants anything."

"Did anyone ask her if she's got any allergies? I forgot to say I was cooking us all a chilli tonight."

"Mins, I switched off from the riveting convo, to be honest. Found myself very preoccupied with an interesting little spider spinning its web in the corner. Just go up and ask her if you're worried. I need to get back to my essay for a bit of grounding after all that excitement."

Minnie laughed. "Point taken. I'll just stick my head round the door to ask her about dinner, that's all."

"See you in a bit."

Minnie carried on up the next flight of stairs to where Angela would be staying. She tapped on the door cautiously. "Erm Angela – I'm doing a veggie chilli this evening if you'd like some?"

The door opened, just enough for Angela to show her face. She gave Minnie a tepid smile. "Th-thanks, but I'm not really a f-fan of spicy f-food. I'll g-get myself something l-later."

"Okay, no worries." Minnie paused. "If you need anything just give one of us a shout, won't you."

Angela gave a slight nod of her head, smiled very briefly once more and closed the door again. Minnie stood for a moment, shrugged and headed back towards the stairs. Oh well, at least she'd offered.

As she reached the bottom, Sonia stuck her head out of her own room, waving something in the air.

"Mins, I was just coming to see you – I've got your phone here."

"Oh, cheers." She padded down the landing to take the mobile from her. "Where was it?"

"Halfway up the bloody stairs – I nearly trod on it."

"Shit. I'll have to be more careful." Minnie pursed her lips. "I left it on the bench in a lecture yesterday, too."

"Well, you have seemed a bit distracted lately, to be fair. Since meeting that new guy. Beguiled by his Irish charms, I expect." Sonia pushed her tongue into her cheek playfully.

Minnie laughed. "Hmm. Maybe. Thanks anyway – I need to check my WhatsApp."

Sonia was about to close her door again. "Oh, it did ping a couple of times, actually. I didn't look, of course, in case it was something personal." She threw Minnie a wink and disappeared into her room once more.

163

Minnie opened her WhatsApp, her heart lifting as she saw there was a message in an old group chat she rarely contributed to anymore and something from Jake.

Minnie proceeded to open it, doing a little jig to find an invitation to go for a drink again the following night.

Teasingly, she replied with:

Have to check my diary – will let you know later x

She went straight to her wardrobe to find the perfect outfit. She could hardly wait.

Chapter 18

Georgia

Thursday, 29 September 2022

Georgia woke to the sound of the usual morning activity outside, the scent of the freshly painted walls filling her nostrils. The cathedral clock chimed in the hour. It was only 8am, but even though she felt slightly queasy and muzzy-headed, she was grateful to have slept through again with no disturbances. Stiff from the previous day's exertions, she eased herself from the bed and peered through the curtains. The sky was clear, the autumnal display around the graveyard vivid in the early sun. It was so strange, the different complexion that the weather put on the whole place.

She glanced round the bedroom, blearily admiring the fruits of her labour once more, before going downstairs to put the kettle on. She needed coffee to function, strong and black. Something to shake off the fog that the medication had left her with. Georgia opened the sitting room curtains, revealing dust motes dancing in the shaft of light that flooded through the nets. Though they were still grimy, Georgia was reluctant to wash them owing to the extra privacy they lent the room. Maybe she needed to invest in some blinds at some point. Her laptop still lay on the armchair where she'd left it the previous morning. Though she knew she should probably ignore it, she felt an irresistible urge to check. Her fingers tingled as she placed it on the side table, then lifted the lid, waiting for everything to load. Hesitantly, she clicked the emails icon, a wave of relief washing over her to see nothing more to concern her. Leaving the laptop open on the table, she went through to the kitchen to make breakfast, returning with her coffee and a bowl of Weetabix. She drank the coffee, then placed the mug on the hearth. Feeling slightly less dazed, she settled in the armchair nearest the window, her gaze drifting constantly to the laptop as she ate her cereal.

Georgia's pulse quickened. The blue notification flashing suddenly at the bottom of the screen was too irresistible to ignore. She put down the dish and craned forwards to see who the sender was.

Borealis.A1082@gmail.com

Georgia felt as though all the strength was draining out of her. She almost tripped in her haste to pick up the computer, her heart thumping, eyes darting across the display. Without even opening the message, she could guess the gist of what it would convey.

The subject line read:

Re: Not Such Good Friends Reunited

This time, she didn't delete the email, but didn't open it

166

either. Dismissing the notification, she snapped the lid shut. Her appetite had disappeared completely. She took the bowl and empty mug back into the kitchen, scraping the waste cereal into the bin. She needed to get dressed. Even if she didn't tell him exactly what was going on, she really had to see if Yiannis could advise her what to do about the messages.

*

Georgia took a deep breath as she walked towards the Orb and saw Cole leaning against the wall outside, well before opening time. Though she wasn't working until the following evening, her anxiety to speak to Yiannis about the emails was overwhelming. But seeing Cole, she hesitated, wondering whether to turn back. He'd made her feel small and she had no desire to speak to him after he'd given her the brush-off. Especially after having learned that he had some sort of connection to Jethro Jackson.

Cole wore a hangdog expression. He looked pale and drawn, as though he hadn't slept. His clothes were crumpled, his chin unshaven. He looked a *mess*. Georgia gritted her teeth and continued to head for the entrance. She would ignore him, walk straight past. Looking round to see her approaching, he straightened, forcing a weak smile.

"Hello. I'd been hoping to see you. I – I wanted to apologise. About the other night."

Georgia's arms folded across her chest. "There's no need," she replied tersely. "If you didn't want to come round, that's fine by me. At least I know where I stand."

"No, no. It's not like that at all. I did – *do* – want to accept your invitation. It's just, well, something . . . came up. If you'd just let me explain . . ."

He turned to face her properly. Georgia was shocked to see

167

a bruise blooming around his left eye, a cut at the corner of his mouth. Cole didn't strike her as the sort to get into brawls.

"What happened to you?" In spite of herself, she flooded with concern, her eyes widening.

"I'm a bit behind with the rent again. Let's just say my landlord's not particularly tolerant." Cole ran a hand through his hair, dropping his gaze.

Georgia winced internally. "Your landlord – is he Jethro Jackson, by any chance?"

Cole nodded miserably. "Unfortunately, yes."

So that explained that, then. Georgia pictured Jackson's pumped-up physique, his self-satisfied expression. He was a vile bully. That woman's swollen face in the photo flashed behind her eyes. Something twisted in Georgia's gut as she wondered more than ever exactly what had happened to her, and just what Jackson might be capable of.

"So he got heavy-handed with you? But that's assault – you should report him to the police."

Cole shrugged. "I've no proof. He sent me a – shall we say, a very direct message the other night, saying he'd be waiting at my flat for his money, but I was jumped on the way home. It was dark and the guy was wearing a face mask. Could've been him or one of his heavies, but could just as easily have been a random attack."

For late payment? Jackson had done this for a measly few quid when he owned so much. Was this how he treated all his tenants? Georgia was incensed. "And the money? Did you pay him?"

"He wasn't actually there when I got back. I think it was meant as a warning. I caught a bus and took a few items to that Cash Converters place in Stoke first thing yesterday – managed to scrape enough to keep him off my back until next month." Cole blew out his cheeks. He looked utterly wretched. "I'm sorry – I know I must've seemed a bit, well, rude, clearing off like that. But all I could think about after the text landed was what I'd need to do to get the money for Jackson. The offer's still open, if you could do with a hand with the decorating."

Georgia regarded his earnest face, softening. "I worked my backside off, but I got it done by myself, thanks." She thought for a moment. Maybe . . .

"I'm too achy to do any more today. I was actually on my way to ask Yiannis something, but – actually, do you know much about computers?"

Cole nodded. "Yeah, I know my way round a motherboard – sort of. Wrote a few articles for *Tech Weekly* in my journo days."

Georgia arced an eyebrow. *How fortuitous*. "Really? I'm impressed. A jack-of-all-trades, then."

"Hmm. Master of none," he countered, smiling with one side of his mouth.

She drew in a breath. "Listen, d'you want to come back to my house now, if you're not busy? I can make us some lunch in a bit if you wouldn't mind helping me with something."

Cole brightened. "Absolutely. Lead on." Though she had been craving company, it still felt slightly uncomfortable, bringing a man into the house. Especially an attractive one. But if Cole knew his way round a computer, she had to get over it. It wasn't as if she was inviting him to spend the night or anything. Men and women could just be friends, after all, even if it did feel alien to her.

Georgia sensed Cole's surprise as she paused to put the key in the door.

"I hadn't realised you lived quite so close." He looked around, almost hesitantly, before crossing the threshold.

From the kitchen doorway, she watched awkwardly as he wandered round the sitting room, taking in every nook and cranny.

"I love these old places. So much character." His eyes shone. "My home in London was a Victorian terrace – nowhere near as old as this, but still lots of original features. The flat I'm in's all 1970s. One of those soulless boxes, you know, partitions so thin you can hear the loo flushing next door."

He ran a hand over the wall above the fireplace, smiling wistfully. "One day, when I write my bestseller, I'd like somewhere just like this. I'm very envious."

"Yes, but it's draughty and I'm expecting to be frozen once the cold weather hits, even with the radiators. There's woodworm in places, too – and God knows what's underneath the floorboards."

"As long as it's not a body, eh," Cole laughed.

Georgia puffed out her cheeks. "Don't even go there. You never know with a building this ancient." Once more, she thought about the previous tenant. The suggestion, even in jest, was not something she wanted to contemplate.

"What about Ned's ghosts? Any sign of them?"

Despite his jokey tone, she felt a sudden prickle of unease pass through her as she pictured the hooded figure from the other night. It may have been her imagination, but it seemed as though the temperature had dipped slightly.

For God's sake. Georgia gave herself a mental shake. She was being ridiculous; she needed to focus on reality. There were far more earthly things to worry about. She was spending too much time alone: it was skewing her judgement.

"Ha. Don't be daft. Right, that's enough about bodies and ghouls, thank you very much. How d'you take your coffee?"

*

While they finished their drinks, Georgia asked Cole to explain how emails worked.

"If I open a message by mistake, have I opened myself up to a possible threat? Or, I don't know, a virus or something?"

"That depends on the email. If there's malicious intent behind it, and you click a link or open an attachment, you could introduce malware to your system. Worst case scenario would be if you did it without thinking and enabled someone to instal spyware on your phone or laptop – these clever little bastards can actually access your camera and microphone. They can even get screenshots of you while you're using your computer."

Georgia's head swam. Get *screenshots* of her? It didn't bear thinking about. She considered the messages she'd received. She hadn't even opened the latest and there weren't any attachments or links in the first one to click on. But the thought that it was possible for someone to zoom in, watch her through her laptop camera, made her want to smash the thing to bits.

"But – if I haven't opened a link or anything – I should be okay?"

Cole nodded. "You should be fine. The only emails which are potentially dangerous are those with an HTML format. They can trick the webmail browser into loading a script code and executing it. Very sneaky. And they work by just opening the email – no link needed."

"Fuck." Georgia was filled with sudden panic. She racked her brains. Had the email address begun with HTML? She didn't think so, but she'd need to double-check the notepad she'd copied it into. This was a nightmare.

Cole's brow knitted. He put down his mug and sat forward.

"You look worried to death. D'you think you could've received something iffy?"

"I don't know. I stupidly opened an email from an unknown sender without thinking. The thought of someone actually spying on me when I'm on my computer is horrible."

"Have you still got the email? I could have a look for you." He nodded encouragingly.

Georgia hesitated. The first message should be in her deleted folder; the second remained unopened, but she didn't want Cole to see either in case it prompted questions.

"No," she lied. "I deleted it, then emptied the folder."

He studied her face, not looking convinced. "You can easily restore deleted emails if you want, you know."

"No, it's fine," Georgia replied, a little too quickly. "I wrote down the address somewhere just in case – I'm fairly sure there wasn't any HTML in it anywhere."

He leaned back once more, his eyes narrowing slightly. "Oh. Okay. Well, you should be fine, then. Just bear it in mind for the future. And if you want to stop any more messages from the same sender, just right-click the email and you'll be given the option to block them – simple as that. And make sure your virus protection's always up to date – very important."

"Thanks. That's put my mind at rest. Yeah, Minnie – my daughter – updated the virus protection for me about six months ago, so that's all fine." Georgia forced a smile. She would block the sender as soon as Cole had left. She still felt anxious about it and was worried now Cole was going to start quizzing her further.

"How's the book going?" She hoped a change of subject would stop the slightly suspicious way he seemed to be looking at her.

Cole's face fell a little. "Not brilliantly, if I'm honest. I've been a bit distracted; you know, with the rent situation and everything. I still need to complete the research and it's been hard to focus lately. The old mojo's gone. It's like I'm up against it to get the manuscript submitted, and even then I'm not guaranteed a big pay-out. Think I need to revert to plan B."

Georgia felt sorry for him. She could easily have wiped his

debts, but it might seem odd, since she'd only known him five minutes. Nor did she want to reveal how much she actually had in the bank. She would have to wait and see how things panned out before she even considered making such an offer, or letting him know just how well she'd been left provided for. She didn't like to think that he might suddenly become extra keen just because she could support him financially.

"Could you get a part-time job – you know, to supplement your income?"

Cole gave a hollow laugh. "What income? I'm living off what's left of my savings and praying the publishers actually want the book when it's complete. Although it's starting to feel more and more like a pipe dream right now."

"So what about this plan B?"

"I've written freelance articles for magazines and newspapers in the past. The shorter pieces aren't so time-consuming. If I can do a few of those to keep me ticking over, put the book on the back-burner for a bit, hopefully I can get myself straight and pick it up again before I'm back to square one."

"At least you have options. Look at me – all I can do is pull pints."

"It's a much underrated skill." Cole tipped his head as he looked at her, his eyes twinkling warmly. "Look. I'm sorry – I haven't much to offer I know, but I would like to see you again."

Georgia studied him. He was handsome: far more good-looking than Trevor had been. And nearer her own age – not that that should have mattered. But the way he looked at her told her he found *her* attractive, too. She had been wary initially, yes. It was inherent in her, this natural mistrust of strangers; even of people she knew. But he listened to her, seemed to be genuinely interested in what she had to say. And he clearly had a similar background, and pressing current problems of his own. She'd taken an instant disliking to Jethro Jackson, and it seemed her instinct was justified. But all the stuff which had been plaguing her recently was definitely linked to her past in some way. To someone who wanted to make her suffer. And she'd never even seen Cole until the other day. She'd have recognised someone like him at once. Plus, he was from the other end of the country to her. There couldn't be any historical connection between them.

Georgia had spent years with a husband who often criticised and belittled her, years of feeling looked down on. Years of pent-up anger and frustration. She'd put up with it more for the sake of stability for their daughter than anything else, if she was honest with herself. After the way she was brought up, what she wanted more than anything was to create a safe, loving home environment for Minnie. Georgia hadn't any friends; had never been with another man since she was a teenager. Her whole adult existence had been dictated by her status as Trevor's wife. And Minnie was clearly concerned about her being alone now; had said that she ought to meet and engage with people. Maybe that's what she needed to do. Maybe it was time she put herself first for a change.

She drew in a breath. "Yes, I'd like that too. Very much. And I always pay my own way, so don't worry on that front. I don't . . ."

The lips planted suddenly on her own made her gasp. Bringing Cole back to the house, the way he kept looking at her, she'd wondered if this could happen: of course she had. But it had been so long since anyone had kissed her, even Trevor, who had never, even in their early years, been especially passionate, that her response felt clumsy, like an inexperienced schoolgirl. When they finally drew back, she dropped her eyes, feeling ridiculously shy. Cole reached out a hand to stroke her hair.

"I can feel my inspiration coming back already," he said softly, lifting her chin and grinning as his eyes searched her face. "Maybe the plan B won't be necessary after all."

174

Georgia cleared her throat, straightening her blouse. She was finding it hard to look him in the eye and started towards the kitchen. "Um – I think I should make us something to eat. I'd say put the telly on, but the picture's not great. I think it must be the signal we get round here."

Cole smiled knowingly. "Leave it with me."

When she came back into the room ten minutes later, he'd done something to adjust the TV set and it was broadcasting perfectly, both sound and vision.

Georgia stared in surprise. "How did you manage that?"

He grinned, tapping his nose. "That would be telling."

It made her laugh. It dawned on her that she hadn't done that, not really, in a very long time. They ate a lunch of omelette and salad from trays on their laps, Georgia's accompanied by a large glass of chilled Pouilly-Fumé, which had Cole raising an eyebrow.

"You know your wines, then?"

She smiled, more relaxed now after a few glugs. "Trevor – my husband – was a bit of a wine buff. Well, a wine snob, to be more accurate. But I know what I enjoy and always like to have a bottle or two in."

His face clouded.

"For a treat – not every day, of course," she added hastily, glancing at the water he'd asked for and worried he might think she sounded too high maintenance. If only he'd known where she started off. What she'd survived on during her miserable childhood. There was always lager in the fridge and whisky in the cupboard, but providing for his family was never high on her dad's agenda. No wonder she'd been so scrawny.

Cole pursed his lips. "I used to enjoy it, back in the day. But for some of us, it's best left alone."

"Ah." Georgia nodded, flinching internally as she recalled her father's regular drunken outbursts. A brutish hand swiped hard and often across the back of her head for some perceived misdemeanour. How glad she was that that particular gene had bypassed her. "It's when it becomes a necessity rather than a pleasure, I suppose."

They chatted well into the afternoon, until Cole announced that he needed to get back and try to do some work.

"Thanks for the lunch. It's been – well, nice." He rose from his chair, smiling awkwardly. "Are you working tomorrow?"

"Yes. Starting my first proper week. I need a good night's sleep tonight."

"I'll be in. Funnily, I'm finding it's the best place for me to focus on the book. And somehow, seeing other people getting drunk and making idiots of themselves strengthens my resolve to stay away from the booze. Christ, there'll be a table in there with my name on soon, like old Ned's." He grimaced, prompting a laugh from Georgia.

"All you need now is the canine companion."

"Trust me, I'd have one, but the bloody landlord doesn't allow pets."

They shared another kiss, more relaxed on her part this time. Light-headed from the wine and this recent embrace, Georgia watched from the door as Cole made his way across the quad, turning to wave before disappearing towards Holy Trinity Church and the shops. She went to wash the plates, humming to herself without even realising. A warm feeling tingled through her as she began reflecting on the way he'd lifted her face towards him, the way he'd looked at her. Wondering what it might lead to. Until the memory of the emails resurged suddenly, dampening her mood.

Leaving the crockery to drain, she went back to her laptop, compelled to check again. But almost as soon as she'd lifted the lid, a notification appeared. Her chest tightened.

176

Borealis.A1082@gmail.com
Re: I'm getting warmer!

Georgia's trembling finger hovered above the sender's address. There was no HTML – that was something. For a moment, she was tempted to open the message. No. That would be a stupid thing to do. She was allowing whoever it was to get under her skin, which was clearly the intention. It was an email, nothing more. As far as she knew, they hadn't found out where she was living. But then – she couldn't be sure of that, could she? Now that Cole had left, the feelings of angst started to build again.

Closing the notification, Georgia hurriedly opened her emails and scanned the inbox for the offending message. Right-clicking the address, she went through the list of options, then selected *Block Sender*. The line vanished immediately. She let out a long breath, shutting the lid abruptly as if it might inhibit any further unwanted communications.

Hopefully that would be the last she would hear from BorealisA, whoever they were.

Shaken into sobriety once more, Georgia sat back in her seat, turning it all over in her mind. She felt the sudden urge to get out of Cuckoo Cottage. She needed company.

She needed Minnie.

Pulling on her coat, Georgia peered anxiously through the net curtains, her eyes sweeping the quad. The thought now that someone could have been observing them, waiting until she was alone again before sending another email, filled her with dread. Someone was watching her; who and from where, she didn't know. But her suspicion was that they were aiming to rake up something she'd spent the best part of the last three decades trying to bury. They had her at a total disadvantage: she didn't have a clue who she was looking for, or where to find them.

Unless – unless it *was* them, hiding in that house across the street. Unless they were in cahoots with Jethro Jackson.

The feelings of dread were suddenly superseded by rage. How *dare* some bastard attempt to intimidate her. To reduce her to a feeble, frightened female, living in fear of her own shadow. Flinging the front door wide and not even stopping to close it behind her, Georgia marched across the quad and hammered on the door of the property in question, then stood back to look up at the window.

"Who the fuck do you think you are?" she screamed, without a thought for how she must look to the people passing by who were pausing to stare. "Well, you aren't going to scare me off, if that's what you're hoping. Do your worst. I'm ready for you, you piece of shit. Bring it on!"

No one answered the door. The light was hitting the window above, so that it was impossible to see if anyone was looking out at her. But whether the occupant had heard or not, Georgia felt oddly emboldened, lighter for having vented. She turned, her fingers still curled into fists at her sides, glaring at an elderly woman who was standing beside the graveyard wall giving her disapproving looks.

"Can I help you?" Georgia asked, widening her eyes sarcastically.

The woman huffed and walked away. Georgia smiled to herself. But turning to look back at Cuckoo Cottage, her stomach clenched as she saw the open door. The realisation that she'd dropped her guard for a moment made her feel sick. She was playing into someone's hands.

Georgia rushed back across the cobbles, locking the door hurriedly behind her. She stood for a moment, taking deep breaths. She *had* to keep a clear head.

She was allowing herself to be provoked and it could be the undoing of her. Arming herself with the small shovel from the fireplace, she went through each room, checking that nothing appeared to have been disturbed: that no one had taken advantage of her momentary lapse and entered the house. Though everything appeared just as it had done, Georgia still felt compelled to check every corner, every cupboard. Once satisfied that nobody had slipped in, she sank into the armchair, burying her head in her hands. What was happening to her? It felt as though she was losing her grip.

She had run from Warchester to escape persecution and this felt no better. Worse, even. Yet she couldn't return. She'd begun to wonder if whoever was on her trail might have followed her here: and if so, they could just as easily follow her back again. And now these emails – were they connected? Her head throbbed with the enormity of what might be in store for her. Of the thought that someone knew her secrets and was relishing the power over her that it gave them.

That wherever she went, they would be close behind.

Chapter 19

Georgia

Friday 30 September 2022

Nothing more had happened the previous day. But Georgia had slept badly, despite taking a sleeping pill. The depth of her anxiety seemed to have overridden its effects, and she'd spent the whole day in the house, groggy and restless, unable to get off the ground. She had kept the back door barricaded, the sitting room curtains partially drawn, with just enough of a gap to peep through the nets if anyone passed by. To frequently scan the frontage of the terrace opposite in case she was being watched again. The laptop remained closed on the table. Georgia's fingers itched to check it, but she forced herself not to. She didn't need anything else to feed her feelings of unease. This evening was to be her first proper shift in the Orb and as the day wore on, she was finding the prospect of coming home alone after dark once more increasingly daunting. Even the smallest noise set her pulse racing.

It was early days, and she wouldn't feel comfortable asking him to stay the night yet, but she was praying that Cole would be around to walk her back at the end of the evening. Although the small excitement she allowed herself to feel at the thought of seeing him again was quickly subdued by the memory of everything else that had been going on. The knowledge that someone out there was probably already planning their next move.

She kept fluctuating between feelings of panic and incensement that someone was inflicting this on her. She couldn't stay inside like a prisoner forever, for God's sake. Giving herself a mental shake, Georgia decided to stroll up to see Minnie for an hour before starting work. It was overcast, though not cold, and almost 4pm: time enough for a cuppa and a chat before she went to the Orb. She dropped Minnie a quick text to make sure she was home.

The response was disappointingly brief.

Sorry. Late pm tutorial. Not back till gone 6 xx

Georgia's heart sank. She was desperate for company. She decided, whether she would look inordinately keen or not, to go to the pub early. At least she'd be surrounded by people.

Having double-checked the back door and windows, Georgia locked up and turned to make her way up the street. But a voice from across the quad rooted her to the spot.

"Mrs Parnell! How are you?"

Georgia shot a look over her shoulder to see Jethro Jackson approaching. Remembering Cole's battered face, the photographs concealed in the wall, anger rather than fear coursed through her. She gritted her teeth.

"I'm fine, thank you."

He was within a few feet of her now, chest pushed forward, a leering smile spread across his face.

"All settled in okay? No more . . . problems with anything?"

Was there an underlying hint of something there? Jackson looked smug, almost amused. But maybe that was his default expression. Georgia bristled.

"Not so far, no." She began to walk and was perturbed to find him falling into step beside her.

"How are you liking the city?"

Georgia pulled up, studying him coldly. "I'm reserving judgement."

"Oh? I hope nobody's . . . bothering you or anything."

His brow had folded into an overtly concerned frown, but Georgia was sure she detected a hint of glee in his eyes. Rather than feeling intimidated, it needled her further.

"Nothing I can't handle. Now if you'll excuse me, I'm meeting someone."

He moved aside and spread his hand wide. "Don't let me hold you up. But don't forget, any issues and I'll have someone round like a shot."

I bet you will, she thought.

"Have a good evening," he called after her, as she carried on towards the Orb. Georgia pretended not to have heard. She was sure she could feel his eyes on her back. The man made her skin crawl.

Georgia walked into the pub, scanning round for Yiannis. There were several people queuing, dirty plates and glasses waiting to be cleared from tables. Yiannis appeared suddenly from behind the bar, looking sweaty and flustered. Seeing Georgia, his face lit up.

"*OMG* am I glad to see you!" He glanced up at the clock, frowning. "You're not due in till later, though."

Georgia smiled, wondering what was afoot but equally glad to see him. She indicated the tables.

"What's going on?"

"Freddie's gone on a jolly and won't be back until this evening. Bloody Lucas threw all his toys out of the pram halfway through his shift and walked out – two of the lunchtime staff called in sick with stomach bugs, so I've been juggling food orders and trying to serve drinks. I've closed the kitchen now, but as you can see, everything's gone tits-up." He tipped his head towards her beseechingly. "Would you mind taking some of those plates through for me please, sweet?"

Georgia was more than happy to assist. Being busy always helped to take her mind off things, and she was still brooding over the encounter with her landlord. She hung up her jacket and began clearing the debris at once, then wiped down the tabletops and distributed fresh beermats.

Ned called over from his regular corner, "Good job you're here, love – he's been in a right flap."

Yiannis glowered in his direction. "Wouldn't have killed you to offer a helping hand, seeing as you almost bloody live here," he muttered under his breath.

Georgia grinned. "I'll find you a dishcloth if you'd like to muck in," she said to the old man, winking aside at Yiannis.

"Who, me?" Ned looked startled. "Nah – it's the old arthritis, you know. I'm not much use with owt like that." He held up his knobbly fingers by way of an excuse.

Yiannis grunted but ignored him, and continued pouring a pint for the sour-looking man waiting in front of him. Soon order had been restored and Yiannis blew out a breath as he paused to rest against the bar.

"You're a diamond," he beamed as Georgia joined him.

She laughed. "Don't worry, I'm sure you can return the favour some day."

Georgia looked up suddenly as the main door opened. At once, the smile fell from her face at the sight of Jethro Jackson sauntering in, mobile clamped to his ear, brow creased in apparent irritation.

"Fuck," she whispered to Yiannis. "Now he's going to know I work here."

Yiannis gave her a gentle push. "Quick, get out the back – I don't think he's clocked you."

Georgia didn't hesitate. She whisked through the swinging door, and stood behind it for a few moments before turning to peer cautiously through the small pane of glass at the top. Jackson had finished his phone conversation and had one elbow on the bar now. She could see him speaking to Yiannis, casting about as he did so. Georgia shrank back to avoid being seen, wondering if he'd watched her entering earlier.

She felt a surge of pure loathing for the man. Here he was, all shiny shoes and tacky gold, oozing arrogance and ill-deserved wealth, when he was inflicting misery on people like Cole. And God knows what he'd done to that woman in the photo. Well, he'd have his bubble burst soon enough. Those pictures would be sure to prompt an investigation into his dodgy activities, wouldn't they? Georgia knew now that she needed to let the police have them, even if anonymously. A few well-chosen words in an accompanying note would point them in Jackson's direction – though she suspected he'd be well known to them already. The thought bolstered her. It would be the first thing on her to-do list the following day.

She waited behind the door, stealing intermittent glances until she saw the unsmiling Jackson down his pint and march back towards the exit. Once certain the coast was clear, she came back out.

"What was he saying?" Georgia asked, peering across through the window to ensure Jackson had really gone.

"Well, you've clearly made an impression." Yiannis shook his head. "Described you to a T – asked if I'd just seen you at all as he thought he'd spotted you coming in. Some cock and bull story about a maintenance issue with your house that he needed to discuss with you."

Georgia snorted. "Yeah, right." She lowered her voice. "Have you seen Cole?"

Yiannis raised an eyebrow. "Not since the other night." He regarded her quizzically. "I thought you weren't interested anymore?"

Georgia puffed out her cheeks. "He explained – about his connection to Jackson and everything. He's his landlord – and Cole got on the wrong side of his fists after he left here on Tuesday."

Yiannis widened his eyes. "Shit."

"Exactly. Well, I . . ." Georgia considered a moment. But maybe it would be better not to mention the photographs and what she was planning. Yiannis seemed a really nice guy, but she'd realised he did like to gossip, and she couldn't risk it getting back that she'd been the one to take them to the police.

"Anyway, as far as Jackson asking about me, I'll just have to hope I manage to dodge him if he starts coming in here looking for me. Not the kind of attention I want."

Yiannis smiled. "Don't worry, sweet. If he starts hassling you, Freddie'll bar him. He won't put up with anyone causing bother in his pub."

"I'm more concerned about what he might do when I leave at the end of the night." Georgia's stomach dropped at the thought that Jackson might be waiting for her when she got home. That maybe he *was* the one observing her from the house opposite.

"Concerned about what who might do? Not me, I hope?"

Georgia turned to see Cole walking towards them via the archway from the lounge. He must have been working on his book in a quiet corner. He greeted her with a hesitant smile, the black eye now very much in evidence.

At the sight of him, Georgia's heart gave a little skip. "No, 'course not. Our friendly mutual landlord. And I don't mean Freddie." Her eyes narrowed to angry slits as she pictured Jackson's expression, his conceited stance.

Cole's face hardened as he reached the bar. "Has Jackson – he hasn't done something to you, has he?"

"No. He obviously saw me coming in earlier though, and he's been in looking for me under some pretext."

"*Bastard.*" The muscles in Cole's cheeks twitched.

"Blimey, he did a proper number on you, didn't he?" Yiannis winced as he studied Cole's face. "Did you report him?"

Cole shook his head a little sheepishly. "No proof, unfortunately." He turned to Georgia. "I'm more worried about you, if he's on your case."

Georgia threw him a smile. "Don't be. Forewarned is forearmed. I'll have the police on him if he starts making a nuisance of himself."

Whether Jackson was planning on being a nuisance or not, she wasn't going to wait to find out. The thought of the photos and what she could do with them gave her a sudden rush of adrenaline. Yes, she'd have the police on him soon enough, all right. She looked at Cole, a smile spreading across her face.

"Right. Let's have no more talk about Jethro Jackson for now, eh? A large Coke, was it?"

Thankfully Cole stayed in the Orb until the bitter end and, as she'd hoped, walked Georgia back to Cuckoo Cottage, waiting until she'd opened the door and had a quick check everywhere downstairs, closing the curtains and the kitchen blinds. The back door was still barricaded, the windows firmly closed. But she needn't have worried about wriggling out of asking Cole to stay, as he made his excuses, saying he wouldn't come in for coffee as he had an early start the following day.

"Crap timing I know, but I've got to go to London to clear up some outstanding business, so won't be back until Monday, unfortunately. But don't forget, if Jackson shows his face or anything happens, *call me.*" He'd pressed a slip of paper bearing his mobile number into her hand. "And if it's something really bad, promise me you'll dial 999."

Georgia had promised. But a phone call to the police wasn't what she had in mind, more a visit to the station to drop something of interest through the letterbox.

They had shared a goodnight kiss and Cole had disappeared into the night, leaving Georgia to lock up and heave the doorstop into position, as had become part of her nightly ritual. But alone in the house, a crawling sense of disquiet started to build once more. Georgia washed down a sleeping pill with some of the whisky. The level in the bottle was going down rapidly. Though it still made her shudder a little, she was becoming more accustomed to the stuff, which worried her. Its calming effect, along with the medication, was something she was beginning to crave: the slightly anaesthetised, detached sensation it lent her. She went straight to the fireplace, easing out the loose brick and carefully removing the old toffee tin containing the photos.

Georgia clutched the container to her chest, smiling to herself and feeling suddenly more positive as she thought what might be set in motion once its contents had reached the hands of the police. She needed to get to bed. The sooner she fell asleep, the sooner she could carry out her mission and thus hopefully eliminate any concerns regarding the odious Jethro Jackson once and for all. She climbed the stairs, tucked the tin beneath her pillow and, too tired to even bother to undress, crawled beneath the duvet.

Georgia had fallen asleep quickly. But something had roused her and her heart was aflutter. Discombobulated, she sat up, looking round. Light was trickling through the curtains, but there was no evidence from outside of the usual early morning activity, telling her it must be before 8am. She peered at the bedside clock and groaned. Only 6:15.

What had disturbed her?

Georgia looked down at her crumpled blouse and grimaced. She hadn't slept in her clothes since she was a teenager. She felt like a slob. Fully awake now, she decided she might as well get up and take a shower. Peeling everything off, she slipped on her dressing gown and made her way downstairs. But as she reached the bottom, she drew back with sudden trepidation. A small brown jiffy bag had been posted through the letterbox. It had landed squarely on top of the iron doorstop, almost as if by design.

No name, no address.

Georgia froze for a moment, staring at the envelope where it lay, wondering if she dared open it. Steeling herself, she stooped to pick it up, feeling the packaging tentatively to try to guess what was inside. It was as light as a feather, soft and flexible. She sat back on the stairs and peeled back the seal with trembling fingers, opening it wide to examine the contents.

Georgia caught her breath. She inverted the bag and allowed the thing to fall to the floor. It was a straggly hank of human hair, maybe six inches in length, mousey brown and tied at one end with a thin blue velvet ribbon. Georgia felt suddenly cold. Her mind whirred. Why the hell would someone send her this? Between finger and thumb, she picked the coil of hair up by the ribbon and dropped it back into the bag, then carried it into the kitchen where she dropped the packet into the pedal bin. Georgia washed her hands repeatedly as if it might expunge the memory. An uncomfortable notion began to burrow from somewhere deep in her subconscious. But was this something to do with her own past – or was it in some way connected to the woman who had lived in the house before her?

Neither thought gave her any comfort at all.

The sooner she took the photos to the police, the better.

Chapter 20

Georgia

Monday, 10 October 2022

A whole week had come and, with the exception of the persistent emails, passed without incident. At 7.30 on the previous Saturday morning, Georgia had donned sunglasses and piled her hair beneath a baseball cap to drop the wallet of photos off at the police station. Dismayed to find no letterbox, she had wandered in as casually as possible given the adrenaline pumping through her, placed the envelope marked for the attention of the officer in charge on the fortuitously unattended counter in Reception, then hurried away up Little Park Street. Inside the envelope she had placed a hand-scrawled note, implying that Jethro Jackson might be a person of interest. All she could do now was sit tight and hope that whoever opened it had the presence of mind to take some sort of action. If the woman in the photo had been reported missing, at least they would have someone to connect to

189

her. Georgia thought about confiding in Cole about the photos, but decided it was best kept to herself. Better if no one else knew at all: she didn't want any casual slip of the tongue linking them back to her and Jackson getting wind of it. And she definitely wasn't going to tell Yiannis.

Apart from Cole, Georgia hadn't mentioned the emails she'd received to anyone either. But even after blocking BorealisA, whoever the hell they were, more had begun to arrive daily, all with increasingly direct subject lines. The latest one, declaring: *THE TRUTH WILL ALWAYS OUT* made her retch.

Each time another landed, the email address altered slightly to give it the appearance of being from a different sender, Georgia blocked it immediately. She felt sickened by it, but at the same time, compelled to check her messages constantly. It was clear that each of these bogus accounts was being set up with the sole purpose of bombarding her with horrible messages, intended to grind her down. There was no doubt in her mind now that they were connected to the anonymous letter she'd received just before leaving Warchester; the gnawing suspicion that they might also be behind the appearance of the little clay figure and possibly the coil of hair, meaning that they really *were* aware of her address, didn't bear thinking about.

The person responsible clearly knew more about her past than Georgia was comfortable with; they must be watching her constantly, revelling in her distress. She was on tenterhooks, wondering what they might have in store for her next. On top of all this was the nagging worry about the previous tenant in the house and what might have become of her. Georgia really hoped the police would find her safe and well somewhere but feared the worst.

The appearance of the ghostly monk had almost been enough to tip her into the abyss. She'd managed to obtain prescriptions from a couple of online pharmacies for more sleeping tablets and tranquilisers, after filling in their health questionnaires – dubious, maybe, and worryingly easy, but necessary and far less hassle than having to explain her plight and justify her needs to a GP. The Zopiclone had become a nightly fixture; though she'd been trying to resist the diazepam, they were just about keeping her on an even keel during the day – and she couldn't keep drinking whisky and risk turning up to work stinking of alcohol fumes. It was becoming intolerable. Georgia's eyes were sunken, her face drawn; no amount of concealer could disguise how haggard she was looking. Even Yiannis had asked if she was okay, and did she need a few nights off. But right now, the distraction of serving in the Orb was the only thing keeping her sane.

In an attempt to occupy her mind, Georgia had been throwing herself into organising the house, and it was becoming something of an obsession. She missed Minnie: hoping that it might tempt her to come round more, Georgia was trying to create a welcoming space, ordering bits and bobs to make Cuckoo Cottage feel more homely. The box room had proved useful for storing all the online orders she was making, until she found the perfect spot for them. Lamps and ornaments. New curtains and rugs; mirrors to reflect light and make the rooms less dingy. She'd managed to wash the living room walls in a warm-white emulsion and got to grips with the log burner, and, during the daytime at least, it all felt somewhat cosier. Now for the dark, windowless shower room, which currently felt like an oubliette. She was awaiting the arrival of yet another order and then she could make a start on that.

A loud rap at the door and a quick glance through the net curtains told her from the parcels heaped on the front step that her new rainfall showerhead and wicker towel stand had turned up. Georgia opened the door to the gum-chewing courier, who held out an electronic pad for her to sign with a stylus, nodded disinterestedly and disappeared back into his van.

Georgia carried the pile of packages into the hallway, pushing the door shut with her foot. She frowned at the number of boxes. She'd only been expecting two. Maybe the parts for the towel storage had been packed separately. Placing everything on the floor, she went to fetch the kitchen scissors, eager to open her new purchases. The showerhead was perfect – exactly like the picture on the website. Minnie would appreciate that – she'd always loved the one at Warchester. She unpacked the towel stand. All good, too. But everything seemed to be present. Why the third box?

She shook the remaining parcel gently. It was quite big – at least eighteen inches square, maybe nine in depth – but very light. Something was rattling around inside. Maybe it was extra fixings for the shelving. Georgia sliced through the parcel tape and lifted the lid.

As she looked inside, she recoiled in horror. Still with the roots attached were a handful of what appeared to be human adult teeth. Her eyes scanned the otherwise empty box in shocked disbelief. There were six in all, yellowing and with hairline cracks in the enamel, one having wedged in the corner flap of the cardboard. There didn't appear to be anything else inside, and when she turned over the lid, she saw that it was completely blank. Hurriedly, she checked the other packaging over, but each had her name and address clearly typed on a white label on the top. Had someone slipped the box into the pile with the others without the courier noticing? Or had he himself left it there?

She rushed back to the window, hoping to catch the man, but the delivery van had gone. Georgia took the box and its contents out into the courtyard round the back and deposited it into the wheelie bin. As the box fell, she noticed a flash of something white peeping from beneath one of the flaps inside. Reaching into the bin, with finger and thumb she gingerly pulled out a slip of paper. As Georgia held it up, her stomach dropped. Five typewritten words, in bold, red capitals.

AN EYE FOR AN EYE . . . Followed by a winking emoji.

Georgia finished the saying in her head. *A tooth for a tooth*.

Bile rose in her throat. Slamming the lid of the bin shut, Georgia re-entered the house, fumbling with the key in her haste to lock the door. She stared at her hands. They were quivering. On unsteady legs, Georgia went upstairs, shakily removed a diazepam tablet from the packet in her bedside drawer, then sat back on the bed for a moment. It worried her that she might grow dependent on the things, but she had to take something. Her heart had been beating so fast she feared she was at risk of passing out. This whole thing was pushing her to the limit.

Georgia lay on the bed, curled into the foetal position. *Think*. A lock of hair. And now *teeth*. What could it mean? Who would send her something so gross? She stayed there for about an hour, her mind a blur as she allowed the tablet to gradually render her numb.

*

It was mid-morning before Georgia felt calm enough to go back downstairs and make a start on the shower room. She kept flitting between feelings of horror and anger, that someone was having such fun at her expense. All the time she tried to think who might be sick enough to target her like this, racking her brains to remember things that she'd prefer not to think about.

Things that she lived in fear of anyone else, especially Minnie, ever discovering.

*

Georgia was washing up after lunch when the jangle of a text came through. She dried her hands and went to check her phone.

MUM NEED YOU URGENTLY. VERY BAD. AT HOME. PLEASE COME RIGHT AWAY

Oh God. Minnie was so independent. Something must be very wrong for her to ask for help. And the way the message tailed off . . .

Her heart racing, Georgia threw on her jacket and shoes, grabbed her bag and ran out of the house, slamming the door behind her. She headed hell for leather to the taxi rank, only stopping to ring Minnie when she was in the car and already on her way. There was no reply. An increasing feeling of cold dread began to build in Georgia's chest as she tried repeatedly, but each time it went straight to voicemail. What could have happened? Had Minnie had an accident? All sorts of scenarios ran through her head. She could be injured and no longer able to answer. In the back of an ambulance, even.

On the verge of tears, Georgia paid the driver, hurling herself out of the cab and up the drive to the student house. She shouted Minnie's name through the letterbox as she hammered on the door, standing back to look up at the windows. Her nerves were in tatters now, the sheer terror of what was going to greet her once inside. Through the living room window, she could see a figure hovering further back in the room, then coming out into the hallway and approaching. Fatima unlocked the door, looking half-asleep and perplexed.

"Hello. Everything all right?"

"What's happened? Is Minnie okay?" Georgia's eyes flew round the hall as she rushed into the house, almost knocking Fatima over in her haste.

"Minnie? As far as I know – some of the archaeologists were

giving a presentation this afternoon about the artefacts they've turned up recently by the Belgrade Theatre car park. I had a migraine so I bailed."

"So – she's not here?"

"No. Mins has been out since late morning – she went into town with Ajab and Sonia. They said they were going for lunch in the Town Wall Tavern first. Dunno where the newbie is." She indicated up the stairs, clearly referring to their new housemate.

Georgia stared at her, open-mouthed. "But she sent me an urgent message to come here – it sounded like something was really wrong. And she's not answering her phone."

"Probably switched off while they're at the talk." Fatima eyed her curiously "So you say she told you she was at home?"

"Yes. Look." Her hands still trembling, Georgia pulled out her phone and showed Fatima the message.

The girl's brow furrowed. "Weird. I wouldn't have thought Mins'd be one for pranking anyone, either. Doesn't seem like her style. Least of all you." She cocked her head. "Come on, I'll make you a tea. You look like you've had a proper scare."

"I have."

Georgia went into the living room and perched anxiously on the edge of the sofa to wait, while Fatima went to make the tea. She tried Minnie once more, but there was still no reply.

"There you go." Fatima reappeared, handing over a steaming, weak-looking brew.

Georgia sniffed the mug, screwing up her nose. "Smells a bit like pee."

Fatima laughed, but was insistent. "It's chamomile. Very soothing. Just what you need right now."

She sat in the armchair opposite Georgia. "So you say this message came through a short while ago?"

"Yes. I came straight here. I thought something terrible must've happened."

Fatima pursed her lips. "Tell you what, I'll message one of the others just to put your mind at rest. Maybe one of them'll pick up."

Within seconds, a text bleeped on Fatima's mobile. She peered at it, smiling up at Georgia. "Yep. They're all still at this talk. Sonia's getting bored now." Fatima flashed her the weary face emoji on her screen, grinning. The phone pinged again. "She says they're just wrapping it up."

"Are they coming straight back?"

"Yeah. They shouldn't be more than twenty minutes or so. Wait here and hopefully you can find out what's gone on."

Georgia felt drained but relieved. She sipped the revolting tea out of politeness and chatted to Fatima about whether she was enjoying living away from home and how the studies were going.

"Oh – how's your new girl settling in, by the way?"

Fatima arched one eyebrow. "She's not a girl exactly."

"Minnie mentioned she was a mature student. How old is she, exactly?"

Fatima looked round, pressing a finger to her lips. She got up and closed the living room door. "Not sure if she's in or not – she's so quiet, you can never tell," she explained.

"About your age, I think," Fatima went on. "She's on a different wavelength from the rest of us, to be honest. Harmless enough, but definitely a bit odd."

"Oh, that's a shame. The rest of you all get on pretty well, don't you?"

"Yeah. We have our moments, but who doesn't?" Fatima sipped her tea. "Mins is great, though. Definitely the calming influence." She grinned.

The turn of the key in the door followed by chattering voices made Georgia jump to her feet, rushing to greet a surprised Minnie the moment she entered the room. She threw Fatima a questioning look as she returned her mum's hug.

Georgia's relief turned suddenly to confused anger. "What the hell was that text all about? I've been worried sick."

"Whoa – what text?" Minnie drew back, staring at Georgia. "I haven't sent you anything today."

"But I got *this* . . ." Georgia fumbled her phone from her coat pocket, opened the message and thrust it towards her daughter.

Minnie read the words aloud, her brow knitting. She looked up at Georgia. "Mum, I never sent this."

"But that's your number, isn't it? It's there in my contact list under *favourites*."

"It may well be, but I definitely didn't send it. Look." Minnie rummaged through her bag and withdrew her own mobile. "See?" She opened her messages, looked for Georgia and clicked her profile picture, handing the phone over to Georgia.

"There it is!" Georgia waved the thing back at her triumphantly. Minnie screwed up her eyes as she read, then reread the capitalised sentence. Her mouth fell open, the colour draining from her face.

"I didn't send this, I swear. Someone's obviously played a joke on the pair of us."

"Well, it wasn't funny. I thought something terrible must've happened." Georgia sank back into the armchair, shaking her head. "But if you've had your phone on you the whole time, how could they do that?"

"A timed message, maybe?"

Everyone looked round at Ajab. He smiled uncertainly.

"Here, let me see." Holding out a hand, he took the phone from Minnie. They all looked on expectantly as he tapped various icons. "Yep, here it is. See that little clock symbol? It means it's been scheduled. Could've been written any time and then fired off when the sender wanted it to be."

Minnie looked uncomfortable. "But I definitely didn't send it. I didn't even know you could do that."

"Well somebody did," said Fatima, grimacing. "Maybe someone at uni's having a laugh at your expense. Have you upset anyone you can think of?"

Minnie chewed her lip. "I don't think so. The only person I can think of is that quiet boy with the long hair I keep seeing in lectures, the one who always stares at me. Could be him, although I can't think why he'd want to do something like that. And when could he have got hold of the phone, anyway? It's always in my bag on the floor when we're in the lecture theatre."

"He – or someone else – could've easily lifted it when you weren't looking, then slipped it back in," suggested Sonia. "It's not impossible."

"The main thing is, you're okay." Georgia stood up again and went to wrap an arm around Minnie's shoulders for a moment. "I'm sorry I got cross, love. It just wasn't very nice. But please make sure you keep your phone somewhere safe in future."

"I will. And I'm sorry you were so worried. That was a pretty sick thing for anyone to do."

Georgia looked up at the clock. "Well, I'd better be getting back. I've got work later." She turned to Fatima. "Thank you for the tea. You're right, I think it did make me feel a bit less fraught, even if it does taste like dishwater."

Fatima laughed. "You're welcome. I'll get more in for next time you call round, then."

Georgia couldn't help notice Minnie throwing her friend a warning look. But right now, she wasn't in the mood to challenge her. She was just glad that her daughter was safe and well.

Wishing everyone goodbye, Georgia headed out of the house, hoping a walk back would help to clear her head. Though ultimately relieved that the text had only been a sick joke and Minnie was okay, a heavy, nauseated feeling had begun to build in her chest as realisation dawned. Whoever was responsible for the prank message had targeted both herself and Minnie. It seemed now more likely than ever that this was the work of the same person who'd sent the email; the bizarre 'gifts'. And if they knew who Minnie was, and where she lived, maybe they intended to reveal her sordid past to her daughter. Minnie was all she had. She couldn't bear the thought that the single most important person in her life might turn her back on her.

Hadn't she suffered enough?

*

Tuesday, 11 October 2022

Georgia had thought about mentioning the horrible Monday she'd had to Yiannis, but he was unusually subdued that evening and the timing didn't feel right.

"It would've been my dad's seventieth birthday today. He's been gone five years now. I was on the phone to my mum earlier – did I tell you she went back to Greece after he died? She's always in a bad way on anniversaries and things. She actually broke down. I feel so bad I didn't make the effort to go home to Athens and spend a couple of days with her. She's not getting any younger herself." He smiled sadly. "Isn't life like that – full of regrets? What is it they say – about the road to hell being paved with good intentions?"

Georgia nodded sympathetically. She didn't dare dwell on everything she regretted. *Never look back.* It could drive you mad. But she'd spent the evening with her stomach in knots, certain that something – *someone* – from her past was the source of her current torment. Who were they? And why had all this started now, after so many years?

It had been quiet in the Orb. Sometimes on nights like this, Freddie would stay open late for some of the regulars, but Yiannis really wasn't up for it. Georgia had seen Freddie giving him a hug when he went out to the back and he'd looked on the verge of tears a couple of times.

Georgia would have welcomed some company after hours. She felt more anxious than ever about going home. If someone knew where Minnie was, was it only a matter of time before they started sending her hints about her mother's past? The thought appalled her. Though Minnie had thought the text could have come from a strange boy at uni, Georgia wasn't convinced.

As she left the pub, Georgia felt more nervous than usual walking down Bayley Lane. She walked briskly, imagining eyes everywhere, scanning round to make sure she wasn't being followed. The quad was quiet, a fine drizzle misting the air and creating fuzzy halos around the old-fashioned street lamps. Only one couple were walking slowly arm in arm towards Holy Trinity, their eyes trained on the cobbles, paying her no attention. Once they had gone, the space was deserted.

She had her key at the ready, and with fumbling fingers turned it in the lock. But as she turned to close the door behind her, she almost stopped breathing. Beyond the wall of the graveyard and immediately in her line of sight, a darkly-hooded figure was standing beside a tall, leaning tombstone. Motionless. Plainly observing her, but with no eyes visible. Where it had come from, she had no idea – there had been no one there a moment ago.

Heart banging inside her chest, Georgia slammed the door, bolting it at once. Her whole body quaking, she had to use both hands to guide the key into the lock and turn it. She heaved the doorstop across, then stood rigidly in the vestibule, listening. Hardly daring to breathe. For the briefest moment, she thought she heard faint chanting; a strange, soulless male voice. And then all was quiet once more.

Georgia had already closed the curtains before leaving the house earlier, and this time she wasn't going to torture herself any more by looking out into the quad. Her head reeling, she

stumbled through to the kitchen to ensure all was secure at the back of the house, then poured herself an extra large whisky. She had started on her third bottle now. Popping a sleeping pill from the blister pack she kept in the cupboard, she swallowed it with a mouthful of the liquor. It was the only way she was ever going to sleep tonight. After the day she'd had, the thought that she was being observed by Ned's ghostly monk was the final straw. She really did wonder if she was going mad.

Chapter 21

Georgia

Friday, 14 October 2022

Georgia wondered about the pattern in the perpetrator's behaviour, whether a brief lull could mean they were out of town or simply allowing the dust to settle before making their next move. To lure her into a false sense of security, then catch her completely off guard. Pull something even nastier out of the bag.

Things had been ticking along steadily with Cole. She felt as though she'd regressed about twenty-five years, a teenager with a new crush, a small thrill running through her each time she caught sight of him. He'd even turned up at Cuckoo Cottage with a colourful bunch of chrysanthemums the other day.

"Cheap and cheerful," he'd said, smiling almost apologetically as he handed them over. "Sorry I couldn't do the dozen roses bit."

But Georgia was touched. She couldn't remember Trevor

ever buying her flowers spontaneously. And the fact that Cole could ill-afford them made the gesture even more meaningful.

The few afternoons she'd spent with Cole had been lovely. On one unseasonably warm day, they'd held hands as they explored the old, narrow streets close to the cathedral, where he'd shown her the beautiful, half-timbered building known as Ford's Hospital, alms houses built for impoverished local people during the sixteenth century. As they ambled through the flag-stoned courtyard, Georgia had raised an eyebrow at the strict rules for its inhabitants still written above the threshold. Apparently, residents would be ejected for: 'haunting alehouses, making strife or other notable misdemeanours'. Cole had laughed, saying that the pair of them had scuppered their own chances, then.

Another time, when the weather had been wet, Cole had grabbed the copy of the *Guardian* from the table in her living room and they'd worked through the 'Quick' crossword sitting on cushions on the floor together. Georgia had put her hands over her eyes when he'd initially suggested the cryptic one and he'd grinned, stating he'd always preferred the quick one himself. She didn't believe him for a minute. As they pored over the clues, he'd slid an arm around her shoulder and kept turning to her, his eyes warm, the closeness of him making her tingle.

They'd drunk tea and talked, Cole opening up more about his past and his difficult relationship with his father. He had this endearing habit of raising a hand to the back of his head when he was reliving anything uncomfortable. Georgia wanted so badly to tell him about her own childhood. But it was ingrained in her to stick to the narrative: that there was nothing significant to impart. That she'd had a very ordinary, safe upbringing.

As always, they hadn't shared more than a kiss before they parted company. It was sweet. *He* was sweet.

Apart from the Tuesday, Cole had been into the Orb every evening she'd been at work, but Georgia was so wrapped up in her own anxiety now that even his presence failed to take her mind off things. Every time the pub door opened, her heart quickened, expecting to see Jethro Jackson striding in. Or worse still, to find him, or someone else, lurking in one of the alleyways that led from the quad, hanging back until Cole had walked her home, leaving her alone and vulnerable once more.

Although a fortnight had passed now and she had seen nothing more of Jackson. Maybe – *just maybe* – the police had actually arrested him. But Georgia didn't dare hope that she'd seen the last of the man. Her thoughts kept flitting between Jackson, or someone else connected to the woman in the photo, being responsible for her unwanted 'gifts', or the root cause being something even darker rearing its head from her past. Of course, it wasn't impossible she was being tormented simultaneously by different people, for different reasons. Regardless, she was in turmoil, bracing herself for the next thing, whatever that was going to be. She was on pins whenever she was alone at home, her senses on high alert. If the aim was just to intimidate her, they were doing an excellent job so far. She was living on her nerves, popping tranquilisers during the day, swilling whisky and sleeping pills at night. Any noise, any evidence of footfall outside Cuckoo Cottage after dark sent her flying to the window in fear of what she might find. Each night as she left the house to go to the Orb, she found herself frantically scanning round, straining to see beyond the graveyard wall, checking every window, every doorway that looked out onto the quad. Cole knew about the emails, but not any of the other stuff. She felt it would raise too many questions. And potentially questions about her own past, the thought of which made her stomach churn.

Despite promising Minnie she'd try to give her space, Georgia's anxiety after the spurious text message had driven her to message and ring the girl constantly, desperate for reassurance that all was okay. She'd tried, *really* tried, to keep her distance. But rather than wait for Minnie to contact her to deliver bad news, or worse still, one of her housemates to say something terrible had happened to Minnie, she felt compelled to check and had even gone to her digs a couple of times. Georgia had noticed Minnie's housemates exchanging meaningful glances when she'd called round, as if they thought she might be a little unhinged. Which, in fairness, she must have seemed. But the worry was all-consuming, a thick shadow threatening to engulf her. In the end Minnie had threatened to block Georgia's number and refuse her entry to the house if she persisted, saying it was doing neither of them any good.

"You need help, Mum." She'd actually said those words to her and it had felt like a slap in the face.

Georgia had been completely taken aback. Minnie had never spoken to her like that before – not in such an angry tone of voice, anyway. The previous evening, Georgia had contacted Yiannis to tell him she'd be late, in order to call round to the house when Minnie hadn't responded to her messages, just to check she was okay. Minnie did seem a bit harassed, to be fair. Maybe she'd caught her at a bad time. Although the constant fear Georgia was living under, the pills – it was inevitable that they'd have an effect on her mental state. She was beginning to feel desperate and wondered if Minnie was right. But then – at least Minnie felt able to speak her mind to her. That was a good thing, wasn't it? Georgia thought back to her relationship with her own parents, how she would never have dared talk back to them, nor challenge them about anything. She winced at the memory of her father slamming her face hard into her dinner on one occasion, when she'd had the temerity to question whether the foul-smelling meat on her plate had gone off; of how her mother had jeered and told her she'd asked for it by being such a fussy eater. But she wasn't, she really wasn't. Though according to her parents, she was ungrateful, spoiled. A whingeing brat. An encumbrance – not that they'd have used that term. A pain in the arse. A waste of space. They'd told her so constantly. Never a word of encouragement or affection.

Then worse, far worse, was how her dad had reacted to the stray black and white kitten she had smuggled into the house. The poor creature had been bedraggled, mewing plaintively, cowering beneath a hedge. It was so small, so helpless. All Georgia wanted was something to love, something to cuddle; some company. She'd hidden her in a cardboard box under the bed whenever she went out, sneaked scraps of food up to her room, a saucer of milk when nobody was looking. Every day, she had been excited to get back from school to see how the little cat was doing. But at some point, her father had clearly cottoned on to the kitten's presence. After just a few days, she'd come home one afternoon to find the sweet soul limp and lifeless on her bedroom floor, a trace of blood at the corner of her tiny pink mouth. Georgia had cradled the kitten in her arms and wept for hours. She knew without doubt that her father was responsible and couldn't bear to think what the evil bastard had done to the poor defenceless creature. Hate wasn't a strong enough word for how she felt about him. Looking back, Georgia realised that this was the turning point for her. The final straw: the event that had truly hardened her heart. That had turned the worm.

It wasn't until Minnie's arrival that she'd started to look at things differently. Here was someone who she could love without fear of rejection; who would love her back forever, unconditionally. Or so she had thought. But although Georgia worried now in her more rational moments that her own erratic behaviour was driving a wedge between them, she simply couldn't help herself.

If Minnie resented being under scrutiny, Georgia realised she would have to keep her distance and watch from afar. Minnie had stormed out of the living room and up the stairs after her little outburst the previous night, leaving Georgia staring after her in dismay. Fatima had been hovering in the doorway but made a sharp exit, casting Ajab a grimace as she went. Georgia sat in the armchair opposite Ajab, who looked decidedly uncomfortable.

"I think Minnie's just a bit stressed out by everything at the moment, Mrs Parnell," he offered. "You know, with her coursework and everything. And she didn't say too much, but I think that thing with the text messed with her head a bit."

"You get how I feel, don't you Ajab?" Georgia had searched his face in anguish. "She's my world and I'm beside myself. I mean, if someone pulls a stunt like that, what else are they capable of? It was downright malicious." The memory of how that text had made *her* feel made Georgia shudder.

He looked dubious. "I suppose – I mean, I know you're anxious and everything, but maybe . . ."

"Listen, I'm just looking out for her. I need to know she's okay. For my own peace of mind. I'm all on my own now and she's all I've got – you do understand, don't you?" She felt a bit guilty for using the poor-little-me defence, but desperate times called for desperate measures. "You're a good friend to Mins – will you keep an eye on her for me? Let me know if there's anything odd going on? But keep it between the two of us, yes?"

Ajab looked aghast. "Mrs Parnell, Mins is my friend! I can't spy on her. It just wouldn't be right."

"I'm not asking you to spy on her. Just to look out for her – and let me know if anything else odd happens. I know she won't want me to worry, but it's worse for me if I'm being kept in the dark. *Please.*"

He'd finally agreed, albeit reluctantly, to keep her informed of any potential developments and gave her his mobile number. "But please, for emergencies only," he had stressed.

Over a message to Ajab that morning, Georgia had eventually managed to establish that he was finishing an assignment at home, but Minnie had a one-hour tutorial at 2pm. Georgia resolved to follow her to uni; watch to see if anyone appeared to be trailing her or paying her undue attention.

Dressed in an old grey hoodie and the obligatory sunglasses, Georgia had left Cuckoo Cottage just before 1pm and walked to the Kenilworth Road, then waited on the opposite side of the street from the student house. She leaned against a wall, trying to look suitably casual and unobtrusive, phone in hand as a useful prop. The occasional person walked past, but no one paid her much attention, nor did they appear to be looking in the direction of Minnie's house. Spotting her daughter emerging from the front door at about 1.20pm, Georgia paused for a few moments before crossing the road, and began to follow at a safe distance.

Georgia was exasperated to see Minnie using the pedestrian underpass to approach the town centre. And the girl had her head down – no doubt checking her phone as she walked. Didn't she realise how dangerous that could be – that someone could easily jump out on her unawares? Did she use that same route every time?

Silly, silly girl. Georgia felt exasperated. She lagged well behind but pursued Minnie through the tunnel and up towards Warwick Row, glancing from left to right and over her shoulder constantly.

Suddenly, as if from nowhere, a tall figure came running from somewhere to the right and across the grassy area beyond the exit from the underpass, grabbing Minnie by the shoulders. Minnie let out a loud shriek.

Her heart hammering, Georgia broke into a run. She couldn't remember ever moving so fast.

"Let her go, you bastard!" she screamed.

To her horror, Minnie whipped round, the colour draining from her face as her eyes landed on Georgia. At once, Georgia recognised the person hanging onto Minnie's shoulders as her housemate, Sonia. The two girls stared at her.

"Were you – were you *following* me, Mum?" Minnie looked horrified.

"I – I was just . . ."

Sonia looked from one to the other, grimacing. She released her grasp on Minnie, stepping away a fraction and throwing her a sympathetic look. "Erm – I'll leave you two to have a little chat. Sorry if I scared you, Mrs Parnell."

As Sonia walked briskly away, Minnie turned to Georgia, her face a mixture of anger and incredulity. "What the hell were you doing?"

Hot tears spilled from Georgia's eyes. "I'm sorry, love. I'm *so* sorry. I'm just so anxious about you all the time, and you're not talking to me, and . . ."

"Pfft – and you wonder why?" Minnie shook her head, her jaw tight.

Georgia reached for her hand, but Minnie pulled back sharply.

"I can't cope with this, Mum. I'm here to study, find my feet, and yet I'm feeling exactly as I did when we were in Warchester. Like I'm wearing a bloody tag."

Georgia dropped her gaze in shame. She'd had no idea she was making Minnie feel that way. She cleared her throat.

"Will you at least let me explain? After last night, I was worried I'd pushed you to the limit, so I thought if I kept an eye on you from a distance, I'd know you were okay without hassling you all the time. I feel like you're growing away from me, and it's killing me. And after that thing with the text, it brought it home to me even more what it would mean if anything happened to you. You're so precious to me, Mins. But I never meant you to feel stifled. Please forgive me."

Minnie stared at her for a moment. She blew out a breath, seeming to relax a little.

"Mum, I get that you're anxious. And I'd had a crap day yesterday and probably overreacted. But you really have to take a step back. I'm fine – and I promise I'll be the first to let you know if anything else weird happens. You're blowing it out of all proportion. I don't go out on my own after dark; I don't take stupid risks."

"But the subway!" protested Georgia, wiping her eyes with her cuff. "You shouldn't cut through there on your own."

Minnie rolled her eyes. "For goodness' sake, it's broad daylight. I wouldn't walk through there by myself at night. I'm not that daft." She sighed. "Look, we need to come to some sort of arrangement. I'll call you at an agreed time, just so you know I'm all right. We can meet up – but at an agreed time. But you can't spy on me, Mum, it's an invasion of my privacy. I'm not a child anymore."

Georgia nodded sheepishly. "I won't. I promise."

"And by the way – please don't get bothering Ajab again. I saw your number come up on his phone, so he had to spill the beans." Minnie managed a small grin. "He couldn't keep a secret to save his life."

She peeled back her sleeve suddenly and pulled a face. "I am *late*. Come on, walk with me. Or maybe we can run – I'd no idea you could sprint like that."

Georgia forced a laugh. "Neither did I."

They linked arms and continued together at a swift pace up towards Broadgate. It gave Georgia a warm feeling. At least their encounter, however ill-timed, seemed to have cleared the air. But it would take a lot more than that to set Georgia's mind at rest permanently.

Because it had only been Sonia jumping out on Minnie on this occasion. But what if the next time it wasn't?

Chapter 22

Minnie

Thursday, 20 October 2022

From the moment she had moved into the house, it had quickly become apparent that Angela was quite content with her own company. At uni, she chose to sit on her own at the back during lectures, and even when in the house, would spend most of her time in her room. On the odd occasion Minnie had tapped her door to see if she wanted a hot drink, or to come and watch a movie on Netflix with the rest of them, she would decline politely. She seemed almost obsessively focused on the course and always had textbooks spread out across her bed and the laptop open, though was quick to conceal the screen, almost as if, Minnie thought, she was embarrassed for anyone to see her work. Or on the other hand, perhaps, she thought they'd copy her ideas. It was hard to know. Angela would use the facilities in the kitchen (mainly the kettle and the microwave), but chose to eat in her room. No one had really got to know her at all. It seemed a bit of a shame.

"Well," Fatima said, as they sat down cross-legged on the rug, digging into boxes of pizza and bottles of beer in front of the TV. It was the third Thursday after Angela's arrival and Minnie, in a buoyant mood as things were going so well with Jake, had decided to treat everyone. They had all agreed on watching *The Woman in the Window* on Netflix, as it was one film none of them had seen. Yet again, Angela had made a polite but firm excuse not to join them, saying she had to finish an essay for the following morning.

"Dunno what I was worried about," Fatima went on, taking a huge bite of pizza and peeling a string of cheese from her chin. "She might just as well not be here, for all we see of her. I s'pose I can't complain. It's almost like having a phantom housemate."

Ajab frowned. "D'you really think she's okay? I mean, she doesn't have visitors; she never mixes with anyone at uni either, as far as I've noticed. She's never mentioned anyone she's close to, apart from her mum, and she hasn't even got her now."

"It seems a bit sad," agreed Sonia. "But what can we do if she doesn't want to socialise? It's her prerogative."

Minnie had to agree. She was slowly becoming resigned to the fact that Angela just didn't want to be part of their little group. With the apparent lack of any other friends, she'd have thought Angela might have welcomed some company. At least they'd all made the effort, even if Angela hadn't. Part of her still wondered if maybe Angela had some sort of personality disorder, but whatever the reason for her social ineptitude, there wasn't much they could do about it if she insisted on shutting herself away all the time. Outwardly at least, the woman seemed happy enough, so Minnie resolved to just let her get on with it. But still she felt concerned that Angela wasn't really looking after herself. She was very thin and didn't seem to eat much, apart from the odd McDonald's she'd have delivered, or some quick processed snack. Maybe she was one of those people who were phobic about eating in public.

Puffing out her cheeks, Minnie rose to her feet and went through to the kitchen, returning with a plate.

"I'll take her up a couple of slices of pizza. We'll never eat all this lot and at least she'll have had something a bit more substantial than those bloody Pot Noodles she seems to live on."

Fatima rolled her eyes. "Personally I wouldn't bother," she said through a mouthful of food. "If the lazy cow can't be arsed to make herself anything to eat, it's not our problem."

Part of Minnie agreed, but she still felt she ought to offer. She knew how it felt to lose a parent. Maybe Angela was depressed. Grief wasn't something you could shake off overnight. She climbed the stairs to the top floor, pausing to take a breath as she reached the landing.

She pricked up her ears. It sounded as if Angela was talking to someone on the phone. Intrigued, Minnie tiptoed across the carpet to listen.

"Not yet. I've already told you." Angela's voice was low, slightly impatient. "I can't – no, I need . . ." There was a lengthy pause as whoever she was talking to responded, the voice muffled and unintelligible at the other end of the line. "Look, this is getting us nowhere. I'll call you tomorrow. I can't really talk now. It might not . . ."

It might not *what*? Minnie was intrigued. She shifted her weight unintentionally and the floorboard beneath her creaked. She gritted her teeth and froze for a moment, aware that Angela had probably heard. Thinking it might be best to announce her presence rather than be found out, Minnie rapped on the door.

"Angela? I've brought you a bit of pizza."

The door opened a fraction. Angela looked flustered.

"Oh. I – I'm not really h-hungry."

"Go on, take it. You might fancy some later." Minnie thrust the plate towards her, peering surreptitiously past Angela's figure in the doorway. The room was a mess as ever: the laptop open next to the lamp on the small desk, piles of scrawled notes laid out randomly across the floor. Various empty cartons and packets had been discarded next to the bed; dirty laundry was piled in one corner. The air smelled stale.

Angela smiled sheepishly. "I need to t-tidy up, I know. Just t-trying to f-finish this assignment – you know how it is." She almost snatched the plate from Minnie's hand. "Th-thanks for this. I p-probably will w-want it in a bit – just need to f-focus at the moment while I'm in f-full flow, so— " She began to close the door, but not quickly enough to prevent Minnie from hearing a message pinging through on the phone lying on the bed.

"P-probably my cousin up in Yorkshire." Angela's eyes darted to the mobile, clearly feeling the need to explain. "I ought to s-switch it off really – too much of a d-distraction when I should be g-getting on with s-stuff."

Minnie glanced at the phone. The case was distinctive. She recognised the design as *The Tree of Life* by Gustav Klimt, one of Trevor's favourite artists. It wasn't the sort of thing she would have expected to appeal to Angela, somehow. She could imagine her preferring a Disney princess, or something equally cute and kitsch.

"Give yourself a break. You know what they say – all work and no play . . ." Minnie trailed off, seeing a look of blatant irritation pass across Angela's face. "Sorry if I disturbed you. I'll leave you to it."

As the door closed abruptly behind her, Minnie stood for a moment, slightly put out. Angela's behaviour was bordering on rude. Fatima was right. Maybe she shouldn't bother in future. It was Angela's loss.

She rejoined the others, who looked up questioningly as she came into the living room.

Minnie shrugged. "She's still working on her bloody essay. Christ knows how long it must be. And her room looks like a bomb's hit it." She pulled a face, lowering herself to the floor and reaching for the bottle of beer she'd left on the coffee table. "And by the way, it sounds as if she's got one cousin she talks to at least, so she's not all alone in the world after all."

Sonia grinned. "There you go, you don't have to feel so worried about her then."

Minnie nodded. But her slightly odd exchange with Angela had dampened her earlier upbeat mood. She wanted to put all thoughts of it out of her mind.

"Yep, Angela's a big girl. She can take care of herself." Taking a large swig of beer, she ran the back of her hand across her mouth. "Who's got the remote? Half the evening's gone already. Let's get the film on."

Chapter 23

Minnie

Wednesday, 26 October 2022

Though she had been seeing Jake for almost a month, Minnie had yet to invite him round to the house. And the flat he was sharing with his co-workers was cramped and 'not ideal', he'd told her, wrinkling his nose. They were taking things slowly, and that suited her fine. So far, their dates had all consisted of a few hours in various local pubs, Minnie being very careful to steer clear of anywhere straying too close to the Golden Orb. The Old Windmill had become a favourite.

Jake had a good sense of humour and she found him easy company. The age gap didn't even enter her head: he certainly didn't look old and their shared taste in music and TV programmes meant there was always something to talk about. But though he kept things generally lighthearted, the topic of his childhood always seemed to cast a cloud over things. If he volunteered stuff, that was fine. But Minnie resolved not to ask any more questions. She'd hoped that sharing stories with him about her own background might have got him to open up, but had given up trying to coax things out of him, as it was clearly a sore point. Reading between the lines, he'd had a miserable existence, particularly owing to the attitude of his adoptive father. The man sounded like a complete shit. She wondered what had happened to Jake's real parents. It only made her feel more for him, somehow, this knowledge that he'd had such a raw deal.

Jake would usually be waiting for her whenever they arranged to meet. But for the first time ever, he was more than fifteen minutes late. It was quarter to eight, the evening air was chilly and damp, and though she didn't really want to go in on her own, she'd decided to stand inside the doorway of the Old Windmill rather than braving the cold. Now she was frequently having to move aside for people coming and going as the pub filled up. Minnie was beginning to worry. She checked her phone again in case she'd missed a message, but there was nothing.

"Hello! I'm *so* sorry."

She jerked her head up to see Jake, breathless and slightly ruffled-looking, walking briskly towards the entrance from across the street.

Minnie flooded with relief. "I was beginning to think I'd been stood up." She managed a small smile. "What kept you?"

"Bloody gaffer. Asked me to do a repair job for one of his tenants at the last minute and it took a lot longer than I thought. He's been in a foul mood today – home from a fortnight in the sun and obviously pissed off to be back." He smiled uncertainly. "Did you not want to wait inside?"

Minnie pulled a face. "I felt a bit conspicuous on my own." She touched her hair and Jake grinned.

"You'd turn a few heads even with that covered."

217

Minnie felt her cheeks warm and dropped her eyes. She never knew quite how to react to a compliment. The sudden touch of Jake's hand on her arm made her jump slightly.

His voice was soft. "What d'you say we get one in here, then try elsewhere for a change?"

"Sure. It is a bit busy tonight – shall we go somewhere quieter?"

Jake paused. "We could go back to mine, if you like. The other lads are out on the lash this evening – probably won't be back till late. I've got a bottle of wine in the fridge, unless they've helped themselves."

Minnie thought for a moment. She suddenly realised she didn't actually know where Jake was staying. "Is it far?"

"Nope. Quite near the cathedral." He studied her face with a smile. "Don't look so worried! I can call a cab to get you home later." He steered her into a nook with a free table. "Have a seat for a bit and I'll go to the bar."

Within half an hour, they were walking up through the town centre. The streets were fairly empty; there was fine drizzle in the air, and the pavements shone with the blurred reflection of the street lamps. Minnie began to feel apprehensive as they crossed Broadgate and approached the quad at the back of the old cathedral and the Orb. She knew her mum would be working that evening and didn't want to risk being seen. It felt too soon to explain that she was seeing someone – especially someone almost ten years older than herself. She and her mum had reached a sort of truce after their confrontation when Minnie had caught Georgia following her, but Minnie still wanted to keep her distance for a bit. It was as though every time she saw or spoke to her mum, it seemed to reignite this irrational anxiety in her about Minnie's welfare. Hopefully Georgia would realise eventually that no news was good news and start to relax about things. Out of sight, out of mind. If she saw her with

Jake, it might lead to a whole new interrogation that she could do without and increase Georgia's ridiculous paranoia further. "D'you want to go in there for one?" Jake turned to her as they drew nearer. "I've been in a few times before. Looks pretty laid-back tonight." He guided her over to peer through the window, cupping his hands around his eyes against the glass. Minnie's stomach turned over as she spotted her mum moving around behind the bar.

"No, no. Let's just go to yours." Minnie smiled briefly, hooking her arm into his and tugging him away. She drew back sharply from the window and began to steer him towards the Guildhall. "Is it this way?"

Jake looked a little surprised. "No, back over there." He indicated vaguely to their left. "But we can go down here if you want, have a quick look and see if there's anything going on in the Guildhall. I hear sometimes they have ghost tours and stuff around Halloween. Might be a laugh."

They were virtually outside Georgia's front door now. Minnie kept her eyes trained straight ahead, anxious not to draw attention to the building in any way. The curtains were drawn, but she noticed that Georgia had left a light on in the sitting room. Minnie felt a pang of guilt as she thought of her mum going home later to an empty house. But then – it had been Georgia's choice to move into the cottage. Apart from the histrionics that time about the monk, she seemed to have settled in well, as far as she could tell. It seemed to be her fixation with what Minnie was up to that was the problem.

As they reached the entrance to the Guildhall, Jake stopped. He puffed out his cheeks. "Nah. It's all in darkness. We'll have to try another night." He paused. "Hey, d'you want to take a look at the old priory? It's all lit up at night."

Normally Minnie would have been hesitant. There were occasionally some really dodgy-looking characters hanging around in the old quarter after dark. But keen for any reason to get him away from the quad, she agreed with enthusiasm. "Yeah – that'd be good."

They turned tail and crossed the square diagonally. In spite of herself, Minnie couldn't help casting a glance to her left and through the leaded windows of the Orb once more. She could see Georgia speaking to a dark-haired man, who was leaning on the bar and laughing. Flirting, even, judging by the way he was looking at her. From Georgia's relaxed body language, they appeared to know one another well. Minnie felt a knot form in her stomach. She was at once curious as to who he might be. Georgia hadn't mentioned anyone in particular that she'd got to know; only Yiannis and Freddie. But asking the question would give away the fact that Minnie had been on the doorstep and hadn't called in, and would undoubtedly have led to a grilling from her mother. It would have to wait until the next time she visited with Ajab – hopefully the man would be a regular. It felt strange, inappropriate even, to think that her mum might be involved with someone with the memory of her dad's loss still so raw. Minnie knew that her mum would need to move on eventually. She was still a relatively young woman; it was a bit much to expect her to behave like a nun for the rest of her days. But it still seemed too soon for Minnie's liking. She wanted her mum to make friends, of course she did. But the thought that she could be so quick to replace Trevor left Minnie with an unpleasant taste in her mouth. It felt – disrespectful.

Jake led Minnie by the hand through a small entry at the end of the terrace of houses opposite the Orb. The area was dark and secluded, and smelled faintly of urine and weed. It made Minnie want to hold onto him more tightly. The passageway opened out into another cobbled, dimly-lit street. They were the only people about, and she felt suddenly nervous, as though someone might be lurking in the shadows waiting to jump out on them. She stalled for a moment, her eyes darting anxiously as she pulled him back.

"What's up?" Jake turned to her, his eyebrows slanting in a question.

"Are you sure this is a good idea?"

He smiled. "It's fine, don't worry. We're nearly there now. This way." He motioned with his free hand towards yet another dark corridor between the buildings ahead.

Though she had seen the excavation of the Benedictine priory before, everything looked different in the dark and Minnie hadn't quite got her bearings. Clinging onto Jake's hand, she allowed him to guide her through the alleyway, the other end of which led to a clear view of the old monastery's uneven sandstone wall straight in front of them, and the faint glow of lights shining up from below ground-level. They crossed the deserted square, passing an Indian restaurant to their left, shuttered and in total darkness.

"Early closing," remarked Jake. "They do a mean biriani. I'll have to take you there some time."

The pair made their way to the rediscovered priory, which offered a view of the old refectory through its huge glass wall. They stood side by side, staring down into the depths of the undercroft. Some of the restored stone walls had been limewashed for effect. Mannequins dressed as monks had been placed around the building, recreating a typical scene from their era: one standing, hands on hips next to a pillar, one posed as if warming his hands next to the remains of a huge stone fireplace; another climbing a short flight of steps, a lighted candle leading his way. There was an odd sense of other-worldliness, as though the monks might actually spring to life at any moment.

Cloaked in darkness and with the damp chill of the night air, their surroundings had taken on an unpleasantly menacing atmosphere. Minnie shivered. "It feels a lot more eerie here than it did in the daytime."

Jake jerked his head round. "Not spooked are you, Minnie Mouse?" He studied her for a moment, an unreadable look on his face, not a glimmer of a smile. His pupils were dilated in the dim.

Suddenly unnerved, Minnie released his hand and took a step backwards. "Okay, I think I've seen enough. Can we go now?"

Jake seemed not to have heard. He turned back to the window, placing his palms flat against the glass. "They say it's haunted, you know. Do you believe in ghosts?"

His voice sounded oddly faraway, as though he was deep in thought.

Minnie's chest tightened. "I – I don't know."

"I see them. Everywhere. But mostly up here." He tapped his head, still staring straight ahead. She studied his glazed expression with apprehension. It was as though he was a million miles away, haunted by something from his past. Any evidence of his usually happy-go-lucky demeanour had vanished.

"*Hell-o!*"

The bellow of a male voice came from behind, almost making Minnie leap into the air. Her heart thumping, she spun round to find a man, his head covered by a dark woollen hat, standing just a few feet away. He seemed to have appeared from nowhere. Fearfully scanning his hands for a weapon but seeing only a lit cigarette, she still grabbed Jake by the arm, moving into the protection of his shadow.

Apparently unperturbed, Jake turned to see who was addressing them, his face breaking into a grin. The man's rude interruption seemed to have shaken him from his reverie. "Hello yourself, you feckin' eejit. Where'd you spring from?"

"I'm just heading home. Left Eric chatting to some bird in Wetherspoon's," he glanced at Minnie, grimacing. "Sorry – some

222

young lady. I nipped in the club but it was dead, so thought I'd call it a night. Taking the short cut." He waved back towards the alleyway Minnie and Jake had just passed through.

Minnie looked from Jake to the man, whose eyes had travelled to her. He too was grinning. It had taken a moment for her to realise that the pair knew one another.

Jake spread out a hand. "Minnie, allow me to introduce one of the reprobates I have the misfortune to share a house with – and call a friend."

The man drew on his cigarette, blowing the smoke skyward, then leaned towards her, extending his free hand. She shook it hesitantly, glancing back at Jake for reassurance.

"Pleased to meet you at last, Minnie. I'm Heggs."

"You nearly gave me a heart attack," she said, her breathing gradually settling once more.

"Sorry. I thought you'd've heard me coming, like."

"Well, we didn't. Anyway, I'm just glad you're not intending to rob us or anything." Minnie forced a smile, though she was still a bit annoyed that Heggs had crept up on them like that, even if Jake was clearly unshaken. It was a pretty stupid thing to do, given the number of muggings and rapes reported after dark.

"So, where're yous two off to, then?" Heggs looked from one to the other quizzically.

Jake hesitated, shooting a look at Minnie. "Erm – just on our way for another bevvy somewhere. Thought I'd bring Minnie here to see this all lit up first."

It seemed Heggs's appearance had put paid to Jake's plans of taking her back to the house. But by now, any earlier thoughts of a cosy couple of hours alone with him no longer seemed so appealing. All Minnie wanted to do was go home.

She turned to Jake, trying to keep her tone light. "Actually, I think I'd better be getting back, if you don't mind. I'm a bit knackered and I've got a lecture first thing tomorrow."

Jake looked deflated. "Oh." He pursed his lips. "Okay, fair enough. I'll walk you."

"Just to the taxi rank will be fine – I'll get a cab." Minnie said quickly. She nodded at Heggs. "Nice to meet you, anyway. Do try not to scare the shit out of me next time though, please."

The man gave a gravelly laugh. "I'll bear it in mind."

The three of them walked through the passageway in single file, Jake leading, with Minnie close behind and Heggs at the rear, back the way they had come. Finally they reached the alley leading to the quad behind the cathedral. Heggs pulled up abruptly.

"Well, this is me then. See you again I hope, Minnie." Heggs tapped his temple with a forefinger, winking briefly. He turned to Jake. "Expecting another heavy day tomorrow. Old Jethro's got one on 'im – he says the bizzies are still sniffing around for some reason. He's still going on about those photos – he reckons someone's trying to frame 'im. I wouldn't fancy being in their shoes if he catches up with 'em. I reckon that's why he took off, hoping it'd die down. He thought he was being tailed when he landed yesterday and he's been like a bear with a sore head. Friggin' paranoid, I reckon."

He rolled his eyes and Jake laughed. "Tell me about it. And even if they were watching, it'll blow over, I'm sure – his pal in CID will calm it down for him."

Heggs nodded, smirking. "Hopefully. Can't stand 'im when he gets all twitchy – feels like you're treading on eggshells all the time. Anyway, I'll let you go. See ya later, mate."

"Yeah, see you in a bit."

Minnie watched as Heggs walked off to their left, disappearing through the narrow doorway of a house at the far end of the terrace opposite her mum's new home. She felt her stomach turn a somersault.

"Do you – is that where you live?" she asked Jake. Her eyes travelled to the light in the window at Cuckoo Cottage, her heart quickening. Everything seemed slightly unreal.

"Yep. Told you it was near the cathedral, didn't I?" Jake grinned. He pointed up at the tower. "That feckin' bell goes off all the time, though. Can't remember the last time I had a lie-in."

Minnie forced a laugh. She looked across the square at the light and movement coming from inside the Orb, wondering suddenly if her mum and Jake had ever met in total ignorance of their connection. It was too weird.

"Look, sorry about Heggs – I thought the pair of 'em'd be out for the whole evening."

"Can't be helped." Minnie chewed her lip. "Um . . . your boss – is he a bit dodgy?"

"Jethro?" Jake scratched his head. "He does a bit of wheeling and dealing, I think. Maybe sneaks the odd lorry-load of booze and fags through customs now and then. Nothing really bad, though."

Minnie paused. "He doesn't ask you to do anything . . . you know, iffy, does he?"

"Me? God, no. I'd give the game away if I got stopped. I mean, would you trust a man with a face like this?" He pulled a goofy expression and Minnie couldn't help but laugh. She couldn't really imagine Jake being involved in anything illegal. He was too – well, nice.

She wasn't sure she liked the sound of his boss, though. "What was that Heggs said about photos?"

"Dunno – Jethro reckons somebody had given the cops some snaps of him; said he'd been made to look like he was up to something when he wasn't. Not porn or anything, if that's what you're thinking." He chuckled. "Bit of a storm in a teacup, I think."

Jake took both of her hands in his own suddenly. "You sure you're not wanting to go in there for one before you go?" He tipped his head towards the pub, widening his eyes hopefully.

"No, no thanks. I really am pretty wrecked, to be honest. Another time, maybe."

"No problem." His smile faltered. "Let's get you that cab, then."

As they began to walk from the quad, Minnie glanced back at the house Heggs had entered. A light had gone on in the upstairs window, though she could see no one. But in the adjoining house, still in darkness, her eyes were drawn to a hint of movement. A shapeless figure appeared to be standing, or maybe sitting – she wasn't sure, behind the glass, lit briefly by what looked like the flash of a torch, which was quickly extinguished. The distraction caused her to stumble a little on the uneven paving slabs, and she let out a nervous laugh as Jake grabbed her.

"Whoa – steady now."

"I need to look where I'm going – people will think I'm drunk."

Shooting another look over her shoulder, Minnie saw that the figure had receded from view. Shuddering a little, she wondered if she could have imagined it.

*

Jake stood awkwardly beside her as they waited at the taxi rank, his hands pushed deep into his trouser pockets. "Sorry – it's been a bit of a wash-out tonight, hasn't it?"

Minnie squeezed a small smile. "It's okay. We can do it another time."

A black cab pulled in. Jake opened the rear door for her to enter. "I'll call you, shall I? Maybe do something on Friday?" His expression was a little sad, his voice tentative. All thoughts of his slightly disconcerting behaviour outside the priory melted away as she looked into his dark eyes.

"Yeah, for sure." She leaned forwards for him to kiss her gently on the mouth and felt the familiar tingle that it always invoked. "I'll look forward to it."

As the taxi pulled away, she watched through the window as Jake shaped his hands into a heart, his face lit with that disarming grin that never failed to turn her to jelly. She felt a warm rush pass through her as she sat back in her seat.

It had been a blip, she told herself. Jake had had a miserable childhood. It must be something he still wrestled with. She couldn't expect him to be permanently upbeat, given everything he'd had to contend with. Maybe it was time she invited him to her house instead, so that he could meet her friends; make things a bit more official.

Maybe she needed to bite the bullet and introduce him to her mother.

Chapter 24

Minnie

Thursday, 27 October 2022

Minnie awoke abruptly to an almighty shriek coming from somewhere in the house. Daylight streamed through the blinds, but it took her a moment to realise the sound hadn't come from her dream. Hoisting herself up in bed, she strained to listen.

"It's gone under there – look!"

She could hear Sonia's muffled but slightly panicky voice, followed by another scream from Fatima.

"Oh my God – get it *OUT*!"

Slipping out of bed, Minnie pulled on a hoodie over her pyjamas and padded out onto the landing.

"What's g-going on?"

Looking up, she saw Angela peering down the stairwell from above, wrapped in a dressing gown.

"Dunno. I've only just woken up." Minnie made her way down the stairs, followed closely by Angela.

Fatima was half-concealed behind the living room door, peeping through the gap.

"Has it gone out?"

"What? What the hell's up?"

"It's a little mouse." Sonia appeared from the kitchen, red-faced and flustered. "It was running around in here when I opened the door first thing. I've been trying to steer it towards the back door, but it squeezed under that gap in the corner, below the cupboards."

"We've *got* to catch it and put it back outside!" Fatima sounded hysterical, her eyes looking as though they were in danger of popping out of their sockets. "It could be pregnant – they have loads of babies. We could get a frigging infestation!"

"Calm down. It's only a mouse." Minnie let out a groan of exasperation. "Just stay in there if you're so freaked out." She steered the quivering Fatima into an armchair, then went into the kitchen. Angela followed tentatively, closing the door behind them. Sonia was on her hands and knees now, her face near the gap in the corner, the torch on her phone activated.

"C-can you see anything?" Angela looked on with mild interest.

"No. The kickboard runs right along here – it could be down at the other end by now, or even in the wall cavity. We're stuffed if it's got into there."

Angela was leaning now, stony-faced, against the wall next to the refrigerator, her eyes continuing to scour the floor. Minnie glanced at her, wondering what was going through the woman's head. She appeared strangely detached.

"Look! There it is!" Minnie spotted the tiny creature reappearing suddenly at the far end of the row of cupboards. Grabbing a tea towel, she threw it, hoping to cover the mouse, which promptly darted across the floor and underneath the huge fridge-freezer, close to where Angela was standing.

"Shit." Sonia hauled herself to her feet. "Good try, though, Mins." She swiped a hand across her sweating brow, rolling her eyes. "Exciting start to the day, eh."

Minnie grinned. "I wondered what all the racket was about." She looked down at the dark space where the mouse was hiding. "We could try tempting it out with a bit of bread or something." Minnie cast around, then picked up a slice of toast that had been abandoned on the worktop and broke off a corner. She stooped to place it on the floor, a short distance from the fridge. Opening one of the cupboards, she pulled out a colander.

"I'll get ready to cover it with this when it comes out. It can't stay under there for long. We just need to keep still – and quiet."

"As a mouse?" Sonia smothered a giggle.

Minnie grimaced. "Haha."

The kitchen door opened a fraction. Ajab stuck his head through, his eyes surveying the room. "Is this a private party or can I come and get my breakfast?"

"Very funny. Either come in and shut the door, or close it and stay where you are," said Minnie in a hushed voice. "We have a mouse issue."

"Eugh. No. Imagine all those droppings." Ajab pulled a face. "And they just squirt pee as they go, don't they? I think I've lost my appetite. I'll come back in a bit." He quickly closed the door, the sound of his retreating footsteps echoing down the hallway.

Sonia raised an eyebrow. "Another wuss," she whispered. "You certainly get to know who you can count on in a crisis."

The three of them hovered close to the fridge, eyes trained on the ground. Angela had remained quiet throughout, observing the proceedings.

Minnie wasn't sure quite what happened next. Angela had clearly noticed the movement before her and, quick as a flash, her foot, shod in a wooden-soled mule, came down hard. There was a sickening crunch as every bone in the little creature's body was shattered.

Sonia cried out. "*No!*"

"What the fuck have you done?" Minnie turned to Angela in shocked disbelief.

"I g-got rid of it. That's what this w-was all about, w-wasn't it?" Angela lifted her foot, revealing a glistening mass of giblets, and, to make matters worse, evidence of tiny foetuses. The mouse had indeed been pregnant.

Calmly removing her shoe, on tiptoe, Angela carried it to the sink, then rinsed the offending matter from the sole, leaving Minnie and Sonia staring in horror at the carnage spread across the kitchen floor.

Sonia had begun to sob. "Oh God, the poor little thing. And it was having babies, too. That's *horrible*. We were just going to catch it and put it back outside."

Angela glanced back over her shoulder dismissively. "It was a m-mouse. Vermin. There are f-far too m-many of them, anyway."

"That was a really vile thing to do, Angela." Minnie put an arm around the weeping Sonia, revulsion and anger rising in her. "We weren't intending to kill it."

An odd, almost chilling smile spread across Angela's face as she looked down at the blood-spattered ceramic tiles, the little heap of gore. It was almost as though she was pleased with herself. Minnie felt something twist in her gut. At that moment, she wanted to punch Angela more than she'd ever wanted to hit anyone.

Angela slid the mule back onto her foot. "You're c-completely over-reacting. I've d-done us all a f-favour." Ripping off a few sheets of kitchen towel from the holder near the sink, she crossed the room and scooped up what remained of the mouse and the majority of its entrails, examined them with satisfaction, then deposited the whole thing into the stainless-steel swing bin. "Now excuse me, I've g-got to g-get ready."

Minnie and Sonia stared after her as she clopped out of the kitchen, back through the hall and up the stairs.

"Sick *bitch*," muttered Sonia, wiping her eyes with the cuff of her cardigan. "How *could* she?"

Fatima called out to them suddenly, still from the safety of the living room. "What's happening in there? Have you caught the mouse yet?"

"You can come out now." Minnie, fighting tears herself, crossed the hall and opened the door. "Angela . . . stamped on it."

Fatima's brow creased into a frown. "I thought you were just going to take it into the garden."

"Apparently Angela had other ideas. She smashed it to smithereens."

"*Eww!*" Fatima came out into the hallway cautiously, peering past Minnie into the kitchen with a look of disgust. "I mean, as you'll have gathered, I'm not exactly a rodent fan, but I didn't think . . ."

"Neither did we." Sonia stared miserably at the floor, shaking her head.

Minnie shuddered as she remembered the look of gratification on Angela's face, the eyes devoid of warmth. The bizarre way the woman had behaved: her whole disconcerting reaction to the situation.

An unwelcome coldness had begun to seep into her bones as it suddenly occurred to her that none of them really knew Angela, or what made her tick, at all.

Chapter 25

Minnie

Friday, 28 October 2022

Minnie had turned down a pre-Halloween party invitation extended to her and her housemates from one of the girls on their course in favour of spending the evening with Jake. The others (with the exception of Angela) were all keen to go, and had hired their fancy dress outfits. Fatima, thoroughly enjoying herself as a green-faced witch, had bought a bottle of sambuca and the party-goers had all had a couple of shots to get themselves in the mood before leaving the house.

Ajab looked uncomfortable in his vampire suit, even though Minnie tried to persuade him it looked hot.

"Come off it, I look like a prize muppet," he had grumbled, adjusting his fangs and the stand-up collar of his cloak in the hallway mirror.

"Everyone will look like a muppet." Minnie rolled her eyes. "It's fancy dress; quit stressing."

"Can't you blow whatsisname out just for this evening? *Please*?" Fatima put on her best cajoling voice, pouting in mock disappointment as Minnie waved them all off at the door. "It'll be a laugh. Karaoke and everything."

"A very good reason not to go, when you've got a voice like mine," Minnie said with a grin. "Nah. You lot go and enjoy yourselves. I think I need to try and cheer Jake up – he looked pretty down in the dumps the other day."

"Hmm – and how d'you plan to do that, I wonder?" Fatima folded her arms, lifting an eyebrow. "Just don't do anything I wouldn't do, eh."

Minnie spluttered. "Well that doesn't rule much out, does it!"

"Are you casting aspersions about my good character, Miss Parnell?" Fatima's mouth gaped in feigned horror.

"What are you trying to say, Mins?" laughed Sonia. "That our Fatima is some sort of Jezebel?"

"I think that accolade goes to you, darling," retorted Fatima, winking at Minnie. Sonia pretended to punch her on the nose.

"Watch it, you. Although actually, I think I quite like the idea of being a Jezebel, whoever she may have been." She tossed her long Morticia Addams wig theatrically from side to side, making the others howl.

Minnie watched in amusement as the three of them weaved down the road, wondering what sort of state they'd be in after a couple of hours, given the fact they were already far from sober. Especially Ajab, who never usually drank much.

She closed the front door and went straight back upstairs to finish getting ready. Jake had arranged to meet her at the Old Windmill at 8pm, so she had half an hour. Minnie had been toying with the idea of bringing him back to the house later, but thought better of it as Angela was going to be in all evening. She'd decided they would have to go somewhere else and had been aquiver with anticipation all day.

She brushed her teeth, finished putting on an extra coat of mascara and a generous spray of her favourite perfume, and pulled on her burgundy fake fur jacket. A quick look in the full-length mirror on the landing told her she looked acceptable. She felt a shiver of excitement as she tapped the app on her phone and made the payment. The Uber was only two minutes away.

Minnie was at the front door when she suddenly thought of Angela, alone in her room as ever. Despite still feeling pissed off with her about the mouse incident, it seemed a bit rude not to acknowledge her, especially as the others were all out, too. She retreated a few steps and called up to the top floor.

"I'm off now, Angela. I might not be back later, so I'll see you tomorrow, I expect."

Angela appeared at the top of the stairs. She gave her a brief smile. "Oh, okay. S-see you, then. H-have a nice t-time." She seemed hesitant. "Erm – w-will the others b-be coming home tonight?"

Minnie laughed. "Who knows? They're all six sheets to the wind already, I think. Hopefully at least one of them has remembered to take a key, so hopefully they won't drag you out of bed. See you."

She closed the door behind her, all thoughts of Angela and the others pushed immediately aside as she climbed into the waiting Uber and headed for the pub in Spon Street. Though she hadn't told Jake, she had a clear plan of how the evening would pan out.

And the perfect, romantic place to take him, just far enough away from the city to feel like they had escaped.

Chapter 26

Minnie

Saturday, 29 October 2022

Fatima seemed agitated as she hovered in the bedroom doorway.

"Mins, you got a minute?"

"Hmm?" Minnie, sitting on her bed and hunched over her laptop, was trying and failing to focus on her essay, and slightly irritated at having her first fluent paragraph interrupted mid-flow. It was frustrating coming back to something later, having completely lost the thread of what she wanted to say. She was still on a high after her night with Jake, her stomach filled with butterflies, her thoughts punctuated frequently with the delicious memory of his touch. The feel of his arms holding her close; the way his lips had brushed her neck and left her weak. The way he had held her in his gaze and told her she was the most beautiful thing he had ever laid eyes on.

She had woken before dawn, lain awake just watching him

until he'd opened his eyes and greeted her with that beguiling grin. They'd made love again, then ordered croissants and coffee, before catching a taxi back into town. After one more lingering kiss, they had gone their respective ways, with the promise of meeting up the following evening. Even though hungover after several glasses of cider the night before, Minnie had walked home as though floating on air.

He'd seemed surprised when she'd suggested taking the Uber straight to the quaint Old Mill Hotel in Baginton, some four miles outside the city centre – even more so, when she announced that she'd booked them a room. But she had been more than ready, and the night was everything she'd hoped it would be. She couldn't wait to repeat it. Any earlier thoughts of introducing Jake, whether to her mother or friends, had been put on the back burner for the time being. Minnie wanted to enjoy having him all to herself for as long as possible.

Minnie was determined to finish her assignment, so that she could see Jake again on Sunday as they'd arranged, without it hanging over her. She needed to seize the chance to work before the impetus deserted her again completely.

"Two seconds and I'll be with you." She finished typing the sentence, pressed 'save' and looked up. "What's the problem?"

"Okay if I come in?"

"'Course." Minnie straightened, her brow creasing into a frown as she noted Fatima's troubled expression. She patted the bed next to her. "Park your bum and tell me what's bothering you."

Fatima closed the door and came to sit beside Minnie. She was flicking her lower lip with her front teeth. "D'you think there's something a bit, well, weird about Angela?"

"Weird how? Like, that she's completely antisocial and lives on shit? That she seems to prefer talking to herself rather than anyone else? Or when she's not in a lecture, she devotes her whole existence to her bloody coursework."

"Well. Partly." Fatima shifted a little, turning her face to Minnie's. "Mins, I found her in here late last night when I got back from the party. While you were out with whatsisname."

"*What?* In my *room?*" Minnie's mouth fell open. "Doing what?"

"I don't know. I'd got a splitting headache after that bloody sambuca, and came back just gone eleven. I fetched myself a glass of water and was just coming up the stairs. I don't think she'd heard me come in – her hearing's obviously not brilliant. Ajab left the bash even before me – he's such a lightweight. His door was shut, so I assumed he'd already turned in, and Sonia was still out partying, so there was no one else about. Anyway, Angela seemed to be wandering around; picking stuff up, putting it down again. And then she turned round and saw me. Well, I *think* she saw me. It was like she looked straight through me." She paused. "I asked what the hell she thought she was doing, but she never said a word. Just floated about a bit more with this really glazed expression, and then walked past me as if I wasn't here. It was bizarre."

"Shit." Minnie shook her head, trying to picture it all. "Where did she go then?"

"Back up to her room. I watched a bit more – she was kind of swaying as she went up. Seemed to be mumbling to herself, too." She grinned. "Nothing new there, mind you."

They had all noticed with some amusement that Angela muttered to herself sometimes. Out of earshot, Fatima had remarked that she must have invented a friend to talk to, as she didn't appear to have any. Minnie had laughed guiltily. It was funny in a way, but she felt a bit sorry for Angela if she was that lonely.

Minnie thought for a moment. "D'you think she could've been sleepwalking? I mean, I'll have a proper look obviously, but I haven't noticed that anything's missing."

Fatima pulled a dubious face. "It's possible. She did look a bit kind of vacant, I s'pose."

"Maybe I need to ask her outright. The fact she didn't even register you were there points to something like that."

Fatima studied her for a moment. "You don't think – I dunno, I don't want to freak you out, but you don't think she's a bit – well, obsessed with you, do you? She does seem to watch you a lot. Sonia commented on it, too."

Minnie felt a sudden chill pass through her. "I hadn't noticed. I mean, when you say she watches me, how, exactly? And what's Sonia said?"

"It was just a feeling she's had for a while, now. And then the other afternoon, she said you were going into the living room and Angela was coming out of the kitchen behind you. Sonia clocked her just staring. Sort of looking you up and down. She said the look on Angela's face creeped her out."

"Well, it's fucking creeping me out now, too." Minnie shuddered. "I'll keep my door locked from now on, I think. Thanks for the heads-up."

"I just thought you should know, mate. Watch your back, eh? It might be nothing, but at the end of the day, we don't really know anything about her."

Fatima got up, forcing a smile. "On that happy note, I'd better get on myself. I'm meeting an old friend in Brum for lunch – she's travelling through so we're having a catch-up." She stood at the door. "I mean it, Mins. Do keep an eye on Angela – maybe better to let her know in a roundabout way that you're onto her, if she *is* up to something."

It was pointless trying to continue with the essay now. Minnie sat staring into space as Fatima closed the door behind her. So two of her housemates thought Angela was preoccupied with her. It gave her a peculiar nauseated feeling. She wondered if Ajab had suspected anything, too.

She began to scour her room, trying to remember where everything was kept; opening each drawer in turn and riffling through the contents, scanning all the items left on top of her desk, and at the bottom of the wardrobe, where she kept her shoes and bags. Everything seemed in order. Whatever Angela had been doing, it didn't look as though she'd taken anything.

Sighing, Minnie closed her laptop and grabbed her towel from the radiator. She would take a shower, get some breakfast. And then she needed to have a word with the woman upstairs.

*

"In your r-room? W-was I?" Angela's face flushed scarlet. She was just climbing the stairs as Minnie headed down to the kitchen.

"Well, yes. Fatima saw you in there. I'd be grateful if you could explain what you were doing." Minnie smiled tightly. She hated confrontation and was trying to be as assertive as she could without sounding accusing. She watched as Angela's eyes flickered nervously, her knuckles blanching as she gripped the banister.

"I'm so s-sorry. I m-must have b-been sleep-w-walking. I used to d-do it a lot as a child, a-p-parently. I th-thought I'd s-stopped. It's usually b-been if I'm p-particularly s-stressed about s-something, and I've g-got this assignment to d-do which I've r-really b-been s-struggling w-with."

Minnie felt suddenly guilty. The woman seemed quite distressed, her stammer more pronounced than ever. Maybe she had a genuine problem. It seemed feasible that anxiety could bring on something like that.

"Oh dear. That's not good. Well, if there's anything any of us can do to help with your coursework, do give us a shout."

Angela's expression relaxed, and with it her grip on the handrail. She smiled briefly, nodding.

"Thank you, you're very k-kind. I think I've t-turned a c-corner with it this m-morning, but if I n-need advice in f-future, I'll be s-sure to ask."

Before Minnie could say anything else, Angela continued briskly on her way, leaving Minnie standing staring up after her. She let out a long breath. Maybe it had been something and nothing. But she would keep her door locked in future, anyway. Sleepwalking or not, she didn't like the idea of Angela wandering into her room in the dead of night. Nor of her watching her as intently as Fatima had implied.

It was an unsettling thought.

*

"Fancy going to the Orb for a coffee?" Minnie stuck her head round Ajab's door.

"Do bears shit in the woods?" He dropped the book he had been poring over onto the bed and let out a groan. "I think if I try to absorb anything else about Industrialisation and the Making of the Modern World with this banging head, I'm actually going to have an aneurysm."

Minnie laughed. "Get your coat, then."

Ajab jumped up, grabbing the jacket that was hanging on the back of his swivel chair. "Your mum working today?"

Minnie blew out her cheeks. "Yeah, she's doing a couple of hours this afternoon. She mentioned it when she messaged me yesterday, but I forgot to reply. I feel a bit bad – I keep fobbing her off. She's been a bit better over the last couple of weeks; you know, since I had a go at her for following me."

Ajab grimaced. "That was a bit mean, to be fair. I think she was just really worried after that prank text thing. That's what mums do, isn't it – get themselves in a flap about stuff. Make mountains out of molehills."

Minnie smiled sheepishly. "S'pose so. It was just getting to me a bit. Every time my phone went off, I kept thinking, *fuck's sake, what now*. But we had a good talk in the end, and she seems less fraught now. I've still been keeping my distance, though – trying to stop her being too clingy again. And I've had a lot on, to be fair."

Ajab raised an eyebrow. "A lot on your mind, that's for sure. How was the date?"

She closed her eyes, smiled secretively. "Ah. Let's just say things are moving along very nicely."

He mimed putting his fingers down his throat. "Spare me the details."

Minnie and Ajab walked up through the town, the sky a bleak dove grey, mizzle dampening their hair and clothes. The streets were busy despite the inclement weather. Shoppers milled in and out of doorways, clutching carrier bags and trudging over the wet pavements. Ajab bought a copy of the *Big Issue* from a smiley-looking lady standing close to the statue of Godiva outside Cathedral Lanes.

As the pair reached the quad behind the cathedral, Minnie's eyes furtively scanned the terrace where Jake shared the house, wondering if he was inside. If he'd been thinking about her as much as she'd been thinking about him. She decided not to mention where he was living to Ajab – and definitely not to her mum. Her eyes were drawn suddenly to a flicker of movement in the upstairs window next to Jake's digs and a thorn of discomfort passed through her as she thought she saw a figure, half hidden by the curtain, peering down. It was so difficult to discern anything other than a vague outline with the way light reflected off the glass. Minnie found it disturbing to think someone was observing them unseen.

The Orb was fairly busy, its windows misted with condensation. It seemed people were seeking refuge on such a miserable Saturday afternoon. The place had been decked out in Halloween decorations. Fake cobwebs and spiders hung from the ceiling and a plastic skeleton had been propped on a chair in the corner. The pair stood in the doorway as Minnie cast around for Georgia, who appeared suddenly from the lounge area carrying a stack of dirty pint glasses. Her face lit up as she saw them.

"Hello you. What've you been up to this last week? I've missed you." She put down the glasses on the bar and came over to give Minnie a hug.

"Sorry. I've been studying a lot – trying to get on top of stuff, you know." Minnie squirmed a little as she thought of her unfinished essay.

"I can vouch for that, Mrs Parnell," chipped in Ajab, a little too eagerly. "She never has her nose out of her books."

Minnie recognised Ajab's attempt to look earnest and tried to avoid eye contact with him. He was a hopeless liar.

Georgia laughed. "Hmm. I'm sure. Well, as long as she's keeping herself out of mischief, that's the main thing. And call me Georgia, please – you're making me feel ancient!" She ushered them in, away from the door.

"Find yourselves a table and I'll bring you a drink over."

"Can we just have a couple of Americanos, please Mum?" Minnie looked over at Yiannis, who was serving a woman. He waved at them from behind the huge pumpkin at the far end of the bar. She glanced at Ajab in amusement, as he waved back, smiling coyly.

"Not hungover, by any chance?" Georgia raised a sardonic eyebrow.

Minnie covered her eyes. "Maybe a bit."

Her mum gave a wry smile. "I'll get the coffees in a minute. Shall I ask Lucas to make you some cheese and tomato toasties?"

The pair nodded enthusiastically and Georgia grinned.

"Plenty of carbs, that's what you need." She disappeared into the kitchen.

They sat down to wait at a corner table to the right of the bar. Yiannis was just coming over to say hello when he was met halfway across the floor by a dark-haired man who had just emerged from the toilets. Yiannis's face lit with a smile.

"Ah, Cole. You haven't met Minnie, have you – Georgia's daughter?"

The man turned, a look of surprise on his face. Minnie stiffened. She recognised him at once as the person who'd been chatting to her mum, the night she had been passing with Jake. She tipped her head, the corners of her mouth lifting tensely.

"Hello."

"Hello! Good to meet you. I've heard a lot about you." Cole smiled broadly.

"Oh? I haven't heard anything about you." There was an awkward pause.

Cole cleared his throat. His eyes travelled to Ajab. "Erm – who's your friend?"

"This is Ajab." Minnie prickled with irritation. Her mum reappeared from the doorway behind the bar, carrying two plates. Seeing Cole, she hesitated briefly, flicking a look from him to Minnie and meeting her gaze. Minnie widened her eyes reproachfully.

"I see you've met Cole," Georgia said, smiling uncertainly as she approached to put the toasted sandwiches on the table. Minnie dipped her head curtly. Her mum quickly went back to the bar, throwing Yiannis a grimace as she did so. It didn't escape Minnie's notice.

"Cole's a historian, so you'll have plenty in common," Yiannis announced, throwing Ajab a wink. Ajab looked flustered, taking a bite from his sandwich and wincing from the hot cheese. He fanned his mouth, making Cole laugh.

"So you're both studying history, then?" Cole was still smiling.

Minnie found it hard not to show her animosity. She appraised him. He was quite good-looking; a lot younger than her dad had been. She wondered how close Cole and her mum had actually become. Minnie felt conflicted. It was really none of her business, she knew that; but the thought of Georgia being with someone else other than Trevor really upset her.

"Yes," Ajab responded, throwing Minnie an awkward look.

Maybe her face was betraying her hostility. Minnie made a conscious effort to relax her features. She was being childish, she realised, but she really couldn't help how she was feeling.

"We're on the same course," she managed, glancing at Ajab.

"D'you mind if I join you?" Cole looked hopeful. Without waiting for a reply, he dragged an empty stool from the next table and sat down opposite Minnie, who drew back a little further against the wall.

Georgia had returned with the coffees. She placed them in front of Minnie and Ajab, then hovered behind Cole, smiling encouragingly at Minnie.

"Cole's writing a book about the history of the city," she told the pair. She smiled, her hand travelling towards Cole's shoulder as if to rest it there, but then withdrew it hurriedly.

"Oh, yes?" Ajab's face lit up. "I'm from Birmingham originally – I thought I knew Coventry pretty well before I came here, but I've found out loads since I started my degree. It's got a fascinating past."

"I'm learning more every day." Cole nodded enthusiastically. "The research I've been doing has thrown up so many things I didn't have a clue about. At this rate, the book's going to be a tome by the time I've finished."

Minnie shifted in her seat. As keen as she was on history, she wasn't interested in hearing Cole prattling on about it. She felt sure he was just trying to impress her mum, constantly throwing her sideways glances. She even caught him winking at one point. But more annoyingly, her mum kept locking eyes with him. Throwing him secret smiles.

Thankfully, the old man, Ned, who Georgia had introduced Minnie to the first night she'd come into the Orb, came over to say hello. Minnie loved his dog, Charlie, whose tail was slicing the air as ever. She bent forward to scruff the fur behind his ears. Charlie rewarded her with a huge lick across the back of her hand.

"*Good boy.* I'm going to have a dog one day," she announced, glancing up at Georgia. "Mum and Dad wouldn't let me have one."

Georgia looked uncomfortable. "Your dad was the one who wasn't keen. He was never really an animal person."

Minnie stared at her. "Really?"

"Yes. He didn't even want a cat. But a dog was a complete no-no. He said he couldn't be doing with the smell and slobber, and cleaning up mess all the time."

Minnie was taken aback. She hadn't realised her dad didn't like dogs. He'd never told her. She'd always thought of him as being an animal lover.

"I'd have quite liked a dog myself," Georgia went on. "But I was worried how you'd be if anything happened to it. Look how upset you were after you lost Thumper."

"Thumper?" Ajab turned to Minnie questioningly.

"My rabbit. I was heartbroken," admitted Minnie. "But I was only eight. I've never been allowed to forget it, though."

"Dogs can live a lot longer than rabbits," Ned declared. "Every home needs a dog, in my book."

"See, Mum?" Minnie was wearing a smirk now. "And it wouldn't be a bad idea for you to get a little guard dog yourself, especially after seeing that monk outside your door . . ."

246

"What monk?" Ned's ears pricked up. He turned to look at Georgia, his eyes wide. "You never said anything."

Georgia shot Minnie a grimace. "Oh, it was nothing. Probably just my imagination running away with me – you know, after that conversation we'd had when I first met you."

"Well, just you keep your curtains closed and don't go looking out after dark. You don't want to see him again." Ned looked genuinely alarmed.

"Why's that, then?" Ajab sat forward eagerly, his eyes travelling from Ned to Minnie.

All the while, Cole had been looking on, tight-lipped after his earlier ebullience. It was satisfying that he didn't seem to want to contribute to this discussion. Minnie was already irritated by him blowing his own trumpet about his bloody book. The best he could do was stay quiet, or she was likely to say something rude eventually.

"Ah. Well," Ned dropped his chin, looking at them from beneath his unkempt eyebrows. "I was telling your mum here, Minnie. There's a ghostly monk who roams around this area, close to the Guildhall. But legend has it if a person sees him three times, then it's very bad luck for them."

"Bad luck? Oh dear. In what way?" Minnie was trying to keep a straight face. She felt Ajab dig her in the ribs.

Ned was full of it now. "This monk's supposed to be the ghost of one Friar Benedict. I was speaking to this young student chap in here last week. He'd seen a figure in one of them cowl things the monks wear, up by the old priory one night. Proper shaken up about it, he was. Anyway, this lad I was speaking to, he'd been reading up on it all after his own experience. That Benedict was a wrong'un, the story goes – excommunicated for sorcery – they reckon he could tell when people were going to snuff it." Ned's face was grave. "I know lots of people scoff about such things, but you can't take no chances. I remember my old dad saying, when I was still a nipper, a chap he knew had seen the friar twice, and not long after the third time, the poor bugger popped his clogs."

Minnie pulled an appropriately shocked face, but decided it was time to change the subject. Poor old Ned was so earnest about it all, there was little point trying to suggest the possibility that the unfortunate man in question had been unwell and his time would have been up anyway. It was all totally farfetched.

"That's awful," said Ajab, his eyes landing on Yiannis, who was quite clearly giving him the eye. His cheeks flushed. "I – I mean, probably wise not to tempt fate, eh?" He nudged Minnie again, averting his gaze from Yiannis.

"Definitely." Minnie nodded. She glanced up at the clock. "Oh God, is that the time? I've just remembered I need to get some stationery bits for uni."

"You do?" Ajab's brow knitted.

"Yes," she said, turning to him pointedly. "To print off my essay?"

"Oh." His face fell.

"Nothing to stop you staying for a bit longer if you want," Minnie said, glancing from Ajab to Yiannis.

"No, it's fine. I need to finish my assignment anyway."

Her eyes travelled to Charlie. She patted him again. "I'd better just wash my hands before I finish my sandwich and then we'll go."

Georgia waved her in Yiannis's direction. "Use the toilets behind the bar. It's warmer in there."

Minnie got up, smiled tightly at Cole who moved aside to let her pass, then went through to the cloakroom behind the bar. It was silly, she knew that, but she felt more than a bit annoyed with her mum. Her new friend Cole seemed full of himself, and Georgia saying that stuff about her dad not liking animals had

248

made him sound a bit, well, hard-hearted. It felt like a dig and Minnie didn't like it.

As she left the cloakroom to return to the bar, Minnie paused to peer through the glass in the top of the door. She could see her mum, laughing, smiling at Cole again. Was she being unreasonable, begrudging her happiness? But then she thought of her beloved dad, the awful way he had died. Anger bubbled inside her again.

Seeing Yiannis approaching, she pulled back, taking a deep breath.

"You okay?" he asked as he swung through the door, his brow creasing slightly. "Your mum's nattering – thought I'd come and check on you. You looked a bit, well, peaky."

"Just feeling crappy today. Self-inflicted." She grimaced.

He laughed. "We've all been there, sweet. Some of us more than others."

She followed Yiannis back into the bar, made a tight-lipped apology to her mum that she really couldn't manage the toasted sandwich after all and nodded pointedly at Ajab to finish his. More than ever, the only thing she wanted to do was to get away from the Orb as quickly as she could.

*

After they'd left the pub, Minnie asked Ajab if he'd mind very much if they just went home. "I don't feel too good," she'd explained. "Actually don't think I can face going round the shops just now."

Ajab pursed his lips. "Okay. You do look a bit barfy, I guess. But I thought you were desperate for paper and stuff?"

"It'll keep. I think I just need to have a lie-down for a bit."

Ajab cocked his head, studying her for a moment. "What's up? You seemed fine before. Apart from the hangover, I mean."

Minnie sighed. "Look, to be perfectly honest it was seeing my mum fawning over that creep. It feels like my dad's only been gone five minutes and – I don't know, it just doesn't seem right. Am I being oversensitive?"

Ajab sucked air through his teeth, considering her words. "I can quite understand where you're coming from," he said slowly. "It must be hard, when you were so close to your dad. But try to see it from your mum's point of view. You've left home; you're making it clear her contacting you all the time is intrusive, but from everything you've told me, she hasn't really got anyone else. At least her seeing a guy will give her something else to think about, take the heat off you. And it's not like she's announced they're getting married or anything, is it? I mean, it was pretty obvious she likes him, but she wasn't fawning over him, as you put it. It's probably just a nice distraction for her after everything she's been through. I think maybe you've blown it up a bit in your head."

Minnie summoned a small smile. "I guess you're right. Maybe I need to grow up a bit."

"Mins, you're the most mature and sensible of all of us. What happened to your dad – it was truly awful. Tragic. It's perfectly natural to feel the way you do. Just give yourself time for it to sink in that your mum needs to move on."

"Thanks, mate. It'll take a bit of getting used to, but that's made me feel a bit better about it." She let out a long breath. "Changing the subject completely – about Yiannis. He's a lovely guy and everything, but I think you're better steering clear. I'd hate to see you hurt."

Ajab looked taken aback. "I wasn't – you know, expecting to get into a relationship or anything . . ."

"No one ever is at the start. But from what Mum says, he and Freddie are pretty solid, even if they both fool around now and then. Maybe best to stick to looking, not touching."

He nodded resignedly, puffing out his cheeks. "You're probably right. I'm just keen to meet someone, that's all."

"And you will. I know you will. But you deserve more than to be someone's bit on the side. It's better to start off on a level playing field, isn't it?" Minnie gave his hand a squeeze.

Ajab leaned in suddenly to peck her on the cheek.

She looked at him in surprise. "What was that for?"

"You're a good friend, Mins. You know that?"

Minnie responded with a playful punch on the arm. "And so are you."

Together they began to head home. But all the way, Minnie's stomach still churned. She tried to shake the thought of the smarmy Cole, of her mum's silly, girlish expression whenever he'd spoken. Of the way her eyes shone as she looked at him. Why had she never looked at her dad that way? Why had she seemed so agitated, rather than heartbroken, in those first weeks after he'd died? Why had Minnie never seen her crying her eyes out?

Maybe Georgia had just been worried about how she was going to deal with everything after he'd gone. Or maybe things between her parents hadn't been as perfect as Minnie had believed.

For God's sake, people dealt with grief in different ways, didn't they? She was being irrational now. Maybe her mum had shut down emotionally as it was all too much for her to bear, and she'd simply internalised it all.

Then why had a niggling, uncomfortable feeling begun to weave its way through Minnie's gut?

Chapter 27

Minnie

Monday, 31 October 2022

Monday wasn't the best day for Halloween and the weather was awful – incessant rain and high winds, which whipped the fallen leaves around the pavement into a mini cyclone. But as everyone, except Minnie, had been to the party on the Friday, no one was really bothered about going out in the evening, so the housemates had agreed to order a takeaway and watch spooky films instead.

"I've borrowed the DVD of *The Night House*," Sonia had said excitedly. "So we could start with that and then put the original *Halloween* on afterwards, as it's on mainstream telly tonight."

Fatima groaned. "I've seen it about a hundred times already. What about one of the *Saw* films instead?"

"Too much blood and guts." Minnie pulled a face. "Can't we

just stick with Sonia's suggestion? I've seen *Halloween* loads of times too, but it's sort of a tradition, isn't it?"

Fatima huffed, then agreed that it probably was a tradition so she'd put up with it, if that was what everyone else wanted to see.

Ajab appeared from the kitchen, smiling broadly. "What d'you think?" He held a huge pumpkin aloft, one side carved into a toothless grinning face, the eyes sinister-looking crescents slanting upwards at the outer corners. "I copied a YouTube tutorial."

"Love it," laughed Sonia. "Let's sit him in the window and light a candle."

"D'you think we should ask Angela to join us?" ventured Minnie dubiously. "I mean, it is Halloween, after all."

"Huh. You can ask if you really must, but it'll be a first if she says yes," muttered Fatima. "Can't imagine her being a horror movie fan either, can you?"

They all agreed on Chinese food. Once everyone had put in their various requests, Ajab went to call in the order, while Minnie took the stairs to the top floor, listening for a moment to see if Angela was otherwise engaged. All seemed quiet, so she knocked loudly on her door.

"Angela, we're just getting a Chinese takeaway and watching creepy films for Halloween – d'you want to come down?"

Angela's door burst open, startling Minnie.

The woman's cheeks were sweaty and red, her eyes oddly wild. Through the doorway, Minnie could see evidence of some sort of sorting: paperwork in piles, clothes strewn across the bed. The usual stale smell of fried food and unwashed bedding wafted onto the landing.

"I – I'm sorry – I hope I'm not interrupting you . . ." Minnie studied her face apprehensively. Angela looked as though she might self-combust at any moment. It was utterly bizarre.

"Look. I *don't* like Chinese food," Angela hissed. "I *don't* share your infantile taste in cinema. I *don't* celebrate Halloween. Please. Don't. Ask. Me. *Again*." The last word was delivered with such angry emphasis, it made Minnie shrink back.

Before Minnie could respond, Angela slammed the door in her face, making Minnie recoil further, stunned by this irrational outburst. Clearly Angela's irate mood, whatever had caused it, was sufficient to eliminate her stammer, and had revealed a decidedly more assertive side to the woman's character than had ever surfaced before. Though Minnie wasn't especially keen on Angela, she liked this new persona even less.

Minnie thundered back down the stairs and straight into the living room, pausing to catch her breath as she stared at her friends. The others, camped on the rug with tea trays ready for their food, all turned to look at her, open-mouthed.

"Jesus. What's the rush? What did she say?" Fatima's brow had creased into a baffled frown.

"She doesn't want to join us. Not now, not ever, from the way she just spoke to me." Minnie shook her head, confounded by Angela's unwonted viciousness. "Absolute frigging weirdo. I think Angela has finally lost the plot."

Chapter 28

Minnie

Tuesday, 1 November 2022

While Angela generally made very little noise and the lack of her presence in the rest of the house was nothing out of the ordinary, Minnie had the odd sense that something was awry as she turned the key in the front door. It was the day after Halloween, approaching dusk, and the house felt unusually cold. She couldn't put a finger on it, but the place seemed somehow emptier, the way it feels when someone has just vacated. She hadn't seen Angela in the lecture theatre earlier, either. After class, Fatima and Sonia had gone for a drink and Ajab had taken a walk to return some books to the library. Perhaps Angela wasn't feeling well. It was very unlike her to miss a lesson. She always appeared to be so conscientious about her studies. And her behaviour had seemed odder than ever the previous night. Maybe she'd been coming down with something.

Minnie made herself a cup of tea and took it through into the living room, plonking down onto the settee and picking up one of the fashion magazines from the pile that Fatima was forever adding to. She leafed idly through the pages and, finding nothing of any great interest, replaced it on the coffee table, listening all the time for any movement elsewhere in the house. She felt restless. Draining her mug, she returned it to the kitchen then came back out into the hallway. A blast of cool air wafted from somewhere above, followed by an unidentifiable clattering noise, stopping Minnie in her tracks. Maybe she ought to go up and see if Angela was okay. Cautiously, she began to climb the stairs. The clattering repeated intermittently, growing louder as she reached the landing.

"Angela? Is everything all right?" There was no response.

Minnie rapped on Angela's door. Still no answer. She knocked again, then put an ear against it but all seemed quiet. *Too* quiet.

"Angela? Are you in there?"

She waited for what she considered an acceptable length of time, then tentatively depressed the door handle.

The window was thrust wide open, causing the roller blind to flap against the frame and a blast of chill air to waft through. Minnie froze in the doorway. She reached in and switched on the light, recoiling as she tried to make sense of what she was seeing. The used bedding had been piled onto the floor next to the usual debris Angela always accumulated. Each of the drawers in the tallboy had been pulled out and emptied. The door to the small wardrobe was open, revealing a row of empty coat-hangers. Minnie entered the room, turning slowly as her eyes darted from one corner to the other. She drew in a breath, clapping a hand across her mouth. It was clear that every one of Angela's belongings had been removed.

Descending the stairs two at a time, she rushed to find her phone which she'd left in the living room. Retrieving it from the table, with trembling fingers she tapped out a text to Ajab.

Angela's done a bunk!!! X

Within seconds, a reply flashed back. WTF??!! X

She pressed Ajab's number and he answered immediately. "So are you saying she's actually *gone*? For good?" Ajab's voice was breathless, as though he was on the move.

"It certainly looks that way. I mean, she's taken all her stuff. No note, no message. Nothing."

"But she was paid up for another six months at least. Why the hell would she just clear off?"

Minnie could hear the rush of traffic in the background, accompanied by the sound of Ajab's footsteps slapping against the pavement. She flopped down onto a chair, her mind reeling.

"No idea." She blew out a long breath. "Maybe she decided she couldn't hack it, living with us lot. Let's face it, she didn't really gel with any of us, did she?"

"But what about the course? I mean, she still needs somewhere to stay. You'd think she'd have said *something* . . . "

"She never gave anything away. I feel like we never really got to know her." Minnie sighed, one palm pressed against her forehead. "I feel awful now. Maybe I should've tried harder, you know, to talk to her and that. Got her to open up a bit . . . "

Ajab snorted. "Come off it, Mins – you've always tried to make her feel included. I mean, I felt a bit sorry for her, with the stammer and everything. But all that aside, she's just a bloody weirdo, if you ask me."

Minnie didn't like to think that Angela, weirdo or not, had been so unhappy that she'd felt compelled to move out. "I'm a bit worried about her, to be honest."

Ajab had paused for a breath. "Look, I'll be back in ten. Stick the kettle on, will you. We can always ask at the uni reception – there'll still be someone there. Why don't you give them a quick call? Maybe she's given them another address. I'm sure we can track her down and persuade her to come back."

Minnie brightened at this suggestion. "Brilliant. I'll ring now. See you in a bit."

The receptionist who answered Minnie's call sounded harassed. Raised voices in the background implied frustration from a couple of her colleagues.

"Sorry, we've been having a mare with our system today. All sorts of problems. I'll be glad to go home."

Minnie could hear her muttering to herself and the tapping of keys as she logged into the history faculty's student list.

"Tandy, you say? I've scrolled right to the bottom of the register and I can't find anyone by that name at all."

"Angela Tandy?"

"No. I can't see anyone called Angela anything. You sure she doesn't go by a different name?"

"Not that I know of." Minnie paused. "D'you think it could be a computer glitch? I mean, you said you've been having issues . . ."

"I doubt it very much. The list looks intact." The woman sounded impatient. There was more tapping. "Well, I've been right to the bottom and back twice now and there's definitely nobody with either the name Angela or Tandy registered with us at all, I'm afraid."

Minnie racked her brains. "Oh, wait – she got a place through clearing. Would that make a difference?"

"No. If anything I'd have spotted her more quickly, as she'd have been highlighted here with a late offer letter being sent out."

"That's very odd. Thanks for your help, anyway."

Minnie hung up. So if Angela wasn't even registered at the uni, what the hell had she been up to? Her mind whirring,

Minnie went to put the kettle on. A slightly queasy feeling had begun to bubble in her stomach. Hearing the rattle of the key in the door, she went cautiously out into the hall, but was relieved to find Ajab unhooking the backpack from his shoulders.

"Any luck?" He studied her face, raising his eyebrows questioningly. "What's up?"

"You're not going to believe this. There's no record of her at the uni. Sounds as if she's never been assigned a place with them at all."

Ajab put down his bag, his mouth gaping. "You're kidding me. So what the fuck has she been doing all these weeks, locked away in her room? Why would she pretend?"

He shook his head, his brow settling into a worried frown. "And more to the point, just who the hell *is* Angela Tandy?"

Chapter 29

Georgia

Thursday, 3 November 2022

Things had been coming to a head for a while, but Tuesday night had been the final straw. Though the pub hadn't been packed, there had been a steady stream of customers, which had left Georgia with little free time. But Cole had sat patiently all the while, frequently smiling up at her with his eyes from his table as he scribbled notes for his manuscript, his brow furrowed in concentration. It touched her that he was content with the fragments of conversation they could share whenever she had a moment to spare. Though he'd called on her at the house a few times now, he made no demands on her, never overstepped the mark. He seemed to be waiting for her to take the lead, but the thought of intimacy was slightly terrifying. What if she was a disappointment? What if they weren't really compatible?

He'd been so candid with her, about his upbringing and his

ex-wife, his money worries. His doubts about the quality of his work. She felt guilty she couldn't be completely open with him about everything. About the demons of her past, her marriage. But there were things that she just couldn't reveal, not to anyone. And still she wasn't ready to invite him to stay the night.

"You really are beautiful, you know," he'd told her only days earlier as they'd parted, lifting a strand of hair from her face. "I don't know why, but you seem to lack confidence and you've no need to. I think you're amazing."

She didn't know how to respond. How could she be beautiful or amazing? Nothing about her was real. Not her looks, not the persona she presented to the world. Rather than bolstering her, the compliment left her awash with shame.

At the end of her shift, Cole had walked her home as he always did when he'd been in the Orb. They'd kissed goodnight and she'd paused to watch fondly as he made his way back across the quad. Reaching into her pocket for the key to Cuckoo Cottage, Georgia's fingers had come into contact with what felt like stiff, slippery paper. Drawing it out, she'd stared at the item in her hand, cold horror enveloping her as it dawned immediately what she was holding. The glow of the street lamp revealed a slightly battered tarot card. Georgia caught her breath. It bore the faded image of a skeleton dangling by one ankle. The Hanged Man. Georgia was under no illusion as to the message it was meant to convey. And someone had clearly slipped it into her jacket while she worked – they must have actually been in the pub. She might even have served them. The thought sent a sliver of ice through her veins. The one place where so far she'd felt relatively safe, and her stalker had been in there – might have been in several times, for all she knew. It was a wake-up call.

Although working at the Orb had provided Georgia with brief respite from the unsettling events at home, she knew now she needed to move on; and the sooner, the better. But she had mixed feelings about it. The regulars were a nice enough bunch and she got along well with Yiannis. Though he was in a relationship with Freddie, she'd learned soon after meeting the pair, it seemed to be a pretty flexible arrangement and neither appeared to mind if the other flirted with, or even dated, other people: something Georgia couldn't quite fathom, as there seemed to be genuine affection between them. Freddie was still away, having booked a long weekend in the Cotswolds – 'with an old friend', he'd said. Georgia wondered how Yiannis really felt about it all.

"It is what it is," Yiannis had told her with a shrug. "We both like a bit of fun. But I'd never leave the old sod and I know he'd never try to hoof me out. We're agreed on what's acceptable and what's crossing a line. We've been through quite a bit these last few years, always been there for one another when it counts. Freddie lost his mum, I lost my dad. It's that time together, isn't it? The shared history. That's what builds the bond."

Georgia had reflected on her marriage to Trevor. The more years that had elapsed, the further apart they seemed to have grown. It obviously wasn't the case with every relationship that shared experiences drew you closer. Trevor could be impatient, insensitive even at times. Overly critical. But she recognised that there had been fault on both sides. Maybe it was partly the fact that she'd never been able to be completely honest with him about her past either. Georgia shut down the memory. It wasn't helpful to embark on that train of thought. Never look back: that had always been her motto. Because if she didn't dwell on everything that had happened, it was almost possible to believe that none of it had been real.

Almost.

She didn't know what the future held for her, only that she needed it to involve Minnie. Wherever Minnie went, eventually she would have to follow. But she was living in dread of something happening to damage their relationship irreparably in the meantime. Though it would break her heart and she wanted more than anything to be close to her daughter, she'd concluded it would be best to move on, to put some distance between them for a while for both their sakes. To disappear until whoever had been plaguing her gave up eventually. Because surely they couldn't sustain this level of persecution indefinitely. Being threatened herself was one thing. But knowing that whoever had it in for her now knew about Minnie, she was growing increasingly fearful for the girl's safety. And equally fearful for the safety of her own secret.

Georgia was starting to formulate a plan, to think of somewhere she could go without leaving a trail. She'd begun searching online again for somewhere else to live. There were plenty of remote properties tucked away in the Warwickshire countryside. Oxfordshire; Wiltshire, even. It might be best to lie low completely, not to attempt to integrate into the community if she wanted to remain completely anonymous.

She hated that she was being forced to think this way once more. That her life plan was being dictated by some malicious bastard. But to protect her sanity and her relationship with Minnie, she felt it was her only option.

After ruminating over a shortlist, Georgia had settled on another Airbnb – an old gatekeeper's cottage in Oxfordshire, set back from the main road and surrounded by acres of land. It was the best option she could find: newly posted on the website and available instantly. She could block the booking for the next three months and take things from there. She had only to click the payment for the deposit and she could catch a train, pick up the keys the following afternoon. Take just the essentials and leave most of her belongings behind – after all, the rent was paid on Cuckoo Cottage for a good while yet. But her heart felt heavy.

She didn't want to run out on Minnie. Georgia kept the Airbnb tab open on her laptop but closed the lid. She would return to it after the night out she had planned with Cole, a sort of farewell present. Not that she would tell him that's what it was. Georgia had swapped her evening off, telling Yiannis she would work the next Monday instead. She'd grown fond of Yiannis and felt a bit guilty, knowing she wouldn't be around to honour it.

Cole had looked drawn and tired the previous evening. Whilst still trying to research and build the contents of his book, Georgia knew he'd also been working hard to bring in some income writing for an online magazine to keep Jethro Jackson off his case. Mercifully, Jackson had kept himself scarce since that evening he'd come into the Orb looking for her, but she'd heard through the grapevine that he was spotted in town only a day or two earlier, so he obviously wasn't in police custody. Maybe he'd just been away somewhere. It was frustrating that her efforts with the photos appeared to have amounted to nothing.

Georgia knew Jackson was bound to start hassling Cole again soon for the rent money. She felt angry that Jordan was making things so uncomfortable for him. She was even toying with the idea of bunging the arsehole some money to cover Cole's rent for a few months before she left, but wasn't sure how best to go about it. An anonymous donation would be certain to raise a few questions from Jackson and she didn't want to arouse suspicion from Cole, either. But she hated to think of him being under so much pressure. He was a really lovely, gentle man and she could easily have fallen in love with him. She was going to be sorry to leave him behind. Georgia couldn't help but draw comparisons between Trevor and Cole: the attentive way he spoke to her, the way he seemed to respect her as a person. Though she hadn't known him long, she was sure he didn't have it in him to behave in the way her husband sometimes had. She

264

recalled one occasion when she'd been at a business awards party with Trevor, who'd deliberately ignored her for most of the evening, sulking over something petty as he often did. After a few drinks, he had actually pulled an attractive young cocktail waitress onto his lap and nuzzled her neck in front of everyone, as Georgia looked on, squirming in humiliation, while the girl laughed as he tucked a twenty-pound note into her cleavage. It was as though he wanted to remind Georgia constantly that he was the one in control; that, although she never really believed he would, he could trade her in for a younger model at the drop of a hat if he wanted to. It was a power thing, that much she realised. But she'd hated him for it.

Georgia planned to take Cole for a nice meal. They had seen one another in the pub most evenings for the last fortnight, as well as the few afternoons they'd spent together at Cuckoo Cottage.

Before they left the previous evening, Cole had told her he'd be in the pub by about 7.30pm on Thursday, so she gave him strict instructions not to eat before coming out. He'd looked at her quizzically.

"Is Lucas doing a curry night?" he'd asked, tipping his head in the direction of the kitchen from where the temperamental chef would flit in and out occasionally, usually red-faced and barking expletives at Yiannis.

"No. We're not eating in here, though. It's a surprise."

Cole had looked uncomfortable. "I should be treating you, not the other way around."

"Huh – whatever happened to gender equality?" Georgia jutted her lower lip in mock indignation. "Anyway, I've had a little windfall. A few hundred quid on the lottery," she'd lied. "I thought it would be nice. But if you don't want to come, I'm sure I could invite someone else . . ."

She'd looked at him teasingly and Cole had laughed.

"Well, when you put it like that. I'll look forward to seeing you tomorrow, then."

*

It was 7.20pm.

From the darkened street, Georgia peered through the harlequin window of the Orb before entering to see if Cole had arrived yet. There were only a couple of regulars standing at the bar, but it was relatively early. She scanned the room, smiling a little sadly as she saw the back of his head, then noticed he was sharing a table with someone. A woman – and not one she recognised. They seemed to be engrossed in conversation. Georgia froze. She paused to observe them for a moment. The woman appeared animated, and was nodding frequently. Suddenly she arose, leaning forwards to shake Cole by the hand. Georgia drew back at once, worried that she might have been seen.

Taking a breath, Georgia approached the entrance. As she crossed the threshold, the woman was making her way out of the door. She seemed to hesitate, staring at Georgia. They must have been a similar age. Though not what Georgia would have deemed overly attractive, the woman had done everything possible to enhance her appearance, her make-up subtle and perfectly applied, her sleek, shoulder-length honey-brown hair immaculate. She was dressed in classic, expensive-looking clothes. Georgia was pretty sure the single-breasted camel coat she wore was from Prada. She noticed the tan leather bag hooked over her shoulder, which bore a gold Louis Vuitton motif. It looked like the genuine article. Georgia was familiar enough with designer labels to recognise several thousand pounds' worth of gear when she saw it.

For the briefest moment, Georgia thought she saw the woman

smile. Not at her, but to herself. And then the door swung behind her and she was gone.

That smile. It had looked self-satisfied – almost malicious, for want of a better word. Georgia felt suddenly cold.

Cole looked round as she walked into the bar. "Hello. You look lovely." He stood up, approaching Georgia to kiss her cheek. "And you smell delicious."

Georgia smiled tightly. "Thank you." She locked eyes with Yiannis behind the bar and gave an almost invisible tip of her head towards Cole's table, her eyebrows knitting in a question. Yiannis beckoned her across surreptitiously.

Apparently oblivious to the sudden tension in the room, Cole asked if she would like a drink.

"No, I'm fine. We'll go in a minute. I just need to speak to Yiannis about my hours next week. Won't be a sec."

Georgia took Yiannis through the door behind the bar. "Who was *she*?" she asked, her voice low.

Yiannis shrugged. "Search me. Never seen her before. She wafted in about fifteen minutes ago and made a beeline for him."

"Really? Did – did Cole buy her a drink?" Georgia hated herself for sounding so suspicious and jealous, but she had to know.

"He did, actually. A vodka martini. She downed it in one." He laughed, giving her a playful nudge. "Good job I'm here to keep an eye on things on your night off, eh. Wondered for a minute if you might've had a rival for his affections. Mind you, don't think *she* was up for it anyway. I've seen her sort before. Accepts the drinks but her eyes are elsewhere the whole time. Always looking for that better offer. No idea what she wanted with him."

Yiannis studied Georgia's crestfallen face, his brow furrowing. "Hey, don't look so worried. I was joking." He placed a hand gently on her arm. "Cole's not a player, sweet. I can always tell.

He's nuts about you. And if he *was* up to anything, he'd hardly be doing it in here, would he? You know what they say. Don't shit on your own doorstep."

Georgia managed a half-hearted laugh. They went back through into the bar, where Ned had just come in with Charlie. The old man's face broke into a smile as he saw Georgia.

"Well, don't you look a picture." He nodded towards Cole. "Lucky fella, this one."

"And don't I know it." Cole approached to slip an arm around Georgia's shoulders. She felt herself stiffen and he obviously sensed it. He turned to look at her in surprise.

"Everything okay?"

Georgia forced a smile, still not entirely convinced. "Yeah, all good."

She glanced at Yiannis, who threw her a wink, nodding encouragingly. She tipped her head in acknowledgement, then took hold of Cole's hand.

"Come on. I've booked us a table for eight o'clock. We'd better get a shift on."

The pair wished everyone a good night and stepped outside, their breath fogging in the chill November air. Georgia steered him to their left, past Broadgate and towards the Burges.

Try as she might to shake it off, seeing Cole with the woman had dampened Georgia's mood. She felt as if the surprise she'd planned for him had fallen flat, though he seemed unaware of her frame of mind.

"Where are you taking me? Or is it a secret?" Cole asked good-naturedly.

"The old *Evening Telegraph* newspaper offices have been converted into a hotel and restaurant," she said bleakly. "I thought – given your journalistic leanings – it might make for an interesting evening. The food gets really good reviews."

"Oh wow – I've passed it a few times and wondered what it

was like. Looks very plush. Thank you – it sounds perfect. And I'm starving."

They walked in silence for a few minutes. Georgia had to ask. She couldn't let the evening carry on like this with a knot tightening in her stomach. Her appetite had vanished completely. Better to let her feelings be known.

"Speaking of secrets, that woman you were sitting with – who was she?"

He stopped, his expression a blend of surprise and annoyance. "I didn't realise you'd seen me with anyone. She left shortly before you arrived."

"I . . . I just looked through the window. Before I came into the pub." Georgia cringed inwardly. She didn't want it to sound as if she'd been spying on him.

"Oh." He regarded her uncertainly for a moment. "I was going to tell you all about it later. Well, she's actually looking for someone to ghostwrite a book for her. An autobiography. Said she'd read some of my online articles and liked my writing style. She'd been in touch with the publisher and they passed on my contact details, so she rang me this afternoon and asked to meet up, more to put a face to the name at this stage, as far as I could gather. No specific details from her as yet, but apparently her father was a hugely wealthy, high-profile figure from what she was saying, and not everything people thought he was. Sounds like she's going to dish the dirt. Not my usual kind of thing, but it could be an interesting venture and she's offering ridiculously good money, so I might have to shelve the Coventry history project a bit longer."

"That's brilliant." Georgia tried to look enthused. "So – you accepted her offer, then?"

"Absolutely. Beggars can't be choosers and I've got rent to pay. Hopefully if it takes off, I might even be able to get the deposit for a house of my own."

Georgia nodded, painting on a smile. They continued walking down the Burges, towards Corporation Street. Still all she could think of was the mysterious woman. The more she considered what he'd said, the more implausible it seemed. If she was so wealthy, why would she approach Cole with his limited resumé, rather than some well-established author?

"Who is she then, this woman?" The way in which she blurted it out was unintentional, but left Cole in no doubt about her feelings. He pulled up sharply, turning her to face him, his eyes ablaze.

"I'm sorry – do you have a problem with me having dealings with someone of the opposite sex? Only if there's one trait I can't bear in anyone, it's jealousy."

"*No.* No, of course not." Georgia threw up her hands in dismay. "That's not it at all. It just seems a bit, well, strange, don't you think? I mean, selecting you to write her life story on the basis of some article she's read. Are you sure it's all above board?"

This was going from bad to worse. Georgia didn't want Cole to think she was being dismissive of his ability. But common sense told her there must be more to it.

"I've got no reason to think otherwise. It's an excellent opportunity for me – if the book sells well, it could lead to other openings. I've been stuck in the doldrums so long, I can't afford to pass up the chance of something that could potentially give my profile a boost."

Georgia feared this was exactly the case – Cole was in dire financial straits; he was so desperate for this to be his big break that it was clouding his judgement. But trying to reason with him, she realised, would only make her sound petty and possessive.

"I'm sorry." She rested a hand on his arm, her eyes searching his face earnestly. "I didn't mean to rain on your parade. You're right, of course. It'd be madness not to bite her hand off. Just trying to look at it from all angles, that's all."

He seemed to relax slightly. "In case you hadn't noticed, the offers haven't exactly been rolling in for me. I can only take her at face value and she seemed sincere. I'm actually bloody excited about it – I'd hoped you would be, too."

"I am – of course. I'm just concerned about you, that's all. You're decent and kind – I'd hate anyone to take advantage of you in any way." It sounded lame, Georgia knew that. But the sentiment was genuine. She thought of the weird way the woman had smiled in the doorway and goosebumps rose along her arms.

Cole gave an odd laugh. "That's very good of you, but I don't know if I'm worthy of that description. My ex-wife'd probably beg to differ."

Georgia blew out a long breath. "Look, let's forget about it for now, shall we? I'd been looking forward to us spending time together somewhere new. Can we just go and enjoy our food and talk about something else? Please?"

Cole shrugged. "Sure, fine by me." But his taut body language told a different story. They carried on to the restaurant making occasional small talk, but an awkward atmosphere had descended, which showed no sign of lifting even as the evening progressed.

Cole was polite but unwontedly quiet throughout the meal. They ate their food in silence, and any subsequent conversation felt stilted and awkward. Georgia noticed his eyes travelling regularly to the clock on the wall.

He walked Georgia back to Cuckoo Cottage at the end of the night, and though he held her hand, it felt as though he was doing it out of courtesy.

"Do you want to come in?" she'd asked hopefully, even if only to end the evening on a less sour note.

Cole puffed out his cheeks. "I think I'll pass, if you don't mind."

He shuffled back a little, his hands clasped behind him. "Listen, it's nothing personal but I think maybe we should cool things for a bit. I mean, I'm going to be even busier than usual focusing on the new book, so I probably won't be free to keep popping into the pub any more. I don't want to keep you dangling when you could be seeing someone else. It's nothing personal," he added, seeing her dejected expression.

"It's because of what I said about that woman, isn't it?" Georgia couldn't disguise her disappointment. Though she knew she wouldn't be seeing him again, she didn't want things to end between them like this. "I meant it, it was nothing to do with me being jealous. I'm always wary of people's motives until I know otherwise – it's just how I am."

Cole sighed. "I'm sure you mean well. But I wish you'd shown more faith in me. I'm not stupid – if I thought she was anything other than genuine, I'd run a mile."

Georgia seriously doubted this, but made no comment. Cole was blinkered, dazzled by the thought of the money he'd been promised to write the book. Flattered, too, that this woman was clearly impressed by his ability as a writer. Even his usual ethics seemed to have gone out of the window. Before she could say anything else, he leaned forwards to give her cheek a perfunctory kiss.

"Goodnight." His voice was cool. "And thank you for the meal. It was a nice idea."

He fell short of adding that the reality had been something else. Georgia watched helplessly as he turned and walked away, disappearing out of the quad without a backward glance.

Blinking back angry tears, she turned the key in the lock. She would probably never see Cole again and his abiding memory of her would be as a jealous bitch.

Once inside, she paused to collect her thoughts. Maybe it was for the best, complicated things less. But she would sit on the cottage in Oxfordshire for a night or two. Maybe leave it until the weekend. She still had to see Minnie before she left. She'd agreed to join her for lunch and Georgia wanted to make it special. A nice memory.

After her nightly routine of locking up and barricading the doors, Georgia poured herself a whisky, took a sleeping pill and went straight to bed. She needed to put the unfortunate evening with Cole out of her mind. She should be feeling more positive about things now. She was taking action: she had an actual, viable plan.

Soon enough she would set things in motion with the move, and then she could be looking forward to a safer future. Away from Cuckoo Cottage. And away from Coventry.

Even if it meant leaving her precious daughter behind.

Chapter 30

Georgia

Friday, 4 November 2022

The morning air was chilly, but thankfully it was a dry, crisp day, the sky clear. Damp weather always seemed to make Cuckoo Cottage feel even colder, somehow. Georgia had lit the log burner anyway. The heat it threw out warmed the whole house and made it cosier and more welcoming. Georgia was sitting in the front room about to eat breakfast, when she heard the slap of post landing on the doormat. As she rose from her chair, there was a sharp rap on the door. She peered from behind the nets to see the postman standing on the step, looking round and clutching a package.

She stooped to pick up the handful of post from the vestibule, then unlocked the door.

"Morning. Sorry – hadn't realised there was this parcel for you, too." The man smiled, handing it across. "Don't need a signature, but it was too big to push through the letterbox."

Georgia thanked him and closed the door. The package wasn't wide, but quite bulky, and soft. She squeezed it gently. It felt like lots of bubble wrap, or something similar. As she peered curiously at the label, her heart sank.

J. Jackson. Something for Jethro, presumably. But why would it be coming to her address? Georgia didn't want to have to seek him out to give it to him. The fewer encounters she had to have with the man, the better. She didn't even feel inclined to hand it over if she saw him in the street. She didn't see why she should have to put herself out. He ought to have made sure his post was properly directed. But thankfully he seemed to have been giving her a wide berth – she hadn't seen him at all since that day he'd been into the Orb looking for her. The more she'd considered it, the more she'd begun to think that maybe he wasn't connected to the weird things happening to her. She suspected his style would be much less subtle.

Propping the package against the wall next to the front door, she went back into the sitting room to finish her cereal, leafing through her own post as she did so. An electricity bill, a statement from the water board. Nothing of any great interest. Georgia dropped them onto the little side table, knocked back her cup of tea and went to take a shower. She was due to meet Minnie for lunch in Bistrot Pierre, a final get-together before her departure from the city. Though Minnie didn't need to know that. Not yet.

*

The bright weather of the morning had given way to showers, but the residual warmth from the wood-burning stove was still throwing out enough heat to make everywhere in the house feel toasty. Slightly drowsy, her stomach full after a hearty lunch, Georgia went upstairs to rest for a while. She checked her phone before settling down, smiling wistfully at the message from Minnie thanking her for a lovely afternoon. It had been so nice to see her and she'd looked so well – so *happy*. Georgia had fought back tears as they'd said goodbye. Clung to her a little longer than she would normally, making Minnie ask if everything was okay. She didn't have a clue how long it would be before they'd see one another again. But it was for the best; she knew that. Minnie had been coy and a little evasive when Georgia asked if she was seeing anyone, which made her suspect that she was. Georgia felt a sudden burst of anxiety, knowing that she would no longer be able to keep such a close eye on her and who she was involved with. But little by little, she'd have to let go; she knew that. After all, Minnie was nineteen now, a similar age to herself when she'd fallen pregnant. And she had a good, supportive group of friends. Georgia felt sure they'd look out for her.

Georgia set an alarm for 5.15pm, to give herself time to wake properly from her nap and get ready to go to the Orb by six o'clock, then nestled under the quilt to close her eyes. The room was still so warm that she threw the covers off and lay atop the duvet instead. Thank God for the log burner. Despite the draughty windows, it was a lifesaver when the temperatures dropped.

It was dark by the time the alarm went off. Georgia groped for the switch on the clock and cancelled the persistent bleeping which had left her heart pounding, having fallen into a deeper sleep than she'd intended. She sat up slowly, rubbing her eyes, then stretched as she made her way from the bed to the door.

Georgia stopped suddenly. What was that godawful *smell*? She put a hand over her nose as she descended the stairs. The odour was offensively pungent and definitely emanating from downstairs somewhere.

Georgia looked all around the sitting room, but there was nothing obvious. She went into the kitchen and checked the pedal bin, in case there was something at the bottom that had gone bad. She opened the fridge but the contents all smelled quite fresh, then leaned over the sink and sniffed. Not the drain, either.

She went back into the sitting room. The smell was definitely stronger in here. And then she remembered Jethro Jackson's package. As she went into the hallway and bent towards the parcel, still leaning against the wall, she recoiled, almost gagging. Reluctantly picking the thing up with one hand, the other pinching her nostrils, she carried it into the kitchen, trying not to retch. Whatever was in there, whether foodstuff or otherwise, had obviously gone rotten – probably helped on its way by the warmth of the house. She couldn't imagine Jackson would want it now, whatever it was.

Georgia took a pair of scissors from the cutlery drawer and, placing the parcel in the sink, cut through the tightly-bound layer of Sellotape wrapped around its opening. She tore back the thick paper, revealing, as she'd suspected, reams of bubble wrap. Georgia pulled it out, holding her breath. It was like that party game, 'pass the parcel': layer upon layer of wrapping until the prize was finally revealed. Georgia kept opening more and more bubble wrap, equally intrigued and repelled by the smell, which was growing stronger by the second.

As she reached the final layer, Georgia let out a scream.

There at the centre, its once vibrant plumage like oil on water, the eyeless head barely attached, lay the corpse of a starling, a maggot-infested cavity in its bloodied side. Completely repulsed, Georgia dropped the thing onto the floor. Sending someone a dead bird – wasn't that some sort of sinister message? A warning – a foreshadowing – that's what it was called. She'd read about it once. Her heart hammering, she cast around for something to dispose of it with. There was a plastic bag hanging from the hook on the back of the door. Trying not to heave, Georgia grabbed it, putting a hand inside like a glove. Steeling herself, her stomach turning over both from the shock and sheer revulsion, she scooped up the bird and the bubble wrap, inverting the bag. With shaking hands, she unlocked the stable door and took it out into the yard, then thrust the whole thing into the wheelie bin.

Locking the door behind her, Georgia leaned back against it for a moment. Her eyes landed on the outer wrapper of brown paper, still in the sink. *Urgh*. Her skin crawled. Everything would need to be bleached; she felt she needed to throw all her clothes into the wash and take a hot shower to rid herself of the stench which seemed to linger around her, whether in her imagination or not, she couldn't be sure.

Returning to the sink, Georgia gingerly picked up the paper between finger and thumb. As she did so, she noticed some wording scrawled in red capitals on the underside. Trying not to get too close, she turned it round so that she could read it.

Georgia clutched the edge of the sink, her chest suddenly tight, legs wobbling so much she thought she might keel over.

YOU CAN RUN BUT YOU CAN'T HIDE, BITCH

And then she knew for certain. That the parcel had never been intended for Jethro Jackson at all. That, like the clay figurine and the teeth, it was meant for her. And the sooner she got out of this hellhole, the better.

278

Chapter 31

Georgia

Saturday, 5 November 2022

Frustratingly, as she'd dragged her heels, the gatekeeper's cottage in Oxfordshire had been booked for a long weekend, delaying her planned escape. Georgia was kicking herself for procrastinating. But hopefully the following Wednesday would be soon enough. She'd paid the deposit now, and it had lifted her spirits a little. She felt she was seeing light at the end of the tunnel. But Georgia had begun to rely on the diazepam to get her through the day, more than ever now. She'd noticed Yiannis giving her strange looks as she served people that evening, and realised her hands had developed a tremor. Georgia gripped the handle on the beer tap more tightly in an attempt to conceal the fact. She was going to have to try to break the habit once she was in a calmer frame of mind. She prayed it would be soon.

Finding the tarot card had made her completely paranoid and she found herself scrutinising every customer, male or female, with wariness and hostility.

"Lighten up a bit, will you. You'll frighten all the punters away if you keep looking at them like that," Yiannis had hissed at her at one point. But Georgia really couldn't help it. The Orb had been the one place she'd felt relatively safe and now she couldn't even find refuge in there.

*

Fireworks had been going off late into the night. Georgia hated them, had always done so, even as a child. Something which Minnie seemed to have inherited; although for Minnie it was more about empathy for the animals, the wildlife who were being terrorised and even killed. Georgia hated the sudden bangs, the smell left hanging in the air. The smog they created, which seemed to hang around for days afterwards.

Even with a sleeping pill, it had taken hours before she'd finally drifted off, plugging her ears with cotton wool to deaden the sound. Georgia found herself suddenly, abruptly awake, as though someone had shaken her. She sat up, her heart pounding. There was a rattling noise coming from downstairs. She took the cotton wool from her ears and strained to listen, trying to locate the direction it was coming from. It seemed to be at the back of the house; maybe the kitchen, or even the shower room.

Frantically, she reached into the drawer in the bedside cabinet and withdrew the carving knife she'd taken to keeping in there as a precaution, placing it on the tabletop next to her mobile.

Pulling on her dressing gown, she slipped the phone into her pocket, grabbed the knife and headed for the stairs. She could feel blood pulsing in her ears, every one of her senses on high alert.

The noise continued, more insistent than before. Clutching the knife, Georgia descended the stairs slowly. She peered through the sitting room door. The noise abated suddenly. Georgia held her breath. From beyond the open kitchen doorway at the far end of the room, she could see movement through the gloom. Frozen with fear, Georgia watched as a shadow, cast through the roller blind, passed back and forth across the cupboards opposite the window. Someone was outside. Pacing. The shadow vanished, then the rattling sound began again, louder and more urgently than ever, as though the person was growing angrier by the minute.

Horrified, Georgia realised that the intruder was trying to gain access through the stable door at the back of the house. It was locked and she'd definitely remembered to wedge the poker through the latch: it had become part of her nightly routine. The concern was that the vigorous, repeated rattling could dislodge it, and without something bracing it, even with the sturdy new bolt, the door would probably yield if any reasonable force was applied to it.

It wasn't a chance she wanted to take.

Georgia took the stairs two at a time. Desperately, she reached into her pocket for the phone. Her shaking fingers felt thick and clumsy as she jabbed at the keys.

The response came down the line immediately: professional, efficient-sounding.

"Emergency. Which service, please?" The woman at the other end waited as Georgia tried to collect her thoughts. "Hello?"

Attempting to keep her voice as steady as possible, Georgia whispered back. "Police, please. Someone's trying to break into my house. I'm on my own."

Georgia crouched in terror behind the bedroom door, willing the police to arrive before the intruder actually managed to get through the back door. The rattling had given way to the sound of something hard thudding against the wood, whether an implement or a boot, she couldn't tell.

There was an almighty crash, and with it the thudding stopped. Georgia hardly dared breathe. Following the brief silence, she could hear the sound of someone moving around downstairs. It felt as though her heart might actually burst out of her chest. She curled into a tight ball, bracing herself for the footsteps on the stairs which were sure to follow.

Georgia realised that the noise had desisted. She turned her head towards the door to listen, fear oozing through every pore. Had the intruder gone – or were they standing, listening, waiting for the right moment to pounce?

A sudden hammering on the front door almost made her jump out of her skin.

"Mrs Parnell, it's the police. Open up."

Georgia's legs were trembling so much, she could barely stand. She hauled herself to her feet, clinging first to the bedroom furniture, then the banister, as she wobbled down to open the front door. Two uniformed male officers came straight in, ensuring her well-being first, before rushing through to the back of the house.

"He's gone," she heard one call. "Must've heard us. Can't have got far, though. I'll get out there."

Georgia heard something crack, the sound of boots trampling over wood.

She managed to get herself into the sitting room. Switching on the light, she went towards the kitchen in a daze, stopping in her tracks as she saw the mess that had been made of the stable-door. The top half lay on the ground, ripped from its hinges, its wooden panels splintered and dented. The bottom swung open, the poker dangling uselessly from the latch.

"Are you all right, Mrs Parnell? You're not harmed in any way?" The remaining policeman, standing in the middle of the kitchen floor, turned to look from the debris to her, his face concerned.

Georgia shook her head. All she could reflect on was what might have happened had the police not arrived when they did. She staggered slightly, covered her mouth, thinking she might be sick.

The policeman guided her into the nearest armchair.

"Is there anywhere you can stay for tonight? Until this lot can be patched up?"

Georgia thought of Minnie but quickly squashed the idea. It wouldn't be fair to wake her in the middle of the night and anyway, she didn't want to worry her. She rubbed at her forehead, trying to clear the tangle of thoughts coursing through her mind.

"I – I think my insurance company will send somebody out to repair the door. I need to dig out my paperwork."

On autopilot, she got up and went back through the sitting room to climb the stairs, hardly knowing how her legs had taken her there. She couldn't even remember who she was insured with. Who had the letting agency recommended? She recalled Stephen saying it wasn't compulsory, as the landlord ought to be fully insured, but possibly advisable to cover herself just in case.

Trevor had taught her well. "If something can go wrong, it probably will. Never take chances. Never make assumptions."

Georgia could hear him now. *Belt and braces, Georgie.*

Especially after finding out about Jethro Jackson's reputation, she had organised premium insurance for her personal belongings before moving them into the house, and had been persuaded by the agent she'd spoken to over the phone to take out basic cover for the building itself, too.

"Some landlords are unscrupulous," she'd advised. "You don't want to find yourself paying out for damage if it's not your fault."

In a moment of clarity, she remembered the documents that had arrived in the post. She reached them from the top shelf of the wardrobe and tapped their number into her mobile. After a call which lasted only a few minutes, she sank back onto the bed. Someone would be round within the hour to patch up the door.

Georgia went back down to tell the police officer, who was speaking to someone over his walkie-talkie. He ended his conversation and turned to her.

"The perpetrator seems to have disappeared into thin air – my colleague radioed for back-up and they've been all round the side streets but nada, unfortunately. We'll dust for prints but I'm not hopeful. Most of these buggers are pros and wear gloves. The best we can hope for is boot prints, but we'll need daylight, so it'll have to be tomorrow, I'm afraid. Any joy with the insurance company?"

She nodded weakly. "They're sending someone out as soon as possible to make the door secure."

"Well, that's something. Good job you were on the ball with your policy, eh?"

The second policeman reappeared through the back door, slightly breathless, a smudge of dirt on one sleeve of his jacket. He looked defeated.

"He was one step ahead of us. We've searched all the alleyways, in sheds and behind bins. He must know the area, I reckon. Main thing is, he didn't get away with anything. He won't be back tonight, that's for sure."

Georgia said nothing. It was her own safety she was concerned for, not her belongings. Whoever it was would have been welcome to anything if they'd just left her alone. But in her gut, she felt sure her possessions weren't of any interest to them. She was the target. Her nerves were in tatters.

She made tea for the officers, who waited with her until the repair man turned up. By the time they had all left, it was almost 5.30am. Georgia felt physically and emotionally exhausted.

It was only after everyone had gone that Georgia saw it. The workman had piled the splintered pieces of wood from the broken door in the back yard, but one piece had been missed, kicked inadvertently beneath the cooker. As she was checking the back door a final time before going back to bed, Georgia noticed the corner poking out from beneath the oven. Stooping to slide it out, her heart almost stopped.

The message, three hateful words, scrawled in chalk capitals, left her in no doubt that her suspicions were very much justified.

NEXT TIME, BITCH

Chapter 32

Georgia

Monday, 7 November 2022

Sunday had been dire. Georgia had spent the entire morning cleaning up the kitchen thoroughly and in a state of constant anxiety, jumping at the slightest sound or the sight of someone passing the house from the corner of her eye. Yiannis had asked if she wanted to stay at the Orb after the pub quiz in the evening, seeing how jumpy she was.

"Not nice, someone trying to break in like that," he'd said, studying her with concern. "Freddie's more than happy for you to stay here for a few nights until the door's been fixed properly. My mum was broken into once. Nothing much taken, but she had to move after that – said the house just didn't feel the same anymore."

Georgia thanked him but declined. Though her nerves were in tatters, she felt she needed to stay in the house the night after the attempted break-in, or she would never return. Like getting back onto the proverbial horse after a fall. She needed to keep in mind that soon she would be leaving it behind for good.

But even as she'd awoken on Monday morning, Georgia had had a terrible feeling that the day wasn't going to go well. That maybe it would have been better to stay in bed and shut out the world, keep out of sight. After leaving the Orb the night before, she'd bolted the doors; slid the carving knife from the block in the kitchen to take upstairs again, this time tucking it beneath her pillow. She knew that if it came to it, she would use the thing without hesitation.

NEXT TIME, BITCH. Whoever it was would be back, there was no doubt about it.

All night Georgia had tossed and turned, worrying about the intruder; the revolting package she had received, the tarot card, and what might be in store for her next. Someone out there hated her with a passion: that much was clear. She tried to shake the thought, to carry on with her daily routine as usual.

But looking out of the window at the clear sky, the glorious autumnal foliage shimmering in the early morning light, Georgia felt suddenly defiant. She had things to do, a life to live. Why should she allow some bastard to terrorise her in her own home – let them win? She wondered if the attempted break-in was just another way of putting the wind up her, whether there was ever any actual intention of meeting her face to face. She just needed to keep her wits about her and ensure the house was secure before going anywhere. Just two more days, and Cuckoo Cottage and everything that had been happening to her there would be in the past.

A grocery delivery from Waitrose that Georgia had ordered earlier in the week was due to arrive between 10.00 and 11.00am. She'd booked it before finalising her move and then stupidly forgotten to cancel the order. She could always leave a message for Yiannis, hide the key somewhere and tell him to help himself. After the stuff had arrived, she resolved, she'd take a walk to see Minnie again. If she wasn't able to leave yet, she wanted to make the most of any remaining time she'd be able to spend with her. The thought of potentially not seeing her for months was eating her up inside.

When the delivery driver knocked on the door at 10.50am, she was ready to go out once she'd put away the shopping. But upon opening the door, Georgia heard raised voices. As she looked to her left, she saw a small gathering outside the Slug and Lettuce, the bar adjacent to the Orb. The people all appeared to be staring at something on the wall, turning frequently to talk among themselves, shaking their heads and looking around. As others passed through the quad, they looked over and began to gravitate towards the group, seemingly curious.

The driver placed the final crate of groceries just inside the door, gesturing towards the crowd. "Dunno what's going on up there. Something's caught their eye by the looks of it."

Georgia strained to look beyond the sea of heads. She gave a small shrug. "Maybe it's one of those guided tours or something and they're waiting for their guide."

"Yeah, maybe." He cast a look over his shoulder, his brow folding slightly. "They all look a bit – worried, I'd have said. Not too pleased, either."

"Oh, maybe it's the plaque about the hanging. I suppose some people might be a bit disturbed by it."

He grimaced, staring at the building uncertainly. "What, someone was actually *hanged* up there?"

"A long time ago. Pretty gruesome, I know."

The man shuddered. "Eugh. Rather you than me, living that close to it. And the graveyard. Doesn't it bother you?"

Georgia laughed, a little bitterly. Her eyes travelled to the terrace opposite. "I didn't think it would when I first came here. Not so sure now, to be honest."

He gave her an odd look. "Oh dear. Still, you could always move . . ." The man's mouth curved upwards, though the frown was still in evidence. He glanced at the list in his hand then down at the bags of shopping, now removed from the containers. "Right, no substitutions in this lot, so I think that's everything, then."

"Thanks very much. Have a good day."

The man gave a small nod, smiled tightly and retreated into his van. Georgia noticed him slow down to take a closer look as he passed the cluster of people outside the bar. She closed the door and went to put the shopping away, then slipped on her coat to make her way to Minnie's. She knew she'd be at home, as she'd told her the other day she didn't have any lectures until the afternoon.

There were even more people there now, a crowd of at least fifteen, snatches of conversation audible as she walked up across the cobbles.

"It's a bloody disgrace," she heard one woman say.

"I remember seeing it on the news at the time – shocking case," said an elderly man, shaking his head.

"People have the right to know who's living next door to them," said another woman angrily. "What are they trying to do to our community?"

Intrigued, Georgia approached to see what all the fuss was about.

Pasted to the wall of the old jailhouse was an A1 poster, a grainy black and white newspaper article pixellated and clearly blown up from a much smaller image. Georgia's stomach dropped. Printed in large, bold capitals beneath the picture, the words swam before her eyes.

WARNING!!!
INFAMOUS JUVENILE OFFENDER
RELOCATES TO COVENTRY
– DO YOU KNOW WHO YOUR NEIGHBOUR IS?

The photograph showed the sullen-looking, hollow-eyed face of a child, captured at his or her worst, the headline diagonally across it declaring GUILTY – then the accompanying caption: Custodial Sentence for Remorseless Baby-faced Killer

"I'm telling you," the first woman resumed adamantly, "People like that don't change. Dangerous kids turn into dangerous adults. They should never be allowed to roam free – and definitely not when no one knows what they're capable of. We should've been told if there's someone like that on the loose."

"Yeah." Another man nodded. "The law's gone soft." He waved a hand towards the old jailhouse. "They should've done what they did to that Mary Ball, kid or not. People like that are the scum of the earth." He spat on the ground as if to emphasise his point.

"Too right," agreed someone else. "They need a proper deterrent, not this half-soaked approach."

The atmosphere among the crowd was becoming increasingly agitated, each feeding off the anger and vitriol of the others.

A young man with tanned skin and close-cropped dark hair, his sleeves rolled up, appeared suddenly from the doorway of the bar. Taking one look at the poster, he pushed his way through and ripped it from the wall.

"Oi, what did you do that for?" an irate male voice shouted from somewhere in the group.

The man turned to cast them all a look of disgust, crumpling the paper between both hands. "For God's sake! Haven't you got better things to do with your morning than standing here baying for the blood of someone who's already paid their debt

290

to society? We all make mistakes. Even if this person is grown up now, they were only a child at the time. Think about it! Or are you all still living in the Dark Ages? I'd've hoped we'd all moved on from that by now."

The people's cries of indignation grew quieter. Though some still appeared riled, the majority of voices had been reduced to a mumble, glancing at one another shamefacedly. Gradually they started to disperse. The young man looked on, arms folded, until the last of them had drifted away.

His gaze landed on Georgia, who was still rooted to the spot, staring after them.

"Honestly. I despair."

Georgia managed a curt nod. A sick feeling was churning in her gut. "I – I just came to see what all the fuss was about."

The man shook his head sadly. "I thought the UK was better than that. My mother came here from Iran over twenty-five years ago, trying to get away from exactly this sort of attitude. Her younger brother – he was hanged when he was still a minor. Mum works for Amnesty International now, supporting oppressed people and trying to change attitudes. Some of the stories she's told us would make your hair stand on end."

Georgia stared at him. "Your mum's brother was *hanged*?" Her voice was strained, her throat dry.

"Yes. For being gay." The man's eyes were glassy with tears. "He was only fourteen. Can you imagine?"

"I'm so sorry," Georgia whispered.

"So am I – and I'm sorry that people everywhere don't find the idea of execution for whatever reason abhorrent." He screwed up the ball of paper in his hand viciously. "I'd like to get my hands on whoever put this thing up. I don't know what their game is."

Georgia knew *exactly* what the game was. Her eyes flew round the quad, wondering whether the culprit was still close by, observing them with spiteful glee. Suddenly the desire to see Minnie had vanished.

The young man wished her good morning and went back into the bar. She assumed he must be one of the staff. With another sharp glance about her, Georgia retreated into Cuckoo Cottage. She bolted the door and pushed the doorstop against it, something she only usually did at bedtime.

It felt as though the net was closing in around her. Georgia's mind was racing. Though she was desperate to leave, she couldn't go until the house was available. Maybe she should do what she'd done before, book something else until the place was ready. She'd thought another couple of days wouldn't have made too much difference, but she knew now she had to get out and fast. If she'd had any idea where her tormentor was, she'd have confronted them – or better still, taken them unawares. As it was, their anonymity had given them the upper hand. She felt like a wild animal, caught in a snare. Waiting for the trapper to come back and finish the job.

Georgia sank into the armchair by the window, her mind racing. Where could she go? She pulled her laptop out of its case and lifted the lid. She could book a last-minute trip to somewhere at the other end of the country – even catch a plane to Europe. But what about Minnie? With the way things were escalating, she really feared that whoever it was might target her next. Georgia's head felt as if it was bursting at the seams. She would have to think of a plausible excuse, persuade Minnie to accompany her. She couldn't abandon her daughter. And if Minnie refused to come, then maybe Georgia really *would* have to stay and face the music. The thought made her gut churn.

She was about to search for flights for both of them, hoping the lure of some winter sun might be too good an offer to pass up, when an email notification popped up at the bottom of the screen.

Borealis.A.1082@gmail.com

Angrily, Georgia opened her emails, this time preparing to reply. Her fingers hovered, poised to type as she thought what she should say, when the subject line pulled her up sharply:

Re: Time for that catch-up Tuesday 8th 7.30 pm?

So Borealis.A actually wanted to meet. She sat back for a moment, wondering what she should do. Maybe this was the only way to make it all stop. To bring things to a head, confront her tormentor and find out what they wanted from her; to see if some sort of agreement could be made.

Steeling herself, Georgia opened the email to see what the sender was proposing. Tomorrow evening. She would finally see who had been trying to scare her these past few weeks. Who had been metaphorically sticking pins in her effigy.

Georgia took a deep breath and began to type her response. Tomorrow evening. She would be ready.

Chapter 33

Minnie

Saturday, 12 November 2022 – Five days later

Minnie was sitting at the breakfast bar in the kitchen, flicking through her emails on her phone and eating toast, when she heard the slam of the front door. Her eyes flew to the clock. Still only 8.40am. Plenty of time before she was due to meet her mum for coffee.

Fatima's eyes were wild as she tore into the kitchen.

"Oh my God, Mins. Oh. My. Frigging. God." She shook her head repeatedly, pulling up a stool next to Minnie as she slapped a newspaper down on the countertop along with the carton of milk she'd just been to buy.

"What? What the hell's up?" Perplexed, Minnie looked from Fatima to the newspaper, twisting it round to read the headline that Fatima was jabbing a shaking finger towards.

WOMAN FOUND MURDERED
IN QUIET WARWICK CUL-DE-SAC IDENTIFIED AS
WEALTHY CONSTRUCTION HEIRESS

Minnie screwed up her eyes to read the smaller print and drew in a sharp breath. She began to read aloud.

"'*Police are continuing their appeal for witnesses following the discovery of a woman's body in a quiet residential road, close to Warwick town centre, in the early hours of Wednesday morning. The death is being treated as murder, although no details have been released as yet. From items in her possession, the victim has now been formally identified as Aurora Trelawney, aged thirty-nine, from the Oxford area. Miss Trelawney is believed to be the only daughter of the late William Trelawney, founder of the successful Trelawney Construction Company, who passed away two years ago. Miss Trelawney's mother is thought to have pre-deceased him by some twenty-five years. It is not clear at this stage whether the crime is in any way connected to Miss Trelawney's status or merely a random attack. If anyone has any information, please call the Crimestoppers hotline on . . .'*"

The picture beneath was a grainy enlargement of what appeared to be a driving licence photograph. Though minus glasses, in full make-up and with her highlighted hair piled high, the image in front of her was unmistakeably that of Angela, albeit a much more glamorous version.

Minnie's mind whirred. She stared at the photo in disbelief, reading and rereading the text in her head. *An heiress.* And her mother had been dead years, by the sounds of things. It was all too much to take in.

"We've got to go to the police," she said eventually, her voice no more than a croak.

Fatima threw up her hands. "And tell them what, exactly? None of *us* had anything to do with this. I always thought there was something not right about her. Why'd she lie about who she was? That's a pretty major deception."

"I have no idea. But I'm really wondering now if she was involved in something dodgy. We should've been more careful about checking her out before she moved in, made her go through the agency instead of just putting up that poster." Minnie thought back to Angela's secretive behaviour, the phone calls to an unnamed cousin. "What a horrible way to finish up though, whatever she'd done."

Fatima slid off the stool and went to one of the cupboards high on the wall. "I need my Rescue Remedy," she announced melodramatically, standing on her toes and scrabbling around on the shelf until she found a small brown bottle. She unscrewed the top and dripped some of its contents straight into her open mouth.

"This has absolutely fucked with my head. Christ, if she was an actual target, we could *all* have been at risk having her living here. We might've had a narrow escape."

Minnie turned to her, blowing out her cheeks. "I can't see why we'd have been in any danger. And it could just as easily have been a mugging that went wrong or something. But I mean it, we really should tell someone she'd been living with us. It might be important."

Fatima straightened, clutching at her head with both hands. "I don't want to be dragged into anything, Mins. I think we should just keep schtum. I mean, it's not like anything happened to her while she was under the same roof as us. And we never really had much to do with her, did we?"

"Yes, but the fact she'd lied about her name, about being on the course. Maybe the police might be able to make sense of it, if they know more about her background than we do."

"About whose background?"

The pair looked round to see Ajab standing in the doorway, still in his pyjamas and rubbing sleep from his eyes with the heels of his hands. Before Minnie had a chance to speak, Fatima grabbed the newspaper and thrust it towards him. "That bloody Angela's. But get this – she wasn't even *called* Angela."

Ajab stared at the page, his eyes wide, then looked up at Minnie open-mouthed. "Shit." He shook his head in disbelief. "Wonder what the hell she was mixed up in?"

"Exactly." Fatima chewed her lip. She hopped from one foot to the other in agitation. The Rescue Remedy clearly hadn't kicked in yet. "I – I'm telling you, extra rent or not, I'm not having anyone else living here after this. It's made me realise just how dangerous it could've been, allowing her to move in before we'd had any proper paperwork off her. I was just getting a bit desperate to be honest, with my dad on at me about having to pay the extra rent." She shook her head. "Remember that time I saw her in your room, Mins? Sleepwalking, my arse."

Minnie had to admit it had all been very peculiar. As had Angela.

"Could've been something to do with her dad's money, though," she suggested. "Sounds as if he was minted."

"Well, that explains how she was able to stump up the rent money no problem, at least," Ajab said slowly. "But what it doesn't explain is why she pretended to be studying for a history degree – and more to the point, why she singled *us* out. 'Cause that's looking exactly like what she did. I mean, if money's no object, why would you move in with a group of students young enough to be your offspring, then hide yourself away all the time and make out you're totally focused on your non-existent coursework? Looks like she told us a pack of lies from the word go."

"Wait," said Fatima, her eyes widening suddenly. She turned to Minnie. "Wasn't your dad something in construction, Mins?"

"Well, sort of." Minnie's brow folded into a frown. She wondered where this was heading.

Fatima leaned forwards eagerly. "D'you think – d'you think there could've been a connection there of some sort – you know, with her old man's business and everything?"

"But my dad had a few different ventures on the go, not just building contracts." She pulled a face, feeling suddenly uncomfortable. "I can't see what that'd have to do with anything, though."

Ajab looked thoughtful. "Yeah. It's a bit tenuous." He tapped the newspaper. "And why now, if it was something to do with Angela's dad? I mean, from what it says here, he's been dead a couple of years."

"And so has Minnie's!" Fatima arched an eyebrow almost triumphantly. "What if – I don't know, they had some sort of deal and it went wrong, or Angela's dad was double-crossed and she was looking for revenge or something . . ."

"That's enough now." Ajab's voice was sharp. He moved to slip an arm around Minnie, whose eyes were bright with tears. The thought that her beloved dad could have had any sort of connection with Angela or her family was completely unpalatable.

"You're upsetting Mins and it all sounds totally far-fetched, anyway." Ajab glowered pointedly at Fatima, whose shoulders sagged.

"Well, I don't know, do I?" Fatima glanced at Minnie. "Just trying to think of possible scenarios, that's all. Sorry, Mins," she added, a little sheepishly. "I didn't mean to dis your dad or anything."

"That's okay," Minnie sniffed. "It always upsets me talking about him. And Dad was a good man; he'd never have stitched anyone up, I'm sure of it."

Trevor had been a good father: that much was true. But

Minnie couldn't put her hand on her heart and say that every one of his business deals had been entirely above board. She couldn't say it aloud, not even to her mum, but some of the paperwork she'd found after his death had seemed a bit, well, irregular. Figures crossed out and amended; cryptic notes in the margins. Minnie could never not love her father, but it had given her a weird feeling in her gut, to think he might not have been quite as worthy of her idolisation as she'd always believed. She'd pushed the notion away, tried not to dwell on it.

Ajab let out a long breath. "Look, I reckon we should stop trying to do the amateur sleuth bit and let the police do their job. But I really think we need to inform them about Angela moving in with us for a while. I'd rather do that than have them banging on our door in the middle of the night and demanding to know why we didn't come forward."

Fatima shrugged. "Okay. I guess you're right. Just hope we don't get the press camping outside the door, that's all. My dad's not a fan of negative publicity."

"I'm sure no one will get a whiff of anything – and even if they do, it'll all be a flash in the pan." Ajab looked thoughtful. "And Angela barely lived here five minutes. The press'll be far more interested in digging up dirt on her and her family."

Or mine. Minnie cleared her throat. Trying to shake any thoughts of her dad having done something unscrupulous, she picked up her phone and went to her news app. The same photograph of Angela was at the top of the day's headlines. She scrolled down the page, her eyes flicking over the various accompanying captions.

"Good God, it's all over the tabloids. The vultures are speculating already." She looked beyond Fatima, into the empty hallway. "By the way, where's Sonia? Wonder if she's seen the news."

"Stayed at some bloke's she picked up the other night."

Fatima rolled her eyes. "I'd drop her a text to tell her what's gone on, but she'll probably be otherwise engaged."

As if on cue, Fatima's phone began to ring from somewhere in the house. "'Scuse me," she muttered, making her way out of the kitchen. "She probably heard me."

"You okay?" Ajab studied Minnie with concern. "She's got foot-in-mouth syndrome, that one." He tipped his head in Fatima's direction.

Minnie smiled. "Yeah, I'm fine. Just a bit, well, touchy about my dad, you know . . ."

He nodded, wrinkling his nose sympathetically. "Listen, d'you want to go to the cop shop, or shall we just call the number they've given in the paper?"

"Probably best to just ring them. I'm sure if they want to interview us properly, they'll call round." Minnie exhaled. "No time like the present, I s'pose." She peered at the newspaper once more and began to tap in the telephone number provided, but was halted abruptly by the sound of Fatima's suddenly amplified voice, coming from the living room.

Minnie looked up to see Fatima reappear in the doorway, her expression even more shocked than before.

"Guys, that was Sonia." There was an odd tremor in her tone. She crossed the kitchen and leaned against the breakfast bar as if her legs were in danger of giving way. "She'd already seen the headline on her phone. But get this." She took a deep breath. "The lad she's staying with – he's studying criminology. And his latest module was on crimes committed by juveniles. They'd tried to keep a lid on it, but one of her fellow inmates found out her true identity and leaked it to the press about ten years ago." Fatima's eyes grew wide. "He reckons Angela – aka Aurora Trelawney – was banged up for several years, from the age of twelve. For drowning her baby brother in the bath. Showed no remorse at all, apparently. The psychiatrist who assessed her said she displayed classic psychopathic tendencies. How the hell they released her so early when she'd done a thing like that is anybody's guess."

"*Jesus Christ*." Ajab turned to Minnie, who was sitting with a hand clapped to her mouth. She recalled the cruel way Angela had killed the mouse; the bizarre, almost gleeful satisfaction she seemed to derive from its suffering. Whether she had been a child or not when she'd killed her brother, some remnant of that earlier character clearly still persisted. And as terrible as it was, she could quite easily believe Angela capable of such a thing now.

"I think you were right in what you said, Fatima," she said shakily. "I think we may all have literally dodged a bullet."

*

After her telephone conversation with Fatima, Sonia had hot-footed back to the house, arriving wild-haired and breathless, still reeling from the news about Angela. Her latest boyfriend had given her a printout of the information he'd discovered about Aurora Trelawney. The others had read in stunned silence the details released by one of the least salubrious tabloids. Apparently, Aurora's solicitor had applied for an immediate gagging order, even though she'd been given a new identity. Despite them being the ones directly affected by her crime, it seemed that the fear of dragging the family name through the mud again outweighed the disgust the Trelawneys must have felt towards their daughter.

Following Ajab's call to the Crimestoppers number, the officer he was directed to had asked to come to the house to speak to everyone later that afternoon, much to Fatima's concern.

After lunch, the four of them had gravitated to the living room, where Fatima began to pace nervously.

"Do I need to be in? Only I really don't want to get dragged into anything."

"For God's sake, sit down will you – you're putting me on edge." Sonia threw herself back into the armchair, her eyes travelling to the ceiling. "I just can't believe we were sharing our home with an actual *murderer*. Makes me feel all – I don't know, creeped out." She gave an exaggerated shudder. "There's something really disturbing about the idea of a child who's capable of a thing like that. And then you wonder what they might be capable of as an adult."

"I don't know. I mean, what percentage of people who've committed murder as a minor actually go on to kill again in later life?" Ajab, looking ponderous, sitting on the sofa next to Minnie, who had half an ear on the conversation while texting her mum. Feeling slightly derailed by it all, she had cancelled their coffee date, telling Georgia she'd call her later to explain. It wasn't something she wanted to talk about over a message.

Naturally Georgia was concerned.

Are you OK? Do you want me to come over? xx

All good. Just a bit of drama at the house. Nothing to worry about. Will ring in a bit xx

*

"So hard to know what could motivate anyone to do a terrible thing like that – she might have had some sort of mental health issues or anything," Ajab went on.

"Exactly. Angela was definitely a fruit loop. And if she did that as a kid – and twelve's more than old enough to know right from wrong – could there have been other stuff she's done in the meantime and the family's kept a lid on it? Money can help cover up a whole heap of shit." Sonia gave one emphatic nod of her head, her mouth set into a grim line.

Fatima stopped pacing and raised a finger. "I think that's the door." Everyone paused to listen. The echo of the bell rang out through the hallway. Fatima shot a panicked look at Minnie. "Oh God, it must be the police."

Minnie rose from her seat, hitching up the waistband of her leggings. She crossed the room to peer through the window. A short, slightly harassed-looking man with greying hair and a tall, slender woman with an impressive Afro carrying herself like a catwalk model, neither in uniform but official-looking and wearing lanyards, were staring up at the building.

"I'll get it. Don't flap." She turned back to Fatima, frowning. "It's not like we've done anything. I don't know why you're so jumpy."

"I've got a record, all right," Fatima blurted out, her cheeks flushing crimson.

Everyone froze, all eyes landing on her.

"What d'you mean?" Sonia asked eventually, shooting a look from Ajab to Minnie. It was as if they were all suspended in time for a moment, no one quite believing what they had just heard.

"A police record. I – I got arrested when I was in sixth form." She bit her lip, dropping her gaze.

"Jeez – now you tell us." Sonia blew out a long breath. She regarded Fatima with narrowed eyes. "What did you do?"

"It – it wasn't anything – I mean, it was nothing that bad. It's just made me really wary of the cops. And I don't want anything coming out in the papers. It could wreck everything."

The doorbell rang again, several times in quick succession now, as though the callers were growing impatient.

"Sorry, guys. I know I should probably have told you before. It's – it's just not one of those things you bring up in casual conversation." Fatima stood wringing her hands. She looked genuinely anguished.

Minnie sighed. "Okay, just try to calm down. We'll talk about it later. In the meantime, I think we'd better answer the door. We don't want to piss them off."

The police officers announced themselves with a flash of their ID as Detective Sergeant Navpreet Gill and Detective Constable Enya Maitland. Minnie showed them through into the living room where the others were all waiting, perched on the edge of the settee like errant pupils about to be reprimanded by their headteacher. The officers took an armchair each, absorbing the plush surroundings with slightly raised eyebrows.

"Nice place you've got here," remarked DS Gill. "It's a far cry from the cruddy flat I shared when I was at uni."

In unison, the housemates laughed awkwardly, unsure how to respond.

"Still, times change, I suppose," he went on. "And Cov's very geared up for students these days, isn't it?" It was a rhetorical question. The city skyline was testament to the vast amount of student accommodation now available. Nonetheless, they were all aware how lucky they were to have found such a comfortable house, and in a pleasant area.

Minnie offered the police officers a hot drink, but they declined. She proceeded to introduce everyone in turn. The atmosphere in the room was charged with nervous energy. Fatima looked as if she was having to hang onto her seat to prevent herself from bolting.

DS Gill glanced at his colleague, his lips twitching at the corners. "There's really nothing to worry about. This is just an informal chat."

DC Maitland smiled reassuringly. "We understand Aurora Trelawney was living here for a time and wondered if there's anything you could tell us about her time with you – any visitors she may have had; anything she might've said to imply all wasn't well with her?"

Everyone shook their heads in unison, then looked pleadingly at Minnie as if making her their spokesperson. She widened her eyes at Ajab, who nodded in encouragement.

Minnie cleared her throat. "Angela Tandy – or Aurora Trelawney, as we now know she was called – gave very little away about herself, to be honest. She didn't mix with us, and never brought anyone here – and from what we've just found out, it sounds as if things she *did* tell us might not have been entirely true." Minnie hesitated to say that Angela had told them a pack of lies from start to finish. It seemed inappropriate, given the way the woman had ended up.

DS Gill nodded. "Uh-huh. I think one of you told my colleague over the phone that she was here for about five weeks in all – is that correct?"

They all looked at one another, nodding in agreement. "Yes, give or take." Ajab seemed to have finally found his voice. He wriggled upright, his manner suddenly more assertive. Minnie was happy for him to step in. She squeezed between Sonia and Ajab on the sofa, and sat back, glancing at Fatima on Sonia's right, who was still fidgeting in her seat as though desperate for the toilet.

"Can you clarify the circumstances under which she came to move in with you all?" DS Gill tipped his head a fraction towards DC Maitland, who had taken out a notebook and was scribbling feverishly.

"Another girl who was supposed to be sharing with us dropped out at the last minute, and we had to plug the gap in the rent," Ajab confirmed. "The woman we knew as Angela responded to a notice we'd put up in Reception at uni. She came round really quickly after her initial phone call, and said she was a mature student from up north. Told us she'd come into some money after her mum died not long before, and was able to stump up nine months' rent, so we were pleased to let her move in – especially as no one else had shown any interest."

DC Maitland lifted her eyes. "So – she actually told you her mother had passed away relatively recently?"

"That's right. Said she'd gone back to college afterwards to do her A levels, to give her life some purpose again, or words to that effect."

The two officers exchanged quizzical looks. The sergeant gave his colleague the briefest of nods.

"I'm sure you'll all have seen today's newspaper headlines by now," said DC Maitland. "Mrs Francine Trelawney has been dead for almost a quarter of a century."

Everyone shook their heads to feign disbelief, though they had since all read every inch of information available about the Trelawney family.

"Is it true that Angela – or Aurora, or whatever she was really called – killed her baby brother?" Sonia blurted out.

"I'm afraid we aren't at liberty to discuss Miss Trelawney's past." DS Gill's response was curt. "There will, no doubt, be plenty of rumours circulating among the gutter press. Our job currently is to find out as much as we can about her recent history in order to apprehend her killer. We don't want anything to muddy the waters."

"But surely that might be relevant," Sonia persisted. "I mean, if she *had* murdered her own brother, it could—"

DS Gill raised a palm. "No good surmising at this point. All we need to establish for the time being is what's been happening in her life more recently."

Sonia leaned back in her seat, tight-lipped.

"You didn't think to ask her for references before you gave her the go-ahead?" DC Maitland scanned their faces.

"Well, no." Ajab looked sheepish. "I s'pose we should have.

We did it all without involving the rental agency, which with hindsight was pretty stupid. But she seemed a bit, well, pitiful, to be honest. She certainly didn't ring any alarm bells to think she could be trouble in any way."

Minnie cast her mind back to that first encounter with Angela. She remembered the odd feeling she'd had about the woman, that she had readily dismissed as being paranoid. She squirmed a little but said nothing. It was a bit late in the day to voice her concerns.

"And she was able to hand over cash for the rent, which was our primary worry at the time." Ajab added. Yes, that had been the main criterion, Minnie thought. Their personal safety should have been top of the list. But hindsight was a wonderful thing.

The policewoman nodded slowly. "You say she didn't really mix with any of you. What about at the university – did she appear to have any friends there?"

Minnie shook her head. "She always sat at the back in lectures, on her own. And she was always the first one out. I did ask her about it one day – she said she got anxiety and liked to sit near the exit. Of course, we found out after she cleared off that she'd never actually been enrolled on the course at all."

"Interesting." DS Gill fired a look at the constable. "Can you think of any reason why she might've lied about something like that?" The sergeant's eyes searched Minnie's face. She felt her cheeks flush in reaction, even though she had nothing to hide.

"Not a clue. I mean, she'd spend hours on her own, up in her room; told us she was working on an essay. We were all a bit freaked out when we learned she wasn't actually a student at all."

DS Gill sat forward in his seat. "And to the best of your knowledge, none of you, or your families, have any past connection with Miss Trelawney or her family – that you're aware of?"

Everyone shook their heads vehemently. This was beginning to feel more like an interrogation than a friendly chat, despite the sergeant's original assurances.

"Did Miss Trelawney leave any belongings when she moved out?" he went on.

"Nope." To the surprise of her friends, Fatima had opened her mouth for the first time. "Just her dirty sheets for us to wash. And a stinking pile of takeaway containers."

Minnie glanced sideways and noticed Sonia giving Fatima's hand a gentle squeeze. Fatima responded with a tentative smile. Minnie felt warmed by this small gesture of solidarity. She wondered what it was that Fatima had done to get herself arrested. She couldn't believe it would have been anything that awful, or surely she'd have been locked up.

The sergeant stood up suddenly, gesturing towards the door. "D'you think we could have a look at the room she was allocated?"

Minnie heaved herself off the sofa. "Sure. Follow me."

The police officers followed Minnie up the stairs, leaving the others still in their seats, staring after them. She pushed open the door to Angela's room and stepped back to allow them access. Apart from the removal of the soiled bedding, everything had been left just as Minnie had found it the day Angela left.

She watched as, both putting on vinyl gloves, they opened drawers and cupboard doors, felt on top of the wardrobe; looked behind the furniture and blinds; under the bed. DS Gill even lifted the mattress. Minnie wondered what on earth they could be expecting – no, it seemed more like hoping – to find.

DC Maitland turned to her. "You say she never brought anyone here?"

Minnie shook her head. "She didn't seem to have any friends or family, as far as we could tell." She thought suddenly. "Oh, wait. I did overhear her chatting on her phone a couple of times. And on one occasion she told me her cousin was messaging her. I s'pose it could've been them she was talking to."

The sergeant's face lit with sudden interest. "Cousin? Was it a man or a woman?"

Minnie shrugged. "I've no idea, I'm afraid. I came up here once to ask if she wanted some pizza and she was having what sounded like a heavy conversation with somebody. I could only hear her end of what was being said though, and she cut the call once she'd realised I was outside the door."

She recalled Angela's obvious discomfort at finding her on the landing. And what was it she'd been saying? Something about not being able to talk right now? Had she been worried she might give something away if she was overheard?

"Thinking back, it seemed like she didn't want anyone to hear what she was talking about. I didn't think too much of it at the time."

DS Gill had been on his hands and knees, stretching one arm to feel behind the wardrobe and sliding his hand up and down.

"Hold on, what's this?" He grappled with something for a moment. There was a sudden ripping sound. He retracted his arm and sat back on the floor, slightly ruffled and brandishing a blue A4 hard-covered scrapbook. It was still attached to a length of silver gaffer tape.

"Well, we'd been hoping to find something of interest. Let's hope this contains just that." He waved the book in the air. "Either Miss Trelawney forgot it, or she left it behind deliberately – maybe in the hope someone would find it eventually."

Minnie racked her brains, casting her mind back to the night she'd heard Angela talking on the phone, the numerous pieces of paper strewn across the floor. The laptop permanently open. Even if she hadn't been working on a thesis, she'd definitely been very focused on something. But Minnie didn't recall seeing any kind of notebook.

DC Maitland produced a large plastic evidence wallet from the cross-body bag she was wearing, unfolded it and handed it to the sergeant, who peeled over the first page carefully, frowned a little, then closed the book before placing it inside.

"We'll take this with us, have a proper look at it at our leisure."

"Does it – d'you think it might give you a lead?" asked Minnie hopefully.

"Too soon to say. But anything that's been deliberately hidden away, for whatever reason, needs proper scrutiny in these circumstances." He turned to DC Maitland. "I think that'll be all for now. Let's get back to the station."

*

Minnie saw the officers out, then went to rejoin the others. Sonia had gone to put the kettle on. She stuck her head through the kitchen doorway as Minnie came down the hall. "Did they find anything?"

Minnie told her about the scrapbook. "They said they'll have a proper look at it later." She shook her head. "I can't take it all in."

"Me neither." Sonia tipped her head towards the living room, lowering her voice. "Our Fatima's a dark horse. I shouldn't have been surprised though, knowing what her temper's like when she's roused. She was just telling Ajab and me what happened. You know, why she got into trouble with the police."

"And?" Minnie leaned forward with interest.

"This sleazebag teacher tried it on with her when she was on her own in a classroom after an open evening. Had her pinned against the wall. Sounded like he had a history of that sort of thing, but he'd never actually been caught out. She trashed his car – spray-painted it with 'nonce' and put a brick through the windscreen."

Minnie threw back her head and laughed. "Good for her. Seems unfair, though, if he'd done something to her."

"Yeah, but it was her word against his and she had no proof. They classed it as criminal damage. She got a forty-hour community payback order and a fine that her old man had to pay."

Minnie puffed out her cheeks. "I bet that went down like a lead balloon."

"Yep. And he cleared it all with the owner of this place, stumped up extra for him to turn a blind eye, plus he signed a contract to act as guarantor for the full year's rent and more besides if she stepped out of line again. You can see why she doesn't want to do anything else to get in his bad books." Sonia grimaced. "Anyway, at least we know now it wasn't anything we should be worried about. Unlike bloody Angela."

Minnie shook her head. "I still can't believe it. I'm wondering what's in that book the coppers took away with them. Don't expect they'll be keeping us in the loop though, somehow."

Minnie's words seemed to hang in the air. Though neither said anything, both she and Sonia prayed that that would be the last they would see of DS Gill and his colleague. Even if they hadn't exactly been fond of Angela, the whole situation had left a very nasty taste.

Chapter 34

Aurora

Monday, 7 November 2022 – Five days earlier

Reclining against the memory foam bolster, Aurora Trelawney stared up from her queen-size bed at the ornate plasterwork of the ceiling in her suite. She'd needed a stopgap for a few days before returning home, and the old but elegant Georgian hotel just outside Stratford-upon-Avon had outstanding reviews on Tripadvisor. She fancied spoiling herself for a while anyway, after putting up with that poky room for all those weeks. But it had been worth it. She knew she'd track the bitch down eventually. It had actually been quite fun. And she'd only just started.

The tentative knock told her Room Service had arrived with the meal she had ordered. Aurora got up slowly, then padded in her bare feet across the immaculate, thick-pile cream carpet to open the door. She watched as the pasty-looking maid, dressed as if she had stepped straight from the nineteenth-century, wheeled the trolley in with a polite nod. The silver cloche was lifted from the tempting platter of hors d'oeuvres Aurora had ordered, the small oak table set with silverware and a pure white napkin, the Veuve Clicquot uncorked and a measure poured carefully into a flute before the bottle was placed in the silver ice bucket. All so terribly civilised. How she had missed being waited on.

"Will that be all, Madam?" The maid smoothed her starched white apron, smiling primly.

"Yes. For now." Aurora handed over a ten-pound note, waving her away. The woman nodded her thanks and retreated, closing the door behind her. Aurora settled herself down to enjoy her food, chewing each mouthful carefully, then recalling her mother's words with sudden bitterness.

"Small bites, keeping one's mouth closed at all times. Place the cutlery at the sides of the plate when not in use, meeting in the centre when you have finished eating. Manners maketh man, Aurora." It was always said with a warning glower.

But table manners, nor any of the other principles of etiquette that her parents went to such pains to teach her, hadn't mattered one iota when she arrived at Caulmoor. Aurora couldn't have been less prepared for the harsh, dog-eat-dog environment she was thrust into. The immediate and unwavering ridicule her behaviour had attracted from the other girls. Being unloved and ignored was one thing. Having people seeking you out daily to abuse and degrade you for their own sadistic amusement was another altogether. Aurora shuddered, shutting down the memory.

Still with a mouthful of partially chewed food, she lifted the champagne flute to her lips and glugged thirstily, draining the glass and running the back of her hand across her mouth. She belched loudly. How Mummy and Daddy would have disapproved of *that*. The thought brought a sneer to her lips.

She had never been enough for either of them. Particularly her father. Her every action seemed to merit disappointment or reprimand.

It had quickly become apparent exactly how much of a disappointment she was once Rupert had arrived. Perfect little Rupert. Apple of his daddy's eye. She'd even heard her father cooing those very same words to the little brat. Aurora had never been sure if it was just that she was born the wrong sex, or if it was just her in general, that they had never taken to. But once her baby brother came onto the scene, she might just as well not have existed.

Well, she'd shown them, hadn't she? Yet despite their anger and grief, the stupid family name was more important to them than anything. They would probably have hushed it up completely, had it not been for the nanny. Stupid, hysterical woman. Aurora had been frustrated to learn that she was now in a nursing home, suffering from dementia and in the latter stages of cancer. Too late for any thoughts of retribution there now.

Finishing the last of the champagne, she pushed the trolley aside and went to take her laptop from its case, setting it on the leather-topped desk against the wall.

Aurora sat down. She opened her emails and clicked on the contact list. No time like the present. She would be leaving for Yorkshire again soon. Throughout her little campaign, she had wondered how to proceed once she'd left that house. Things could easily continue from a distance. But the more she'd thought about it, the more she wanted to look the bitch in the eye. Let her know who had been responsible for unnerving her enough to make her abandon her perfect home. For putting the fear of God into her these last few weeks. And now for the *pièce de résistance*. Her very public, very humiliating unmasking. All before passing on the baton for someone else to pick up where

Aurora had left off, and do whatever they saw fit. A little white lie about identity along the way would ensure the right person, at least from her perspective, was going to get everything they deserved. Aurora felt a shiver of delight as she thought of her ultimate revenge. It was perfect.

There was a pub in the heart of Warwick. A sort of mid-point between where Aurora was staying and the centre of Coventry. It would make a good place for a rendezvous. And tomorrow evening would be perfect.

Unable to keep the smile from her face, Aurora began to type. She read what she had written twice, nodded in self-approval, then clicked 'send'. She snapped shut the lid of the laptop and sat back for a moment, a warm feeling running through her. Picking up the old-fashioned phone from the desk, she dialled 1 to summon Room Service once again.

Another bottle of champagne was in order. She had earned it.

Chapter 35

Georgia

Thursday, 10 November 2022 – Three days later

Georgia had decided she needed to carry on as normal. She'd turned up for work in the Orb on the Wednesday, put on her best smile, laughed with the punters. Told Yiannis she was feeling much better after her migraine the previous night. But the whole evening had been a strain, as though she was just going through the motions, the thought of her encounter in Warwick the night before leaving a queasy feeling in her gut.

But with two nights' sleep, albeit fitful, now behind her, things were beginning to feel a little better. Thursdays were always a bit busier, people building up to the freedom of the weekend. Even for those who didn't work, it was as if a cloud was lifting as they put distance between themselves and the long-associated misery of a Monday morning. It was a cold, wet evening, but the pub was warm with body heat and a lively atmosphere, the jukebox pulsing with Freddie's now familiar 1980s playlist.

"You seem a bit brighter today," Yiannis remarked, as Georgia swept towards the bar with another stack of empties, whistling along to the Pet Shop Boys' rendition of 'Always On My Mind'. "Not moping over Cole any more, eh?"

"Nah." She smiled, a little wistfully. "I think that ship's sailed, I'm afraid. Got to move on."

"Never mind, sweet. Plenty more fish in the sea."

But whenever the door to the bar opened, Georgia's head still jerked up, wondering if she'd catch a glimpse of Cole. He'd been true to his word and was staying away, whether he had a new book to write or not. She felt genuinely sorry about the way things had ended between them. Maybe given a few weeks he'd forgive her for what he'd perceived as an exhibition of jealousy. But whether he did or not, from her point of view, there was no going back now.

Georgia wondered if Cole was growing concerned yet that the woman hadn't contacted him again. With any luck, it would make him reflect on what she herself had told him. That he ought to have been more cautious about taking everything a complete stranger had told him at face value. She would still have liked to help him out financially. Maybe that was something she could rectify in the future.

At the end of the evening, Georgia was ready to leave the pub and looking forward to falling into bed. Yiannis wished her good night and locked the door behind her. But as she stepped out onto the cobbles, about to open her umbrella against the downpour, old Ned, who had sat in comparative silence for most of the evening, appeared suddenly from round the corner. His clothes were soaked and he was shivering.

"Oh!" Georgia put a hand to her throat, her heart quickening. "You made me jump. I thought you'd left ages ago."

"I wanted a word with you," he said, his eyebrows slanting anxiously, rain droplets trickling down his cheeks. "I've been worried."

Georgia stopped to pat an equally drenched Charlie, who was looking up at her, his tail thrashing as usual despite it all, filling the air around him with fine spray.

"What about?"

"About you. After what you said – you know, about seeing the monk."

Georgia straightened to look at him. She knew now that she had nothing to fear from any monk. That it had all been just another part of an elaborate plan to make her existence as unpleasant as possible.

"You mustn't worry, Ned," she said, smiling. "It's lovely that you're concerned about me, but I've had a good think since. You know, I reckon it's all been because I'm living on my own and in such an old building. Especially after listening to your creepy tales." She arched an eyebrow in mock consternation. "I'm pretty sure it's probably all been a figment of my imagination."

He turned his head to one side, regarded her with troubled eyes. "Well I don't. And I may be a silly old man, but I don't think these things come from nowhere. There's no smoke without fire."

"What d'you mean?"

"The stories. About that monk, Friar Benedict, appearing three times . . ." He tailed off, looking genuinely anguished, pulling a huge white handkerchief from his pocket and mopping at his face.

Georgia suppressed a smile. He was taking everything very literally. "And because I thought I'd seen it twice, you're worried something bad could happen to me if it reappears, is that it?"

He reached out a gnarled hand and pressed hers, his expression imploring.

"I don't want you to take that chance, love. Maybe – maybe if you moved somewhere else? I mean, it doesn't have to be far, but you've always been in that house when you've seen him, haven't you?"

Georgia sighed. He was obviously completely obsessed with the idea of the mythical monk, and nothing she was going to say would make any difference.

"Look. I'll think about it. But thank you for thinking of me. I'm very touched." She leaned forwards and dropped a kiss onto the old man's wet leathery cheek. "Now you get yourself and poor Charlie off home – the pair of you're going to catch pneumonia out here in this."

Ned squeezed her hand again earnestly. "Promise me? That you'll think about what I've said?"

"I promise. Now off you go and I'll see you tomorrow. Good night."

She watched for a moment as he hobbled away, then made her way back to Cuckoo Cottage, now soaked to the skin herself. Too tired to light the log burner, she peeled off her wet coat, draped it over the sitting room door, ensured everywhere was locked, and made her way wearily up the stairs. Once in bed, her eyes closed the second her head hit the pillow.

*

It was the knock that stirred her. A loud, insistent noise that echoed unnaturally throughout the whole house. Georgia sat bolt upright. She screwed up her eyes to look at the bedside clock. Only 3.45am.

A second knock. A dull, ominous thud: as though someone was striking the door with a heavy instrument. She held her breath, turning her head towards the window. The sound was coming from the front of the building. The third, louder still.

It was almost rhythmic, seeming to reverberate through the walls, striking fear into her. She climbed from the bed to peer down onto the empty quad, onto the graves of people long gone. People who might even have lived in this very house at some time in the dim and distant past.

It was then that she saw him. The same dark, cowled figure. Head bowed. Just standing there, motionless, right outside her front door. As though it was waiting for something.

And then the head was raised, up and to one side. Though she could see no face, it appeared to be looking straight at her. One arm lifted slowly, and an invisible hand appeared to be pointing right at her, before the whole apparition seemed to melt into the darkness.

Georgia pulled back from the window, her heart thumping hard in her chest, trying to gather her thoughts. After everything that had happened, why was she seeing the monk once more? She had thought it just another part of a vindictive game. Why had he come back?

A feeling of cold dread wriggled its way through her torso.

A sudden flicker of light from the house opposite drew her gaze immediately. There, yet again, was that figure. Watching. Hovering for a moment, before disappearing from view. Had they too seen what she had just witnessed? Or were both things merely figments of her recently stoked imagination? Had *anything* over the past few torturous weeks been real? She was beginning to doubt her own sanity.

Crawling back under the covers, Georgia curled into a ball, her hands over her ears. She tried to steady her breathing, to reason with herself. Stress could cause all sorts of issues. Hallucinations, auditory disturbance. This had been a particularly rough few days; her brain must be playing tricks on her. Hearing noises, seeing things that weren't there. And Ned's concerns had obviously been uppermost in her mind when she'd fallen, exhausted, into bed. But the monk – it had looked so real. *Solid*.

Georgia took in a sharp breath. A feeling of panic rose from her gut as it occurred to her that this was nothing to do with her tormentor at all. This was very much to do with *her*. It felt now to Georgia as though it was some kind of judgement, a reckoning. She had done terrible, unforgiveable things, and yet here she was, her life outwardly perfect. She had her health, a beautiful daughter. More money than she could ever need. She'd led a charmed existence.

And she deserved none of it.

Was she about to be thrown off a precipice?

Chapter 36

Georgia

Friday, 11 November 2022 – One day later

It had rained, heavily and steadily, for the last two days and throughout the night, continuing into the early morning. Falling like a friend from the heavens; washing away her sins. Quite literally. Georgia relished the sound as it thrummed rhythmically against the window, even enjoying the fresh chill on her face from the whistling breeze gusting through the gap in the ancient frame, wrapped as she was in the warm duvet. She hadn't lit the log burner yet and Jethro Jackson's apparently 'innovative' plastic shields were pretty useless, but right now she didn't care. She'd cancelled her booking at the house in Oxfordshire now. It didn't matter that she'd lost the deposit. There was no need to flee; nothing to fear any more. In the cold light of day, her terror about the monk she'd seen again seemed ridiculous. Though she hadn't been as overwrought, there had still been that underlying unease, that nagging doubt that she wasn't out of the woods yet.

Despite the draught, Georgia felt almost cocooned within the room this morning. Could she – *dare* she hope she might just have weathered the storm? There had been no knock at the door, no one asking uncomfortable questions. Though she had spent the previous couple of days in a fluctuating state of anxiety, a kind of clarity filled her head now, a strange sense of calm. She didn't even feel the need to reach for the diazepam today.

As she lay staring at the ceiling, she thought absently of Cole. Poor Cole. After her enlightening meeting the other night, she knew now for certain that he had been duped; there would be no lucrative ghost-writing project for him. No boost to his flagging career. He was a decent man and he had been cruelly manipulated. But there was no going back there for her now. She'd moved on.

Georgia couldn't believe how stupid she herself had been, not twigging it had all been part of the plan to get to her. She knew something didn't feel right about it all. But it was that chance remark from Yiannis, that one small observation that had made her reflect afterwards. That, when she had finally made the connection, had made her spine tingle.

"Good job I'm here to keep an eye on things on your night off. Wondered for a minute if you might've had a rival for his affections," he'd said with a laugh. "Mind you, don't think *she* was up for it. I've seen her sort before. Accepts the drinks but her eyes are elsewhere the whole time. Always looking for that better offer."

A better offer – or for someone else to walk through the door and see her and Cole together. A worm of discomfort wriggled through her veins as she remembered meeting those eyes as they'd passed in the doorway – and that glimmer, that indefinable feeling, of what she now realised had been mutual recognition.

And then the email had landed, illuminating everything and sending her into turmoil.

She remembered wondering vaguely about this Angela person when Minnie had mentioned her initially – why would someone so much older want to move in with a bunch of teenagers? But she'd dismissed the notion. The woman was lonely, a mature student in a strange city. And since everyone else on Minnie's course was still in their teens, there was probably no one else available she could relate to. Minnie had always been good like that: able to talk to people on any level. She'd never like to think anyone was feeling excluded. She would have been the one to make sure Angela was always made to feel welcome, even if the others hadn't been that enthused. Always thinking the best of people, never occurring to her to question their motives.

Dear, guileless Minnie. Georgia wondered sometimes about her biological father. She'd never known him properly – it had been a brief, physical relationship. Nothing more. Maybe their daughter took after him.

Georgia thought back to her meeting with 'Angela' in the pub in Warwick three days earlier. She remembered how her stomach had dropped as she walked in and saw her sitting there, the smug smile tugging at her annoying mouth. The woman had turned up looking well-groomed, in full make-up: a far cry from the timid, dowdy little mouse Minnie described. As she talked, there had been no evidence of the stammer Minnie had mentioned. She'd oozed self-assurance. From her almost triumphant demeanour, 'Angela' had clearly been ready to confront her. But Georgia knew her as someone else. And she'd had questions of her own.

"How did you find me?"

Aurora's thin, pink-tinted lips had curved into a dislikeable sneer, creating two crescent-shaped grooves either side of her mouth. She had lost the padding that used to fill out her face. But without glasses and with her hair pulled back, she'd become instantly recognisable. Georgia remembered the girl staring at her vacantly from across the dining hall the first time she'd noticed her. There had always been something creepy about her. Finding out what she was doing time for had come as no great surprise.

"It's probably not the best idea to have your picture in the papers when you want to stay under the radar, you know. Raising funds for your local hospice, too – commendable."

The slant of the woman's eyes and her sly, knowing expression made Georgia want to slap her face. The knowledge that this psycho had been living under the same roof as Minnie filled her with revulsion and anger.

Georgia kept her voice low. "Yes, but after I moved. How did you know where to look?"

"Well, I'd already discovered the name you'd assumed, hadn't I? It wasn't hard. I hung around the village for a bit and asked a few people, said I was an old school friend trying to get in touch. I mean, Trevor was well known in the area. A proper philanthropist, by all accounts."

Aurora's fixed gaze seemed to be boring into Georgia's head. It felt like termites burrowing beneath her skin.

"Poor Trevor. He really didn't want to believe me, you know. Good job I'd saved the press cuttings." Very deliberately, Aurora swirled the red wine in her glass, lifting it to her nose to inhale the aroma.

"I do appreciate a good Malbec, don't you?" Aurora's tongue pressed against the inside of her cheek. Her focus never deviated from Georgia's face. "And the way he died – tragic. It must have been devastating for you."

The room seemed to spin suddenly around Georgia. She gripped the edge of the table in an attempt to steady herself.

"So if you knew where I was when Trevor was still alive, how come it took you so long to approach me?"

"I've had a lot to contend with these last two years," Aurora snapped in response. "Dealing with the fallout of my father's estate. So much paperwork, you've no idea. Oh – but maybe you *have*." She arced an eyebrow pointedly. "I mean, Trevor must have left you in a similar position, I imagine. The downside of owning a successful company. Or did you let the lawyers deal with all that?" She smiled thinly, leaning back in her seat, pausing for a moment. Georgia made no reply.

"And then I had to go to Switzerland for yet *another* operation on my tibia," she continued. "The rehabilitation has been a painful and protracted process." Her eyes flickered, their pupils dilated. "But I never stopped thinking about you. About the *good old days*." Aurora's tone was caustic.

"Oh, by the way, I've brought you a memento." The woman reached into her coat pocket, producing a folded piece of paper, and slid it across the table. Georgia stared at it. A creased, yellowing sheet from an old newspaper. It seemed to dance before her eyes. She really didn't want to look but knew she must. Her fingers feeling oddly clumsy, she opened the page out. Seeing the photograph and caption, Georgia felt her heart jump into her throat. The same image that had been blown up and pasted to the wall outside the Slug and Lettuce.

Georgia had to restrain herself. If they hadn't been in a public place, she would have gladly throttled the woman. She forced herself to look at the photograph once more. The memory of it was still fresh, though the faded image had been printed almost thirty years earlier.

Aurora was smiling, a sinister leer weighted with ill intention.

"Anyway, where were we? I was disappointed to find you'd

moved out of your lovely home so suddenly. But even before you'd left Warchester, I'd been doing my homework. One man pointed me in the direction of your nice cleaning lady. She seemed quite put out you hadn't kept her on after Trevor died, you know. I got the impression you're in her bad books. She was very helpful, though. Gave me your email address. *Very* chatty, too. Told me she'd heard Minnie had a place at Coventry University. It was a no-brainer, if you were ever to go AWOL. Find the daughter, find the mother." Her brow twitched. "The woman told me plenty about you, too, by the way. Quite the lady of leisure, she said. Really moved up in the world, didn't you?"

There was an edge of steel to her voice, her eyes glinting with malice. "Anyway, I made my way to Coventry. Got myself a little cleaning job at the uni at the start of the new term. Didn't take me too long to find Minnie from your own cleaner's description. Let's face it, she's hard to miss with that hair. And then I spotted her in the reception, putting up the poster advertising the room! What a *gift*!"

She gave a high, fluting laugh, which went right through Georgia, like nails scraping on a chalkboard.

"What the hell d'you want from me? Are you after money?" Georgia's voice had lowered to a growl. She glanced round sharply, but no one appeared to be paying them much attention.

Aurora leaned forwards. She fixed her eyes on Georgia's, splaying her manicured fingers across the table. There was no hint of a smile of any sort now, just a look of pure contempt.

"I don't need a penny from you," Aurora hissed. "In spite of everything, I was left well provided for." She cleared her throat. "Just as well, with all the things I've had to fork out for. Dental implants. Private medical consultants; speech therapists. It's taken me years just to overcome the stammer."

Georgia remembered the stories circulating at Caulmoor that Aurora – (or Porky, as she was cruelly nicknamed – a reference to the stammering cartoon pig; Georgia had never actually learned her real name) – had come from a seriously wealthy family. How ironic that her parents hadn't ensured she never received her inheritance, after what she had done.

Porky. The connection suddenly dawned. The memory of the pottery class and the stumpy little figure Georgia had made – it was Susan who'd pointed it out. An ugly little mug it had, she'd said. Had she modelled it on Porky? Everyone had joined in, taunting the girl. And not wanting to be the odd one out, to her shame, Georgia had laughed with them.

"Besides," Aurora went on, drumming her coral shellac nails on the tabletop. "No amount of money could ever make up for what that place did to me. What you and the others subjected me to. No. I wanted to burst your cushy little bubble. I wanted to make your life the living hell that mine was for six interminable years."

Georgia drew in a breath, an unpleasant tingling spreading through her. She thought back to her time in Caulmoor, to the 'residents' who had come and gone. She had formed alliances of sorts – she could never have thought of them as friendships – with some of the more ruthless girls. The hard nuts. It was all about self-preservation. Conform or go under. And so she had conformed. She'd been small for her age, light on her feet and sporty: that always seemed to elevate the girls' status among their peers to some extent. That, and being able to handle themselves. And because Georgia hadn't been particularly strong, not when she'd first arrived there at least, she had made sure she stayed on the right side of those who were.

Georgia remembered Aurora well. For all the wrong reasons. She'd been physically awkward, ungainly. Overweight. And undoubtedly a bit strange. She would mumble to herself, stare at people for no apparent reason, as though she had no control over it. A target for the bullies. Everyone knew that you needed to keep your head down, never to draw attention to yourself. She was asking for it. Georgia wasn't about to put herself on the line for someone she didn't know, or even like the look of, come to that. And so she'd gone along with the rest when they'd singled Aurora out. She recalled one occasion when a group of them had pinned the girl down in the dorm and urged Georgia to lop off her ponytail with a pair of scissors one of them had stolen from the kitchens. Another when one of the bigger girls, Susan, had yanked back her hair at the dining table and force-fed her cold semolina. It had made Aurora puke all down her tracksuit. Maybe the worst of all was when Susan had put her face close to Aurora and screamed right into the girl's ear. Everyone had watched as she'd been sent, clutching her head, to see the nurse. One of the older girls had overheard the woman telling another member of staff that Aurora had a ruptured eardrum and that they'd need to keep an eye on her, though the advice didn't appear to have been heeded.

It wasn't nice, when Georgia thought back. But then, being locked up with a group of frustrated and often unstable adolescent females probably wouldn't have been nice under any circumstances, let alone those with violent or otherwise criminal tendencies. Caulmoor had been an absolute snake pit. The staff constantly reminded them all that they were there to be punished for whatever misdemeanour they'd committed; that it wasn't a holiday camp. They turned a blind eye to bullying, many of them seeming to actively condone it. And the consequences for some of the girls were grim.

"So you decided to try and tip me over the edge?"

Aurora's smile was chilling. "It's been such fun, thinking of all the ways you could be rattled. I mean, that little old house. And you all alone. What a perfect scenario."

Georgia thought about the monk, her fears she was being haunted. That was clearly part of Aurora's vendetta, too. The latest apparition must have been a hangover from that, an illusion summoned from the recesses of Georgia's own mind after her conversation with Ned. Possibly even brought on by the medication she'd been taking so frequently.

She thought of the spiteful but unquestionably earthly twenty-first-century emails, the text that was supposed to have come from Minnie. The message chalked on the broken door. The dead bird.

But the clay figure. The lock of hair. The *teeth*. They should have spelled it out to her. How could she have been so *stupid* not to remember about Porky?

"But why me? There were plenty of others that did worse. Why'd you single me out?"

"Oh, believe me, I've got my list. But you were right up there. Literally." Aurora leaned to one side, tapping her left leg. "I wonder if you can remember why?" She narrowed her eyes. "I'm never likely to forget. I can only ever drive an automatic – even the latest round of surgery wasn't a riotous success."

Georgia squirmed. The shameful memory of something that had long haunted her flashed through her mind. The others egging her on as she stood at the top of the stairs. Susan pushing her forwards, whispering in her ear, questioning whether she had the bottle to do it. And then her horror as she watched Aurora's arms flailing inelegantly, crashing heavily against each stair as she fell. Lying howling in agony at their foot, blood pouring from her mouth. They'd learned later that some of the girl's teeth had been knocked out as she'd smacked against the concrete floor. Georgia remembered how sick she had felt. The terrible realisation of what she had done. The wave of guilt and self-loathing for inflicting something so needlessly cruel on someone so pathetic.

But Aurora didn't seem pathetic now. She seemed controlled and dangerous. And vengeful.

"Plus, you'd made yourself very accessible," Aurora went on. "My father held a keen interest in his competitors and what they were up to. When I came across that article among his files and saw how very comfortable you are now, it made me see red. You needed to be knocked off that undeserved pedestal." She ran a tongue over her glossy upper lip, then sat back in her seat. "I had an interesting conversation with that Cole chap, by the way. I'm sure he'll be fascinated to hear about your colourful past. Did you know he was actually a journalist before trying his hand at being an author? Gave it up as he wasn't that successful, apparently. Well, he seemed pretty keen when I asked if he'd like to help me write my autobiography. Even better, I'm thinking of including your sordid little story as a sort of bonus. Our *connection*. It could even be a bestseller. *Imagine*."

A horrible coldness flooded Georgia's whole body. "What – what have you told him?"

"Nothing. Yet." Aurora smirked, dropping her eyes to study her own hand. "I bet Minnie hasn't a clue about any of it, has she? You being a juvenile offender and everything . . ."

A sick feeling rose in Georgia's chest. "You keep Minnie out of this."

"Actually, I think Minnie deserves to know. I mean, she's so interested in history, isn't she? I'm sure she'd be really fascinated to learn all about her own family tree."

Blinded by rage, Georgia reached across the table and grabbed Angela by the wrist.

"Stay the fuck away from my daughter. Or you'll regret it." Her voice was louder than she'd intended, attracting raised eyebrows and disapproving glances from some of the other customers.

Evidently ruffled, Aurora yanked back her arm, adjusting her sleeve. She cast a sideways look at the people observing them, then back at Georgia, drawing herself upright in her seat.

"I wouldn't start throwing your weight about, if I were you. I'm the one with the upper hand here, and we both know it."

Her tone was light, but Georgia detected a slight tremor. It bolstered her. Rising from the table, she leaned towards Aurora once more in as menacing a fashion as she could muster. "I mean it. Stay away from my daughter, you freak, or there'll be consequences."

Without waiting for a reply, she picked up her bag and marched out of the pub, leaving the door swinging in her wake. Pausing for breath, Georgia stood against the wall, her head spinning. Aurora had gone to great lengths to track her down. To try to scare her out of her wits. Was the woman really vindictive enough to bring her whole world crashing down?

Georgia knew the answer before she'd even asked the question.

Chapter 37

Minnie

Sunday, 13 November 2022 – Two days later

"Has my mum arrived yet?" Minnie sat anxiously on a punitively uncomfortable chair bolted to the floor in the windowless interview room, chewing a hangnail from the side of her thumb. She had pulled on a parka over her tiger-striped onesie before leaving the house so abruptly earlier, hoping to be back at home shortly, but was beginning to think she was there for the long haul.

DS Gill was sitting opposite her, DC Maitland to his right, waiting to record their meeting. The constable had explained Minnie's rights and entitlements, something which Minnie had found alarming, but went on to stress that this was not, at this stage at least, an interview under caution; that she was there voluntarily and was free to leave at any time; that she could have legal representation if she wanted it, but they didn't deem it necessary at the present time. If they were to be believed. The gist of it all was, as far as Minnie could gather, that they would simply welcome her assistance to clarify some information that the scrapbook had brought to light. Nonetheless, Minnie was all too aware of cases of gross miscarriages of justice. Everyone was.

"Don't let them browbeat you, Mins." Fatima had clutched Minnie's arm anxiously as she was about to leave the house. "And don't trust them. Be careful what you say. In fact, don't say anything at all without a brief present."

Minnie was terrified of her words being twisted and then being accused of something that she'd had no part in. Even though they'd insisted she was free to leave, she feared that lack of cooperation on her part might make the police suspect she'd actually done something wrong. Would they think she looked guilty if she asked for a solicitor? An increasingly sick feeling was building inside her. Where was her mum? How could she leave her hanging like this? It was so unlike her.

The sergeant glanced up at the clock. It was over an hour now since Minnie had been brought into the station. The officers had agreed to wait for confirmation that her mother had arrived, but their patience was obviously wearing thin.

"Miss Parnell, you are not a minor." DS Gill let out a long breath, leaning back in his seat. "You've called your mother four times now. I think the best thing all round is if we proceed whether she's on site or not. We've wasted enough time as it is. If we consider it necessary to take the interview further, you're entitled to have a solicitor present."

By now, Minnie was on the verge of tears. "Mum said she'd be here in twenty minutes. I'm really worried something's wrong. She's never late for anything." She looked pleadingly at the faces of the two police officers. "Please – can I just try calling her once more?"

The sergeant gave a brief, slightly irritable nod. "All right.

One more call and then we really need to get on with things. We haven't got all day."

With trembling fingers, Minnie took the phone from her pocket, went straight to her recent call history and dialled Georgia's number yet again. It rang, emptily and persistently, then went to voicemail. Minnie had already left her three messages; it seemed pointless to leave a fourth. She ended the call.

"I'm sure something's happened," she said, her voice cracking. Minnie's eyes sought DS Gill's, hoping her desperation was evident. "I know my mum. She'd never let me down. Can someone please go and check on her? She's living in Cuckoo Cottage, on Bayley Lane. Just along from the Golden Orb."

DS Gill glanced sideways at his colleague, jaw clenched, his eyes indicating the door.

DC Maitland rose from the table, straightening her grey blazer. Minnie noticed dispassionately that there was a stain of some sort on the lapel. A hurried breakfast, maybe.

"I'll make a quick call." The constable smiled at her reassuringly. "Can I get you a coffee – or some water or something?"

"No. No, I'm fine, thanks." Minnie's hands fidgeted in her lap. She surveyed the stark room helplessly. Despite her thick parka, she felt suddenly cold. Everything seemed surreal, like a nightmare she couldn't wake from. Things appeared to be going from bad to worse. She sat in silence, avoiding eye contact with the sergeant, whom she could feel observing her constantly.

Within minutes, DC Maitland was back. She put her head round the door and beckoned to DS Gill, her eyebrows raised.

"Excuse me one moment." DS Gill gave Minnie a tight nod, then left the room, closing the door behind him. Minnie turned to see the pair, just visible through the panel of safety glass near the top of the door, discussing something. DC Maitland was shaking her head, her face grave.

They came back into the room and resumed their seats. From DC Maitland's awkward body language, something was clearly afoot, though she forced a brief smile.

"Miss Parnell, unfortunately your mother still hasn't arrived, but if we could just ask you a couple of quick questions, we can all go about our business for the rest of the day."

"Has anybody been to check on her?" Minnie's eyes darted between the two officers, who looked decidedly ill-at-ease.

"Someone will update us soon – we have a couple of officers located close to your mother's address."

"Has something happened to my mum?" Minnie could feel panic building in her chest. There was an odd undercurrent between the two police officers, some development they weren't divulging; she felt sure of it.

"Please try to stay calm." DS Gill cleared his throat. "If you can just tell us what you know about Aurora Trelawney's connection to your mother, it could be enormously helpful to our inquiry."

"My *mother*'s connection to her?" Minnie stared at them, incredulous. "What on earth d'you mean?"

The two officers exchanged stony-faced glances. "The entire contents of Aurora Trelawney's scrapbook seem to be devoted to information relating to your mother. Photographs, notes. Press cuttings. A proper dossier. Miss Parnell, what, if anything, do you know about your mother's personal history?"

Chapter 38

Georgia

Tuesday, 8 November 2022 – Five days earlier

Once outside the pub where she had left Aurora, Georgia had paused for a moment, taking stock of the situation. Rage bubbled inside her, blood pulsing in her temples. How *dare* the woman start issuing her with threats? She stood just round the corner from the pub's entrance, concealed in a doorway between two shops, waiting to see which direction Aurora would take. There was little time to decide how she was going to play this. It was clear that Aurora's silence couldn't be bought. Georgia couldn't risk her telling Minnie about her past, nor could she take the chance that she wouldn't spill everything to Cole. Above all else, the thought of what it would do to her daughter – to their relationship – made her feel physically sick. She couldn't allow anything – *anyone* – to come between them.

Only minutes after Georgia had left the building, Aurora

appeared. Georgia shrank back into the shadowy recess of the shop doorway, watching. The woman paused to wrap a scarf around her neck, glanced from right to left and back, then crossed the main road and started to walk slowly down a narrow side street towards the high boundary walls of the castle. The street lighting was dim and a mist had descended, making visibility poor.

Maintaining a safe distance, Georgia had followed. She noticed Aurora's slightly lopsided gait, the foot which dragged a little behind the other over the cobbles. Any sympathy or guilt Georgia might have felt for what she had inflicted all those years ago had vanished. Now she could see only a vengeful, bitter individual who threatened her own and Minnie's future. She knew she had no choice.

Aurora paused to pull her phone from her handbag and dialled, then began to speak to someone as she walked. Georgia was too far away to hear what she was saying, but the woman was engrossed in conversation, her head bowed, making Georgia's task all the easier.

Fortuitously, there was a distinct lack of surveillance cameras anywhere along the little side streets which meandered downwards towards the castle. Georgia followed as Aurora plodded on, realising the woman was heading for the bottom of a cul-de-sac just outside the castle walls. A single, unidentifiable car was parked at the far end, shrouded beneath the overhanging branches of a large sycamore. She assumed it must be Aurora's.

It took only seconds for Georgia to reach a decision. Fuelled by loathing and anger, she pulled a pair of gloves from her coat pocket and slipped them on. She moved quietly, stealthily, behind Aurora, never allowing her to disappear from view but keeping far enough back to evade detection, her eyes darting all the time for anyone appearing, her breath coming in rapid, shallow gasps.

Still on her mobile, Aurora reached the car, the handset now wedged between one shoulder and her good ear as she fumbled through her bag for her keys, her back to Georgia; still focused on her call and oblivious to Georgia's presence. She had parked at the far end of the close, away from the other houses and beneath a cluster of trees, making Georgia's mission so much simpler than she could ever have hoped.

Adrenaline coursed through Georgia's veins. Electric with energy, cold sweat beading on her upper lip, she knew it was now or never as she lunged towards her victim.

Aurora's phone clattered to the ground as, her heart hammering, Georgia took hold of the scarf around the woman's neck and drew it taut. Aurora was unable even to cry out. She clawed at the fabric with both hands, trying desperately to pull herself free. But Georgia, driven by a physical strength she didn't know she possessed, continued to pull the scarf ever tighter. Aurora's throat gurgled, her mouth spluttering saliva as she fought for breath. Within what felt like hours but must have only been seconds, Georgia felt Aurora's body grow limp. Releasing the scarf, Georgia looked on as the woman slumped to the ground, the phone beside her where she lay, its screen smashed. Stooping to put her exposed wrist in front of Aurora's mouth, Georgia recoiled as she felt no breath.

Aurora lay like a toppled scarecrow, motionless, limbs askew, her dishevelled hair spread across the pavement. Georgia stared down at her. The woman's swollen tongue lolled from her open mouth, her eyes bulging and bloodshot.

The realisation of what she'd done made Georgia double over suddenly, heaving violently. She managed to reach the grass verge before a stream of vomit poured from her. Composing herself, she straightened, knowing she had to move fast. The key fob lay close by: she toyed with the idea of bundling Aurora into the car, to prolong the length of time before she was discovered, but quickly abandoned the idea when she rationalised how heavy and cumbersome Aurora's lifeless body was likely to be. And then there was the risk of leaving her own DNA in the vehicle. No, better to leave her where she lay; make it look as though she'd been robbed.

Georgia grabbed Aurora's phone reflexively, shoving it deep into her pocket. She cast about her frantically, but there was still not another soul in sight. With trembling, uncoordinated hands, she tipped out the contents of Aurora's handbag, lifting the coin purse and a separate wallet containing credit cards. She would leave the car. But the emptied bag and absence of money would hopefully make it look like a mugging gone wrong. A vulnerable woman, walking the streets alone in the dark . . .

Summoning every ounce of strength she had, Georgia forced her jelly-like legs to carry her, staggering, along the road, past the castle to her right and in the direction of the main road. If anyone *were* to see her, they'd probably think she was drunk. Her mind swam. The mizzle had given way to rain, fine at first but growing gradually more persistent. Georgia pulled her coat tightly around her, kept her eyes trained on the ground. She needed to get as far away from the place as she could – and fast. But she needed to keep a cool head, too.

Think.

No traceable card payments. She hadn't bought anything in the pub. Good. No sightings anywhere near the scene of the crime – she was certain no one had seen her. It was almost two miles away, but she would make her way to Warwick Parkway Station rather than walk to the nearer one just outside the town centre. Less likelihood of bumping into someone who might have noticed them arguing earlier. Plus, booking an Uber was out of the question and she couldn't even risk flagging down a cab. Taxi drivers could be nosy. She just prayed no one in the pub remembered her and made the connection when Aurora's body was found. Georgia looked down at the scarf still clutched in her hands and shuddered. She knew little about DNA transfer, but feared it could contain incriminating fibres from her own gloves. She would have to dispose of it, that and the phone. She'd worry about that later. But she'd been sick – would that give her away? She had a feeling that she'd read somewhere rain would wash away any such evidence, but couldn't be sure. Her mind was racing. She would have to look it up.

Her mind reeling and barely conscious of her surroundings, Georgia tapped the postcode for the train station into her own phone and began to follow the directions. It was still only 9.15pm. Soon she was on the largely empty train and heading back to Coventry. Sitting with her forehead pressed against the glass, she stared unseeingly through the window, a tidal wave rolling in her gut.

How was she ever going to get past this if the police *did* catch up with her? And what would it all do to Minnie – and to their relationship? The realisation suddenly hit her: that if caught, her actions would ultimately reveal her true identity, bring about the very thing she'd been so terrified of happening. That her lies, her every calculated word and deed throughout her whole adult life would have been for nothing.

What had she done?

Chapter 39

Georgia

Sunday, 13 November 2022 – Five days later

The phone rang out, cutting through Georgia's thoughts as she lay in bed. Though she had been awake a while, she'd been content to relax, not feeling the same urgency she usually did to start making herself busy. The knowledge that there would be no further attacks on her felt as if a ten-ton load had been lifted from her shoulders. It was like having an excruciating pain which had suddenly vanished. Her gaze shifted to the small clock on the bedside cabinet. It was only 8.30am. She picked up the handset, smiling as she saw Minnie's name flash up.

"Hi, love. Everything okay?"

There was a lot of noise in the background, as though she was calling from an office or something similar. Minnie's voice was slightly breathless, almost panicky.

"Mum, I'm at the police station. They came to get me just

now. All this business with . . . with Angela . . . I can't . . ." she tailed off for a moment, her speech ragged as though she was struggling to think coherently. "They found this kind of – this scrapbook in her room – it contains lots of pictures; jottings and stuff. I don't know what exactly, they didn't tell me. But for some reason they seem . . . they seem to think Angela moved in with us all because of me. The one thing they *have* said is that there's a photo at the front, of me – of *us* as a family: you, me and Dad. I'm really worried they think I had something to do . . . to do with . . ." Her voice cracked. She began to sob. "Mum, can you – can you come down?" she whispered. "Please? They wouldn't let Ajab come with me. I don't want to be here on my own. I'm scared."

Georgia's whole body had turned to ice. Her mind flew to the scrapbook Minnie had mentioned. She didn't dare contemplate what it contained. What the police may have gleaned about her own connection to Aurora.

"Which – which police station are you in?"

"The one in town," sniffed Minnie. "The police officers are from Warwickshire, but they brought me here as it's nearer. Can you *please* come down? I know you can't sit in on the interview, but I'd feel so much better if I knew you were close by."

"Yes, of course I can. Give me twenty minutes and I'll be there."

"Thank you. I'm so sorry to drag you into this . . ."

Georgia felt a sob rise in her own throat. "Oh, sweetheart – you have nothing to be sorry about. We'll sort this out together. I'm sure everything'll be fine. Try not to worry. I'll see you very soon, I promise. Just sit tight."

Georgia rang off, her mind reeling. Swinging her legs off the side of the bed, she sat with her head in her hands, her eyes squeezed shut, taking deep breaths. She needed to think clearly, stay calm. Hopefully she'd be able to speak to one of the police officers before they interrogated Minnie. What an absolute nightmare this whole situation was. Assuming they'd already put all the pieces together, she could only hope they would agree not to disclose everything about her past to her daughter. Though surely, if they *had* made the connection, they'd have been knocking on *her* door . . .

But then – what was worse? Knowing your mother had been locked up for murder as a damaged, neglected child, or discovering that as a grown, supposedly responsible adult, she had the capability to take a life with her own bare hands, rather than owning up to what she had done in the past? Surely even if she wasn't currently a suspect in Aurora's murder, it was only a matter of time before the police's attention turned to her, given what the spiteful witch was sure to have pasted into that bloody book. She could only hope and pray that the downpour over the days following Aurora's death had removed any traces of her DNA from the crime scene. But was circumstantial evidence enough to secure a conviction?

Georgia knew she was going to have to bite the bullet, step up to support Minnie when she needed her. With limbs like lead, she stood and flung open her wardrobe, riffling frantically through the hangers to find something suitably professional-looking. Even if she was trembling like a leaf within, she had to present a perfectly poised front. This was no time to crumble.

"Always power-dress when you mean business," Trevor had once told her. He was putting on his favourite blue Canali suit, slapping his cheeks with Creed Aventus, in preparation for an important meeting with some potential clients. "Lets people know you're no pushover."

Poor Trevor. She wondered what he'd have made of it all. What a fucking fiasco everything had turned into. With hindsight, it would've been so much better to have come clean with him from the start. If he'd rejected her, she'd have just had to live with it. She would still have had her daughter. Anything would have been better than this.

Georgia's grandmother's words of warning rang in her ears.

"Oh, what a tangled web we weave . . ."

If only Trevor hadn't been so aggressive. *If only* he hadn't had so much vodka: she knew he'd have been far more rational sober. But he had pushed and pushed – verbally and then physically. And she had pushed back. Hard.

Trevor never had been steady on his feet after a drink or two. She recalled dispassionately how he had slipped on the wet tiles, the terrible crack as his head hit the side of the pool; the splash as he entered the water. How, still reeling from his words, she had watched, relieved initially that silence had been restored. That the echo of his stinging rebuke had ceased. Shaken to her senses, for the briefest moment she had considered jumping in to haul him to the side, to turn him over so that, even though unconscious, he could still breathe. But common sense, or at least, that was how she'd thought of it at the time, had prevailed. Someone had told him her secret – and now he was threatening to share it with Minnie. She couldn't allow that to happen.

And so she had sat back in her lounger, necked her gin and tonic, and waited for his life to ebb away before calling for an ambulance. Never once thinking of the consequences for poor Minnie. Never once dreaming that less than two years later, she herself would have taken yet another life.

This was no time for reflection. Georgia pulled out her favourite Paul Smith trouser suit and a cashmere polo neck, and laid them on the bed. If she hurried, she would just have time for a quick shower, a slick of lipstick. She would book an Uber: as a rule, they were virtually on the doorstep within five minutes. She wondered fleetingly whether to call Trevor's solicitor, but thought maybe that was being pre-emptive. Best to find out the lie of the land first.

Her legs felt like water as she headed for the stairs. A tangle of thoughts careened through her mind. She couldn't afford to become flustered. Minnie needed her now; needed her to be the calm, rational one. The parent.

Hesitating on the top step, Georgia thought about retrieving her phone, in case Minnie tried to call again. The poor kid had sounded beside herself.

Georgia wasn't sure what happened next. A loud knock on the front door caught her unawares. Georgia froze. Torn between answering the door and collecting the phone, in her already agitated state, Georgia felt herself pulled, almost comedically, in both directions. The caller hammered again. She hesitated, then decided to grab the mobile first.

In that briefest of seconds, as she twisted towards the bedroom doorway, her bedsock caught on a nail jutting from the floorboard. The sudden stab of pain in her sole caused her to retract her foot sharply and somehow lose her balance. Everything seemed to happen in slow motion. Her other foot slid, causing her head to whip sharply backwards. She seemed to have lost all coordination. Though she tried to grab the banister, it remained just out of reach. Her arms flailing like windmill sails, Georgia began to fall, colliding heavily and brutally with each stair as she went.

Back, back. Until the heavy iron doorstop waiting in the vestibule met with the crown of her head.

And then there was nothing but empty blackness.

Chapter 40

Minnie

Sunday, 13 November 2022

"I just don't *get* it." Cheeks streaked with tears, Minnie sat on the sofa, shivering as much from shock as cold, her head in her hands. Ajab prised one hand from her head and pressed a steaming mug of tea into it.

"Here, drink this. It'll warm you up."

She looked up at him, her face a picture of confusion and angst. Ajab sat beside her, rubbing her back, studying her with concern. He had been the only one home when she arrived back and Minnie was glad. His calm, gentle manner was just what she needed.

After a gruelling half-hour that morning discussing the contents of Angela's scrapbook, the police had finally told her that her mum had been rushed to hospital and a patrol car had taken Minnie directly there. Everything she'd learned about the woman's fixation with her mum was bouncing round in her head like a pinball. She had been shown photographs of some of the book's contents: years' old newspaper cuttings from various events with her dad; photographs of Warchester taken from outside the gates, one in which she herself was walking up the drive. More worrying were recent images taken of Georgia leaving the Orb, obviously captured without her knowledge. And then one particularly sinister picture, showing the front door of Cuckoo Cottage with a red, hand-scrawled X right across it. She just couldn't take it all in.

Arriving at the hospital and seeing her mum like that, blood seeping through the dressing around her head, the wires and bleeping machines, Minnie had been left reeling. It was a complete, surreal nightmare. A kind lady doctor had taken her into a side room; explained that, whilst everything looked pretty scary and the CT scan had revealed a linear fracture to one of the parietal bones at the back of Georgia's skull, the first signs were that she should make a good recovery – it was just going to take time. They were monitoring her closely and keeping her under mild sedation to keep her comfortable.

Drained after several harrowing hours sitting at Georgia's bedside with nothing happening other than regular checks being made on her mum's vital signs, Minnie had been advised to go home and rest.

"There's nothing you can do at the moment, my love," the nurse had explained. "Why don't you go home; get a good night's sleep and come back tomorrow when you're feeling a bit better? Hopefully we'll have some updates for you by then, too. And with a bit of luck, your mum might've actually woken up properly, too."

In a haze, Minnie had caught a taxi back to the house, her mind spinning with the unreal turn of events. Desperate to speak to Jake, she'd tried to call him several times throughout the day, but there had been no reply. That was all she needed, for him to have gone cold on her. The week had gone from bad to worse. She wondered what else it was going to throw at her.

Since arriving home, though still churned up about her mum's accident, Minnie had begun to mull over everything that she'd learned at the police station again. Fatima had been half right – *Minnie* had been the reason Angela had moved in with them. But it had been her mum, not Trevor, as Fatima had suggested, who was the focus of Angela's attentions. It was completely mystifying.

"The cops think Angela must've used me to track Mum down." Minnie turned to Ajab, her hands gradually thawing around the mug of tea. "Sounds like she was completely obsessed with her."

"Bloody hell." Ajab grimaced. "I'm assuming there was some sort of history there? Or was it some stalkerish thing – had she just met her somewhere once and got infatuated? I mean, you hear about these things, don't you. Scary, the number of weirdos there are out there."

Minnie dropped her gaze. She was still trying to absorb what the police had told her and there was clearly more to it than they were letting on. She had asked to see the actual scrapbook, but they'd said it wasn't possible as it was still being checked by the forensics team. At least they'd seemed satisfied eventually that Minnie had no knowledge of any link between Angela and her mum.

She shook her head. "God knows. I'm sure there's stuff they're not telling me. They seemed pretty cagey." She let out a sigh. "Well, at least we know now what Angela spent all her time doing, shut away in her room when we thought she was studying."

The front door slammed. Ajab got up at once as Fatima and Sonia came into the room, stopping in their tracks as they saw Minnie's drawn, solemn face.

"Guys, before you say anything, Mins has had the day from hell. Her mum was taken into hospital with a head injury after falling down the stairs."

Sonia covered her mouth with her hands. "Oh my God, I'm so sorry, Mins. Are you okay? How's your poor mum?"

"She's stable, thankfully. Sounds as if it could've been a whole lot worse if she'd landed differently. Apparently she woke for a short while after they admitted her, but she was asleep the whole time I was there. They've scanned her and said there's no evidence of brain damage, and there doesn't appear to be any cerebrospinal fluid leakage, so they're just keeping her comfortable, and hopefully she'll be well enough to come out in the next few days, even if she won't be 100 per cent for several weeks."

Fatima's eyes widened. "She fell down the stairs, you say? You don't think . . ."

Minnie jerked her head round. "What?"

"They said it could've been a lot nastier, right? I don't want to freak you out, but . . . d'you reckon it might not've been an accident? I mean, after what happened to Angela . . ."

"Thanks, mate. That's made me feel a whole lot better." Minnie glared at her, angry that Fatima would even suggest such a thing. She didn't need anything else to worry about right now.

"Fuck's sake – why can't you just keep your thoughts to yourself sometimes?" Sonia rounded on Fatima, whose cheeks reddened.

She threw up her hands. "I'm sorry, I'm sorry. It – it just crossed my mind, that's all. I mean, we don't know yet what happened to Angela, do we, and if there's a link to Mins's mum, well . . ."

"It was an accident, okay? Could've happened to anyone, especially on those stupid fucking stairs." Minnie stood up abruptly, turning to Ajab. "I'm wrecked. I've got to get myself

350

to bed. I just need to put everything out of my head for a few hours. Hopefully tomorrow will be better."

Ajab gave her a hug which she returned gratefully. "Yeah, fingers crossed. 'Night."

The other two wished her goodnight and Minnie climbed wearily to her room, praying that there would soon be some sort of resolution to the mystery of Angela's death and that the woman's obsession with Georgia had no wider implications. The thought that anyone could wish her mum harm had never entered Minnie's head and Fatima's words niggled at her.

She checked her phone, but there was no message from Jake. Her heart sank.

All she wanted to do was block out the world and sink into oblivion.

Chapter 41

Georgia

Tuesday, 15 November 2022 – Two days later

"Hello, Mrs Parnell. Welcome back."

Georgia blinked against the unwelcome intrusion of bright light. She screwed her eyes up more tightly. The gentle pressure of someone's hand on her own made her flinch. Slowly, she tried to lift her eyelids, but they felt so heavy, it was as though they had been glued shut. She emitted an involuntary groan. The lead weights pinned to her sides must be her arms, she realised. She was supine, her head slightly raised: that much she had gathered, though she seemed to have no real sense of any other part of her body or where it was in relation to the rest of her. As her ears tuned into her surroundings, she became aware of intermittent bleeps and shuffling footfall, voices near and far. Wheels trundling across an unidentifiable surface. The incongruous blend of disinfectant and something like mince in gravy hit her nostrils suddenly. She felt bile rising in her throat, made to put a palm over her mouth to stem it.

"It's fine, don't worry." The hand patted her again, on the shoulder this time. She felt something placed beneath her chin.

"There you go, my love. Better out than in."

The retching caused the crushing pain in her head to grow sharper. She lay back, exhausted from the effort. Something was dabbed across her mouth, the pillow behind her head straightened.

Gradually Georgia's eyes fluttered open, everything blurry initially. As they adjusted to the harsh fluorescent glow above her, she looked slowly from side to side.

"Where am I?" Her mouth felt parched, her lips dry and unwilling to part. The corners of her mouth were sore and crusty.

"You're in hospital. You've been here over twenty-four hours now, drifting in and out. Gave us all a bit of a scare, you did."

A beaming, round-faced lady in a sky-blue shirt-dress, hair slicked back into a bun, was bustling round her, checking the displays on various flashing machines next to the bed and writing notes on a clipboard. It suddenly dawned on Georgia that she must be a nurse. Everything felt strange, disorientating.

"I'm Bernila. I'll be looking after you. Doctor will be round to see you shortly."

Georgia glanced to her side, her eyes following the tube taped to the crook of her arm to a bag of clear liquid suspended next to the bed.

"What happened to me?"

"You fell down the stairs. Hit your head." There was a whirring noise as Bernila pressed something at the foot of the bed and Georgia felt herself slowly elevated to an even more upright position.

"Are you in any pain, my love?"

Georgia responded with a wince, raising her free arm to the

353

back of her skull. She felt a thick wad of dressing beneath her fingers. Her head throbbed like a beacon.

"You've been having multimodal IV analgesia – I'll tell Doctor and we can tweak the prescription if it's not effective enough." Bernila smiled reassuringly. "Don't look so worried. It may take a little time but you'll be okay. Doctor will explain – they did a CT scan when they brought you in and they'll need to keep an eye on you, but usually these things sort themselves out in a few months. You'll just have to take things easy for a while."

The sudden memory of what had happened rushed into Georgia's mind. The heart rate monitor began to oscillate wildly, her breath coming in short, rapid gasps.

"*Minnie*. Is Minnie okay?"

"Your daughter? She's fine. She was here for hours yesterday. Lovely girl."

"And the police?" She had to ask the question but wasn't sure she wanted to hear the response.

Bernila's pleasant face clouded a little. "Don't you worry about the police. They want to speak to you, but I won't be letting them anywhere near until you're feeling up to it. You've had a close call and you're my patient – your welfare's my priority, not helping with their inquiries. Plenty of time for that later."

"But – they've let Minnie go?"

"Oh, yes. She was telling me all about it." Bernila rolled her eyes. "Sounds like a proper mix-up. I'm sure it'll all be straightened out soon." She rubbed Georgia's hand, then guided the spout of a plastic beaker to her lips. "Try and have a little drink for me, my love."

Georgia spluttered, but managed a few sips, her throat painful as the water slid down.

Bernila grimaced. "You were intubated for a short time as a precaution when you were first admitted, so it'll probably be a bit sore for a while," she explained. "Now just you rest and

Doctor will be round in the next half hour or so to talk about the scan results. Let's focus on getting you well again, shall we?"

"Can I call Minnie?" Georgia croaked.

"I'll ring her – let her know you're properly awake now. I'm sure she'll be in to see you soon." Bernila gave her arm a comforting squeeze, then disappeared through the door opposite the end of the bed. Georgia cast blearily around the room. She was in a private bay, a door leading to the bathroom to her right, a large rectangle of glass looking out onto a busy corridor to her left. It felt as though something was pressing down on her head. The effort of sitting up, even for so short a time, had been exhausting. Minnie had been released, that was the main thing. She would be able to see her very soon.

Georgia closed her eyes and allowed herself to drift away once more.

Chapter 42

Georgia

Wednesday, 16 November 2022 – One day later

Georgia opened her eyes to semi-darkness. She peered up at the clock. It was 1.40am. The light in the corridor was dim, the incessant noise of the usual daily ward activity replaced by a welcome calm. Only the occasional cough or creak through the adjoining wall betrayed the presence of other patients. Through the glass, she could see a bespectacled staff nurse sitting behind the reception desk, hunched over paperwork lit by an anglepoise lamp. Georgia hauled herself up into a sitting position and reached for the tumbler of water next to the bed, took a few gulps, then flopped back down, frustrated by the fatigue that even such a minor action induced. The doctor had explained that the rehabilitation process wouldn't happen overnight; she would need to be patient and not overtax herself. Georgia closed her eyes once more. Her thought processes were still muddled, but she knew that soon enough things would improve. This only imbued her with anxiety, knowing that with her recovery would come the inevitable grilling from the police and its implications.

They must know everything by now. Her real name. Her past misdemeanours. As a child offender, Georgia's true identity had been a closely-guarded secret, a High Court injunction having been imposed to prevent the media from hunting her down and exposing Georgia and any family she had to likely persecution, with only a select few police officers who had originally worked on her case kept informed of her status and whereabouts. But Aurora must surely have given the local force every clue they needed in her wretched scrapbook. It wouldn't take a genius to fit all the pieces of the jigsaw together.

Georgia rolled onto her side, away from the window. Worse than facing the police would be seeing Minnie's reaction to it all. She would have to be told; Georgia knew that. The total devastation it would cause her. The horror and shame Georgia had tried to protect her daughter from, her whole life. She felt a tear trickling from the corner of her eye into her ear and swept it away with the back of her hand.

Georgia heard the door open, then close quietly. She tried to compose herself and remained on her side, expecting the nurse to approach and announce the usual observations that they seemed to deem necessary whatever the hour. Muted footsteps squeaked across the floor. She heard the rattle of the privacy curtain being pulled slowly round the bed and groaned a little inwardly, preparing herself for the cuff of the blood pressure monitor, the digital thermometer poked into her ear. Maybe even another blood draw.

"Ah, there you are."

The words sent a shard of ice up her spine. Slowly Georgia turned to see a tall, hooded figure standing next to the bedhead. Her heart quickened. But then she considered everything that had happened, the blow to her head. The confusion that something so traumatic could cause. She thought about the monk. He was hardly likely to have followed her here, was he? She'd been pumped full of God knows what. She must be imagining it. Her irrational fears were grounded in reality, her current stressful situation. She rolled back onto her side and let out a long breath. The figure wasn't real.

"That's very rude, turning your back on a visitor like that."

The voice was only a whisper, but so close now she could feel the warmth of breath on her face. This was no hallucination. This was frighteningly real.

Georgia turned slowly to see someone leaning over her. Her eyes widened in horror. She opened her mouth to scream, but nothing came out. The figure straightened, pressing a gloved finger to its lips, then gave a sinister little laugh. Frantic, Georgia groped for the emergency call button dangling from a cable behind her, but it was out of reach.

"No one will hear you, anyway. Nursey's just gone on her break. She obviously thought she wouldn't be missed for a few minutes while she went out for a crafty fag. I've been keeping an eye on her from out there." The head tipped towards the general direction of the exit. Georgia had seen it when they wheeled her down for another scan. Paralysed by fear, she could do no more than lie there, wondering what was in store for her.

"I believe you and I had a mutual acquaintance. Aurora Trelawney? Or maybe you knew her as Angela Tandy. I think she'd had a couple of aliases in her time. Much like yourself."

There was a pause. Georgia's mouth felt drier than ever. Her pulse was racing. She thought fleetingly that it would have been interesting to see how it was behaving on the heart monitor that had been removed only hours earlier. Maybe it would even have triggered an alarm. She tried to sit up, but was pushed firmly back onto the bed.

"I don't know if you've guessed our connection. All you need to know about me is that you ruined my life. And I don't give a flying fuck whether you were a child. We were all kids once. I'm damn sure *I* knew the difference between right and wrong when I was ten."

Confusion flooded Georgia's mind. Who *was* this person? The voice was low, but the blatant rage and hatred seeping through was terrifying.

"I mean, Aurora was a case in point. She had a proper bee in her bonnet about you, didn't she? It'd taken her months, she said, but she finally tracked me down and pointed me in your direction, so I s'pose I should be grateful to her for that. But I never liked the woman. How could anyone, knowing what she did?" The head shook from side to side, the action vehement. "She did seem pretty disturbed, though. Daddy issues, I'd have said. Ha!"

This sudden exclamation made Georgia start. She curled her fists around the bedsheets, drawing them up to her chin. "Who are you? What – what are you going to do?"

There was no response.

The figure remained motionless for a moment, the silence more unnerving than the vitriol that had preceded it. Then suddenly, the head bent towards her, so close she could detect the sourness of whisky on the intruder's breath. Dutch courage, maybe. The voice reduced further to a menacing hiss.

"I'm going to finally get justice for my family. My mammy and daddy and my big sister. Burned to a cinder in their own home." There was a sudden quaver in the voice, the suggestion of despair through the anger. One hand went to the face as if to swipe away a tear. "The irony is I'd have gone with them, if I hadn't been ill at the time. In hospital with the croup, apparently. 'Course, I don't remember. I was just a wee baby. Not that it would have stopped you even if I'd been at home, I don't suppose."

Georgia felt sickened. "I'm so sorry for your loss," she

whispered. "That's a terrible thing to have happened. But I had nothing to do with your family's deaths. I – I think you've got your wires crossed."

This only seemed to incite more anger. "For fuck's sake, have the guts to admit it. You were found guilty, weren't you? I'm sick of gobshites like you, hiding behind deprived childhoods, whingeing about how abuse and hardship drove them to do terrible things. *Boo-fucking-hoo*. But you're still here, aren't you? You've had a very cushy life, from everything I've been told. Well, now your chickens have all come home to roost."

Georgia turned her face away in despair. Nothing she could say was going to persuade the intruder that she hadn't killed those people. As if from nowhere, she felt the sudden searing pain of something sharp being plunged into the back of her head. The abrupt, violent action occurred so quickly she had no time to react. Though she tried to raise her arms in resistance, she had been rendered pathetically weak after her fall and the prolonged spell in bed. Overwhelming panic was building inside Georgia as she began to fight for breath. Her chest felt as if it were about to explode.

Georgia's head grew fuzzy, consciousness beginning to desert her. She had a vague awareness that this was it; that her life was about to be extinguished. Maybe this was no more than she deserved, anyway: retribution for the terrible things she had done. A roundabout way of making things even. There was a resignation about it all, an odd sense of peace. No more fear, no more guilt. No more lies or living under the constant threat of being unmasked; of Minnie's disgust and devastating rejection of her.

The last thing she heard was the muffled words of her killer, spoken close to her ear.

"Goodbye, Jolene Jackson. See you on the other side."

Chapter 43

Minnie

Sunday, 11 December 2022 – Twenty-five days later

Minnie was glad to have her mum's funeral behind her. It had been a small, private affair in the crematorium: Minnie's friends, Yiannis and Freddie, who'd sent a huge spray of lilies, and a handful of regulars from the Orb. Cole had sat in the back row, looking rueful, but disappeared immediately after the service. Minnie realised sadly that Georgia had not a single close friend from when she was growing up, no family other than herself. It wasn't much to show for almost forty years on the planet.

The inquest had yet to come, but everything pointed to unforeseen complications as a result of the head injury. It was thought that Georgia had suffered a sudden violent seizure, which had led to a dangerous arrhythmia and ultimately a cardiac arrest. The duty nurse had looked in to check on her in the early hours and found her cold. Minnie was heartbroken to think that Georgia had died alone. It was too cruel. The only comfort was that her mum's death must have been painless and that she would have been completely unaware of what was happening.

The past few weeks had been a living hell, but Minnie's friends had really stepped up and she was incredibly grateful. Ajab had been so kind and supportive, and Fatima had been a true rock, helping with arrangements and fending off unwanted press intrusion. Sonia's previously hidden domestic skills had come to the fore – she seemed to have found her vocation as mother hen, making sure Minnie was eating properly and preparing meals for them all. Even if she no longer had any blood family, Minnie felt she could always count on her loyal little crew, who'd turned out to be the best friends anyone could ask for. They had even offered to stay on in the house with her over the Christmas holiday, saying they wouldn't dream of leaving her behind. It was going to be strange, her first Christmas without her mum, though at least she wouldn't be spending it alone. Her mates were absolute diamonds.

But she was devastated about Jake. The timing couldn't have been worse. He'd been distracted since around the time of her mum's death, with worries of his own about his job situation, and only two days before the funeral, had finally told her apologetically that he was returning to Liverpool. He'd seemed genuinely remorseful.

"The contract's finished here and the gaffer's got another major project on in Merseyside. I've got to go where the work is. I can't live on fresh air. I'm so sorry."

"But – but I've got money. Plenty of it. You don't have to worry." She'd looked at him, pleading with her eyes.

"I can't take your money, Minnie Mouse."

There was a tremor in his voice. For a moment Minnie thought he might actually break down, but he'd looked away, composed himself.

"Will you be coming back?" She'd tried to stem the tears, her lip trembling. It was one more blow she didn't need.

"I really don't know. But we'll keep in touch, eh?" He had stroked her cheek fondly, his dark eyes studying her face, trying to coax a smile. They had shared one last bittersweet kiss, and then he was gone. She knew in her heart that she would probably never see him again.

The day of Jake's departure, Minnie had cried until there were no tears left, as much for her mum as for him. For the futures that neither of them were going to have now. She was anxious about Warchester; what she was going to do with the house. But her dad's old solicitor had told her not to worry, that there were no decisions that needed to be made urgently. She was a very wealthy young woman, he'd said, a little patronisingly, and to coin a phrase, the world was pretty much her oyster. As if money mattered to her now. What she wouldn't have given to have her mum back, her dad. And her lovely Jake.

The police investigation into Angela's murder seemed to have reached an impasse. DS Gill had promised to keep her informed if anything came to light.

In the meantime, one thing Minnie *did* need to do was to clear her mum's belongings from Cuckoo Cottage. It had taken every ounce of courage she possessed to cross the threshold again, to see where her mother had lain unconscious, her dried blood still on the old iron doorstop. The event that had effectively sealed her fate.

Ajab had offered to accompany Minnie, but once she'd got past that initial hurdle, she wanted to take her time sifting through stuff, taking in the essence of the place. Of her mum's final weeks. She felt so bad that she hadn't visited more. This was one job she had to do alone. Before entering, Minnie had gazed sadly across at the house Jake shared with Heggs. She wondered how he was getting on in Liverpool. Briefly, she considered knocking on the door later, speaking to Heggs to ask after him. No. It would be a bad idea. If Jake wanted to contact her, he would have done so, and there had been no attempt on his part. He had moved on, and so, sadly, must she.

Minnie took the roll of bin liners she'd brought with her and climbed the stairs slowly. She bit her lip as she looked around the freshly painted bedroom, the new bedding and shabby chic mirror giving it a more homely touch. Her mum had actually done a pretty good job. Latterly, Georgia had surprised her with the things she'd been capable of, given that Minnie had always teased her about being a lady of leisure. It made Minnie wonder about what life had been like for her mum growing up, before she'd had Trevor's money to pay for tradesmen to do all those jobs that Minnie herself never thought twice about. To buy nice things: the little luxuries that she had, to her shame, always taken as a given. She realised she knew very little about her mother's upbringing, other than what Trevor had told her: that she'd been an only child; that her parents had been poor and hadn't treated her very well. That she'd been in care. Minnie felt a pang of misery that she would never be able to ask her those questions now. She didn't even know where Georgia had spent her childhood, other than somewhere in the north west. Her own lack of curiosity about it all astounded and appalled her now.

Opening the wardrobe, she began to lift the clothes carefully from their hangers. Her heart ached as she pressed each of the items to her face in turn, breathing in the faded scent of Georgia's perfume for a moment, then folded them neatly in a pile on the bed. At the front of the top shelf was a pile of sweaters and cardigans. She took them out, one by one, placing them on the bed next to the other clothes. Behind the jumpers and pushed right to the back of the shelf, she noticed an old, navy-blue banker's box, the sort her dad used to store his files in, secured with a length of black cord. Minnie reached in and pulled the box out, then sat on the bed for a moment with it on her lap. Loosening the knot, she lifted the lid. There, right on top of the jumble of papers within, was a creased brown envelope. It bore Minnie's name and date of birth written in blue biro, in Georgia's familiar scrawl. Unfolding the flap, Minnie's eyes filled with tears as she saw a lock of dark hair, an umbilical cord clip. The tiny tag which must have been attached to her own wrist in the maternity ward. She had no idea her mum had kept any of this. A beam of hope lit her mind as she thought maybe she'd find some clues to her mum's past among her mementos.

Minnie wanted to take her time sifting through the items she had just discovered. Placing the box almost deferentially on the floor, she went back down to the kitchen to make herself a coffee. She was interrupted almost immediately by a knock at the door. An unfamiliar elderly man with wispy grey hair stood on the step. He was almost bent double, frail-looking; a stick in one hand, a bunch of red and white carnations in the other.

"I'm sorry to disturb you, love. I heard about what happened and I just wanted to pay my respects. Bought these the other day, but there's been no one here to give them to." He raised the slightly droopy flowers aloft. "The poor lady – she was your mum, wasn't she?"

Minnie attempted a smile. "Yes. Yes, she was. And thank you, that's very kind."

"I never actually got to meet her, but I was sort of a neighbour." He turned to indicate the row of houses on the opposite side of the quad. "I used to see her coming and going, you know. I don't get out myself much these days. Spend half my life staring out the bloody window, living it through everyone who goes by." He laughed sadly. "Life catches up with you. You take my word for it, you never think you're going to get old. And then one day, it dawns on you, you're struggling to do the things you'd always taken for granted. You look in the mirror and wonder where the years have gone."

Minnie studied the old man. His cloudy eyes were sunken, his gnarled hands shook a little. He sounded breathless. He must have been well over eighty.

"Um – I'm just making myself a coffee – would you like one?"

He looked surprised. "I wasn't angling, you know. I really did come over just to bring the flowers . . ."

"I know you weren't." Minnie stepped aside for him to enter. "Please, come in. I'm not in any hurry today. I've got to pack up my mum's things and it's not a job I've been looking forward to."

"Emotional, eh? I know just how that feels." The old man's eyes crinkled into a sad smile. "Well, thank you – I will join you for a quick coffee, then, if I'm not intruding."

He seemed to be taking everything in as he walked into the sitting room. Minnie took the flowers from him, then directed him to the armchair nearest the window while she went to make the drinks.

"Funny isn't it," he called, raising his voice to be heard above the kettle. "I've lived here the best part of sixty years and I'd no idea what this house looked like on the inside."

"Yes. I suppose they're all a bit different, aren't they?" she called back. "Milk and sugar?"

"Just the one sugar, please. Lots of milk, if you've got enough."

"Plenty – I picked up a pint on my way over."

Minnie came back in with the coffees and placed one next to him on the small side table, then sat down in the chair opposite. It wouldn't hurt to spend a little time with the poor old soul, she thought. He must be lonely.

"I'm sorry – I haven't introduced myself. I'm Sam. Sam Zielinski."

"Nice to meet you, Sam. I'm Minnie."

The old man beamed. "Like the mouse."

Minnie nodded, squeezing a sad smile. "Yes, like the mouse."

"And your mum? Georgia, wasn't she? I saw the funeral notice in the *Telegraph*."

"Yes, that's right."

Sam shook his head. "Terrible. So sad. And she was so young, too."

Tears welled in Minnie's eyes once more. "Yes, she was. She should've had decades left."

"I'm so sorry, love – I didn't mean to upset you." The old man reached for his drink, looking a little uncomfortable.

"No, it's fine. I'm like this all the time at the moment. It'll get better, I'm sure, but right now everything's very raw."

"I remember the last young woman who was living here before her. She did a moonlight flit, you know."

"Oh? Oh yes, now you mention it – I think I remember Mum saying something about her."

"Hmm. Very iffy, it all was." He leaned forwards almost conspiratorially. "There was something going on with her, I reckon. Possibly something not legal, too."

"Really?" Minnie's eyes widened with interest. She sipped her coffee. "What sort of thing?"

The old man lowered his voice. "Don't quote me on it, but I reckon there could've been drugs involved." He gave her a slow wink.

"Oh dear. What makes you think that?"

"Well, that blinkin' Jethro Jackson fella had installed her here, hadn't he? Everyone knows what *he* gets up to on the quiet." He screwed up his nose in distaste. "The police hauled him in the other week, apparently. The bugger wriggled out of it, whatever it was they were trying to pin on him. Not enough evidence. The postman was telling me. Not a lot gets past me, you know, even if I rarely get out these days. And I see all bloody sorts from that window and no one's got a clue." He waved towards his house. "Let's face it, I'm pretty invisible sitting up there."

"What did you see? Going on with the woman, I mean?"

"Different people coming to her door at all hours. And I mean *all* hours. I'm always up and down half the night – bloomin' prostate; it's a right nuisance. Yes, going in, coming out again only minutes later. Looking proper shifty. I may be an old codger, but I'm not daft." He scratched his chin, his lips pursed. "It's my guess – and I'm only surmising, mind – that Jackson was supplying and she was doing the selling on. But then she buggered off, didn't she. In the middle of the bloomin' night. I saw her, everything but the kitchen sink with her, getting into a taxi – well, I'd heard the rumble of a diesel engine, so I looked out. Jackson was round there like a shot next morning: searching the place from top to bottom, I reckon he was. Face like thunder when he came out. Whether she took his drugs or his money – or both, I couldn't say, but God help her if he ever catches up with her." He glanced back out of the window. "Let's just say I hear plenty of stuff through my walls. Those lads living next door to me work for him, you know. For all I know, they might be at it, too."

Goosebumps prickled along Minnie's arms. Her hand travelled to her throat. "What – dealing drugs?"

He considered for a moment. "The older two, very possibly. But maybe not the young Polish fella. He seemed decent. Good-hearted. He'd even knock on my door now and again, ask if I needed anything fetching from the shops. He wasn't here all that long." Sam studied Minnie curiously. "Here, didn't I see you with him once or twice?"

Minnie frowned slightly. "I think you must be confusing me with someone else. I was seeing a man called Jake for a while, but not a Polish boy."

Sam's face lit up. He nodded vigorously. "Yes, Jake. It's him

I'm on about." He smiled to himself. "That was how we first met. A letter addressed to me got delivered there by mistake and he brought it round for me. We got talking – he told me his parents were Polish, like mine, but he'd been brought up in Ireland by an auntie after they died. Yes. Jakub Nowak. That was it."

"But – but he never said. That his family were Polish, I mean." Minnie's mind was whirring. "I always thought his surname was O'Connor."

"That was his auntie's husband's name, apparently. Poor kid had had a rotten time of it, from everything he said." He shook his head. "Nowhere else for him to go though, was there, after what happened to his family. Tragic."

"What did actually happen to them? He never told me and I didn't like to pry." Minnie studied Sam's face, which had grown solemn.

"Killed in their own home," he said bluntly. "Burned to death in their beds. His mum and dad and his older sister – and *she* was only about ten, I believe. Some wicked little girl lit a firework – a silent one, so they wouldn't have heard anything – and dropped it through their letterbox one Bonfire Night, along with a rag soaked in turps. Can you imagine?" Sam's jowly cheeks wobbled a little as he spoke. "Evil. They caught up with her thankfully, sent her away for a time. I don't care what anyone says though, a kid who can do something like that should be locked up and the key thrown away. Oh, I'll bet she's probably living the high life somewhere now, with a new name and everyone around her in blissful ignorance of what she did." His mouth had set into a hard line. "Where's the justice, eh? Everything seems to be arse about face these days, if you'll pardon the expression."

They finished their coffees in silence. Poor Jake. No wonder he didn't want to talk about it. His whole family, murdered

369

by a child. A sick feeling turned in Minnie's stomach as she remembered what Sonia's boyfriend had discovered about Aurora Trelawney.

Aurora. Minnie still couldn't think of her as anything other than Angela. But that's what they did, didn't they? People who'd done something terrible in their past. Adopted a different name; tried to distance themselves from it all. Aurora was responsible for the death of her own brother. Even though she'd been punished for it and her family had done everything in their power to protect her identity once she was released, she wondered how they must really have felt about her. Maybe it was more about protecting themselves than Aurora. Their money and power had enabled them to buy the silence of the press. It seemed all wrong.

Whoever had killed Jake's family all those years ago must still be out there somewhere, grown up now. Maybe with children of their own. Minnie considered, if she were Jake, how *she* would feel if she were to come face to face with that person. Would she have it in her heart to forgive? There were restorative justice schemes in place these days: opportunities for victims to confront offenders, to try to help them come to terms with the devastation the perpetrators' actions had wreaked on their lives. She wondered if such ventures ever really worked. For Minnie personally, she felt it would just provide her with a face to haunt her dreams. Thank God it wasn't something she needed to consider.

Sam eased himself to his feet, groaning a little, one hand supporting his back. He gave Minnie a brief smile.

"I'd better let you get back to your sorting, love. Thank you for the coffee – and the company. And please, if you're passing, do give me a knock. It's always nice to see a friendly face."

Minnie saw him to the door. "Thank you very much again for the flowers."

He nodded, pressing her hand gently. "You take care of yourself, now, won't you. Bye 'bye."

Minnie watched as he hobbled across the quad, then came back into the house. Taking a deep breath, she climbed the stairs to the bedroom once more. Tingling with anticipation, she knelt on the rug beside the bed and began to remove every sheet of paper, every cardboard folder, every envelope and letter, from the banker's box. This was going to take hours, but at least things seemed to have been arranged roughly in some sort of chronological order, with the most recent documents nearest the top of the pile.

The best place to start surely was from the bottom up. Because here lay the clues to Georgia's history. To her own heritage. But as she was about to start sifting through, Minnie felt the floorboard beneath her wobble slightly, the hard ridge of its edge digging into to her shin. Sitting back, she lifted the edge of the rug. The board was loose.

And the house was so *old* . . .

Suddenly excited at the prospect of finding something of historical interest beneath, Minnie jumped to her feet, scanning round for a suitable object to prise it up. There was nothing visible. She was about to go back downstairs when her eyes landed on the bedside cabinet. Opening the drawer, she recoiled slightly at the sight of a carving knife sitting right at the front. Why the hell would her mum have something like that in the bedroom? For *protection*? The thought was alarming.

Minnie used the blade to loosen the floorboard, managing to lift it from one edge. As she peered into the aperture below, her heart sank a little. No ancient treasure box or diary. No scrolls. Just an obviously recent M&S plastic carrier bag, which had been wound several times around something and wedged between the rafters. Minnie reached in to remove the bag, tipping out its contents onto the floor. She frowned. It was a scarf. Not her mum's sort of thing at all. Expensive-looking, yes – but more like the kind of thing an older lady would wear. And brown – definitely not Georgia's colour. But the soft thud as it landed told her there was something wrapped inside. As she lifted the fabric, the item fell to the floor with a clatter.

Minnie fell back, her hands shaking. There in front of her lay an iPhone, its screen shattered. But it was the distinctive, vibrant cover that she had recognised immediately. The pale yellow background. The swirling gold branches. The black, red-eyed bird.

Klimt's *The Tree of Life*.

And then she knew, without a doubt. That the phone had belonged to Angela.

Chapter 44

Wednesday, 25 January 2023 – Forty-five days later

Coventry Telegraph

POLICE ANNOUNCE POSSIBLE BREAKTHROUGH IN CONSTRUCTION HEIRESS MURDER

Warwickshire Police have issued a statement regarding the shocking murder of wealthy construction heiress, Aurora Trelawney, whose body was discovered near Warwick town centre in November of last year. Following a thorough examination of certain items belonging to the deceased, they are now trying to locate Jakub Nowak, aged twenty-eight, whom they believe to have been in regular contact with Ms

Trelawney in the weeks prior to her death.

Detective Sergeant Navpreet Gill, speaking on behalf of Warwickshire CID, is urging anyone with information regarding this potential new lead to come forward.

"This has been a baffling case for all those involved, but we believe we may now have a clearer picture of Ms Trelawney's background and the events that may ultimately have led to her death. It has come to light that Mr Nowak's family died in horrific circumstances many years ago. We are considering the possibility that the murder of Ms Trelawney may be linked to those deaths and is the result of a tragic case of mistaken identity. We are appealing for Mr Nowak to contact us, to help eliminate him from our enquiries. Anyone with information which may help us to locate Mr Nowak can call our hotline number. All calls will be treated in the strictest confidence."

Ajab looked up from reading the article aloud on his phone. "So, sounds like they think they've got their killer, then."

Fatima had been leafing through a magazine, her feet curled beside her at the far end of the settee. She raised her eyes, pursing her lips. "Yeah, but whoever he is, they'll have to catch up with him first. He's had two months to make himself scarce – he could be on the other side of the world by now."

Minnie was sitting rigidly next to Ajab, his words dancing through her head, her eyes focused on the floor. The rug seemed to be moving suddenly, rippling like waves; coming up to meet her. She staggered to her feet, heading for the door with a hand over her mouth.

"Mins, you okay?" Sonia was just coming from the kitchen, carrying a tray of mugs. "You don't look a good colour."

Minnie just made it to the toilet in time before retching violently, the door still open behind her.

"Jesus. Was it something you ate?" Sonia had put down the tray in the hallway and was stooping to rub her back.

"No. At least . . . no. I don't think so." Minnie sat back on her haunches for a moment, catching her breath, her head still swimming. She looked up at Sonia's anxious eyes and promptly burst into tears.

"Oh, sweetheart! Whatever's wrong?"

Minnie couldn't even begin to tell her. The nightmare of the terrible secret she'd been keeping all these weeks; about the torment of feeling that she had never really known her mum at all, the discovery that Georgia had even lied about her real name. Of the shocking information in the file about a conviction for murder, the details of Georgia's post-release Licence conditions and Notice of Supervision. But worst of all, of finding Angela's phone and the unthinkable implications of its presence. Of how she was torn by the dilemma of whether or not she should reveal what she knew and thus completely trash her mother's memory. How the sleepless nights were making studying – even *living* – impossible.

And now, on top of everything, *this*. Only a day after her most recent earth-shattering discovery. Minnie had always thought she was resilient, but it was all too much for one person to shoulder alone. If she didn't tell someone, she was going to go mad.

She thought of the white plastic wand with its tell-tale vertical blue line, discarded in disbelief in the bathroom bin only yesterday. Of the ramifications of the police's latest announcement. And once more of what she had found in her mother's secret hiding place.

Minnie allowed Sonia to help her to her feet, leaning to run the tap. She rinsed her mouth, then straightened, turning to look at Sonia, whose kind, non-judgmental face was a picture of concern.

Minnie knew that she couldn't make the past right. But she could at least try to prevent another catastrophic wrong. Taking Sonia's hand, she drew in a long, resigned breath.

"I need to speak to the police. There's something they really need to know."

Chapter 45

Jake

Monday, 5 December 2022 – Fifty-one days earlier

Jake had settled himself towards the back of the half-empty coach to Liverpool in the driving rain that afternoon, his sodden, over-stuffed rucksack wedged into the net luggage rack above his head. He swatted away the slow drips landing on his shoulder from time to time in irritation. He had hooked his rain-heavy combat jacket over the back of the empty seat next to him and was leaning against the window, his wet hair sticking to the cold glass. The downpour had worsened since passing Birmingham, lashing the windscreen so that the driver had the wipers at full pelt, the wheels sending arcs of muddy spray to shower any smaller vehicles in the coach's wake as it ploughed by. The sky was blue-black with cloud, ensuring that any daylight had been obliterated well before dusk should have fallen, making driving conditions even more hazardous. Jake was past caring.

If they'd had a terrible accident, skidded off the road and ended up mangled, then so be it.

But he was being a selfish prick, wasn't he? To the best of his knowledge, no one else on board deserved to die. He had done the worst thing any human being could have done and he was going to have to live with the persistent needling of his conscience for the rest of his life. Too late to realise afterwards that eliminating his family's killer would never bring him the sense of vindication and peace of mind he had craved for so long. How he wished he could turn back the clock. How he wished he had never even heard of Jolene Jackson, that she had remained some faceless hate figure that only resurged whenever the whisky had been flowing. That punching a wall once in a while had been enough to get it out of his system. Ironic, really, that his gaffer had shared her surname. Jethro, who for all his faults had effectively saved him from a life on the streets. Put a roof over his head. Jake had even asked him outright once if he had a relative called Jolene. Of course, he'd never heard of her. But then, Jackson was a pretty common name, wasn't it?

He could have tried to put it all behind him, let bygones be bygones. But once he'd met Aurora and started on that corkscrew of a trajectory, chewed up now by hatred and the burning desire for revenge, it had felt impossible to stop.

Having discovered how his family had died had only been the start of it. Naturally, he had been angry and embittered. Who wouldn't? But once Aurora Trelawney had tracked him down, she had eagerly fuelled his desire for some sort of redress.

"Do you call that justice? That woman took your whole family's lives and now she's living anonymously in the lap of luxury, totally unscathed and smug. Doesn't that make your blood boil?"

And it did: of course it did. He'd been dealt some truly shit cards and yet there was Jolene Jackson, wanting for nothing, her horrendous actions swept neatly under the carpet along with her identity. He wasn't so naive as to think Aurora didn't have her own agenda. The woman had delighted in telling him how Jolene had behaved as an inmate in Caulmoor; how she was a rotten egg from a rotten family, who revelled in the misfortunes of others. A wicked bully of a child who would no doubt have turned into a hateful, malevolent adult. Someone society would be well rid of.

But Jake had never been prepared for how he would grow to feel about Minnie. Aurora had handed him the press cuttings, showing this pampered, privately-educated little shite with tomato-red hair. What the hell was that all about? A nod to socialism? A middle-class stab at rebellion? Pfft. Well, she'd made herself easy enough to find. He'd known the students always hung out at the SU on Friday nights. It was only a matter of time before he'd come across her. And then he could worm his way in there, get her to lead him to her mother.

Then Aurora had had a change of plan. She'd discovered that the house Minnie was sharing had a spare room – she would move in and track Jolene down, she said. It shouldn't take long. Have a bit of fun terrorising her first. Like a cat tormenting its prey. And then Jake could do just as he liked. He'd carried on seeing Minnie anyway, just out of curiosity initially. But it became impossible to stop. He'd found her so unlike any of the girls he'd been involved with before. It was unfathomable that such a lovely human being could be a first-degree relative of someone so vile.

He'd had time to think long and hard about it. About what Jolene had done to his parents, to his sister. About how different his own upbringing could have been, growing up surrounded by a family who loved him. Who hadn't resented his every action, his very presence. After his conversations with Aurora, the only option for a piece of scum like Jolene Jackson, she'd helped him to conclude, would be to wipe her from the face of the earth. And Aurora thought that honour should be his. He just wasn't sure how it would play out. Though Aurora had told him to sit tight, Bonfire Night, the anniversary of his family's murder, had been too much. He'd sat in his room, downed a whole bottle of Jameson, listening to the incessant row of the fireworks, torturing himself with what had happened to them. If he'd succeeded in getting into the house that night, he'd probably have killed her there and then. Hearing the cops arrive, he knew he'd have to run.

He'd managed to leave a message, letting her know her card was marked. *NEXT TIME, BITCH.* She'd have known then that her cover was blown. That that wasn't the end of it. The thought that, at the very least, she'd have been shitting herself had given him a little satisfaction. But by morning he had the hangover from hell, a rip in his jeans from climbing the gate and splinters in his fingers. Not his smartest move. He needed to leave the drink alone.

Jake's alliance with Aurora had been uneasy. She had seemed slightly unhinged anyway, and when he'd made the appalling discovery that she herself had killed her own infant brother, he'd wanted no more to do with the woman. When she'd been found dead, he shed no tears. But he had stupidly accepted money from her when they first met. Aurora had been insistent. To help with expenses, she had said. He hadn't spent it – not a penny. Jake felt sickened now by the thought that he'd accepted what amounted to blood money. She had deliberately stoked his anger, made him think that by killing Jolene, he would have the personal satisfaction of seeing justice done. And that he'd be free of the shadow Jolene had cast over his life. Aurora had even given him the idea about an overdose of insulin, but he'd researched himself about where best to inject and, given the head injury, had decided on the scalp muscle. Fast-acting – plus the needle mark was unlikely to be picked up if an autopsy was carried out. The cut she'd sustained during her fall had been an absolute gift. Jake had been blinded by the hatred he felt towards Jolene. But now he couldn't believe how he'd allowed himself to be manipulated, how low he'd actually stooped.

Before boarding the coach that day, Jake had sought out the young homeless lad he often passed in the town and pushed a roll of banknotes into his pocket. Hopefully it would help to get him back on his feet.

The woman Minnie had spoken of didn't seem to tally with everything Aurora had told him about Jolene. Or Georgia, as she had come to be known. A caring, if sometimes overly-protective mother. A quiet, private person who had been at her most content in the home, creating a safe, loving environment for her child. Who had been a devoted and dutiful wife. Minnie had worried that her mum was lonely as she had no close friends, no family that she knew of. Had felt guilty that she didn't spend more time with her. She'd made Georgia sound like some sort of tragic heroine.

Although – Minnie was her daughter. She was sure to see a different side to Georgia than most. And she obviously knew nothing of her past. But whatever Georgia had been, it didn't give him the right to do what he had. Two wrongs, he now realised, did not make a right. More than anything, it was the thought of what all this had done to Minnie. Beautiful, sweet Minnie. She deserved none of it. She'd been nothing like the spoiled, egocentric brat he was expecting. It just showed, you couldn't judge a book by its cover. He could even have seen himself settling down with her, building a life together. Having a family. But he'd well and truly screwed any chance of that happening, hadn't he?

Jake stared out desolately at the blur of neon against the crow-black of the heavens. He felt hot tears sting his eyes, and thumped the window suddenly with the side of his fist in frustration and self-loathing. The middle-aged scouse guy on the other side of the aisle to his left turned abruptly, regarding him with some apprehension.

"Y'all right, mate?"

Jake twisted round, forcing a small smile of resignation.

"No, mate. I'm not all right. I'm an absolute fuck-up is what I am. But you know what, I've made my bed and I'll just have to lie in it."

He turned his face back to the window. In its reflection, he could see the man's baffled, concerned expression as he watched the back of Jake's head. He wondered what the man would have thought of him if he knew what he'd done. Whether he would look at him with the revulsion and contempt he deserved.

Jake wondered how he would ever be able to look at himself in a mirror again.

Epilogue

Gorton, Manchester

February 2023

Cora Peters heaved herself up in bed, rubbing her eyes as her partner carried breakfast in on a tea tray. Catching sight of herself in the mirror on the opposite wall, she grimaced. She hadn't bathed for three days and her greying hair looked like a bird's nest. Thank God the worst of the symptoms had passed. It had been the worst flu she'd had in years and it had completely floored her. At least she didn't have to worry about going back to work. Retirement had its upsides.

"Morning. How you feeling today?" Bernadette placed the tray carefully across Cora's lap, then opened the curtains, making Cora blink hard against the sudden flood of stark white light.

She blew out a breath, half-heartedly picking up a slice of buttered toast. "Bit better, thanks. I'll try and get up today. I need a shower – and these sheets could do with changing."

"Only if you feel well enough." Bernadette regarded her mock-sternly for a moment, hands on hips. "Oh, by the way, someone called Jasper Browne rang for you. An ex-copper, he said."

Cora's brow furrowed. "Jasper? Haven't heard from him in eons. He transferred to the Met, what, fifteen years ago? Did very well for himself. I thought he'd retired to Spain with a nice fat pension."

Bernadette nodded. "Yeah, he said he was calling from Marbella. Sounded pretty fired up. Said he'd heard something from an old colleague he thought would interest you. Something about a case you worked on back in the nineties. A minor who was sent down for murder, I think? Said it could wait, but he left his number and asked if you could give him a bell as soon as you're up and about." She tipped her head towards the tray. "I've scribbled his details on that bit of paper."

Cora sat back, chewing on the toast. She put down the remainder of the slice, nodding slowly.

"He must be on about Jolene Jackson. That was the girl's name. JJ, they called her. Yeah, awful case. One of those that stay with you. She was one messed-up kid. Came from this huge family, infamous in the community; parents were total wasters. The rest of the children were all taken into care after she was locked up."

Bernadette shook her head. "I've always said most of these things are connected with what's going on at home. Some kids haven't got a hope in hell of ever making anything of themselves."

"Ah, but Jolene did all right for herself in the end. Turned things around; got a new identity after she left the facility, trained to be a primary school teacher. She emigrated – to Peru of all places, I was told. Total fresh start. Had a couple of children of her own. Her probation officer touched base once in a while to let me know how she was getting on. The case really disturbed me at the time. Saw a lot of crap when I was on the force, but that was one that really haunted me. But you can't let these things play on your mind, can you? It'd drive you insane."

Bernadette cocked her head sideways, her expression soft. "Always said you weren't enough of a hard nut to be a copper. I'm so glad you've put all that behind you now."

Cora squeezed a small smile. Whether the job was behind her or not, the cases she'd worked on had left their mark. Bad enough to have had dealings with one pre-adolescent murderer during her career, let alone two. Jolene had been a tough little cookie; she'd always thought she'd survive the system. She wondered what became of her siblings, whether they'd fared better as they grew up.

It had been the other girl, Gail Haywood, she'd always been more concerned about. Only months after Jolene's case. Such a timid, scrap of a girl. Same area, similar background: parental neglect, horrific abuse. But just her; no brothers or sisters to share the load. The father had been a drunk and a complete brute. A big bloke, too. The mother not much better. Something in the kid must have just snapped one day. Plunged a boning knife into her father's jugular when he was asleep. Attacked her mother too, when she'd come after her, but the woman had escaped with lacerations to her arms and hands. Cora never said as much, but she thought the pair got all they deserved.

They'd found cigarette burns on Gail's legs, multiple bruises on her torso. Even then, the girl refused to say where her injuries had come from. Hardly spoke a word, even though she'd been questioned repeatedly for days. Clearly traumatised. In Cora's opinion, it hadn't seemed right to send her down with what she'd been through, but in the wake of the Jolene Jackson debacle, the court had shown no leniency. Murder was murder, apparently, and, as it had for Jolene Jackson, Caulmoor Young Offender Institution beckoned for Gail. Even with clearly mitigating circumstances. Funny to think that the two girls might have even got to know one another in there.

The last Cora had heard, Gail had made good. Under a new name, Georgia, she'd married a wealthy businessman and had a daughter. It sounded as if it had all worked out for her in the end. Cora hoped she was happy now, that she'd managed to put it all behind her. Though it had its flaws, she still believed in a justice system that aimed to rehabilitate. It may not work in every case, but there were many that deserved a second chance, and Gail was definitely one of them.

Cora took a mouthful of tea, then finished her toast. She pushed the tray aside and swung her legs off the side of the bed, pausing before standing shakily. Bernadette took her arm to steady her and Cora rolled her eyes.

"Look at me, I'm like a bloody old woman. Hope this isn't the shape of things to come."

Bernadette grinned. "Well, I'll be here to look after you if it is. Come on, I'll run you a bath. Easier than trying to stand in the shower if you're feeling a bit wobbly. I can strip the bed while you're having a soak."

Cora planted a kiss on her cheek. "You're a diamond, d'you know that?"

She sank back down onto the mattress as Bernadette left the room, listening for a moment to the sound of water hitting the bathtub. Picking up the piece of paper with Jasper's number, she lifted her mobile from the bedside cabinet. Might as well call him now while she was waiting, find out what he was so keen to tell her. It must be something pretty significant, for him to get in touch after all this time.

Jolene Jackson. Yes, she was sure that Jasper must be ringing with news about her. Whatever had she been up to now?

Acknowledgements

First and most importantly, huge and grateful thanks to my wonderful editor, Rachel Hart. This book was our third collaboration and she's been a joy to work with. Her patience, support and guidance throughout have been invaluable and greatly appreciated. Avon's loss is most definitely Wildfire's gain! A big thank you to Anna Nightingale for picking up the baton and for her kind reassurances when I've had a wobble! Thanks also to Laura Gerrard for her meticulous copy-edit and helpful suggestions. To Jess Zahra for pulling everything together at the final hurdle! Many thanks and a big shout-out to the lovely wider team at Avon Books, all of whose input is so vital. There is so much going on behind the scenes to bring the reader the final polished article and all credit to those unsung heroes working away in the background who help this happen, from marketing, to cover design, to being tireless cheerleaders, helping to press books into the hands of readers. You are all stars!

As always, massive gratitude to all the bloggers, reviewers

and booksellers who are so incredibly generous with their time – we authors have so much to thank you for and the value of your hard work is immeasurable. Also to all the lovely writers and Twitter/Instagram friends who are unfailingly supportive and encouraging – writing can be a solitary pursuit and it's comforting to know we're all in a similar boat!

Thanks as ever to the people central to my existence, my wonderful family: to my husband, Mark, my children, Gemma, Natalie and Christopher, and my grandchildren, Olivia, Josh, Isaac, Noah, Oliver and Gracie. You are my light at the end of the tunnel!

Finally, a massive thank you to every reader who has bought and read this book – your support is everything and I'm eternally grateful to you all. I really hope you have enjoyed the story.

**When a young widow's little girl
vanishes, could a dark family secret
hold the answer?**

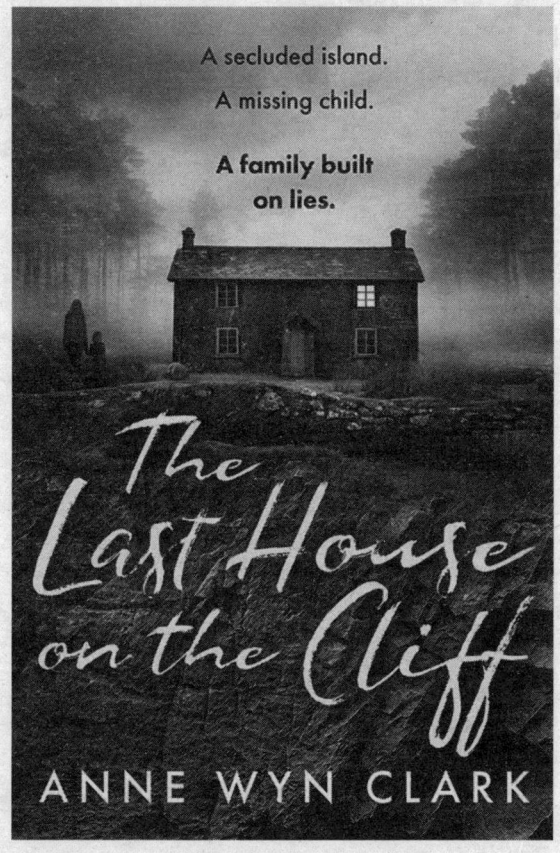

A secluded island.

A missing child.

**A family built
on lies.**

*The
Last House
on the Cliff*

ANNE WYN CLARK

A terrifically dark and twisty tale that asks: *can you
ever really trust those closest to you?* Perfect for fans of
Ruth Ware, Cass Green and C.J. Tudor.

A mysterious figure.
A whispering community.
A deadly secret . . .

A haunting, twisty story about the power of secrets and rumours, perfect for fans of Ruth Ware's *The Turn of the Key* and Lucy Atkins's *Magpie Lane*.

A missing child.
A broken community.
A horrifying secret.

Some crimes should never be uncovered…

The
Secrets of
Mill House

ANNE WYN CLARK

The chilling, stay-up-all-night suspense thriller for fans
of C.J. Tudor, Riley Sager and Stephen King.

Secrets won't stay in the dark forever . . .

An eerie, bone-chilling and twisty thriller about how far we go to protect our darkest secrets, for fans of C.J. Tudor, Riley Sager and Cass Green.